EX LIBRIS:
Stories of Librarians, Libraries & Lore

OTHER ANTHOLOGIES EDITED
BY PAULA GURAN

Embraces
Best New Paranormal Romance
Best New Romantic Fantasy
Zombies: The Recent Dead
The Year's Best Dark Fantasy & Horror: 2010
Vampires: The Recent Undead
The Year's Best Dark Fantasy & Horror: 2011
Halloween
New Cthulhu: The Recent Weird
Brave New Love
Witches: Wicked, Wild & Wonderful
Obsession: Tales of Irresistible Desire
The Year's Best Dark Fantasy & Horror: 2012
Extreme Zombies
Ghosts: Recent Hauntings
Rock On: The Greatest Hits of Science Fiction & Fantasy
Season of Wonder
Future Games
Weird Detectives: Recent Investigations
The Mammoth Book of Angels and Demons
After the End: Recent Apocalypses
The Year's Best Dark Fantasy & Horror: 2013
Halloween: Mystery, Magic & the Macabre
Once Upon a Time: New Fairy Tales
Magic City: Recent Spells
The Year's Best Dark Fantasy & Horror: 2014
Time Travel: Recent Trips
New Cthulhu 2: More Recent Weird
Blood Sisters: Vampire Stories by Women
Mermaids and Other Mysteries of the Deep
The Year's Best Dark Fantasy & Horror: 2015
Warrior Women
Street Magicks
The Mammoth Book of Cthulhu: New Lovecraftian Fiction
Beyond the Woods: Fairy Tales Retold
The Year's Best Dark Fantasy & Horror: 2016
The Mammoth Book of the Mummy
Swords Against Darkness

EX LIBRIS:
Stories of Librarians, Libraries & Lore

Edited by Paula Guran

PRIME BOOKS

Print ISBN: 978-1-60701-489-8
Ebook ISBN: 978-1-60701-490-4

FIRST PUBLICATION DATA:
"The Last Librarian: Or a Short Account of the End of the World" © 2011 Edoardo Albert; 1st Publication: *Daily Science Fiction,* 5 August 2011. | "The Books" © 2010 Kage Baker; 1st Publication: *The Mammoth Book of Apocalyptic SF,* ed. Mike Ashley (Robinson). Reprinted by permission of Kathleen Bartholomew and the Virginia Kidd Agency, Inc. | "In Libres" © 2015 Elizabeth Bear; 1st Publication: *Uncanny* #4. | "The Sigma Structure Symphony" © 2012 Gregory Benford; 1st Publication: *The Palencar Project,* ed. Davd Hartwell (Tor). | "Paper Cuts Scissors" © 2007 Holly Black; 1st Publication: *Realms of Fantasy,* October 2007. | "King of the Big Night Hours" © 2007 Richard Bowes; 1st Publication: *Subterranean,* Issue #7. | "Exchange" © 1996 Ray Bradbury; 1st Publication: *Quicker Than the Eye* (Avon Books). | "The Green Book" © 2010 Amal El-Mohtar; 1st Publication: *Apex Magazine,* 8 November 2010. | "Those Who Watch" © 2016 Ruthanna Emrys; 1st Publication: *The Mammoth Book of Cthulhu,* ed. Paula Guran. (Robinson UK/ Running Press US) | "Death and the Librarian" © 1994 Esther M. Friesner; 1st Publication: *Asimov's,* December 1994. | "If on a Winter's Night a Traveler" © 2015 Xia Jia; originally published in Chinese: *Guangming Daily,* 5 June 2015, Version 14; 1st English publication (translation by Ken Liu): © 2015: *Clarkesworld* #110. | "In the House of the Seven Librarians" © 2006 Ellen Kages; 1st Publication: *Firebirds Rising: An Anthology of Original Science Fiction & Fantasy,* ed. Sharyn November. (Firebird/Penguin). | "Magic for Beginners" © 2005 Kelly Link; 1st Publication: *Magic for Beginners* (Small Beer Press). | "Summer Reading" © 2012 Ken Liu; 1st Publication: *Daily Science Fiction,* 4 September 2012. | "In the Stacks" © 2010 Scott Lynch; 1st Publication: *Swords & Dark Magic: The New Sword & Sorcery,* eds. Jonathan Strahan & Lou Anders (HarperVoyager). | "The Fort Moxie Branch " © 1988 Cryptic, Inc; 1st Publication: *Full Spectrum,* eds. Lou Aronica & Shawna McCarthy (Bantam Spectra). | "The Inheritance of Barnabas Wilcox" © 2004 Sarah Monette; 1st Publication: *Lovecraft's Weird Mysteries* #7. | "Special Collections" © 2015 Norman Partridge; 1st Publication: *The Library of the Dead,* ed. Michael Bailey (Written Backwards/Dark Regions Press). | "A Woman's Best Friend" © 2008 Robert Reed; 1st Publication: *Clarkesworld* # 17. | "What Books Survive" © 2012 Tansy Rayner Roberts; 1st Publication: *Epilogue,* ed. Tehani Wessely (Fablecroft Publishing). | "The Midbury Lake Incident" © 2015 Kristine Kathryn Rusch; 1st Publication: *Magical Libraries, an Uncollected Anthology,* Issue 5 (WMG Publishing). | "The Librarian's Dilemma" © 2015 E. Saxey; 1st Publication: *The Journal of Unlikely Academia,* October 2015. | "With Tales in Their Teeth, From the Mountain They Came" © 2013 A.C. Wise; 1st Publication: *Lightspeed* #32. ❧

Contents

Paula Guran • Ad Librum • *7*

Ellen Klages • In the House of the Seven Librarians • *17*

Kage Baker • The Books • *39*

Esther M. Friesner • Death and the Librarian • *51*

Elizabeth Bear • In Libres • *63*

Richard Bowes • The King of the Big Night Hours • *79*

Ruthanna Emrys • Those Who Watch • *93*

Norman Partridge • Special Collections • *107*

Ray Bradbury • Exchange • *135*

Holly Black • Paper Cuts Scissors • *145*

Ken Liu • Summer Reading • *161*

Kelly Link • Magic for Beginners • *167*

Sarah Monette • The Inheritance of Barnabas Wilcox • *207*

Kristine Kathryn Rusch • The Midbury Lake Incident • *217*

A.C. Wise • With Tales in Their Teeth, from the Mountain They Came • *227*

Tansy Rayner Roberts • What Books Survive • *239*

E. Saxey • The Librarian's Dilemma • *253*

Amal El-Mohtar • The Green Book • *271*

Scott Lynch • In the Stacks • *279*

Robert Reed • A Woman's Best Friend • *313*

Xia Jia • If on a Winter's Night a Traveler • *325*

Gregory Benford • The Sigma Structure Symphony • *331*

Jack McDevitt • The Fort Moxie Branch • *359*

Edoardo Albert • The Last Librarian • *371*

About the Authors • *377*

Ad Librum

—ᴧᴧᴧ—

Paula Guran

That libraries and librarians are often found in fiction should come as no surprise. Cultural reflection aside, writers usually know both well and are fond of them. And, since authors need reading and readers and libraries and librarians nurture such, authors have a vested interest in their ongoing success.

Grant Burns points out in *Librarians in Fiction: A Critical Bibliography* (1997): "Librarians in fiction tend to be unhappy and beset with problems. That fact probably says far less about librarians and their image than it does about serious fiction."

Science fiction and fantasy is, thank goodness, not "serious fiction" (whatever that is). The troubled, gloomy librarian does, of course, occur in speculative fiction, but librarians are also characterized in a variety of other ways.

Descriptions of libraries themselves, in general fiction, are similarly confining. Back in 1904—a time when fiction in libraries and the establishment of public libraries (at least in England) were controversial topics—librarian J.D. Stewart wrote, more than somewhat tongue in cheek:

> Now, it may seem novelists, with few exceptions, are the last persons capable of describing a library . . . The libraries they have described fall naturally into two classes—the gloomy-mysterious and the impossibly-magnificent . . . Sometimes they are places of mystery, with secret passages concealed by sliding bookcases and leading to noisome vaults—vaults where ghastly deeds have been done, and in which heaps of human bones lie mouldering. Some writers have even misinterpreted the phrase, "ghosts in the library," and have turned the place into a haunted chamber, the supernatural inmates having a close connection with the human bones aforesaid . . .

Like those troubled, gloomy librarians, "gloomy-mysterious" and "impossibly-magnificent" libraries certainly exist in speculative fiction—especially the darker sorts!—but again, there's far more diversity in both architecture and atmosphere.

In fantasy, libraries can exist outside time and space and be infinite. Librarians are usually vastly knowledgeable and often greatly heroic . . . and sometimes scary or even evil.

The most-often cited example of the fantastic library is Jorge Luis Borges'
Library of Babel in his 1941 story of the same name.

"The universe (which others call the Library) is composed of an indefinite
and perhaps infinite number of hexagonal galleries . . . " he explains. Each shelf in
these rooms "contains thirty-five books of uniform format; each book is of four
hundred and ten pages; each page, of forty lines, each line, of some eighty letters
which are black in color." Each book consists of different combination of letters,
and in total they contain all possible arrangement of letters. So, the Library as a
whole contains:

> Everything: the minutely detailed history of the future, the archangels'
> autobiographies, the faithful catalogues of the Library, thousands
> and thousands of false catalogues, the demonstration of the fallacy of
> those catalogues, the demonstration of the fallacy of the true catalogue,
> the Gnostic gospel of Basilides, the commentary on that gospel, the
> commentary on the commentary on that gospel, the true story of your
> death, the translation of every book in all languages, the interpolations of
> every book in all books.

Borges (who worked as one) doesn't say much about librarians, although he
mentions the possibility that "there must exist a book which is the formula and
perfect compendium of all the rest: some librarian has gone through it and he is
analogous to a god."

The Library of Dream in Neil Gaiman's graphic novel series The Sandman
is another fictional library existing outside time and space. Librarian Lucien
oversees "the largest library that ever was" (*Vertigo Jam*, August 1993) and even
contains books "their authors never wrote or never finished, except in dreams."
(*Sandman 22*, January 1991). Lucien says he "can remember the title, author, and
location of every book in this library . . . Every book that's ever been dreamed.
Every book that's ever been imagined. Every book that's ever been lost. Millions
upon millions of them. That's what I remember. It's my job. Other things . . . I
forget sometimes." (*Sandman 57*, February 1994).

Earlier, in *Beyond Life* (1919), John Branch Cabell invented a library with
similar books, but it was quite firmly (if fictionally) bound in time and space.
Located in protagonist John Charteris' Cambridge home, Willoughby Hall, its
shelves "contain the cream of the unwritten books—the masterpieces that were
planned and never carried through."

The section includes, he notes, "a number of persons who never published a
line." But there are well-known authors as well: "Thackeray's mediaeval romance

of Agincourt. Dickens, as you see, has several novels there: perhaps *The Young Person* and *The Children of the Fathers* are the best, but they all belong to his later and failing period." The main treasure of this library is an "unbound collection of the unwritten plays of Christopher Marlowe."

Charteris also possesses "books with which you are familiar, as the authors meant them to be." Books read in these "intended" editions are quite different than the works as published.

The Unitary Authority of Warrington Cat (formerly known as the Cheshire Cat—yes, the one with whom Alice acquainted) is in charge of the Great Library in Jasper Fforde's humorous cross-genre Thursday Next series. (Seven books beginning with *The Eyre Affair*, 2001). The Library is a "cavernous and almost infinite depository of every book ever written. But to call the Cat a librarian would be an injustice. He was an uberlibrarian—he knew about all the books in his charge. When they were being read, by whom—everything."

Fforde's Great Library is located on an alternate Earth where literature is quite important and reality is stretched so thin fictional characters can jump from one book to another. The Library's upper twenty-six stories house all published fiction. Beneath it are another twenty-six floors of "dingy yet industrious subbasements known as the Well of Lost Plots. This is where books are constructed, honed and polished in readiness for a place in the library above—if they make it . . . The failure rate is high."

Another library outside the normal limits of space and time is found in Genevieve Cogman's Invisible Library novels. The mission of the Invisible Library—which exists between many alternate Earths—is to save books unique to a particular Earth. Librarians—who can alter reality using the Language— are spies/agents sent to retrieve these books. Librarian Irene is sent on a mission in the first book (*The Invisible Library*, 2015) that proves quite dangerous. The following books expand on the role of librarian as hero.

A truly heroic librarian from outside space/time is found in Liz Williams' little-known *Worldsoul* (2012), which posits the question: "What if being a librarian was the most dangerous job in the world?" Worldsoul is a great city that forms a nexus point between Earth and many dimensions. Its library is a place where old stories gather and forgotten legends come to fade and die—or to flourish and rise again. Librarians are doing their best to maintain the Library, but . . . things . . . keep breaking out of ancient texts and legends and escaping. Librarian Mercy Fane must pursue one such dangerous creature. (Full disclosure: Projected as a trilogy, only this first book was published and I was its editor. I hope Liz Williams will eventually get the sequels published.)

The Extreme Librarians, or Bookaneers, are the heroic keepers of the Wordhoard Pit of UnLondon, an alternate London in China Miéville's *Un Lun Dun* (2007). Young Deeba climbs perilous booksteps and storyladders to the rim of the Pit's brick tower. At least one hundred feet in diameter, it is hollow and lined with books. Retrieving anything from this high-rise universe of bookshelves is challenging; at the very least it requires harnesses, tethering, ropes, and the occasional pickaxe. One Extreme Librarian, Margarita Staples, relates how bookaneers might be "gone for weeks, fetching volumes. . . . There are risks. Hunters, animals, and accidents. Ropes that snap. Sometimes someone gets separated." Sometimes librarians never return.

Miéville also invented Gedrecsechet, the librarian of the Palgolak church in his novel *Perdido Street Station* (2000). "Palgolak was a god of knowledge. He was depicted either as a fat, squat human reading in a bath, or a svelte vodyanoi doing the same, or, mystically, both at once. . . . He was an amiable, pleasant deity, a sage whose existence was entirely devoted to the collection, categorization, and dissemination of information."

Palgolak's library does not lend books, but readers can visit any time of the day or the night, and there were very. The Palgolaki believe "everything known by a worshiper was immediately known by Palgolak, which was why they were religiously charged to read voraciously."

In the second of Garth Nix's Old Kingdom series, *Lirael* (2001), the clairvoyant Clayr have a vast library . . .

> ". . . shaped like a nautilus shell, a continuous tunnel that wound down into the mountain in an ever-tightening spiral. This main spiral was an enormously long, twisting ramp that took you from the high reaches of the mountain down past the level of the valley floor, several thousand feet below.
>
> Off the main spiral, there were countless other corridors, rooms, halls, and strange chambers. Many were full of the Clayr's written records, mainly documenting the prophesies and visions of many generations of seers. But they also contained books and papers from all over the Kingdom. Books of magic and mystery, knowledge both ancient and new. Scrolls, maps, spells, recipes, inventories, stories, true tales, and Charter knew what else.
>
> In addition to all these written works, the Great Library also housed other things. There were old armories within it, containing weapons and armor that had not been used for centuries but still stayed bright and new. There were rooms full of odd paraphernalia that no one now knew how to use. There were chambers where dressmakers' dummies stood fully clothed, displaying

the fashions of bygone Clayr or the wildly different costumes of the barbaric North. There were greenhouses tended by sendings, with Charter marks for light as bright as the sun. There were rooms of total darkness, swallowing up the light and anyone foolish enough to enter unprepared.

The eponymous fourteen-year-old protagonist of the novel becomes a Third Assistant Librarian, explores the library and grows into the young woman she'll need to be as a Second Librarian who saves the world.

The Librarian (his name has been long forgotten) of the Unseen University in the Terry Prachett's Discword series is a wizard. He was once a human. But after being accidentally transformed into an orangutan, he decided to remain a primate. Even though all he ever says is "oook" and occasionally "eeek," other wizards understand him perfectly. The Librarian has the ability to travel through L-Space, which connects every library that ever existed.

The Unseen University and its Library are located in the city of Ankh-Morpork. The Library houses "the greatest assemblage of magical texts anywhere in the multiverse" as well as normal books, books never written, dictionaries of illusionary words, and atlases of imaginary places. Some of its endless shelves are, handily, Möbius shelves. The building does not obey the "normal rules of space and time": "It was said that it went on FOREVER . . . you could wander for days . . . there were lost tribes of research students somewhere in there [and] strange things lurking in forgotten alcoves . . . preyed on by other things that were even stranger." (*Guards! Guards!*, 1989). Luckily it is topped with a dome only a few hundred feet across that helps one get one's bearings.

Somewhat like Borges' library, the Unseen University Library may have book, *The Octavo*, that might be god. It contains the great eight spells the Creator used to create the Discworld.

Another (albeit much junior) academic library is located at the Hogwarts School of Witchcraft and Wizardry in J.K. Rowlings' Harry Potter books. Its librarian, Madame Irma Pince, is a strict and somewhat scary guardian of the library's contents and sometimes not very helpful to students. (Even though all the books in the library are already protected by spells, she has been known to place additional hexes on books for enhanced security.) The Hogwarts Library contains "tens of thousands of books; thousands of shelves; hundreds of narrow rows." (*Harry Potter and the Philosopher's Stone*, 1997). To gain access to the books in its Restricted Section "you needed a specially signed note from one of the teachers . . . These were the books containing powerful Dark Magic never taught at Hogwarts, and only read by older students studying advanced Defence Against the Dark Arts."

Occasionally fantasy librarians are wicked. Rachel Caine's The Great Library series posits a world where the Great Library of Alexandria has survived and evolved into a ruthlessly powerful entity that controls the dissemination of information. Using alchemy, the library can instantly deliver content, but the personally owning books is illegal. Those who govern the Great Library value knowledge and their system far more than human life. "

Science fiction pioneer Jules Verne's (1828-1905) heroes, scientists, and engineers, were human libraries (or at least encyclopedias) brimming with information they could provide from memory. He describes one as being "like a book, a book that solved all their problems for them . . . " (*The Mysterious Island,* 1894); another, a geographer, when told he speaks like a book agrees: " 'That's exactly what I am. . . . You are all invited to leaf through me as much as you like." (*In Search of the Castaways*, 1865).

Verne's imagined libraries reflected—with considerable amplification—the luxurious private libraries of the nineteenth century. He describes Captain Nemo's library aboard the *Nautilus* in *Twenty Thousand Leagues Under the Sea* (1870):

> Tall, black rosewood bookcases, inlaid with copperwork, held on their wide shelves [twelve thousand] uniformly bound books. [The furnishings included] huge couches upholstered in maroon leather and curved for maximum comfort. Light, movable reading stands, which could be pushed away or pulled near as desired, allowed books to be positioned on them for easy study. In the center stood a huge table covered with pamphlets, among which some newspapers, long out of date, were visible. Electric light flooded this whole harmonious totality, falling from four frosted half globes set in the scrollwork of the ceiling.

The library also serves as a smoking room and adjoining "lounges" house masterpieces of art and scientific specimens.

When SF attempts to predict libraries and librarians of the future, the results are widely ranged.

The Cerebral Library by David H Keller, M.D. (*Amazing Stories*, May 1931) tells of a mad scientist who devises a way to acquire, store, and electronically access a library of "the entire range of human knowledge." Not quite the *entire* range; the database for his library was to be obtained from the brains of five hundred college-educated men (and three librarians) who, over the course of five years of reading, read seven hundred and fifty thousand books.

After all that reading, their brains were to be surgically removed, stored in glass jars, and wired together. The scientist could then query by typing on a keyboard, and the audio answer would be relayed through a radio. Luckily for the 503 young men, the plot is foiled before their brains are removed.

Robots are being used these days in some libraries, but nothing like Harry Harrisons' Filer-model robot librarians in his story "The Robot Who Wanted to Know" (*Fantastic Universe*, March 1958):

> . . .very little intelligence is needed to shelve books or stamp cards, but this sort of work has long been handled by robots that are little more than wheeled IBM machines. The cataloging of human information has always been an incredibly complex task. The Filer robots were the ones who finally inherited the job. . . . Besides a complete memory, Filer had other attributes that are usually connected to the human brain. Abstract connections for one thing. If it was asked for books on one subject, he could think of related books in other subjects that might be referred to. He could take a suggestion, pyramid it into a category, then produce tactile results in the form of a mountain of books.

The Galactic Library occupies almost the entire subsurface of eighty-first century Terra in Frank Herbert's *Direct Descent* (1980). The library staff of eight thousand is aided by robots. "The first rule of the Galactic Library Code is to obey all direct orders of the government in power." Preserving the library while still adhering to the Code is a challenge met by clever librarians when governments in power try to destroy it.

But vast libraries need not take up entire planets. In Anne McCaffrey's *Dragonsdawn* (1988) colonists travel on spaceships to their new home on the planet Pern. General Cherry Duff, the colony's official historian and librarian, insists "records of all ethnic written and visual cultures be taken to Pern," since you never know when "old information will become new, viable and valuable." Besides, the "whole schmear . . . takes up no space at all on the chips we've got."

Master Ultan, the blind librarian in *The Shadow of the Torturer* (1980), the first volume of Gene Wolfe's four-volume Book of the New Sun, tells us the books of the great library of Nessus, of which he is in charge, come in every conceivable variety including a cube of crystal "no larger than the ball of your thumb that contains more books than the library itself does."

In William Gibson's *Neuromancer* (1984), "cyberspace" is a matrix of networked information that "cowboys" like protagonist Case jack into. His consciousness then navigates the consensual hallucination. The New York City Public Library is mentioned and, although it is not spelled out, one can extrapolate that the general public may need librarians—at least sometimes—to access the network through libraries. One research library also acts as a dead storage area with a human librarian as its guardian.

In Neal Stephenson's 1992 novel *Snow Crash*, Hiro Protagonist is a freelancer for the Central Intelligence Corporation (CIC), which uploads information to the Library of Congress which has merged with CIC. Hiro gets compensated if someone finds a use for information he has provided to the library. As only one percent of the information in the Library gets used, Hiro doesn't make much from this, so he also delivers pizza. His "indispensable guide and companion" in the post-internet Metaverse is a virtual librarian:

> The Librarian daemon looks like a pleasant, fiftyish, silver-haired, bearded man with bright blue eyes, wearing a V-neck sweater over a workshirt. . . . Even though he's just a piece of software, he has reason to be cheerful; he can move through the nearly infinite stacks of information in the Library with the agility of a spider dancing across a vast web of cross-references. The Librarian is the only piece of CIC software that costs even more than Earth [a geopolitics program]; the only thing he can't do is think.

This idealized reference librarian delivers information and makes connections. He is self-programming, but was originally written by "a researcher at the Library of Congress who taught himself how to code."

Moa Blue in *The Starry Rift* (1986) by James Tiptree, Jr., is another ace SF librarian. When two Comeno students visit the Great Central Library of Deneb University—"asking for a selection of Human fact/fiction from the early days of the Federation, "to get the ambiance"—they meet Chief Assistant Librarian Moa Blue, an amphibian. He recommends three stories for them and his "comments" serve as introductions to the three tales. In an epilogue by the students, they express their thanks and hope they can dedicate their paper to him.

Not all science fictional libraries are useful for the public. In Marc Laidlaw's *The Third Force: A Novel of Gadget* (1996)—one of the earliest tie-in novels based on (what was then) a CD-ROM game, Gadget—a totalitarian United States is ruled by a megalomaniacal dictator. It is difficult access anything as identification codes on each book change, and books are constantly rearranged by an automatic retrieval system to insure book locations cannot be memorized. All searches are recorded and reported to the government. Even the chief librarian of the Imperial Library, Elena Hausmann, cannot access everything. Elena, secretly a member of the resistance, considers the library a "crypt for knowledge now. No one can borrow a book without fearing for their lives."

In Sean McMullen's *Voices in the Light: Book One of Greatwinter* (1994), thirty-ninth century Australia has no electricity; wind engines are leading-edge technology, and steam power is banned by major religions. Zarvorva, the Highliber of Libris (a state library), controls "a network of libraries and librarians scattered over . . . thousands of miles." The library functions as a government controlling education, communication, and transportation. Since there is no predominant religion in the area, librarians perform rituals and ceremonies in addition to teaching classes, distributing and collecting books, and running communication towers. Zarvorva has reorganized and "modernized" her library. "The changes did not go uncriticized, but the Highliber was dedicated and ruthless. She lobbied, fought duels, and had officials assassinated . . . and even had the more numerate of her opponents abducted for a new and novel workforce."

Science fiction has been known to use libraries as literal repositories of all knowledge or metaphors for civilization as a whole. In *Day of the Triffids* by John Wyndham (1951), for instance, post-apocalyptic survivors recover books from libraries to learn skills needed to survive. One character notes: "The most valuable part of our flying start is knowledge. That's the short cut to save us starting where our ancestors did. We've got it all there in the books if we take the trouble to find out about."

However, the protagonist later discovers that farming

> . . . is not the kind of thing that is easily learned from books . . . Nor is book-installed knowledge of horse management, daisy work, or slaughterhouse procedure by any means an adequate groundwork for these arts. There are so many points where one cannot break off to consult the relevant chapter. Moreover, the realities persistently present baffling dissimilarities from the simplicities of print."

Another attempt to preserve civilization after its downfall with a library is made in *A Canticle for Leibowitz* (1960) by Walter M Miller, Jr. Nuclear war has wiped out most of civilization and those left are hostile to learning and knowledge. Roughly paralleling the historical Dark Ages, the monks gather and preserve what books they can find in order to keep "the spark burning while the world slept."

Ken Scholes' Psalms of Isaak series (first book: *Lamentation*, 2009) posits a far-future post-apocalyptic civilization in which the Androfrancine Order has assembled a Great Library in the city Windwir. The order is devoted to the preservation and promulgation of knowledge obtained mostly from archaeological digs. The city and (almost) all in it are destroyed. But as the series continues, it is discovered that the books were also stored, at least partially, in the memory of Isaak, a steam-powered android called a mechoservitor. He and human supporters start collecting whatever books still remain and reestablishing the library.

Neither knowledge nor libraries are always honored and preserved in science fictional futures. In the year AD802701 of H.G. Wells' *The Time Machine* (1895), libraries have been abandoned. An enormous library is described where nothing is left but useless "decaying vestiges of books."

Isherwood Williams, the protagonist of George Stewart's *Earth Abides* (1949), feels libraries offer a store of "the wisdom by which civilization had been built, and could be rebuilt." He realizes people must learn how to read tries to instruct the new generation. But, with the exception of his youngest son, Joey, the younger folks are uninterested. The protagonist eventually abandons the notion civilization as he knew it will ever be rebuilt and, instead of reading, teaches them skills they need to survive.

. . . and that is merely a sampling of fantastic and science fictional librarians and libraries. I've touched on a few titles intended for younger readers, but not really considered books specifically for children, let alone film, TV, gaming, and other media. You'll find plenty more there.

As for the contents of this anthology . . .

Let's start by finding out what it is like to be raised by feral librarians.

Paula Guran
National Science Fiction Day 2017

In the House of the Seven Librarians

Ellen Klages

Once upon a time, the Carnegie Library sat on a wooded bluff on the east side of town: red brick and fieldstone, with turrets and broad windows facing the trees. Inside, green glass-shaded lamps cast warm yellow light onto oak tables ringed with spindle-backed chairs.

The floors were wood, except in the foyer, where they were pale beige marble. The loudest sounds were the ticking of the clock and the quiet, rhythmic thwack of a rubber stamp on a pasteboard card.

It was a cozy, orderly place.

Through twelve presidents and two world wars, the elms and maples grew tall outside the deep bay windows. Children leapt from *Peter Pan* to *Oliver Twist* and off to college, replaced at Story Hour by their younger brothers, cousins, daughters.

Then the library board—men in suits, serious men, men of money—met and cast their votes for progress. A new library, with fluorescent lights, much better for the children's eyes. Picture windows, automated systems, ergonomic plastic chairs. The town approved the levy, and the new library was built across town, convenient to the community center and the mall.

Some books were boxed and trundled down Broad Street, many others stamped DISCARD and left where they were, for a book sale in the fall. Interns from the university used the latest technology to transfer the cumbersome old card file and all the records onto floppy disks and microfiche. Progress, progress, progress.

The Ralph P. Mossberger Library (named after the local philanthropist and car dealer who had written the largest check) opened on a drizzly morning in late April. Everyone attended the ribbon-cutting ceremony and stayed for the speeches, because there would be cake after.

Everyone except the seven librarians from the Carnegie Library on the bluff across town.

Quietly, without a fuss (they were librarians, after all), while the town looked toward the future, they bought supplies: loose tea and English biscuits, packets of Bird's pudding, and cans of beef barley soup. They rearranged some of the shelves, brought in a few comfortable armchairs, nice china and teapots, a couch, towels for the shower, and some small braided rugs.

Then they locked the door behind them.

Each morning they woke and went about their chores. They shelved and stamped and catalogued, and in the evenings, every night, they read by lamplight.

Perhaps, for a while, some citizens remembered the old library, with the warm nostalgia of a favorite childhood toy that had disappeared one summer, never seen again. Others assumed it had been torn down long ago.

And so a year went by, then two, or perhaps a great many more. Inside, time had ceased to matter. Grass and brambles grew thick and tall around the fieldstone steps, and trees arched overhead as the forest folded itself around them like a cloak.

Inside, the seven librarians lived, quiet and content.

Until the day they found the baby.

Librarians are guardians of books. They help others along their paths, offering keys to help unlock the doors of knowledge. But these seven had become a closed circle, no one to guide, no new minds to open onto worlds of possibility. They kept busy, tidying orderly shelves and mending barely frayed bindings with stiff netting and glue, and began to bicker among themselves.

Ruth and Edith had been up half the night, arguing about whether or not subway tokens (of which there were half a dozen in the Lost and Found box) could be used to cast the I Ching. And so Blythe was on the stepstool in the 299s, reshelving the volume of hexagrams, when she heard the knock.

Odd, she thought. It's been some time since we've had visitors.

She tugged futilely at her shapeless cardigan as she clambered off the stool and trotted to the front door, where she stopped abruptly, her hand to her mouth in surprise.

A wicker basket, its contents covered with a red-checked cloth, as if for a picnic, lay in the wooden box beneath the Book Return chute. A small, cream-colored envelope poked out from one side.

"How nice!" Blythe said aloud, clapping her hands. She thought of fried chicken and potato salad—of which she was awfully fond—a mason jar of lemonade, perhaps even a cherry pie? She lifted the basket by its round-arched handle. Heavy, for a picnic. But then, there *were* seven of them. Although Olive just ate like a bird, these days.

She turned and set it on top of the Circulation Desk, pulling the envelope free.

"What's *that*?" Marian asked, her lips in their accustomed moue of displeasure, as if the basket were an agent of chaos, existing solely to disrupt the tidy array of rubber stamps and file boxes that were her domain.

"A present," said Blythe. "I think it might be lunch."

Marian frowned. "For you?"

"I don't know yet. There's a note . . ." Blythe held up the envelope and peered at it. "No," she said. "It's addressed to 'The Librarians. Overdue Books Department.'"

"Well, that would be me," Marian said curtly. She was the youngest, and wore trouser suits with silk T-shirts. She had once been blond. She reached across the counter, plucked the envelope from Blythe's plump fingers, and sliced it open it with a filigreed brass stiletto.

"Hmph," she said after she'd scanned the contents.

"It *is* lunch, isn't it?" asked Blythe.

"Hardly." Marian began to read aloud:

This is overdue. Quite a bit, I'm afraid. I apologize. We moved to Topeka when I was very small, and Mother accidentally packed it up with the linens. I have traveled a long way to return it, and I know the fine must be large, but I have no money. As it is a book of fairy tales, I thought payment of a first-born child would be acceptable. I always loved the library. I'm sure she'll be happy there.

Blythe lifted the edge of the cloth. "Oh my stars!"

A baby girl with a shock of wire-stiff black hair stared up at her, green eyes wide and curious. She was contentedly chewing on the corner of a blue book, half as big as she was. *Fairy Tales of the Brothers Grimm.*

"The Rackham illustrations," Blythe said as she eased the book away from the baby. "That's a lovely edition."

"But when was it checked out?" Marian demanded.

Blythe opened the cover and pulled the ruled card from the inside pocket. "October 17, 1938," she said, shaking her head. "Goodness, at two cents a day, that's . . ." She shook her head again. Blythe had never been good with figures.

They made a crib for her in the bottom drawer of a file cabinet, displacing acquisition orders, zoning permits, and the instructions for the mimeograph, which they rarely used.

Ruth consulted Dr. Spock. Edith read Piaget. The two of them peered from text to infant and back again for a good long while before deciding that she was probably about nine months old. They sighed. Too young to read.

So they fed her cream and let her gum on biscuits, and each of the seven cooed and clucked and tickled her pink toes when they thought the others weren't looking. Harriet had been the oldest of nine girls, and knew more about babies than she really cared to. She washed and changed the diapers that had been tucked into the basket, and read *Goodnight Moon* and *Pat the Bunny* to the little girl, whom she called Polly—short for Polyhymnia, the muse of oratory and sacred song.

Blythe called her Bitsy, and Li'l Precious.

Marian called her "the foundling," or "That Child You Took In," but did her share of cooing and clucking, just the same.

When the child began to walk, Dorothy blocked the staircase with stacks of Comptons, which she felt was an inferior encyclopedia, and let her pull herself up on the bottom drawers of the card catalog. Anyone looking up *Zithers* or *Zippers* (*see "Slide Fasteners"*) soon found many of the cards fused together with grape jam. When she began to talk, they made a little bed nook next to the fireplace in the Children's Room.

It was high time for Olive to begin the child's education.

Olive had been the children's librarian since before recorded time, or so it seemed. No one knew how old she was, but she vaguely remembered waving to President Coolidge. She still had all of her marbles, though every one of them was a bit odd and rolled asymmetrically.

She slept on a daybed behind a reference shelf that held *My First Encyclopedia* and *The Wonder Book of Trees*, among others. Across the room, the child's first "big-girl bed" was yellow, with decals of a fairy and a horse on the headboard, and a rocket ship at the foot, because they weren't sure about her preferences.

At the beginning of her career, Olive had been an ordinary-sized librarian, but by the time she began the child's lessons, she was not much taller than her toddling charge. Not from osteoporosis or dowager's hump or other old-lady maladies, but because she had tired of stooping over tiny chairs and bending to knee-high shelves. She had been a grown-*up* for so long that when the library closed she had decided it was time to grow *down* again, and was finding that much more comfortable.

She had a remarkably cozy lap for a woman her size.

The child quickly learned her alphabet, all the shapes and colors, the names of zoo animals, and fourteen different kinds of dinosaurs, all of whom were dead.

By the time she was four, or thereabouts, she could sound out the letters for simple words—CUP and LAMP and STAIRS. And that's how she came to name herself.

Olive had fallen asleep over *Make Way for Ducklings*, and all the other librarians were busy somewhere else. The child was bored. She tiptoed out of the Children's Room, hugging the shadows of the walls and shelves, crawling by the base of the Circulation Desk so that Marian wouldn't see her, and made her way to the alcove that held the Card Catalogue. The heart of the library. Her favorite, most forbidden place to play.

Usually she crawled underneath and tucked herself into the corner formed of oak cabinet, marble floor, and plaster walls. It was a fine place to play Hide and Seek, even if it was mostly just Hide. The corner was a cave, a bunk on a pirate ship, a cupboard in a magic wardrobe.

But that afternoon she looked at the white cards on the fronts of the drawers, and her eyes widened in recognition. Letters! In her very own alphabet. Did they spell words? Maybe the drawers were all *full* of words, a huge wooden box of words. The idea almost made her dizzy.

She walked to the other end of the cabinet and looked up, tilting her neck back until it crackled. Four drawers from top to bottom. Five drawers across. She sighed. She was only tall enough to reach the bottom row of drawers. She traced a gentle finger around the little brass frames, then very carefully pulled out the white cards inside, and laid them on the floor in a neat row:

She squatted over them, her tongue sticking out of the corner of her mouth in concentration, and tried to read.

"Sound it out." She could almost hear Olive's voice, soft and patient. She took a deep breath.

"Duh-in-s—" and then she stopped, because the last card had too many letters, and she didn't know any words that had Xs in them. Well, *xylophone*. But the X was in the front, and that wasn't the same. She tried anyway. "Duh-ins-zzzigh," and frowned.

She squatted lower, so low she could feel cold marble under her cotton pants, and put her hand on top of the last card. One finger covered the X and her pinky covered the Z (another letter that was useless for spelling ordinary things). That left Y. Y at the end was good. funnY. happY.

"Duh-ins-see," she said slowly. "Dinsy."

That felt very good to say, hard and soft sounds and hissing Ss mixing in her mouth, so she said it again, louder, which made her laugh so she said it again, very loud: "DINSY!"

There is nothing quite like a loud voice in a library to get a lot of attention very fast. Within a minute, all seven of the librarians stood in the doorway of the alcove.

"What on earth?" said Harriet.

"*Now* what have you . . . " said Marian.

"What have you spelled, dear?" asked Olive in her soft little voice.

"I made it myself," the girl replied.

"Just gibberish," murmured Edith, though not unkindly. "It doesn't mean a thing."

The child shook her head. "Does so. Olive," she said pointing to Olive. "Do'thy, Edith, Harwiet, Bithe, Ruth." She paused and rolled her eyes. "Mawian," she added, a little less cheerfully. Then she pointed to herself. "And Dinsy."

"Oh, now Polly," said Harriet.

"Dinsy," said Dinsy.

"Bitsy?" Blythe tried hopefully.

"*Din*sy," said Dinsy.

And that was that.

At three every afternoon, Dinsy and Olive made a two-person circle on the braided rug in front of the bay window, and had Story Time. Sometimes Olive read aloud from *Beezus* and *Ramona* and *Half Magic*, and sometimes Dinsy read to Olive, *The King's Stilts*, and *In the Night Kitchen* and *Winnie-the-Pooh*. Dinsy liked that one especially, and took it to bed with her so many times that Edith had to repair the binding. Twice.

That was when Dinsy first wished upon the Library.

A note about the Library:

Knowledge is not static; information must flow in order to live. Every so often one of the librarians would discover a new addition. *Harry Potter and the Sorcerer's Stone* appeared one rainy afternoon, Rowling shelved neatly between Rodgers and Saint-Exupery, as if it had always been there. Blythe found a book of Thich Nhat Hanh's writings in the 294s one day while she was dusting, and Feynman's lectures on physics showed up on Dorothy's shelving cart after she'd gone to make a cup of tea.

It didn't happen often; the Library was selective about what it chose to add, rejecting flash-in-the-pan bestsellers, sifting for the long haul, looking for those voices that would stand the test of time next to Dickens and Tolkien, Woolf and Gould.

The librarians took care of the books, and the Library watched over them in return.

It occasionally left treats: A bowl of ripe tangerines on the Formica counter of the Common Room; a gold foil box of chocolate creams; seven small, stemmed glasses of sherry on the table one teatime. Their biscuit tin remained full, the cream in the Wedgwood jug stayed fresh, and the ink pad didn't dry out. Even the little pencils stayed needle sharp, never whittling down to finger-cramping nubs.

Some days the Library even hid Dinsy, when she had made a mess and didn't want to be found, or when one of the librarians was in a dark mood. It rearranged itself, just a bit, so that in her wanderings she would find a new alcove or cubbyhole, and once a secret passage that led to a previously unknown balcony overlooking the Reading Room. When she went back a week later, she found only a blank wall.

—∿—

And so it was, one night when she was six-ish, that Dinsy first asked the Library for a boon. Lying in her tiny yellow bed, the fraying *Pooh* under her pillow, she wished for a bear to cuddle. Books were small comfort once the lights were out, and their hard, sharp corners made them awkward companions under the covers. She lay with one arm crooked around a soft, imaginary bear, and wished and wished until her eyelids fluttered into sleep.

The next morning, while they were all having tea and toast with jam, Blythe came into the Common Room with a quizzical look on her face and her hands behind her back.

"The strangest thing," she said. "On my way up here I glanced over at the Lost and Found. Couldn't tell you why. Nothing lost in ages. But this must have caught my eye."

She held out a small brown bear, one shoe button eye missing, bits of fur gone from its belly, as if it had been loved almost to pieces.

"It seems to be yours," she said with a smile, turning up one padded foot, where DINSY was written in faded laundry-marker black.

Dinsy wrapped her whole self around the cotton-stuffed body and skipped for the rest of the morning. Later, after Olive gave her a snack—cocoa and a Lorna Doone—Dinsy cupped her hand and blew a kiss to the oak woodwork.

"Thank you," she whispered, and put half her cookie in a crack between two tiles on the Children's Room fireplace when Olive wasn't looking.

Dinsy and Olive had a lovely time. One week they were pirates, raiding the

Common Room for booty (and raisins). The next they were princesses, trapped in the turret with *At the Back of the North Wind*, and the week after that they were knights in shining armor, rescuing damsels in distress, a game Dinsy especially savored because it annoyed Marian to be rescued.

But the year she turned seven-and-a-half, Dinsy stopped reading stories. Quite abruptly, on an afternoon that Olive said later had really *felt* like a Thursday.

"Stories are for babies," Dinsy said. "I want to read about real people." Olive smiled a sad smile and pointed toward the far wall, because Dinsy was not the first child to make that same pronouncement, and she had known this phase would come.

After that, Dinsy devoured biographies, starting with the orange ones, the Childhoods of Famous Americans: *Thomas Edison, Young Inventor.* She worked her way from Abigail Adams to John Peter Zenger, all along the west side of the Children's Room, until one day she went around the corner, where Science and History began.

She stood in the doorway, looking at the rows of grown-up books, when she felt Olive's hand on her shoulder.

"Do you think maybe it's time you moved across the hall?" Olive asked softly.

Dinsy bit her lip, then nodded. "I can come back to visit, can't I? When I want to read stories again?"

"For as long as you like, dear. Anytime at all."

So Dorothy came and gathered up the bear and the pillow and the yellow toothbrush. Dinsy kissed Olive on her papery cheek and, holding Blythe's hand, moved across the hall, to the room where all the books had numbers.

Blythe was plump and freckled and frizzled. She always looked a little flushed, as if she had just that moment dropped what she was doing to rush over and greet you. She wore rumpled tweed skirts and a shapeless cardigan whose original color was impossible to guess. She had bright, dark eyes like a spaniel's, which Dinsy thought was appropriate, because Blythe *lived* to fetch books. She wore a locket with a small rotogravure picture of Melvil Dewey and kept a variety of sweets— sour balls and mints and Necco wafers—in her desk drawer.

Dinsy had always liked her.

She was not as sure about Dorothy.

Over *her* desk, Dorothy had a small, framed medal on a royal-blue ribbon, won for "Excellence in Classification Studies." She could operate the ancient black Remington typewriter with brisk efficiency, and even, on occasion, coax chalky gray prints out of the wheezing old copy machine.

She was a tall, raw-boned woman with steely blue eyes, good posture, and even better penmanship. Dinsy was a little frightened of her, at first, because she seemed so stern, and because she looked like magazine pictures of the Wicked Witch of the West, or at least Margaret Hamilton.

But that didn't last long.

"You should be very careful not to slip on the floor in here," Dorothy said on their first morning. "Do you know why?"

Dinsy shook her head.

"Because now you're in the non-friction room!" Dorothy's angular face cracked into a wide grin.

Dinsy groaned. "Okay," she said after a minute. "How do you file marshmallows?"

Dorothy cocked her head. "Shoot."

"By the *Gooey* Decimal System!"

Dinsy heard Blythe *tsk-tsk*, but Dorothy laughed out loud, and from then on they were fast friends.

The three of them used the large, sunny room as an arena for endless games of I Spy and Twenty Questions as Dinsy learned her way around the shelves. In the evenings, after supper, they played Authors and Scrabble, and (once) tried to keep a running rummy score in Base Eight.

Dinsy sat at the court of Napoleon, roamed the jungles near Timbuktu, and was a frequent guest at the Round Table. She knew all the kings of England and the difference between a pergola and a folly. She knew the names of 112 breeds of sheep, and loved to say "Barbados Blackbelly" over and over, although it was difficult to work into conversations. When she affectionately, if misguidedly, referred to Blythe as a "Persian Fat-Rumped," she was sent to bed without supper.

—⁓—

A note about time:

Time had become quite flexible inside the Library. (This is true of most places with interesting books. Sit down to read for twenty minutes, and suddenly it's dark, with no clue as to where the hours have gone.)

As a consequence, no one was really sure about the day of the week, and there was frequent disagreement about the month and year. As the keeper of the date stamp at the front desk, Marian was the arbiter of such things. (But she often had a cocktail after dinner, and many mornings she couldn't recall if she'd already turned the little wheel, nor how often it had slipped her mind, so she frequently set it a day or two ahead—or back three—just to make up.)

—⁓—

One afternoon, on a visit to Olive and the Children's Room, Dinsy looked up from *Little Town on the Prairie* and said, "When's my birthday?"

Olive thought for a moment. Because of the irregularities of time, holidays were celebrated a bit haphazardly. "I'm not sure, dear. Why do you ask?"

"Laura's going to a birthday party, in this book," she said, holding it up. "And it's fun. So I thought maybe I could have one."

"I think that would be lovely," Olive agreed. "We'll talk to the others at supper."

"Your birthday?" said Harriet as she set the table a few hours later. "Let me see." She began to count on her fingers. "You arrived in April, according to Marian's stamp, and you were about nine months old, so—" She pursed her lips as she ticked off the months. "You must have been born in July!"

"But when's my birth*day*?" Dinsy asked impatiently.

"Not sure," said Edith, as she ladled out the soup.

"No way to tell," Olive agreed.

"How does July fifth sound?" offered Blythe, as if it were a point of order to be voted on. Blythe counted best by fives.

"Fourth," said Dorothy. "Independence Day. Easy to remember?"

Dinsy shrugged. "Okay." It hadn't seemed so complicated in the Little House book. "When is that? Is it soon?"

"Probably," Ruth nodded.

So a few weeks later, the librarians threw her a birthday party.

Harriet baked a spice cake with pink frosting, and wrote DINSY on top in red licorice laces, dotting the I with a lemon drop (which was rather stale). The others gave her gifts that were thoughtful and mostly handmade:

~ A set of Dewey Decimal flash cards from Blythe.

~ A book of logic puzzles (stamped DISCARD more than a dozen times, so Dinsy could write in it) from Dorothy.

~ A lumpy orange-and-green cardigan Ruth knitted for her.

~ A sno-globe from the 1939 World's Fair from Olive.

~ A flashlight from Edith, so that Dinsy could find her way around at night and not knock over the wastebasket again.

~ A set of paper finger-puppets, made from blank card pockets, hand-painted by Marian. (They were literary figures, of course, all of them necessarily stout and squarish—Nero Wolfe and Friar Tuck, Santa Claus and Gertrude Stein.)

But her favorite gift was the second boon she'd wished upon the Library: a box of crayons. (She had grown very tired of drawing gray pictures with the little pencils.) It had produced Crayola crayons, in the familiar yellow-and-green box, labeled LIBRARY PACK. Inside were the colors of Dinsy's world: Reference Maroon, Brown Leather, Peplum Beige, Reader's Guide Green, World Book Red, Card Catalog Cream, Date Stamp Purple, and Palatino Black.

It was a very special birthday, that fourth of July. Although Dinsy wondered about Marian's calculations. As Harriet cut the first piece of cake that evening, she remarked that it was snowing rather heavily outside, which everyone agreed was lovely, but quite unusual for that time of year.

Dinsy soon learned all the planets, and many of their moons. (She referred to herself as Umbriel for an entire month.) She puffed up her cheeks and blew onto stacks of scrap paper. "Sirocco," she'd whisper. "Chinook. Mistral. Willy-Willy," and rated her attempts on the Beaufort Scale. Dorothy put a halt to it after Hurricane Dinsy reshuffled a rather elaborate game of Patience.

She dipped into fractals here, double dactyls there. When she tired of a subject—or found it just didn't suit her—Blythe or Dorothy would smile and proffer the hat. It was a deep green felt that held 1000 slips of paper, numbered 001 to 999. Dinsy'd scrunch her eyes closed, pick one and, like a scavenger hunt, spend the morning (or the next three weeks) at the shelves indicated.

Pangolins lived at 599 (point 31), and Pancakes at 641. Pencils were at 674 but Pens were a shelf away at 681, and Ink was across the aisle at 667. (Dinsy thought that was stupid, because you had to use them together.) Pluto the planet was at 523, but Pluto the Disney dog was at 791 (point 453), near Rock and Roll and Kazoos.

It was all very useful information. But in Dinsy's opinion, things could be a little *too* organized.

The first time she straightened up the Common Room without anyone asking, she was very pleased with herself. She had lined up everyone's teacup in a neat row on the shelf, with all the handles curving the same way, and arranged the spices in the little wooden rack: ANISE, BAY LEAVES, CHIVES, DILL WEED, PEPPERCORNS, SALT, SESAME SEEDS, SUGAR.

"Look," she said when Blythe came in to refresh her tea, "Order out of chaos." It was one of Blythe's favorite mottoes.

Blythe smiled and looked over at the spice rack. Then her smile faded and she shook her head.

"Is something wrong?" Dinsy asked. She had hoped for a compliment.

"Well, you used the alphabet," said Blythe, sighing. "I suppose it's not your fault. You were with Olive for a good many years. But you're a big girl now. You should learn the *proper* order." She picked up the salt container. "We'll start with Salt." She wrote the word on the little chalkboard hanging by the icebox, followed by the number 553.632. "Five-five-three-point-six-three-two. Because—?"

Dinsy thought for a moment. "Earth Sciences."

"Ex-actly." Blythe beamed. "Because salt is a mineral. But, now, *Chives*. Chives are a garden crop, so they're ... "

Dinsy bit her lip in concentration. "Six-thirty-something."

"Very good." Blythe smiled again and chalked CHIVES 635.26 on the board. "So you see, Chives should always be shelved *after* Salt, dear. A place for everything, and everything in its place."

Blythe turned and began to rearrange the eight ceramic jars. Behind her back, Dinsy silently rolled her eyes.

Edith appeared in the doorway.

"Oh, not again," she said. "No wonder I can't find a thing in this kitchen. If I've told you once, Blythe, I've told you a thousand times. *Bay Leaf* comes first. QK-four-nine—" She had worked at the university when she was younger.

"Library of Congress, my fanny," said Blythe, not quite under her breath. "We're not *that* kind of library."

"That's no excuse for imprecision," Edith replied. They each grabbed a jar and stared at each other.

Dinsy tiptoed away and hid in the 814s, where she read "Jabberwocky" until the others came in for supper and the coast was clear.

But the kitchen remained a taxonomic battleground. At least once a week, Dinsy was amused by the indignant sputtering of someone who had just spooned dill weed, not sugar, into a cup of Earl Grey tea.

Once she knew her way around, Dinsy was free to roam the library as she chose.

"Anywhere?" she asked Blythe.

"Anywhere you like, my sweet. Except the Stacks. You're not quite old enough for the Stacks."

Dinsy frowned. "I am *so*," she muttered. But the Stacks were locked, and there wasn't much she could do.

Some days she sat with Olive in the Children's Room, revisiting old friends, or explored the maze of the Main Room. Other days she spent in the Reference Room, where Ruth and Harriet guarded the big important books that no one could ever, ever check out—not even when the library had been open.

Ruth and Harriet were like a set of salt and pepper shakers from two different yard sales. Harriet had faded orange hair and a sharp, kind face. Small and pinched and pointed, a decade or two away from wizened. She had violet eyes and a mischievous, conspiratorial smile and wore rimless octagonal glasses, like stop signs. Dinsy had never seen an actual stop sign, but she'd looked at pictures.

Ruth was Chinese. She wore wool jumpers in neon plaids and had cat's-eye glasses on a beaded chain around her neck. She never put them all the way on, just lifted them to her eyes and peered through them without opening the bows.

"Life is a treasure hunt," said Harriet.

"Knowledge is power," said Ruth. "Knowing where to look is half the battle."

"Half the fun," added Harriet. Ruth almost never got the last word.

They introduced Dinsy to dictionaries and almanacs, encyclopedias and compendiums. They had been native guides through the country of the Dry Tomes for many years, but they agreed that Dinsy delved unusually deep.

"Would you like to take a break, love?" Ruth asked one afternoon. "It's nearly time for tea."

"I *am* fatigued," Dinsy replied, looking up from Roget. "Fagged out, weary, a bit spent. Tea would be pleasant, agreeable—"

"I'll put the kettle on," sighed Ruth.

Dinsy read *Bartlett's* as if it were a catalog of conversations, spouting lines from Tennyson, Mark Twain, and Dale Carnegie until even Harriet put her hands over her ears and began to hum "Stairway to Heaven."

One or two evenings a month, usually after Blythe had remarked "Well, she's a spirited girl," for the third time, they all took the night off, "For Library business." Olive or Dorothy would tuck Dinsy in early and read from one of her favorites while Ruth made her a bedtime treat—a cup of spiced tea that tasted a little like cherries and a little like varnish, and which Dinsy somehow never remembered finishing.

A list (written in diverse hands), tacked to the wall of the Common Room.

10 Things to Remember When You Live in a Library

1. We do not play shuffleboard on the Reading Room table.
2. Books should not have "dog's-ears." Bookmarks make lovely presents.

3. Do not write in books. Even in pencil. Puzzle collections and connect-the-dots are books.

4. The shelving cart is not a scooter.

5. Library paste is not food. [Marginal not in child's hand: True. It tastes like Cream of Wrong Soup.]

6. Do not use the date stamp to mark your banana.

7. Shelves are not monkey bars.

8. Do not play 982-pickup with the P-Q drawer (or any other).

9. The dumbwaiter is only for books. It is not a carnival ride.

10. Do not drop volumes of Britannica off the stairs to hear the echo.

———※———

They were an odd, but contented family. There were rules, to be sure, but Dinsy never lacked for attention. With seven mothers, there was always someone to talk with, a hankie for tears, a lap or a shoulder to share a story.

Most evenings, when Dorothy had made a fire in the Reading Room and the wooden shelves gleamed in the flickering light, they would all sit in companionable silence. Ruth knitted, Harriet muttered over an acrostic, Edith stirred the cocoa so it wouldn't get a skin. Dinsy sat on the rug, her back against the knees of whoever was her favorite that week, and felt safe and warm and loved. "God's in his heaven, all's right with the world," as Blythe would say.

But as she watched the moon peep in and out of the clouds through the leaded-glass panes of the tall windows, Dinsy often wondered what it would be like to see the whole sky, all around her.

First Olive and then Dorothy had been in charge of Dinsy's thick dark hair, trimming it with the mending shears every few weeks when it began to obscure her eyes. But a few years into her second decade at the library, Dinsy began cutting it herself, leaving it as wild and spiky as the brambles outside the front door.

That was not the only change.

"We haven't seen her at breakfast in weeks," Harriet said as she buttered a scone one morning.

"Months. And all she reads is Salinger. Or Sylvia Plath," complained Dorothy. "I wouldn't mind that so much, but she just leaves them on the table for *me* to reshelve."

"It's not as bad as what she did to Olive," Marian said. "*The Golden Compass* appeared last week, and she thought Dinsy would enjoy it. But not only did she turn up her nose, she had the gall to say to Olive, 'Leave me alone. I can find my own books.' Imagine. Poor Olive was beside herself."

"She used to be such a sweet child," Blythe sighed. "What are we going to do?"

"Now, now. She's just at that age," Edith said calmly. "She's not really a child anymore. She needs some privacy, and some responsibility. I have an idea."

And so it was that Dinsy got her own room—with a door that *shut*—in a corner of the second floor. It had been a tiny cubbyhole of an office, but it had a set of slender curved stairs, wrought iron worked with lilies and twigs, which led up to the turret between the red-tiled eaves.

The round tower was just wide enough for Dinsy's bed, with windows all around. There had once been a view of the town, but now trees and ivy allowed only jigsaw puzzle-shaped puddles of light to dapple the wooden floor. At night the puddles were luminous blue splotches of moonlight that hinted of magic beyond her reach.

On the desk in the room below, centered in a pool of yellow lamplight, Edith had left a note: "Come visit me. There's mending to be done," and a worn brass key on a wooden paddle, stenciled with the single word: STACKS.

The Stacks were in the basement, behind a locked gate at the foot of the metal spiral staircase that descended from the 600s. They had always reminded Dinsy of the steps down to the dungeon in *The King's Stilts*. Darkness below hinted at danger, but adventure. Terra Incognita.

Dinsy didn't use her key the first day, or the second. Mending? Boring. But the afternoon of the third day, she ventured down the spiral stairs. She had been as far as the gate before, many times, because it was forbidden, to peer through the metal mesh at the dimly lighted shelves and imagine what treasures might be hidden there.

She had thought that the Stacks would be damp and cold, strewn with odd bits of discarded library flotsam. Instead they were cool and dry, and smelled very different from upstairs. Dustier, with hints of mold and the tang of vintage leather, an undertone of vinegar stored in an old shoe.

Unlike the main floor, with its polished wood and airy high ceilings, the Stacks were a low, cramped warren of gunmetal gray shelves that ran floor-to-ceiling in narrow aisles. Seven levels twisted behind the west wall of the library like a secret labyrinth that ran from below the ground to up under the eaves of the roof. Floor and steps were translucent glass brick and six-foot ceilings strung with pipes and ducts were lit by single-caged bulbs, two to an aisle.

It was a windowless fortress of books. Upstairs the shelves were mosaics of all colors and sizes, but the Stacks were filled with geometric monochrome blocks of subdued colors: eight dozen forest-green bound volumes of *Ladies Home Journal* filled five rows of shelves, followed by an equally large block of identical dark red *Life*s.

Dinsy felt like she was in another world. She was not lost, but for the first time in her life, she was not easily found, and that suited her. She could sit, invisible, and listen to the sounds of library life going on around her. From Level Three she could hear Ruth humming in the Reference Room on the other side of the wall. Four feet away, and it felt like miles. She wandered and browsed for a month before she presented herself at Edith's office.

A frosted glass pane in the dark wood door said MENDING ROOM in chipping gold letters. The door was open a few inches, and Dinsy could see a long workbench strewn with sewn folios and bits of leather bindings, spools of thread and bottles of thick beige glue.

"I gather you're finding your way around," Edith said without turning in her chair. "I haven't had to send out a search party."

"Pretty much," Dinsy replied. "I've been reading old magazines." She flopped into a chair to the left of the door.

"One of my favorite things," Edith agreed. "It's like time travel." Edith was a tall, solid woman with long graying hair that she wove into elaborate buns and twisted braids, secured with number-two pencils and a single tortoiseshell comb. She wore blue jeans and vests in brightly muted colors—pale teal and lavender and dusky rose—and a strand of lapis lazuli beads cut in rough ovals.

Edith repaired damaged books, a job that was less demanding now that nothing left the building. But some of the bound volumes of journals and abstracts and magazines went back as far as 1870, and their leather bindings were crumbling into dust. The first year, Dinsy's job was to go through the aisles, level by level, and find the volumes that needed the most help. Edith gave her a clipboard and told her to check in now and then.

Dinsy learned how to take apart old books and put them back together again. Her first mending project was the tattered 1877 volume of *American Naturalist*, with its articles on "Educated Fleas" and "Barnacles" and "The Cricket as Thermometer." She sewed pages into signatures, trimmed leather and marbleized paper. Edith let her make whatever she wanted out of the scraps, and that year Dinsy gave everyone miniature replicas of their favorite volumes for Christmas.

She liked the craft, liked doing something with her hands. It took patience and concentration, and that was oddly soothing. After supper, she and Edith often sat and talked for hours, late into the night, mugs of cocoa on their workbenches, the rest of the library dark and silent above them.

"What's it like outside?" Dinsy asked one night, while she was waiting for some glue to dry.

Edith was silent for a long time, long enough that Dinsy wondered if she'd spoken too softly, and was about to repeat the question, when Edith replied. "Chaos."

That was not anything Dinsy had expected. "What do you mean?"

"It's noisy. It's crowded. Everything's always changing, and not in any way you can predict."

"That sounds kind of exciting," Dinsy said.

"Hmm." Edith thought for a moment. "Yes, I suppose it could be."

Dinsy mulled that over and fiddled with a scrap of leather, twisting it in her fingers before she spoke again. "Do you ever miss it?"

Edith turned on her stool and looked at Dinsy. "Not often," she said slowly. "Not as often as I'd thought. But then I'm awfully fond of order. Fonder than most, I suppose. This is a better fit."

Dinsy nodded and took a sip of her cocoa.

A few months later, she asked the Library for a third and final boon.

The evening that everything changed, Dinsy sat in the armchair in her room, reading Trollope's *Can You Forgive Her?* (for the third time), imagining what it would be like to talk to Glencora, when a tentative knock sounded at the door.

"Dinsy? Dinsy?" said a tiny familiar voice. "It's Olive, dear."

Dinsy slid her READ! bookmark into chapter fourteen and closed the book. "It's open," she called.

Olive padded in wearing a red flannel robe, her feet in worn carpet slippers. Dinsy expected her to proffer a book, but instead Olive said, "I'd like you to come with me, dear." Her blue eyes shone with excitement.

"What for?" They had all done a nice reading of *As You Like It* a few days before, but Dinsy didn't remember any plans for that night. Maybe Olive just wanted company. Dinsy had been meaning to spend an evening in the Children's Room, but hadn't made it down there in months.

But Olive surprised her. "It's Library business," she said, waggling her finger and smiling.

Now, that was intriguing. For years, whenever the Librarians wanted an evening to themselves, they'd disappear down into the Stacks after supper, and would never tell her why. "It's Library business," was all they ever said. When she was younger, Dinsy had tried to follow them, but it's hard to sneak in a quiet place. She was always caught and given that awful cherry tea. The next thing she knew it was morning.

"Library business?" Dinsy said slowly. "And I'm invited?"

"Yes, dear. You're practically all grown up now. It's high time you joined us."

"Great." Dinsy shrugged, as if it were no big deal, trying to hide her excitement. And maybe it wasn't a big deal. Maybe it was a meeting of the rules committee, or plans for moving the 340s to the other side of the window again. But what if it *was* something special . . . ? That was both exciting and a little scary.

She wiggled her feet into her own slippers and stood up. Olive barely came to her knees. Dinsy touched the old woman's white hair affectionately, remembering when she used to snuggle into that soft lap. Such a long time ago.

A library at night is a still but resonant place. The only lights were the sconces along the walls, and Dinsy could hear the faint echo of each footfall on the stairs down to the foyer. They walked through the shadows of the shelves in the Main Room, back to the 600s, and down the metal stairs to the Stacks, footsteps ringing hollowly.

The lower level was dark except for a single caged bulb above the rows of *National Geographics*, their yellow bindings pale against the gloom. Olive turned to the left.

"Where are we going?" Dinsy asked. It was so odd to be down there with Olive.

"You'll see," Olive said. Dinsy could practically feel her smiling in the dark. "You'll see."

She led Dinsy down an aisle of boring municipal reports and stopped at the far end, in front of the door to the janitorial closet set into the stone wall. She pulled a long, old-fashioned brass key from the pocket of her robe and handed it to Dinsy.

"You open it, dear. The keyhole's a bit high for me."

Dinsy stared at the key, at the door, back at the key. She'd been fantasizing about "Library Business" since she was little, imagining all sorts of scenarios, none of them involving cleaning supplies. A monthly poker game. A secret tunnel into town, where they all went dancing, like the twelve princesses. Or a book group, reading forbidden texts. And now they were inviting her in? What a letdown if it was just maintenance.

She put the key in the lock. "Funny," she said as she turned it. "I've always wondered what went on when you—" Her voice caught in her throat. The door opened, not onto the closet of mops and pails and bottles of Pine-Sol she expected, but onto a small room, paneled in wood the color of ancient honey. An Oriental rug in rich, deep reds lay on the parquet floor, and the room shone with the light of dozens of candles. There were no shelves, no books, just a small fireplace at one end where a log crackled in the hearth.

"Surprise," said Olive softly. She gently tugged Dinsy inside.

All the others were waiting, dressed in flowing robes of different colors. Each of them stood in front of a Craftsman rocker, dark wood covered in soft brown leather.

Edith stepped forward and took Dinsy's hand. She gave it a gentle squeeze and said, under her breath, "Don't worry." Then she winked and led Dinsy to an empty rocker. "Stand here," she said, and returned to her own seat.

Stunned, Dinsy stood, her mouth open, her feelings a kaleidoscope.

"Welcome, dear one," said Dorothy. "We'd like you to join us." Her face was serious, but her eyes were bright, as if she was about to tell a really awful riddle and couldn't wait for the reaction.

Dinsy started. That was almost word-for-word what Olive had said, and it made her nervous. She wasn't sure what was coming, and was even less sure that she was ready.

"Introductions first." Dorothy closed her eyes and intoned, "I am Lexica. I serve the Library." She bowed her head once and sat down.

Dinsy stared, her eyes wide and her mind reeling as each of the Librarians repeated what was obviously a familiar rite.

"I am Juvenilia," said Olive with a twinkle. "I serve the Library."

"Incunabula," said Edith.

"Sapientia," said Harriet.

"Ephemera," said Marian.

"Marginalia," said Ruth.

"Melvilia," said Blythe, smiling at Dinsy. "And I too serve the Library."

And then they were all seated, and all looking up at Dinsy.

"How old are you now, my sweet?" asked Harriet.

Dinsy frowned. It wasn't as easy a question as it sounded. "Seventeen," she said after a few seconds. "Or close enough."

"No longer a child," Harriet nodded. There was a touch of sadness in her voice. "That is why we are here tonight. To ask you to join us."

There was something so solemn in Harriet's voice that it made Dinsy's stomach knot up. "I don't understand," she said slowly. "What do you mean? I've been here my whole life. Practically."

Dorothy shook her head. "You have been in the Library, but not of the Library. Think of it as an apprenticeship. We have nothing more to teach you. So we're asking if you'll take a Library name and truly become one of us. There have always been seven to serve the Library."

Dinsy looked around the room. "Won't I be the eighth?" she asked. She was curious, but she was also stalling for time.

"No, dear," said Olive. "You'll be taking my place. I'm retiring. I can barely reach the second shelves these days, and soon I'll be no bigger than the dictionary. I'm going to put my feet up and sit by the fire and take it easy. I've earned it," she said with a decisive nod.

"Here, here," said Blythe. "And well done, too."

There was a murmur of assent around the room.

Dinsy took a deep breath, and then another. She looked around the room at the eager faces of the seven Librarians, the only mothers she had ever known. She loved them all, and was about to disappoint them, because she had a secret of her own. She closed her eyes so she wouldn't see their faces, not at first.

"I can't take your place, Olive," she said quietly, and heard the tremor in her own voice as she fought back tears.

All around her the librarians clucked in surprise. Ruth recovered first. "Well, of course not. No one's asking you to *replace* Olive, we're merely—"

"I can't join you," Dinsy repeated. Her voice was just as quiet, but it was stronger. "Not now."

"But why *not*, sweetie?" That was Blythe, who sounded as if she were about to cry herself.

"Fireworks," said Dinsy after a moment. She opened her eyes. "Six-sixty-two-point-one." She smiled at Blythe. "I know everything about them. But I've never *seen* any." She looked from face to face again.

"I've never petted a dog or ridden a bicycle or watched the sun rise over the ocean," she said, her voice gaining courage. "I want to feel the wind and eat an ice cream cone at a carnival. I want to smell jasmine on a spring night and hear an orchestra. I want—" she faltered, and then continued, "I want the chance to dance with a boy."

She turned to Dorothy. "You said you have nothing left to teach me. Maybe that's true. I've learned from each of you that there's nothing in the world I can't discover and explore for myself in these books. Except the world," she added in a whisper. She felt her eyes fill with tears. "You chose the Library. I can't do that without knowing what else there might be."

"You're leaving?" Ruth asked in a choked voice.

Dinsy bit her lip and nodded. "I'm, well, I've—" She'd been practicing these words for days, but they were so much harder than she'd thought. She looked down at her hands.

And then Marian rescued her.

"Dinsy's going to college," she said. "Just like I did. And you, and you, and you." She pointed a finger at each of the women in the room. "We were girls before we were librarians, remember? It's her turn now."

"But how—?" asked Edith.

"Where did—?" stammered Harriet.

"I wished on the Library," said Dinsy. "And it left an application in the unabridged. Marian helped me fill it out."

"I *am* in charge of circulation," said Marian. "What comes in, what goes out. We found her acceptance letter in the Book Return last week."

"But you had no transcripts," said Dorothy practically. "Where did you tell them you'd gone to school?"

Dinsy smiled. "That was Marian's idea. We told them I was home-schooled, raised by feral librarians."

And so it was that on a bright September morning, for the first time in ages, the heavy oak door of the Carnegie Library swung open. Everyone stood in the doorway, blinking in the sunlight.

"Promise you'll write," said Blythe, tucking a packet of sweets into the basket on Dinsy's arm. The others nodded. "Yes, do."

"I'll try," she said. "But you never know how long *any*thing will take around here." She tried to make a joke of it, but she was holding back tears and her heart was hammering a mile a minute.

"You will come back, won't you? I can't put off my retirement forever." Olive was perched on top of the Circulation Desk.

"To visit, yes." Dinsy leaned over and kissed her cheek. "I promise. But to serve? I don't know. I have no idea what I'm going to find out there." She looked out into the forest that surrounded the library. "I don't even know if I'll be able to get back in, through all that."

"Take this. It will always get you in," said Marian. She handed Dinsy a small stiff pasteboard card with a metal plate in one corner, embossed with her name: DINSY CARNEGIE.

"What is it?" asked Dinsy.

"Your library card."

There were hugs all around, and tears and goodbyes. But in the end, the seven librarians stood back and watched her go.

Dinsy stepped out into the world as she had come—with a wicker basket and a book of fairy tales, full of hopes and dreams.

The Books

Kage Baker

We used to have to go a lot farther down the coast in those days, before things got easier. People weren't used to us then.

If you think about it, we must have looked pretty scary when we first made it out to the coast. Thirty trailers full of Show people, pretty desperate and dirty-looking Show people too, after fighting our way across the plains from the place where we'd been camped when it all went down. I don't remember when it went down, of course; I wasn't born yet.

The Show used to be an olden-time fair, a teaching thing. We traveled from place to place putting it on so people would learn about olden times, which seems pretty funny now, but back then . . . how's that song go? The one about mankind jumping out into the stars? And everybody thought that was how it was going to be. The aunts and uncles would put on the Show so space-age people wouldn't forget things like weaving and making candles when they went off into space. That's what you call irony, I guess.

But afterward we had to change the Show, because . . . well, we couldn't have the Jousting Arena anymore because we needed the big horses to pull the trailers. And Uncle Buck didn't make fancy work with dragons with rhinestone eyes on them anymore because, who was there left to buy that kind of stuff? And anyway, he was too busy making horseshoes. So all the uncles and aunts got together and worked it out like it is now, where we come into town with the Show and people come to see it and then they let us stay a while because we make stuff they need.

I started out as a baby bundle in one of the stage shows, myself. I don't remember it, though. I remember later I was in some play with a love story and I just wore a pair of fake wings and ran across the stage naked and shot at the girl with a toy bow and arrow that had glitter on them. And another time I played a dwarf. But I wasn't a dwarf, we only had the one dwarf and she was a lady, that was Aunt Tammy, and she's dead now. But there was an act with a couple of dwarves dancing and she needed a partner, and I had to wear a black suit and a top hat.

But by then my daddy had got sick and died so my mom was sharing the trailer with Aunt Nera, who made pots and pitchers and stuff, so that meant we were living with her nephew Myko too. People said he went crazy later on but it wasn't true. He was just messed up. Aunt Nera left the Show for a little while after it all went down, to go and see if her family—they were townies—had made it through okay, only they didn't, they were all dead but the baby, so she took the baby away with her and found us again. She said Myko was too little to remember but I think he remembered some.

Anyway we grew up together after that, us and Sunny who lived with Aunt Kestrel in their trailer which was next to ours. Aunt Kestrel was a juggler in the Show and Myko thought that was intense, he wanted to be a kid juggler. So he got Aunt Kestrel to show him how. And Sunny knew how already, she'd been watching her morn juggle since she was born and she could do clubs or balls or the apple-eating trick or anything. Myko decided he and Sunny should be a kid juggling act. I cried until they said I could be in the act too, but then I had to learn how to juggle and boy, was I sorry. I knocked out one of my own front teeth with a club before I learned better. The new one didn't grow in until I was seven, so I went around looking stupid for three years. But I got good enough to march in the parade and juggle torches.

That was after we auditioned, though. Myko went to Aunt Jeff and whined and he made us costumes for our act. Myko got a black doublet and a toy sword and a mask and I got a buffoon overall with a big spangly ruff. Sunny got a princess costume. We called ourselves the Minitrons. Actually Myko came up with the name. I don't know what he thought a Minitron was supposed to be but it sounded brilliant. Myko and I were both supposed to be in love with the princess and she couldn't decide between us so we had to do juggling tricks to win her hand, only she outjuggled us, so then Myko and I had a swordfight to decide things. And I always lost and died of a broken heart, but then the princess was sorry and put a paper rose on my chest. Then I jumped up and we took our bows and ran off, because the next act was Uncle Monty and his performing parrots.

By the time I was six we felt like old performers, and we swaggered in front of the other kids because we were the only kid act. We'd played it in six towns already. That was the year the aunts and uncles decided to take the trailers as far down the coast as this place on the edge of the big desert. It used to be a big city before it all went down. Even if there weren't enough people alive there anymore to put on a show for, there might be a lot of old junk we could use.

We made it into town all right without even any shooting. That was kind of amazing, actually, because it turned out nobody lived there but old people, and old people will usually shoot at you if they have guns, and these did. The other amazing thing was that the town was huge and I mean really huge, I just walked around with my head tilted back staring at these towers that went up and up, into the sky. Some of them you couldn't even see the tops because the fog hid them.

And they were all mirrors and glass and arches and domes and scowly faces in stone looking down from way up high.

But all the old people lived in just a few places right along the beach, because the further back you went into the city the more sand was everywhere. The desert was creeping in and taking a little more every year. That was why all the young people had left. There was nowhere to grow any food. The old people stayed because there was still plenty of stuff in jars and cans they had collected from the markets, and anyway they liked it there because it was warm. They told us they didn't have enough food to share any, though. Uncle Buck told them all we wanted to trade for was the right to go into some of the empty towers and strip out as much of the copper pipes and wires and things as we could take away with us. They thought that was all right; they put their guns down and let us camp, then.

But we found out the Show had to be a matinée if we were going to perform for them, because they all went to bed before the time we usually put on the Show. And the fire-eater was really pissed off about that because nobody would be able to see his act much, in broad daylight. It worked out all right, in the end, because the next day was dark and gloomy. You couldn't see the tops of the towers at all. We actually had to light torches around the edges of the big lot where we put up the stage.

The old people came filing out of their apartment building to the seats we'd set up, and then we had to wait the opening because they decided it was too cold and they all went shuffling back inside and got their coats. Finally the Show started and it went pretty well, considering some of them were blind and had to have their friends explain what was going on in loud voices.

But they liked Aunt Lulu and her little trained dogs and they liked Uncle Manny's strongman act where he picked up a Volkswagen. We kids knew all the heavy stuff like the engine had been taken out of it, but they didn't. They applauded Uncle Derry the Mystic Magician, even though the talkers for the blind shouted all through his performance and threw his timing off. He was muttering to himself and rolling a joint as he came through the curtain that marked off Backstage.

"Brutal crowd, kids," he told us, lighting his joint at one of the torches. "Watch your rhythm."

By we were kids and we could ignore all the grownups, in the world shouting, so we grabbed our prop baskets and ran out and put on our act. Myko stalked up and down and waved his sword and yelled his lines about being the brave and dangerous Captainio. I had a little pretend guitar that I strummed on while I pretended to look at the moon, and spoke my lines about being a poor fool in love with the princess. Sunny came out and did her princess dance. Then we juggled. It all went fine. The only time I was a little thrown off was when I glanced at the audience for a split second and saw the light of my juggling torches flickering on all those glass lenses or blind eyes. But I never dropped a torch.

Maybe Myko was bothered some, though, because I could tell by the way his eyes glared through his mask that he was getting worked up. When we had the sword duel near the end he hit too hard, the way he always did when he got worked up, and he banged my knuckles so bad I actually said "Ow" but the audience didn't catch it. Sometimes when he was like that his hair almost bristled, he was like some crazy cat jumping and spitting, and he'd fight about nothing.

Sometimes afterward I'd ask him why. He'd shrug and say he was sorry. Once he said it was because life was so damn boring.

Anyway I sang my little sad song and died of a broken heart, *flumpf* there on the pavement in my buffoon suit. I felt Sunny come over and put the rose on my chest and, I will remember this to my dying day, some old lady was yelling to her old man, " . . . and now the little girl gave him her rose!"

And the old man yelled, "What? She gave him her nose?"

"Damn it, Bob! Her *ROSE*!"

I corpsed right then, I couldn't help it, I was still giggling when Myko and Sunny pulled me to my feet and we took our bows and ran off. Backstage they started laughing too. We danced up and down and laughed, very much getting in the way of Uncle Monty, who had to trundle all his parrots and their perches out on stage.

When we had laughed ourselves out, Sunny said, "So . . . what'll we do now?" That was a good question. Usually the Show was at night, so usually after a performance we went back to the trailers and got out of costume and our moms fed us and put us to bed. We'd never played a matinée before. We stood there looking at each other until Myko's eyes gleamed suddenly.

"We can explore the Lost City of the Sands," he said, in that voice he had that made it sound like whatever he wanted was the coolest thing ever. Instantly, Sunny and I both wanted to explore too. So we slipped out from the backstage area, just as Uncle Monty was screaming himself hoarse trying to get his parrots to obey him, and a moment later we were walking down an endless street lined with looming giants' houses.

They weren't really, they had big letters carved up high that said they were this or that property group or financial group or brokerage or church, but if a giant had stepped out at one corner and peered down at us, we wouldn't have been surprised. There was a cold wind blowing along the alleys from the sea, and sand hissed there and ran before us like ghosts along the ground, but on the long deserted blocks between there was gigantic silence. Our tiny footsteps only echoed in doorways.

The windows were mostly far above our heads and there was nothing much to see when Myko hoisted me up to stand on his shoulders and look into them.

Myko kept saying he hoped we'd see a desk with a skeleton with one of those headset things on sitting at it, but we never did; people didn't die that fast when it all went down. My mom said they could tell when they were getting sick and people went home and locked themselves in to wait and see if they lived or not.

Anyway Myko got bored finally and started this game where he'd charge up the steps of every building we passed. He'd hammer on the door with the hilt of his sword and yell, "It's the Civilian Militia! Open up or we're coming in!" Then he'd rattle the doors, but everything was locked long ago. Some of the doors were too solid even to rattle, and the glass was way too thick to break.

After about three blocks of this, when Sunny and I were starting to look at each other with our eyebrows raised—meaning "Are you going to tell him this game is getting old or do I have to do it?"—right then something amazing happened: one of the doors swung slowly inward and Myko swung with it. He staggered into the lobby or whatever and the door shut behind him. He stood staring at us through the glass and we stared back and I was scared to death, because I thought we'd have to run back and get Uncle Buck and Aunt Selene with their hammers to get Myko out, and we'd all be in trouble.

But Sunny just pushed on the door and it opened again. She went in so I had to go in too. We stood there all three and looked around. There was a desk and a dead tree in a planter and another huge glass wall with a door in it, leading deeper into the building. Myko began to grin.

"This is the first chamber of the Treasure Tomb in the Lost City," he said. "We just killed the giant scorpion and now we have to go defeat the army of zombies to get into the second chamber!"

He drew his sword and ran yelling at the inner door, but it opened too, soundlessly, and we pushed after him. It was much darker in here but there was still enough light to read the signs.

"It's a library," said Sunny. "They used to have paperbacks."

"*Paperbacks*," said Myko gloatingly, and I felt pretty excited myself. We'd seen lots of paperbacks, of course; there was the boring one with the mended cover that

Aunt Maggie made everybody learn to read in. Every grownup we knew had one or two or a cache of paperbacks, tucked away in boxes or in lockers under beds, to be thumbed through by lamplight and read aloud from, if kids had been good.

Aunt Nera had a dozen paperbacks and she'd do that. It used to be the only thing that would stop Myko crying when he was little. We knew all about the Last Unicorn and the kids who went to Narnia, and there was a really long story about some people who had to throw a ring into a volcano that I always got tired of before it ended, and another really long one about a crazy family living in a huge castle, but it was in three books and Aunt Nera only had the first two. There was never any chance she'd ever get the third one now, of course, not since it all went down. Paperbacks were rare finds, they were ancient, their brown pages crumbled if you weren't careful and gentle.

"We just found all the paperbacks in the *universe*!" Myko shouted.

"Don't be dumb," said Sunny. "Somebody must have taken them all away years ago."

"Oh yeah?" Myko turned and ran further into the darkness. We followed, yelling at him to come back, and we all came out together into a big round room with aisles leading off it. There were desks in a ring all around and the blank dead screens of electronics. We could still see because there were windows down at the end of each aisle, sending long trails of light along the stone floors, reflecting back on the long shelves that lined the aisles and the uneven surfaces of the things on the shelves. Clustering together, we picked an aisle at random and walked down it toward the window.

About halfway down it, Myko jumped and grabbed something from one of the shelves. "Look! Told you!" He waved a paperback under our noses. Sunny leaned close to look at it. There was no picture on the cover, just the title printed big.

"Roget's. The. Saurus," Sunny read aloud.

"What's it about?" I asked.

Myko opened it and tried to read. For a moment he looked so angry I got ready to run, but then he shrugged and closed the paperback. "It's just words. Maybe it's a secret code or something. Anyway, it's mine now." He stuck it inside his doublet.

"No stealing!" said Sunny.

"If it's a dead town it's not stealing, it's salvage," I told her, just like the aunts and uncles always told us.

"But it isn't dead. There's all the old people."

"They'll die soon," said Myko. "And anyway Uncle Buck already asked permission to salvage." Which she had to admit was true, so we went on. What we didn't know then, but figured out pretty fast, was that all the other things on the shelves were actually big hard books like Uncle Des's *Barlogio's Principles of Glassblowing*.

But it was disappointing at first because none of the books in that aisle had stories. It was all, what do you call it, reference stuff. We came out sadly thinking we'd been gypped, and then Sunny spotted the sign with directions.

"Children's Books, Fifth Floor," she announced.

"Great! Where's the stairs?" Myko looked around. We all knew better than to ever, ever go near an elevator, because not only did they mostly not work, they could kill you. We found a staircase and climbed, and climbed for what seemed forever, before we came out onto the Children's Books floor.

And it was so cool. There were racks of paperbacks, of course, but we stood there with our mouths open because the signs had been right—there were books here. Big, hard, solid books, but not about grownup stuff. Books with bright pictures on the covers. Books for us. Even the tables and chairs up here were our size.

With a little scream, Sunny ran forward and grabbed a book from a shelf. "It's *Narnia*! Look! And it's got different pictures!"

"What a score," said Myko, dancing up and down. "Oh, what a score!"

I couldn't say anything. The idea was so enormous: all these were *ours*. This whole huge room belonged to us . . . at least, as much as we could carry away with us.

Myko whooped and ran off down one of the aisles. Sunny stayed frozen at the first shelf, staring with almost a sick expression at the other books. I went close to see.

"Look," she whispered. "There's millions. How am I supposed to choose? We need as many stories as we can get." She was pointing at a whole row of books with color titles: *The Crimson Fairy Book. The Blue Fairy Book. The Violet Fairy Book. The Orange Fairy Book*. I wasn't interested in fairies, so I just grunted and shook my head.

I picked an aisle and found shelves full of flat books with big pictures. I opened one and looked at it. It was real easy to read, with big letters and the pictures were funny, but I read right through it standing there. It was about those big animals you see sometimes back up the delta country, you know, elephants.

Dancing, with funny hats on. I tried to imagine Aunt Nera reading it aloud on winter nights. It wouldn't last even one night; it wouldn't last through one bedtime. It was only one story. Suddenly I saw what Sunny meant. If we were going to take books away with us, they had to be full of stories that would *last*. What's the word I'm looking for? *Substance*.

Myko yelled from somewhere distant "Here's a cool one! It's got pirates!" It was pretty dark where I was standing, so I wandered down the aisle toward the window. The books got thicker the farther I walked. There were a bunch of books about dogs, but their stories all seemed sort of the same; there were books about horses too, with the same problem. There were books to teach kids how to make useful stuff, but when I looked through them they were all dumb things like how to weave potholders for your mom or build things out of Popsicle sticks.

I didn't even know what Popsicle sticks were, much less where I could get any.

There were some about what daily life was like back in olden times, but I already knew about that, and anyway those books had no story.

And all the while Myko kept yelling things like "Whoa! This one has guys with spears and shields and *gods*!" or "Hey, here's one with a flying carpet and it says it's got a thousand stories!" Why was I the only one stuck in the dumb books shelves?

I came to the big window at the end and looked out at the view—rooftops, fog, gray dark ocean—and backed away, scared stiff by how high up I was. I was turning around to run back when I saw the biggest book in the world.

Seriously. It was half as big as I was, twice the size of *Barlogio's Principles of Glassblowing*, it was bound in red leather and there were gold letters along its back. I crouched down and slowly spelled out the words.

The Complete Collected Adventures of Asterix the Gaul.

I knew what "Adventures" meant, and it sounded pretty promising. I pulled the book down—it was the heaviest book in the world too—and laid it flat on the floor. When I opened it I caught my breath. I had found the greatest book in the world.

It was full of colored pictures, but there were words too, a lot of them, they were the people in the story talking but you could *see them talk*. I had never seen a comic before. My mom talked sometimes about movies and TV must have been like this, I thought, talking pictures. And there was a story. In fact, there were lots of stories. Asterix was this little guy no bigger than me but he had a mustache and a helmet and he lived in this village and there was a wizard with a magic potion and Asterix fought in battles and traveled to all these faraway places and had all these adventures!!! And I could read it all by myself, because when I didn't know what a word meant I could guess at it from the pictures.

I settled myself more comfortably on my stomach, propped myself up on my elbows so I wouldn't crunch my starched ruff, and settled down to read.

Sometimes the world becomes a perfect place.

Asterix and his friend Obelix had just come to the Forest of the Carnutes when I was jolted back to the world by Myko yelling for me. I rose to my knees and looked around. It was darker now; I hadn't even realized I'd been pushing my nose closer and closer to the pages as the light had drained away. There were drops of rain hitting the window and I thought about what it would be like running through those dark cold scary streets and getting rained on too.

I scrambled to my feet and grabbed up my book, gripping it to my chest as I ran. It was even darker when I reached the central room. Myko and Sunny were having a fight when I got there. She was crying. I stopped, astounded to see she'd pulled her skirt off and stuffed it full of books, and she was sitting there with her legs bare to her underpants.

"We have to travel light, and they're too heavy," Myko was telling her. "You can't take all those!"

"I have to," she said. "We *need* these books!" She got to her feet and hefted the skirt. *The Olive Fairy Book* fell out. I looked over and saw she'd taken all the colored fairy books. Myko bent down impatiently and grabbed up *The Olive Fairy Book*. He looked at it.

"It's stupid," he said. "Who needs a book about an olive fairy?"

"You moron, it's not about an olive fairy!" Sunny shrieked. "It's got all kinds of stories in it! Look!" She grabbed it back from him and opened it, and shoved it out again for him to see. I sidled close and looked. She was right: there was a page with the names of all the stories in the book. There were a lot of stories, about knights and magic and strange words. Read one a night, they'd take up a month of winter nights. And every book had a month's worth of stories in it? Now, that was concentrated entertainment value.

Myko, squinting at the page, must have decided the same thing. "Okay," he said. "But you'll have to carry it. And don't complain if it's heavy."

"I won't," said Sunny, putting her nose in the air. He glanced at me and did a double-take.

"You can't take that!" he yelled. "It's too big and it's just one book anyway!"

"It's the only one I want," I said. "And anyhow, you got to take all the ones you wanted!" He knew it was true, too. His doublet was so stuffed out with loot, he looked pregnant.

Myko muttered under his breath, but turned away, and that meant the argument was over. "Anyway we need to leave."

So we started to, but halfway down the first flight of stairs three books fell out of Sunny's skirt and we had to stop while Myko took the safety pins out of all our costumes and closed up the waistband. We were almost to the second floor when Sunny lost her hold on the skirt and her books went cascading down to the landing, with the loudest noise in the universe. We scrambled down after them and were on our knees picking them up when we heard the other noise.

It was a hissing, like someone gasping for breath through whistly dentures, and a jingling, like a ring of keys, because that's what it was. We turned our heads.

Maybe he hadn't heard us when we ran past him on the way up. We hadn't been talking then, just climbing, and he had a lot of hair in his ears and a pink plastic sort of machine in one besides. Or maybe he'd been so wrapped up, the way I had been in reading, that he hadn't even noticed us when we'd pattered past. But he hadn't been reading.

There were no books in this part of the library. All there was on the shelves was old magazines and stacks and stacks of yellow newspapers. The newspapers weren't crumpled into balls in the bottoms of old boxes, which was the only way we ever saw them, they were smooth and flat. But most of them were drifted on the floor like leaves, hundreds and hundreds of big leaves, ankle-deep, and on every, single one was a square with sort of checkered patterns and numbers printed in the squares and words written in in pencil.

I didn't know what a crossword puzzle was then but the old man must have been coming there for years, maybe ever since it all went down, years and years he'd been working his way through all those magazines and papers, hunting down every single puzzle and filling in every one. He was dropping a stub of a pencil now as he got to his feet, snarling at us, showing three brown teeth. His eyes behind his glasses were these huge distorted magnified things, and full of crazy anger. He came over the paper-drifts at us fast and light as a spider.

"Fieves! Ucking kish! Ucking fieving kish!"

Sunny screamed and I screamed too. Frantically she shoved all the books she could into her skirt and I grabbed up most of what she'd missed, but we were taking too long. The old man brought up his cane and smacked it down, crack, but he missed us on his first try and by then Myko had drawn his wooden sword and put it against the old man's chest and shoved hard. The old man fell with a crash, still flailing his cane, but he was on his side and striking at us faster than you'd believe, and so mad now he was just making noises, with spittle flying from his mouth. His cane hit my knee as I scrambled up. It hurt like fire and I yelped.

Myko kicked him and yelled "Run!"

We bailed, Sunny and I did, we thundered down the rest of the stairs and didn't stop until we were out in the last chamber by the street doors. "Myko's still up there," said Sunny. I had an agonizing few seconds before deciding to volunteer to go back and look for him. I was just opening my mouth when we spotted him running down the stairs and out toward us.

"Oh, good," said Sunny. She tied a knot in one corner of her skirt, for a handle, and had already hoisted it over her shoulder onto her back and was heading for the door as Myko joined us. He was clutching the one book we'd missed on the landing. It was *The Lilac Fairy Book* and there were a couple of spatters of what looked like blood on its cover.

"Here. You carry it." Myko shoved the book at me. I took it and wiped it off. We followed Sunny out. I looked at him sidelong. There was blood on his sword too.

It took me two blocks, though, jogging after Sunny through the rain, before I worked up the nerve to lean close to him as we ran and ask: "Did you kill that guy?"

"Had to," said Myko. "He wouldn't stop."

To this day I don't know if he was telling the truth. It was the kind of thing he would have said, whether it was true or not. I didn't know what I was supposed to say back. We both kept running. The rain got a lot harder and Myko left me behind in a burst of speed, catching up to Sunny and grabbing her bundle of books.

He slung it over his shoulder. They kept going, side by side. I had all I could do not to fall behind.

By the time we got back the Show was long over. The crew was taking down the stage in the rain, stacking the big planks. Because of the rain no market stalls had been set up but there was a line of old people with umbrellas standing by Uncle Chris's trailer, since he'd offered to repair any dentures that needed fixing with his jeweler's tools. Myko veered us away from them behind Aunt Selene's trailer, and there we ran smack into our moms and Aunt Nera. They had been looking for us for an hour and were really mad.

I was scared sick the whole next day, in case the old people got out their guns and came to get us, but nobody seemed to notice the old man was dead and missing, if he was dead. The other thing I was scared would happen was that Aunt Kestrel or Aunt Nera would get to talking with the other women and say something like, "Oh, by the way, the kids found a library and salvaged some books, maybe we should all go over and get some books for the other kids too" because that was exactly the sort of thing they were always doing, and then they'd find the old man's body. But they didn't. Maybe nobody did anything because the rain kept all the aunts and kids and old people in next day. Maybe the old man had been a hermit and lived by himself in the library, so no one would find his body for ages.

I never found out what happened. We left after a couple of days, after Uncle Buck and the others had opened up an office tower and salvaged all the good copper they could carry. I had a knee swollen up and purple where the old man had hit it, but it was better in about a week. The books were worth the pain.

They lasted us for years. We read them and we passed them on to the other kids and they read them too, and the stories got into our games and our dreams and the way we thought about the world. What I liked best about my comics was that even when the heroes went off to far places and had adventures, they always came back to their village in the end and everybody was happy and together.

Myko liked the other kind of story, where the hero leaves and has glorious adventures but maybe never comes back. He was bored with the Show by the time he was twenty and went off to some big city up north where he'd heard they had their electrics running again. Lights were finally starting to come back on in the towns we worked, so it seemed likely. He still had that voice that could make anything seem like a good idea, see, and now he had all those fancy words he'd gotten out of *Roget's Thesaurus* too. So I guess I shouldn't have been surprised that he talked Sunny into going with him.

Sunny came back alone after a year. She wouldn't talk about what happened, and I didn't ask. Eliza was born three months later.

Everyone knows she isn't mine. I don't mind.

We read to her on winter nights. She likes stories.

DEATH AND THE LIBRARIAN

~~~

Esther M. Friesner

In an October dusk that smelled of smoke and apples, a lady in a black duster coat and a broad-brimmed hat, heavily veiled, called at Rainey's Emporium in Foster's Glen, New York. She descended from the driver's seat of a black Packard, drawing the eye of every man who lounged on the wooden steps of the crossroads store and attracting a second murmuring throng of idlers from Alvin Vernier's barber shop across the way. The men of Foster's Glen had seen a Packard automobile only in the illustrated weeklies, but to see a woman driving such a dream-chariot—!

However, by the time the lady reached the steps of Rainey's and said, "I beg your pardon; I am seeking the home of Miss Louisa Foster," she had become a middle-aged man in a plain black broadcloth suit, a drummer with sample case in hand and a gleaming derby perched on his head, so that was all right.

"Miss Foster?" Jim Patton raised one eyebrow and tipped back his straw hat as he rubbed his right temple. "Say, you wouldn't be a Pinkerton, now would you?" And the other men on Rainey's steps all laughed, because Jim was reckoned a wit as wits went in Foster's Glen, New York.

The gentleman in black smiled politely, and a trim mustache sprouted across his upper lip to give him a more dapper, roguish air. (This at the expense of his drummer's case, which vanished). "Yes, she's in trouble with the law again," he replied, turning the jape back to its source and stealing Jim's audience along with his thunder. "Lolling on the throne of an opium empire, I'm told, or was it a straightforward charge of breaking and entering?" He patted the pockets of his vest. "I'm useless without my notes." The idlers laughed louder, leaving poor Jim no hope but to drop the cap-and-bells and try the knight's helm on for size instead.

"That's a scandalous thing to say about a lady!" Jim snapped. "And about a lady like Miss Foster—! I can't begin to tell you all she's done hereabouts: church work, the Ladies' Aid, visiting the sick.... Why, she's even turned the east wing of the judge's house into a library for the town!"

"Is that so?" The stranger shot his crisp celluloid cuffs and adjusted a fat ring, pearl and silver, on his lefthand littlest finger. It twinkled into diamond and gold.

His remark was only a remark, but Jim Patton took it for a challenge to his honesty. "Yes, that's *so*," he blustered. "And she's even set aside the money to make the judge's house over to the town for use as a library entire after she's gone."

"What does the judge have to say to all this?"

"What does—?" Jim gaped. "Why, you scoundrel, old Judge Foster's been dead these twenty years! What's your business with his daughter but mischief if you don't even know that much about the family?"

"That would be business that concerns only Miss Foster and me," the stranger replied, and he grew a little in height and breadth of chest so that when Jim Patton stood up to face him they were an even match.

Still, Jim bellowed, "I'll make it my business to know!" and offered fists the size of small pumpkins for inspection. He was farm-bred and raised, born to a father fresh and legless returned from Gettysburg. Caleb Patton knew the value of begetting muscular sons to follow the plow he could no longer master, and Jim was his sire's pride.

The stranger only smiled and let his own muscles double in size until his right hand could cup Jim Patton's skull without too much strain on the fingers. But all he said was, "I am a friend of the family and I have been away." And then he was an old man, dressed in a rusty uniform of the Grand Old Army of the Republic, even though by rights the thick cloth should have been deep navy blue instead of black as the abyss.

The Packard snorted and became a plump, slightly frowzy looking pony hitched to a dogcart. It took a few mincing steps forward, sending the Emporium idlers into a panic to seize its bridle and hold it steady until the gaffer could retake his seat and the reins. Most solicitous of all was Jim Patton, who helped the doddering veteran into the cart and even begged the privilege of leading him to Miss Foster's gate personally.

"That's mighty kind of you, sonny," the old man in black wheezed. "But I think I can find my way there right enough now."

"No trouble, sir; none at all," Jim pressed. "When your business with Miss Foster's done, I'd be honored if you'd ask the way to our farm after. My daddy'd be happy to meet up with a fellow soldier and talk over old times. Were you at Antietam?"

The old man's tears were lost in the twilight. "Son, I was there too." And he became a maiden wrapped in sables against the nipping air. She leaned over the edge of the dogcart to give Jim a kiss that was frost and lilacs. "Tell Davey to hug the earth of the Somme and he'll come home," she said. She drove off leaving Jim entranced and bewildered, for his Davey was a toddler sleeping in his trundle-bed at home and the Somme was as meaningless to his world of crops and livestock as the Milky Way.

The lady drove her pony hard, following the directions Jim and the rest had given. Her sable wraps whipped out behind her in the icy wind of her passage. The breath of a thousand stars sheared them to tattered wings that streamed from her shoulders like smoke. Her pony ran at a pace to burst the barrels of the finest English thoroughbreds, and his hooves carved the dirt road with prints like the smiling cut of a sword. They raced over distance and beyond, driving time before them with a buggywhip, hastening the moon toward the highpoint of the heavens and the appointed hour.

At length the road Jim Patton had shown her ended at the iron gates of a mansion at the westernmost edge of the town. By the standards of Boston or New York it was only a very fine house, but in this rural setting it was a palace to hold a princess. Within and without the grounds trees shielded it from any harm, even to the insinuating dagger of curious whispers. The judge himself had ordered the building of this fortification on the borders of his good name, and the strain of shoring up his innumerable proprieties had aged wood and stone and slate before their time.

The maiden stepped out of the dogcart and shook out her silvery hair. The black kitten mewed where the pony had stood and sniffed the small leather portmanteau that was the only tiding or trace of the dogcart.

The elderly woman gathered up portmanteau and kitten, pressing both to the soft fastness of her black alpaca-sheathed bosom with the karakul muff that warmed her hands. She glanced through the fence's tormented iron curlicues and her bright eyes met only darkened windows. She had ridden into town with the twilight, but now she stood on the hour before the clocks called up a new day.

"None awake? Well, I am not in the least surprised," she commented to the kitten. "At her age, quite a few of them grow tired at this hour. It's almost midnight. Let us try to conclude our business before then. I have a horror of cheap dramatics."

Then she caught sight of a glimmer of lamplight from a window on the eastern side of the house. "Ah!" she exclaimed, and her breath swung back the iron gates as she sailed through them and up the long white gravel drive.

The front doors with their glass lilies deferred to her without the hint of a squeak from latch or hinges. She took a moment in the entryway to arrange herself more presentably. Her black-plumed hat she left on a porcelain peg beside a far more modest confection of gray felt and ivory veils, then studied her reflection in the oak-framed glass the hat-pegs adorned.

"Mmmmmm." She laid soft pink fingers to her lips, evaluating the dimpled, dumpling face and all its studied benevolence. "Mmmmno," she concluded, and the black kitten mewed once more as the handsome young man in gallant's garb took final stock of every black-clad, splendid inch of his romantic immanence. He opened the portmanteau out upon itself, and it turned into an onyx orb. He felt that when a woman spent so much of her life circumscribed by domesticity and filial attentiveness, she at least deserved to depart in more dashing company than that of a fuddy-duddy refugee from a church bazaar. He sighed over the glowing orb before he knelt to touch the kitten's tail. Was that a purr he heard from the heart of the black sword he raised in the silent hall?

He passed through corridors where clutter reigned but dust was chastened out of existence. His gaze swept the house for life and saw the cook snoring in her room below the rooftree, the maids more decorously asleep in their narrow iron beds. A proper housecat patrolled the kitchen, the pantry and the cellar, hunting heedless mice, dreaming oceans of cream. He noted each of them and sent his whispers into minds that slept or wakened:

"If you love him, tell him not to leave the farm for that factory job in New York City or the machines will have him."

"She must be born in the hospital, no matter how loudly your mother claims that hospitals are only for the dying, or she's as good as never born at all."

"Let the silly bird fly across the road; don't chase it there! The delivery man cannot rein back a motor-driven van in time and he does not know that you are a queen."

In certain times, in certain cases, he was allowed this much discretion: he might give them the means to forestall him, if they only had the wit to heed. Would he call it kindness? Ah, but in the end there were no whispered cautions that would avail. He could not change the fact he embodied, merely the time of its fruition. The grand black swan's wings he called into being as a final touch were neither grand nor black enough to hide him from the inevitability of himself.

Still, he thought she would appreciate the wings, and the way he made the black sword shine and sing. He came to the east wing, to the door past which the library lay. He knew the room beyond. Every wall of it was armored with bookshelves, except tor the interruption of a massively manteled fireplace and where a pair of heavy French doors framed a view of the hill sloping down to the town. He had entered that room twenty years ago, wearing somber juridical robes and a bulldog's grim, resigned expression as he informed Judge Foster of the verdict *sans* appeal. Then his hands had been blunt as the words he had spoken. Now his fingers were long and pale as he touched the orb to the doorknob and let himself in.

She looked up from the book she was reading. "Hello," she said, closing the buff-colored volume and laying it aside on the great desk of rosewood and brass. A snowy wealth of hair crowned her finely featured face. Lamplight overlaid with a dappled pattern of roses shone on the fair hands she folded in the lap of her moire dress, a gown so lapped in shades and meanings of black that it left his own dark livery looking shabby by comparison. Her expression held recognition without fear.

"Were you expecting me?" he asked, rather taken aback by the calm she wore draped so gracefully around her.

"Eventually," she replied. Her smile still had the power to devastate. "Isn't that the way it is supposed to be?" She rose from the high backed chair and the bottle-green leather moaned softly to give her up from its embrace. "Father always told me I'd go to Hell, though he'd beat me black and blue if I so much as pronounced the word. Now that I've said it, I assume that's my destination." Her eyes twinkled, and in the air before them fluttered the ghost of a long-vanished fan. "Is it?"

The swan's wings slumped, then trickled away entirely. The gallant's costume diminished to the weedy suiting of a country parson. The sword lingered only long enough for him to realize it was still in his hands, an embarrassment. It shrank posthaste to become a raven that hopped onto the parson's shoulder and croaked its outrage at being transformed into so inappropriate an accessory. At least the orb had possessed the good taste to become a well-thumbed copy of Scripture.

"I—ah—do not discuss destinations."

"Not even to tell me whether it will be all that much of a change from Foster's Glen?" She owned the miraculous ability to be arch without descending to kittenishness.

"I am—er—I am not at liberty to say," he replied, polishing the lozenges of his pince-nez with a decidedly unclerical red kerchief he yanked from a trouser pocket.

"What are you at liberty to do, then?" she asked. "Collect the dead?"

"Er—ah—souls, yes. In specific, souls." He settled the lenses back on the bridge of his nose. "One does one's duty."

"One does it poorly, then," she said, and there was a great deal of bite to the lady's words.

Her vehemence startled him so that he did a little jump in place and bleated, "Eh?"

She was happy to explain. "If souls are what you gather, I said you do a shoddy job of work. You could have had mine twenty-five years ago. I had no further use for it. But to come now—! Hmph." Her small nose twitched with a disdainful sniff that had once broken aspiring hearts.

"Twenty-five years a—?" He made the pages of his Bible flutter as he searched them with a whirlwind's speed. His eyes remained blank as he looked up again and inquired, "I *am* addressing Miss Louisa Foster?"

The lady sighed and moved toward the nearest wall. From floor to ceiling it was a single, continuous tidal wave of books. The musty smell of aging ink and paper, the peculiarly enchanting blend of scents from cloth and leather bindings, sewn spines, and the telltale traces of all the human hands that had turned those pages enveloped her like a sacred cloud of incense as she took a single volume down.

"So it is true," she said, looking at the text in her hands instead of at him. "Death does mistake himself sometimes."

"But you are—?" he insisted.

"Yes, of course I am!" She waved away his queries impatiently.

"Louisa Jane Foster, Judge Theophilus Foster's only child, sure to make a brilliant marriage or Father would know the reason why. A brilliant marriage or none. Father gave me as few choices as you do."

She replaced the book and took down a second one, a cuckoo among the flock of fine leather-fledged falcons. It was only bound in yellowing pasteboards, but when she opened it a scattering of scentless flower petals sprinkled the library carpet. The laugh she managed as she paged through the crumbling leaves trembled almost as much as her smile.

"Have you ever heard of a man named Asher Weiss? More than just in the way of business, I mean. Did you know he was a poet?" She did not look disappointed when her caller admitted he did not. "I didn't think so." Her eyes blinked rapidly. "And the rest of the world is now as ignorant as you.

"There is a poem in here called 'For L.,' " she said. "I don't think seven people alive today ever read it. But I was one who did. He wrote it and I followed a trail of words into his heart, like Gretel seeking a way out of the darkling wood by following trails of pebbles and breadcrumbs." She stopped to gather up the petals in her palm and slip them back between the pages. "Not very brilliant, as matches go; nothing his faith or mine would willingly consecrate, so we made do without consecration. We two—we three soon learned how hard it is to live on pebbles and breadcrumbs." She slid the booklet back onto the shelf.

"May I?" He helped himself to the poet's pasteboard gravestone and read the dead man's name. "But this man died more than twenty-five years since!" he protested.

"And did I ever protest when you took him?" she countered. "At least you left me . . . the other." Her mouth hardened. She snatched the booklet from him and jammed it back between its more reputable kin. "A consolation, I imagined; living proof that God did not solely listen to Father's thundered threats. For a while I dreamed I saw the face of a god of love, not retribution, every time I looked down into his laughing eyes, so like his father's. Oh, what a fine joke!" She plucked a random volume from the shelf and flipped it open so that when she spoke, she seemed to take her words from the printed lines before her. "With all the best jokes, timing is everything."

She held the timorous parson's gaze without mercy. "Is sickness your purview too? Is hunger? Is fever? Or are you only there to settle their affairs in the end? That time—crouching by the bed, holding his hand—I wanted it to be me you took, not him. God knows how he would have gotten on without me—maybe Father's heart would have softened to an orphan's plight . . . " Her smile was bitter as she shook her head. "No. I only read fairy tales. It is for the children to believe in them."

She looked up. "Do you like children, Death?"

Before he could answer, she folded the book shut. "I know," she said. "Ask no questions. Bow your head. Accept." She jabbed the book at the judge's portrait above the fireplace and her voice plunged to a baritone roar: "*Your choices will be made for you, girl! When I want your opinion, I'll give it to you!*" She clapped the book between her hands and laughed. "You would think I would have learned my lessons better than that by now, living with the voice of God Almighty. Almighty . . . whose word remakes the world according to his desires. You know, I never had a Jewish lover, never had a bastard child. When I did not return with Father from New York City, all those years that I was gone from Foster's Glen, I was studying music abroad, living with a maiden aunt in Paris. So I was told. The townsfolk still think I am a lady."

"But you are!" he exclaimed, and the raven sprang from his shoulder to flit beneath the plaster sunbursts on the ceiling.

"You are as happily gulled as they, I see." She extended her hand and the bird came to rest upon it. "I am sorry," she told it. "We have no bust of Pallas for your comfort here, birdie. Father viewed all pagan art as disgraceful, because like my Asher, so few of its subjects seemed able to afford a decent suit of clothes."

"Well, ah—" The parson took a breath and let it out after he had comfortably become a gentleman in evening dress offering his arm and the tribute of a rose. "Shall we go?"

"No." The lady laughed and kissed the bird's gleaming plumage. "Not yet."

"Not—? But I thought—?" He cleared his throat and adjusted the starched bosom of his shirt. "From the warmth of your initial greeting, Miss Foster, I assumed you were quite willing to accept me as your escort tonight."

"How gallant," she said, her words dry as those ancient petals. "And at my age, how can I refuse so fine an offer? I cannot. I only wish to defer it."

"So do they all," he responded. "But this is the appointed time."

She ignored his summons, moving with a smooth, elegant carriage to the portrait above the mantel. She aped the judge's somber look to the last droop of jowl and beetling of brow as she thundered, "*Where is the blasted girl? Will these women never learn to be on time!*" She rested her free hand on the cool marble as she gazed up into the judge's painted scowl. "How long did you wait for me in the lobby of our hotel, Father, before you realized I had flown?" She looked back at her caller. "If I found the courage to keep him waiting, I have little to fear from baiting Death."

The stranger coughed discreetly into a black-gloved hand. "I am afraid that I really must insist you come with me now."

"Why should I come to you when you would not come to me?" Her eyes blazed blacker than the raven's feathers, blacker than the curl of downy hair encased in gold and crystal at the neck of her high-collared gown. "I called you and you would not come. Why? Couldn't you hear me? Was the rain falling too hard on the tiny box, or was the echo from the hole they'd dug for him too loud? I doubt it. They never dig the holes too deep in Potter's Field. Or was it the rumbling of the carriage wheels that drowned out my voice when *dear* Cousin Althea came to fetch me home again? Ah, no, I think perhaps it might have been impossible to hear my cries to you above the fuss she raised because she was so overjoyed to have 'found' me at last."

She slammed the book down on the mantel. "Of course it was impossible for her to have found me earlier, when all she had was my address on any of a dozen letters; letters I sent her pleading for money, for medicine, for the slightest hint of compassion. . . . " She sank down suddenly on the hearthstone, frightening the raven to flight.

He knelt beside her and took her in his arms. Her tears were strong reality against his form of smoke and whispers.

"You have waited so long," she murmured, her breath in his ear warm and alive. "Can't you wait a little longer?"

"How much longer?" He smelled the lavender water that she used after her bath and felt the weary softness of her old woman's skin, her old woman's hair.

"Only until I finish reading." She laid her hands on his shoulders and nodded toward the desk where the buff-covered book still lay.

"Is that all you ask? Not days, not months, only until—?"

"That is all." Her hands clasped his. "Please."

He consented, only half comprehending what he had granted her. All she had said was true: His was the discretion that had assumed there was no truth behind a woman's pleas. So many of them cried out *Let me die!* who thought better of it later. Only when he was compelled to meet them below the railing of a bridge or with the apothecary bottle still in hand was he assured of their sincerity, and Miss Louisa Foster had not sought either of those paths after her cousin Althea fetched her home. *Hysterical* and *She'll get over it* tapped him on the shoulder, leering. He did have memories.

Still dressed for dancing, he helped her to her feet. She returned to her place in the green leather chair and took up the buff-covered book again. "To think I don't need spectacles at my age. Isn't it wonderful?" she said to him. And then: "You must promise not to frighten them."

He nodded obediently, although he had not the faintest idea of what she meant. He recreated himself as a lady of her own age and bearing, a tangle of dark tatting in her hands, a woolly black lapdog at her feet, the image of the poor relative whose bit of bread and hearthfire is earned with silence and invisibility.

The coach clock on the mantelpiece struck midnight.

The French doors creaked as a little hand shyly pushed them open. A dark head peered around the edge of the door. *Mother?* the wind sighed.

She did not look up from the open book as the child blew across the carpet and settled into her shadow. The small head rested itself against her knees and thin, milky fingers that should have been pink and plump and scented with powder instead of mold reached up to close around her hand.

Read to me.

"Why, Danny, I am surprised at you," she said softly. "You know we can't begin without your friends."

The wind blew more phantoms through the open doors, gusts and wracks and tumbling clouds of children. They swept into the darkened library, whirling in eddies like the bright autumn leaves outside, catching in snug corners, in favorite chairs before the breath of their advent died away and left them all sitting in attentive order around Miss Louisa Foster's chair.

The stranger felt a tiny hand creep into hers, a hand whose damp clasp she had last disengaged as gently as she could from the breast of the young, despairing mother fated to survive the plunge the child did not. It was not the stranger's place to ask what became of her charges after she called for them. The child tugged insistently at her hand, then clambered up into her lap uninvited. She settled her head against the lady's shawled shoulder with a contented sigh, having found someone she knew. Her feet were bare and her golden hair smelled of factory smoke and river water.

"Now, shall we begin?" Miss Foster asked, beaming over the edge of the open book. Smiles answered her. "I think that if you are all very good, tonight we shall be finished with Tom Sawyer's adventures, and then—" Her voice caught, but she had been raised with what Judge Foster liked to call "breeding." She carried on. "—and then you shall rest."

She raised her eyes to the patient caller in the other chair. "You see how it is? Someone has to do this for them now. They were lost too young for anyone to share the stories with them—the old fairy tales, and Mother Goose, and *Kim*, and the legends of King Arthur, and *The Count of Monte Cristo*, and—and—oh! How can children be sent to sleep without stories? So I try."

"When—?" The lady with the lapdog wet her lips, so suddenly dry. "When did they first come to you?" The child leaning against her shoulder shifted, then pounced on the tangled tatting in her lap and sat happily creating a nest of Gordian knots as complex and as simple as the world.

"They came soon after I made over this room to be the town's library, after Father was dead. I scoured the shelves of his law books and filled them with all the tales of wonder and adventure and mischief and laughter they could hold. I was seated right here one midnight, reading aloud to myself from Asher's book of poetry, when the first one came." She leaned forward and fondly ruffled the hair of the little boy whose pinched face was still streaked with coal dust. "I never guessed until then that it was possible to hunger for something you have never known."

Then she bent and scooped up the child who held so tightly to her skirts. She set him on her lap and pressed his head to the high-necked, extremely proper sleekness of her dress front. The little ghost's black hair curled around the brooch that held his single strayed curl.

"One night, he was here with the rest. Come all the way from New York City, can you imagine that? And the roads so cold." Her lips brushed the white forehead. "So cold." She set him down again among the rest and gave the stranger a smile of forced brightness. "I've found that children sleep more peaceably after a story, haven't you?" Before her caller could reply, she added, "Please forgive me, but I don't like to keep them waiting."

Miss Foster began to read the last of Tom Sawyer's adventures. The oil lamp smoothed away the marks of fever and hunger and more violent death from the faces of the children who listened. As she read, the words slipped beneath the skin, brought a glow of delight to ravening eyes. In her own chair. Miss Foster's caller became conscious of a strange power filling the room. The ghosts were casting off their ghosts, old bleaknesses and sorrows, lingering memories of pain and dread. All that remained were the children, and the wonder.

At last, Miss Foster closed the book. "The End," she announced, still from behind the stiffness of her smile. The children looked at her expectantly. "That was the end, children," she said gently. "I'm afraid that's all." The small ghosts' eyes dimmed by ones and twos they drifted reluctantly from the lamplight, back toward the moonlit cold.

"Wait."

The stranger stood, still holding the little girl to his chest. He was dressed as a road-worn peddler, with his goods on his back and a keen black hound at his heels. He dropped his dusty rucksack on the rosewood desk and plunged his arm inside. "Here's *Huckleberry Finn*," he said. "You'll have to read them that after they've heard *Tom Sawyer*." He dug more books from the depths of the bag, piling each on each. "Oh, and *The Three Musketeers. Uncle Tom's Cabin. Little Lord Fauntleroy* . . . well, it takes all kinds. And *David Copperfield, Treasure Island, Anne of Green Gables, 20,000 Leagues Under the Sea, Sarah Crewe*—" He stared at the tower of books he had erected and gave a long, low whistle. "I reckon you'll have the wit to find more."

She seized his wrist, her voice urgent as she asked, "Is this a trick? Another joke that Father's own personal god wants to play on me?"

"No trick," he said. "I shall come back, I promise you that, Miss Louisa. I'll come back because I must, and you know I must."

She touched the mourning brooch at her throat. "When?"

"When I promised." His eyes met hers. "When you've finished reading."

He placed the girl-child in her lap, then lifted up her own lost son; together they were no more burden than the empty air. Her arms instinctively crept around to embrace them both and he placed an open book in her hands to seal the circle. "Or when you will."

"I don't—" she began.

"Read."

He shouldered his rucksack and whistled up his hound. The ghostly throng of children gazed at him as he passed through their midst to the French doors. Outside there was still smoke and apples on the air, and a thousand tales yet to be told. He paused on the threshold and turned to see her still sitting there in the lamplight, staring at him.

"Give them their stories, Louisa," he said, his face now aged by winds and rains and summer days uncountable. "Give them back their dreams."

"Once—" She faltered. The children drew in nearer, faces lifted like flowers to the rain. "Once upon a time . . . "

He watched as the words took them all beyond his reach, and he willingly let them go. He bowed his head beneath the moon's silver scythe blade and took a new road, the black dog trotting beside him all the way.

In Libres

~~~

Elizabeth Bear

"I have always imagined that Paradise will be a kind of library."
—Jorge Luis Borges

Euclavia glared down at the sweaty slip of paper crumpled in her left fist. She had managed to shut the door of her tutor's office quietly behind her, managed to walk with soft steps all the way down the hall to the outside door, managed to pass through those great oaken portals (carven as they were with allegorical scenes in relief, involving trees and fauns and one very confused-looking centaur) softly and without force. She paused at the top of the granite steps, panting lightly with the effort of keeping her temper, and whispered under her breath, "One more source, Professor Harvey? One more source to read for my already-finished thesis? One more *fucking* source?"

She stared across the green lawns and pale gravel paths of the university campus, allowing the soft breeze to lift her hair. Morning light limned the roof tiles and rendered green leaves translucent. She forced her breathing to slow, her hand to unclench.

A centaur, much less confused-looking than the one disporting itself with the allegorical fauns, trotted up to the base of the steps. Sunlight—also shimmering on the appaloosa blanket across his shoulders—sparked red highlights off his glossy brown-black skin. He didn't have to crane his head to look up at her, though she stood at the top of the steps to the Biomancy building, as he was the height of a tall man atop a tall horse.

His name was Bucephalus.

"Hey, Eu," Bucephalus said. "What's wrong?"

The paper rustled as her fist clenched again. "I've got to go to the library."

If his face hadn't been the color of an antique cherrywood escritoire, she imagined he might have blanched.

"The library?"

She held the slip of paper out to him. He took it, read it while his mobile eyebrows performed arabesques and oddities, and then said, aloud, "*A Treatise on Adulterations of Food, and Culinary Poisons Exhibiting the Fraudulent Sophistications of Bread, Beer, Wine, Spirituous Liquors, Tea, Coffee, Cream, Confectionery, Vinegar, Mustard, Pepper, Cheese, Olive Oil, Pickles, and Other Articles Employed in Domestic Economy*. By Frederick Accum."

"I need to read a rare book."

"I gathered." His eyebrows said, *but this?!*

"There's apparently," she sighed, "a chapter on poisonous mushrooms. And since my thesis deals with the use of psychoactive plants in thaumaturgy . . . "

Euclavia decided that she needed pastry to take the edge off her irritation. Centaurs were pretty much always hungry, having two stomachs to fill, so the companions set off down the path to the buttery.

Bucephalus's horsey tail flicked unhappily. His hoof clomped as he stamped. "That's just the worst. I thought the whole thing was written!"

"It is," she said. "Professor Harvey wants additional cites, and he thinks I need to rework my mushroom chapter based on some information in this particular text."

His eyebrows were dubious. "Which is in the Special Collections."

"Of course," she said. She paused. He gave her a nervous sideways glance and sidled away. She was pitiless. "I want you to come with me."

"Aw, Eu," he said.

"Hey," she said. "Who'd been helping you with your arcanology lab procedure and grading every week since last semester?"

He stopped short. He tossed his head. He snorted. He folded his arms, glared at her, and when she glared right back he shook out his mane and sighed like a gusty storm.

She didn't drop her gaze. She said, "How dangerous can it be?"

His eyebrows scowled thunderously. "You're an awful person."

"You're all-but-dissertation. And you've been ABD for how long now?"

He didn't look at her.

She said, "How much thesis do you have left to write?"

That stopped him. "You'll help me finish."

"How much is left?"

"I'm stuck," he said. And then, after a few moments, "Two chapters. Maybe. Just the conclusion really. And the bibliography."

Desperation crushed her better judgment. "I'll help you finish," she agreed, regretting it already.

He glared at her, tail flicking. But, "All right," he said.

Euclavia felt a twinge in her better nature, knowing that on some level she'd taken advantage of her predator stare to bully the herd animal. She stepped on her softer emotions ruthlessly. *Pity never made a sorcerer.*

"When do you want to go?" he asked. From the way he was studying the light touching the minarets of an ornate lecture hall on the edge of campus, she knew he was hoping he'd be able to come up with a prior engagement.

They had a study date that evening.

"After lunch," she said. "Today."

"Eu—"

"Soonest begun," she said. "Is first ended. Let's just get this over with before we lose our nerve completely, shall we? Besides. Maybe Dr. Theophilus will be impressed by your initiative. We will *totally* find a book in the Special Collections on your topic, too. We'll check with the reference librarians on the way in."

"I don't believe I'm letting you talk me into this."

"The word you want is *browbeat*, old friend. Come on, let's go eat before all the good stuff is gone."

Euclavia was still chewing on an end of bread when they left the buttery the better part of an hour later. That was a short meal, by centaur standards (two stomachs, one inadequate human mouth to fill them with), and Bucephalus had done his best to draw it out for another hour. But Euclavia (again) had been pitiless.

Even inside her head, the phrase was starting to take on the sonorous quality of a refrain.

Bucephalus ignored her as they walked into the afternoon light, preferring to pointedly argue literature with Joseph, a bull-headed classmate who chewed his cud and contemplated the quadrangle with deceptively mild bovine eyes. They paused in the lavender shade of an ancient, bowering jacaranda tree. Euclavia waited with slowly diminishing grace, rocking from foot to foot, while they continued the conversation.

The shadows had moved a half-inch, and the centaur was saying, "Honestly, as far as poets of anguished masculinity go, I prefer Conrad to Hemingway, but they're both operating from a very narrow construction—" when Euclavia thumped him lightly on the shoulder with the side of her hand and said, "I hate to interrupt, Bue, but if we're going to do this while there's still some daylight to work with, we ought to get a wiggle on."

Bucephalus glared at her, but it was the right threat. Darkness would be worse, for both of them.

"What are you up to?" Joseph asked, and for a moment Euclavia almost hoped he'd decide to join them.

But—"The Library," Bucephalus announced, as if he were informing Joseph of a death. "Eu needs a book. Says her advisor."

Joseph shuddered. "You're braver creatures than I. Do you have the list of supplies?"

Bucephalus said, "It's in the student handbook."

"Right." Joseph whipped a rucksack off his enormous, humped shoulder— Euclavia hadn't even seen it up there—and dug around in it with one horny hand. He stared off into space with a concentrated expression—or as close as a bull's muzzle could get, while still absently cud-chewing—and then came up with a ball of string and a grin.

"Here." He placed it ceremoniously in Bucephalus's hand. "You might just need this."

The Library was not a single building, but rather a complex of buildings on the edge of campus, with only one way in. It was said to have one copy of every book ever written. This was probably an exaggeration, despite the fact that it seemed to have a functionally infinite interior. The Library was bigger on the inside, and it iterated.

It certainly had a great mad pile of things shelved within it. Finding them was another matter: there was no card catalogue, and several attempts to establish one had met with madness, failure, and disappearances.

There were, however, Librarians. Librarians, with their overdeveloped hippocampi, their furled cloaks, their swords and wands sheathed swaggeringly across their backs. The university bureaucracy was nightmarish, Byzantine, and largely ornamental. But those caveats did not apply to the Librarians, an elite informational force second to none. They were lean, organized, and they knew when to turn left and when to turn right.

This one looked dubious, and a little concerned. "I recommend against this," said the Librarian.

It did nothing to settle Euclavia's stomach.

She held up the scrap of paper, with its scrawled note proclaiming: *A Treatise on Adulterations of Food, and Culinary Poisons Exhibiting the Fraudulent Sophistications of Bread, Beer, Wine, Spirituous Liquors, Tea, Coffee, Cream, Confectionery, Vinegar, Mustard, Pepper, Cheese, Olive Oil, Pickles, and Other Articles Employed in Domestic Economy*. By Frederick Accum.

"My tutor wants me to read this for my thesis."

With—she hoped—the outward appearance of calm, she added, "Special Collections."

"Hmm," said the Librarian. She extracted the soggy scrap from Euclavia's grasp and perused it closely. "Have you been sleeping with your tutor's spouse or something? Any reason for him to want you dead? No?"

"No," Euclavia said firmly, wondering. She was aware of Bucephalus falling back from her rear, very silently indeed for somebody with four hooves as big as dinner plates walking on a hardwood floor. She stuck a hand back and grabbed his mane before he sidled completely out of reach.

He snorted. He could have dislodged her easily and made a break for it, but other than leaning against her grip, he didn't put up a fight.

"It has a chapter on mushrooms," Euclavia said helpfully.

"I can't imagine how it would be useful. It's from an interdicted plane, you see. Nonfunctional thaumosphere. Very difficult to get books in and out of a place like that. But we're committed, very committed. Still, that's why it's in Special Collections. The Special Collections Librarian is very interested in such works."

The Librarian pronounced her colleague's title with an upward flicker of her eyes, as if she expected it to make an impression. It was that expectation more than any prior knowledge that gave Euclavia the creeping chills.

"So tell us about this Librarian," said Bucephalus.

The Librarian shook her head. "She doesn't really like to be discussed."

"Tell us about the labyrinth, then," Euclavia suggested.

The Librarian smiled. "It changes without notice. Try not to get caught between the sliding stacks when they move. We can check you out a ball of twine."

"We have one." Euclavia held it up.

"Good," said the Librarian. "Then you're prepared. You'll want three days of food. Pencils and notepaper—pens are not allowed. A sleeping bag or bedroll. No fires. Browse at your own risk. Urination and defecation in designated restrooms only. No shoes on the antique carpets. That goes double for horse-shoes. First aid stations and water are with the restrooms. We say, every five kilometers, but really they move around. Any questions?"

Euclavia and Bucephalus shook their heads.

"Do you need to go back for anything?"

Negative again.

"Please don't feed the books. Some of them will beg."

"Beg?"

"Everybody wants something," the Librarian said. "It's the metric for a successful story." She wrote something down and handed it to Euclavia. It was a number, and it glowed faintly. "Here. This will illuminate your researches."

Euclavia took it and said "Thank you" automatically.

"*In libres! In libres!* Into the books!" the Librarian cried.

An archway did not so much open behind her as become apparent for the first time, as if Euclavia had suddenly noticed it. She glanced over at Bucephalus and found him staring, too, nostrils flared, eyebrows elevated. If his ears were mobile, they would have been pricked tip to tip.

Bucephalus held her gaze for a moment longer, then glanced over at the Librarian. "Say," he asked. "What do you have on alchemically dissolving and later reconstituting skeletons in animatable form?"

"What kind of skeletons?"

". . . mammal?"

"It's always the quiet ones," she said.

And then she issued them a second pass, with another faintly phosphorescent call number scribbled on it.

Bucephalus plucked the ball of twine from Euclavia's palm and tied one end in careful knots, high among the ornate carvings on the archway. "There," he said. "That should be out of the way."

He seemed suddenly cheery. Euclavia didn't trust it. She shouldered her pack and they set off into the stacks, falling into step with one another. Now his hooves clattered cheerfully on the floors, the flash of white stockings on mahogany-black legs showing bright in the gloom.

"Where's the fatalism?" Euclavia asked.

The centaur snorted. His tail stung her shoulders as he gave it a particularly good swish. "This is fatalism," he replied. "I've made the decision to die happy."

At first, the shelves were wooden, widely spaced and low enough to see over. They were crammed with bright, slender, large-format books with hard board covers. Euclavia reached for one with a lavishly illustrated front, the image half-concealed behind its smaller neighbor. The colors were glorious and she itched to touch it.

Bucephalus caught her wrist. "Browse at your own risk," he murmured.

"It's the children's section!"

His eyebrows were shaped like commas, but in their articulation they provided all the punctuation a novelist could desire. "Don't tell me small humans are immune to nightmares."

Euclavia still remembered a few so vividly it didn't seem as if more than a decade had passed. "Point taken," she said, and drew back her hand without stroking that jewel-toned spine.

She glanced down at the scrap with the call number on it. The scrawl still glowed with a faint, silver-violet light. When she turned to the right, she thought it became incrementally brighter.

She held her scrap up and swung from side to side so Bucephalus could see the effect. "Check yours."

He pulled it from the sporran he wore slung around his human waist, hanging against the chest of his horse-part. "To the right," he said after a moment's study.

"Going my way?" she joked.

He snorted, but she thought he felt the same relief that she did. At least they wouldn't have to split up, or make the decision to spend longer in the Library together, to track down both sources. Not yet, anyway.

A black thing, cat-sized—something with wings, or something like a black rag or sack caught up on a wind—flapped and tumbled from above. There might be vaults up there, a groined roof lost in shadows. There might be stars, Euclavia thought. She imagined she caught a glimpse of rectangles of transparent indigo speckled with shimmering lights, but it was like looking upward through water. Everything wavered, as if the shadows were veils of smoke or translucent silk lashed in a wind, half-obscuring.

The thing with the ragged wings—if they were wings—landed atop one of the shelves a few rows off and scuttled along it batlike, spiking elbows above its back. It lowered an indistinct head and sniffed, hard and frequently. It turned, then— just the head, rotating like an owl's—and fixed Euclavia with a fiery green stare, flat and reflective as the glare of light off still water.

She froze and it hissed, or perhaps it hissed and she froze. A moment later, its glare was interrupted. Then it kicked off hard, wings—if they were wings— extended and flurrying, a slim emerald-colored folio depending from its back feet. Euclavia saw that it wore white cotton gloves over what were unmistakably birdlike talons.

"What was that?" Euclavia asked.

"Retrieval system?"

She turned to slap his shoulder, but he was staring after the whatever-it-was, not watching her for a reaction, and his expression looked earnest. Earnest, and concerned. So she patted him instead. His hide was wet already with nervous lather.

They walked on, taking turns trailing the twine behind them, long enough to become hungry and stop at a rest room for food and a nap. The rest was physical only: Bucephalus remained standing up, like an ill-at-ease stallion, and Euclavia managed nothing more than to drift and briefly doze. It didn't leave her refreshed.

After a few desultory hours, they washed their faces, used the facilities, and drank some weak tea made from the hot water tap before continuing. Several more of the black flapping creatures flitted about overhead. Some bore volumes in their white-gloved talons. None of them, after the first, paid any heed to Bucephalus and Euclavia.

They didn't run out of twine, which was a minor miracle. Consider the source, though: they had gotten the ball from a minotaur.

Euclavia was about to campaign for a break for lunch—she had apples and cheese in her bag, and saw the cheery red glow of a restroom sign off to the right—when something ahead rumbled softly, more a shiver through the floor than a real noise Euclavia heard with her ears. She looked at Bucephalus, who was already looking down at her.

"Your hearing is better," she said.

His grin was more of a wince. "The stacks. They're moving."

So they were.

Euclavia and Bucephalus came to a railing. Below it was a drop of at least one story, down to an enormous, possibly boundless room.

As they paused on the edge of the Children's Section, Euclavia strained her eyes to peer into the gathering gloom of Nonfiction. She saw before her serried rank upon rank of gray steel shelves, stretching into haze, dimness, and misty infinity. Even from the elevated height she stood upon, each stack was taller than Bucephalus, and she gave up trying to calculate the number of books that might be visible after a few moments of desultory math that nevertheless left her an ache between the eyes.

They were not in neat rows, but rather formed a sort of irregular pattern of right angles. Like the sort of maze you might draw with a pen, Euclavia thought. Trying to trace it with her eyes made her dizzy.

"So many books," Bucephalus said.

"It's a labyrinth, not a library."

"The path to knowledge follows many strange turnings," he replied. She didn't know if it was a quotation.

The air had a faint, sickly, rancid odor. Something that made Bucephalus snort and stamp. She didn't ask him to identify it.

"Down the stairs?" she asked.

He gave her a haunted look, and followed her along the rail.

But the stairs, when they found them, were spiral. No challenge for Euclavia, but Bucephalus would not be descending in that fashion. They stood there, side by side, frowning down at the wrought steel spiral.

"It's only about twelve feet down," he said at last. "I could jump."

"You cannot jump," she answered. "You'd have to go over the railing. That's three more feet, and onto a hard floor. You'll break your legs."

"If only we had a block and tackle. I could lower myself." He looked around. "This is a public building, right?"

"Technically."

"So it has to be accessible." He paced off toward the nearest side wall, visible because of the glow of yet another sign indicating a restroom.

Euclavia dug out her scrap and glanced down at it as she followed. The silver-violet glow was dimming. "We're going the wrong way."

"Says you. Hah, there it is!"

He gestured. Her eye followed. She blinked. Picked out in cheery red symbols over a filigreed cage door was the word "mezzanine," and through the cage the interior of a lift was just visible.

"You're going to trust that thing?"

"Can't get down the spiral stair," he remarked with casual bravado. "If you're too chicken I'll meet you on the ground floor."

She probably would have taken him up on it, but she could see the foamy white lather worked up in the creases of his joints, and she knew he wasn't any less scared than she. So she tossed the ball of twine over the rail and then followed him in to the lift—he raised and lowered and locked the grate—and waited while he pushed the button marked ground. The thing hesitated for a moment and then started up with a shudder that left her clutching the centaur's arm with both hands. But then it smoothed out, and by the time it (gently) settled level with the ground floor, she was shaking out her robe and trying to pretend to both of them that she was entirely nonchalant.

He raised the grate, and they both stepped out briskly. He left it open behind them, she noticed, and she figured that was a sensible precaution in case they had to leave in a hurry.

"Ugh," he said. "Stinks even worse down here."

"It smells like something rotten," she said, turning to find the string. She handed the ball to him.

He gave her a look that made her wish she hadn't commented. "It is."

They entered the maze. There were more of the ragged black things here, flitting from place to place overhead, occasionally perching atop one of the stacks to glare down at them balefully with their flat, reflective green or gold or orange eyes. Three different books tried to seduce Bucephalus, and two more made passes at Euclavia. They stayed strong, though she admitted to herself that if she'd been alone, she might not have been able to resist running her hands over the one with the copper-tooled limp leather cover.

But Bucephalus caught her looking, and she drew her hand back in time.

"Looks like it might be illuminated," she said, in apology.

He snorted his horsey laugh. "My mother always did say books would be the death of me."

He handed her back the ball of twine to keep her hands busy. It didn't seem much smaller.

They walked on. They chose their direction by the gleam of the call numbers, though Euclavia admitted to some misgivings. What if the papers would try to lead them in a straight line? What if the route through the labyrinth of the stacks was circuitous? What if they starved before they found a way out?

They were quickly out of sight of the mezzanine, and after a few more hours, Euclavia couldn't even be certain she knew what direction it lay in.

But they only found themselves retracing their steps out of dead-ends when they tried to second-guess their simple guides, and in the end they shrugged and decided maybe the Librarian had known what she was doing.

They were actually starting to relax a little bit, and were debating how far to push on past the halfway point in their supplies, when they stumbled across the body.

It wasn't entirely unexpected. The stench had been growing stronger and stronger, and was now gaggingly heavy. When they rounded the corner and found the corpse, though, Euclavia was unprepared for how much worse it was than she'd been braced for. It was humanish, human-sized, but—a small blessing—not really too distinct in the gloom. A flock of the black wing-things perched along it in a ragged single line, their heads bobbing as they gorged.

One looked up. Then another.

Euclavia glanced down at her scrap. Their way led forward.

Bucephalus' tail swished dramatically. His eyes were rimmed with white. Euclavia agreed wholeheartedly.

But Bucephalus said, "We have to go past."

So they edged. The space between the stacks was narrow—three feet or so— and the corpse sprawled across most of it. They got within an arm's length and the biggest wing-thing hissed, reared back, and began to beat its wings aggressively. It wasn't large—the body between the wings was the size of a large house cat—but the teeth in its indistinct shadowy snarl were as long and white as bone needles.

Euclavia wondered if the person on the floor had died of hunger, or of some more direct means.

"Aw, bugger," Bucephalus said. He grabbed her wrist and lunged forward.

Euclavia lost hold of the twine. She found herself dragged into the air, dangling beside his broad, lathered shoulder. The centaur leaped. She swung against his side, arms wrenched, splattered with voluminous horsey sweat. He landed with a jarring thud. She cried out; they had hurdled both the bat-things and the body. Her arm twisted as she spun, and her other side collided with the centaur's barrel.

She threw her other arm over Bucephalus' withers and held on for dear life, facing backwards, her knees drawn up before her in an attempt not to swing under his belly and get trampled or disemboweled. She had a great view backward as the bat-winged things began to rise up, screeching, from their meal.

"Run," she yelled at Bucephalus. "They're coming!"

Her arm slipped off his shoulders as he sprang forward again. Euclavia felt a sudden trembling—strong, now, not the almost subliminal vibration of before. But still nearly silent. The narrow corridor between the stacks on either side, she saw, was tightening.

Euclavia half-expected Bucephalus to pick her up and swing her over his withers, but perhaps centaurs simply didn't think of themselves as beasts of burden. Instead he dragged her—still—by the wrist at a near-gallop, and she bounded along beside him, pulled into impossible leaps, keeping her balance only because he steadied her with his powerful arms. The stacks rolled, closing behind them. Euclavia swore she could feel them clipping Bucephalus' heels, but they were menacingly almost-silent in their well-oiled motion. Only the precise, heavy clicks with which they slid flush and locked together gave away the mass and power of their closing.

"I lost the string!" she yelled.

"Least of our worries! Hang on," Bucephalus called. She wrenched her gaze around and saw that the wall of books had closed in front of them. The stacks were sealing themselves. There was no way out.

Bucephalus coiled himself like a tremendous spring and leaped into the air, hooves reaching spasmodically. She got a fistful of his mane somehow and clung, feeling her body fly out behind him like a banner. He struck the bookcase halfway up, banked off it, and somehow twisted in midair to leap even higher. And then they were cantering along the top of the book cases, a path no wider than the length of Euclavia's forearm, with the bat-creatures flocking in hot pursuit, throwing themselves down to pull Euclavia's hair and try to blind the centaur.

She'd either dragged herself onto Bucephalus' back, or he had tossed her there. She clutched across his chest, fastening her hands together, as bookcase after bookcase slid into the sides of the long rank they ran along and locked there. At least it had the effect of making their path wider.

They came to the end. "Hang on," Bucephalus called again—she would have dinged him for repetition if she'd been able to get half a breath—and he leaped. Down, all that distance to the hard wooden floor below while the ragged wings of the bat-creatures fluttered and jostled and squealed around them.

She'd been wrong. It wasn't too far for him to jump. He landed running, hooves plowing long splinters from the boards, and the shock of it nearly knocked Euclavia's pelvis into her sternum. If she hadn't been gritting her teeth, she suspected she would have bitten her tongue off; as it was, she chipped a tooth and swallowed the sharp shard that resulted.

Then she chipped another, and nearly busted her nose as Bucephalus set his haunches, slithered to a halt, and she smacked into the back of his skull face-first.

"Shit!" she yelled, letting go of him to grab her stinging face. "Shit!"

"Eu," Bucephalus warned, not turning.

She lifted her gaze over his shoulder. He still crouched, half-sitting, weight as far back as he could lean it. His front hooves teetered on the edge of an open lip, a drop down into a pit some thirty feet below. The air was pleasantly dry, cool— the perfect environment for old books. A sign hung above them, in illuminated letters.

The pit was full of books, books housed in an immense spiraling labyrinth of curved cases. And at their center, head bowed over something minuscule, was a creature so gigantic that even from this distance and height, she seemed to tower over them. She had enormous wings like a bat's, folded tight, and she seemed to be holding whatever she was looking at in their two forward-reaching fingers. Her long tail curled around her hind feet, and her crested head was set in a long neck, which she had curved into a serpentine. She was a silvery violet-gray, scaled all over except for the furry patches at her cheeks and along her underbelly. As the bat-things settled on the rim of the pit beside them, their pursuit and harassment forgotten, Euclavia could now see a kinship between them and the giant dragonish thing under the illuminated sign that read *Special Collections*.

"The Book Wyrm," Euclavia said, awed. "I didn't think she was real."

Bucephalus held up the slip of paper in his hand. The call number scribbled on it flamed star-brilliant, achingly silver. "I think we're here," he whispered. "I guess that's the Special Collections Librarian."

The enormous wyrm lifted her head from the tiny book balanced delicately upon her wing-talons. She raised what could have been an eyebrow behind her horn-rimmed glasses.

She said, "Shhh!"

They stood silent for a moment, staring across the space to the Librarian. The Librarian stared back. Euclavia felt Bucephalus's frozen, quivering shock between her knees. She felt the slow drip of blood, thick and sticky, from her nose. She watched the dragon's velvet nostrils flare as if it scented them.

She couldn't look it in the enormous, variegated silver eyes. She looked down, and realized that it was crouched on a pile of bleached bones.

"Why," Bucephalus whispered, "didn't I finish my dis six years ago, when I should have done? I could be tenure track by now somewhere."

"I see you have pull slips," the Librarian said conversationally. "Hand them here, would you?"

A bat-thing swooped down and plucked the paper from Bucephalus' fingers. Another circled, descending toward Euclavia, and she dug hastily in her pockets to find her pull slip before the monstrous little cannibal reached her. She shuddered when the white-gloved talons brushed her flesh.

The wyrm accepted both bits of paper with a delicacy of touch Euclavia, despite herself, found astounding. If she were on the scale the Librarian was, she wouldn't have been able to manage that task with a magnifying glass and tweezers. The Librarian, though, seemed to read both slips without difficulty.

She tapped a pile beside her and said, "Yes, we have these. You can't take them away from here, though. Special Collections don't circulate."

"Oh," said Euclavia.

Bucephalus sidled.

The Wyrm said. "And this one—the food science one—well, it's in my personal to-read pile. Re-read, actually, as I read it when we got it in, but there are never enough new books, are there? I don't suppose you'd mind waiting until I finish?"

"Not at all," said Euclavia, with a sinking feeling. "When do you think you might get to it?"

"Oh," said the wyrm. "Right now it's about five hundred thousand and eleven. Wait, no! Five hundred thousand and four. I forgot—three of those ahead of it are in multiple volumes."

Euclavia laid a hand on Bucephalus's shoulder. To steady herself, not him. He was like a rock. Maybe they could go out and come back later? She shuddered to think about it, and shuddered worse when she remembered that she had lost the twine and they didn't know their way out unless they found it.

She said, "How long might it take you to get through those others?"

"No more than a century," said the wyrm. "I read quickly." She tapped the pile again. "The alchemy book, though. I can pull that one for your friend right now. I just finished rereading it a few years ago and haven't put it back in the hold list yet. Then maybe you and I can have a nice chat while he reads it. It's so seldom that I have interesting visitors." The bones rustled under her weight as she resettled herself. "And they never stay long enough once they get here."

"They leave again?" Bucephalus asked. His voice was steady but Euclavia knew it was an act. She could feel the shivers running through him.

"They usually starve," the wyrm admitted. She stirred her bones.

One of the bat-wing things fluttered down before Bucephalus. It dangled a thin, black-bound quarto in white-gloved claws.

He hesitated and it warbled at him, a funny sound almost too high to hear. He reached out gingerly and accepted the volume. The bat-thing released it and fluttered away, long tail lashing.

Euclavia nerved herself and said to the dragon, "You don't suppose I could just jump ahead of you? I only need to read one chapter. It won't take more than a half hour, I imagine." She held up a pencil. "I won't get any ink near it."

"Well," said the Librarian thoughtfully. "No, I don't think so. I'm ahead of you on the hold list, you see. That wouldn't be fair, would it?"

"No," said Euclavia. "I suppose it wouldn't."

The wyrm raked again at the piles of bones. Euclavia thought of being trapped here forever, too big to leave, for so long that you'd already read every book in an infinite library multiple times.

She thought about what it would be like for her and Bucephalus to sit here and entertain this dragon with conversation until they starved, and then were skeletonized by her—Offspring? Symbiotes? Hench-things?—and were added to the comfortable rakings of her nest.

She said, "What if I traded you something to let me take your place on the hold list? Then you could add yourself again."

"Irregular," said the dragon. She pushed her spectacles up her snout with one hooked talon, though, and frowned as if interested.

"Still," Bucephalus said, who was obviously not as fear-stupefied as Euclavia had thought him.

The dragon said, "What do you have in mind?"

"Well," said Bucephalus, and Euclavia could have kissed him, "Euclavia and I are both writing books, it happens. We need these sources to finish them."

"Hmmm," said the dragon.

"But we can't finish them if we stay here and entertain you until we starve," Euclavia said, picking up the centaur's thread when the wyrm turned her silver eyes on him and he began to stammer. "Let us use the sources and take notes, and show us the way back—and we'll bring you copies of our books before anybody else has read them!"

The dragon settled, folding her wings one over the other. She directed at the both of them a speculative, skeptical look. "You're asking me to trade something that I have, here, today—for something entirely hypothetical. Something that you may never complete."

"But I have," Euclavia said, desperately. "It is completed. That's why I'm here. I gave it to my tutor and he said I needed one more source." She pointed to the pile the wyrm had tapped with her fore-talon. "*A Treatise on Adulterations of Food, and Culinary Poisons Exhibiting the Fraudulent Sophistications of Bread, Beer, Wine, Spirituous Liquors, Tea, Coffee, Cream, Confectionery, Vinegar, Mustard, Pepper, Cheese, Olive Oil, Pickles, and Other Articles Employed in Domestic Economy.* By Frederick Accum. That's it; that's all I need. One cite, and my book is finished."

She waited. She didn't speak. The wyrm didn't speak either. Bucephalus held his breath, his knuckles white on the covers of his alchemy text.

They could try to run. But Euclavia remembered the festering body in the stacks, and guessed in her heart how that would work out.

"New *books*," Euclavia said, temptingly.

Behind her, one of the bat-things giggled and chittered.

"Two books," said the dragon. "New books. Books nobody else has read before me."

"Just us," Euclavia said. "My tutor, but he won't have read the new material. Not until after you do. And nobody's seen Bucephalus's book yet. Have they, Bucephalus?"

He shivered. She squeezed his shoulder. "No," he said. "No, they haven't."

The dragon blinked, slowly, and fluffed her frill. Then she said, in a sonorous tone, "We have a bargain. But if it goes unfulfilled in prompt fashion, I do charge thee, small creatures. Remember that a Librarian makes a very bad enemy."

They read under the dragon's watchful eye.

Then, the bat-things led them back to the twine, which was still whole and, miraculously, waiting for them. And the twine led them out: hungry and exhausted, footsore, leaning on one another, but giddy with the luck of being alive. They clutched their pencil-scribbled notes against their chests. They walked and slept and walked again.

When they came at last through the warrens of the far-flung Children's Section, within sight of the great archway to reception and the eldritch glow of the EXIT sign, only then did Bucephalus turn to Euclavia and say to her in a confiding tone, "You owe me."

And Euclavia, light-headed with giddiness, said, "You mean, you owe me."

"Excuse me?"

"Well," she said, and grinned. "You pretty much have to finish your dissertation now."

The King of the Big Night Hours

Richard Bowes

At the moment the first kid jumped off a library balcony I was on the phone in my office. In what I eventually saw as more uncanny than coincidental, my friend Alex and I were trying to remember the last time either of us had seen the guy who called himself the King of the Big Night Hours.

Alex lives out in Jersey now but years ago he worked with me at the university. "Is the gym still open late?" he asked and chuckled at the memory. "That's where I remember him. He was hot looking."

My answer was, yes it was still open. I remembered the big West Indian who did a lot for the university security uniform he wore. His bearing as much as looks defined the King.

At that instant, shouts echoed in the atrium and I heard a big, hollow thud like a quarter ton of laundry had hit the marble floor.

I did not immediately rush out to see what had happened. It was the Friday of the first week of the fall semester and the library hummed with kids. I thought it was one more damn student thing.

The screams got me off the phone and onto the ninth floor balcony. The center of the university library is a twelve-story atrium. Balconies line each floor and flying staircases connect each balcony with the ones above and below it. Railings of four-and-a-half foot tall vertical brass spikes were all that separated those balconies and stairs from the wide, empty interior space.

Right then those railings were lined with spectators who stared down in silence. The atrium floor is polished marble decorated with in an intricate gray, white, and black geometrical pattern. A man lay sprawled face down on the marble floor surrounded by a splatter of impact blood.

Seeing him, I visualized his downward path, saw the floor flying towards his face. From above, the pattern on the floor can create the illusion it's coming towards the viewer. Staring down at the still body, the pattern seemed to fill my vision. I managed to turn away before I was mesmerized.

At times like these, it helps to have a function, something to do. Some of the students who stared were wide eyed, hypnotized by what they had seen. Right then, acting on impulse, violating university protocol, I touched the students, tapped each one on the back, then put my hands on their shoulders and turned them around. "Don't look," I said. "It doesn't help."

Sirens sounded outside. Uniformed police and EMS medics came through the front doors with their radios blasting.

One kid whom I'd turned around stared straight ahead looking horrified; tears stood in her eyes. "I was on the balcony talking on my cell phone," she told me. "And I saw him climb onto the railing up on the tenth floor. I yelled at him, 'What are you doing?' Then he went over the side. I could have run up those stairs and stopped him."

She repeated this a few times. She told me her name was Marie Rose. Glancing over the railing I saw the medics at work on the body. I kept telling her I knew how she felt but that she had done everything she could.

When the silent crowds on the balconies stirred I looked again and saw they had the jumper on a stretcher. Everyone watched in absolute silence as he was rolled across the atrium and out the door.

"Come sit down," I said.

Yellow crime scene tape was being strung around the area of the floor with the spattered blood. A nursing student who came upstairs said she had heard the EMTs say the kid's heart had stopped but that they had gotten it beating before they took him away.

The Science Reference desk is through a glass door opening from the ninth floor balcony, and it's where I usually worked. The librarian who had been on duty through the whole incident badly needed to get away for a while.

So I sat at the desk with Marie Rose and asked about her studies. She was taking a masters in French lit and I got her to talk about that.

While she did, I found myself wondering what would have happened if I'd jumped up at the first shouts and gone out on the balcony. Could I have gotten to the man before he went over the railing? What if I'd begun moving at the first mention of the King?

Police began to appear on the upper floors. A couple of detectives went through the building asking for witnesses. I looked to Marie Rose. She nodded and went over to them.

A very young uniformed cop had been sent upstairs to find the jumper's personal effects. I took him to the tenth floor and we looked at piles of books and papers, backpacks abandoned as people ran out to see what had happened. Many of them had yet to return. Nobody was even sure if the jumper had been studying on the floor.

The cop was nervous and a little pale and I wondered if maybe he'd been given this assignment because he was having trouble with the blood downstairs. After a while, we found a blue backpack with a bunch of suicide poetry: books by Anne Sexton, Robert Lowell, Sylvia Plath. And I said, "I'm afraid this is what we're looking for."

When I was back at the desk, a young man asked me very quietly, "Is there another way out? I want to leave but I don't ever want to cross the atrium." Flashes came from where the technicians were taking pictures of the spot where the body had landed. Looking down I could see reporters at the front door questioning the people who left.

I asked aloud who wanted to go out the back way. Half a dozen patrons responded and I brought them down in the freight elevator and out past the trash and garbage on the loading dock.

Guard George Robins, who had been at the university as long as I had, was leaning back against a wall with his hand over his eyes breathing hard. It occurred to me as we passed him that Guard Robins had known the King.

I had been working in the building since it had opened almost exactly thirty years before. Even though it was against university regulations, no one thought to stop me when I opened the back door and let out everyone who had followed me.

When I got back upstairs, another bunch of students wanted to leave and I took them down, too, and let them out. Robins was drinking coffee one of the secretaries had brought him. He'd been the first to get to the body. "I just heard he's dead in the emergency room," he told me. This was not the moment to ask him about the King.

The police were through with the site where the kid had landed. I stood at a door that led out into the atrium. The building maintenance foremen spoke in Spanish to one of the porters who refused to look at him.

Hector was the porter's name and he trudged out onto the floor with a water cart and a mop and started to clean up the blood. It was obvious this bothered him.

I saw the head of Reference standing with other administrators and went and told her I'd been letting people out the back way. She said it was fine. I had been there so long that when I did things like this it was assumed somehow I was following precedent.

University grief counselors appeared just as they had on 9/11. The day of the suicide was, in fact, September 11, 2003. We mulled this over, stood in clusters around our information desks, and gathered in corners of the atrium. I made sure Marie Rose got to see the counselors, but I didn't go to them myself.

The one who died, as we learned more about him, as a photo was found in the computer system, turned out to have been someone I half remembered, a silent guy who sometimes used the computers on my floor. Just before the reference desks shut down for the evening, a big, goofy kid who was a regular in this part of the library rushed in and asked, "Did anyone see my backpack?"

When I asked what was in it, he said, "My notebooks, a calculus text. And books for a twentieth century American poetry class I'm taking." I told him the police had it.

The suicide's personal effects, when we found them at closing time, were in a basement study area. They were piled neatly and clearly identifiable as his, as if he was making things easier for us before he went up to the tenth floor and jumped.

Then work was over and there was nothing more to be done. Usually, when I left for the day, I left work behind. That evening walking through the atrium I felt like threads still connected me to the building.

I was supposed to attend a friend's reading in the East Village, but I didn't go. I went home and first sat down, then lay down, aware that I was in a kind of minor shock from the blood and the body.

Sometime later that marble floor came up and hit me in the face with a dull smack and I jerked myself awake in my bed. It was after nine o'clock, too early and too late at the same time.

My last lover and I had broken up the year before. I thought of calling an old friend then thought of something better. I grabbed my bag and got to the university gym just before 10:00 p.m. in the very heart of the Big Night Hours.

The place is often half deserted at that time on Fridays. Passing through the lobby I could look down on a few swimmers doing laps in the pool. A couple of three-on-three basketball games were almost lost on the vast gym floor. From somewhere in the distance I heard a racquetball ricochet and, for a moment, I almost expected to see the King leaning against a wall taking everything in with a little smile on his face.

The spell was broken in the locker room. Students were pulling on their clothes. Their talk was all chatter about missed shots, a girl someone knew from high school and just met again today, an accounting exam, the frat party on Saturday night.

These straight kids are very modest. They rarely take off their garish, shapeless boxer shorts and wrap towels around themselves before they do. Mostly they go back to their rooms to shower.

Some of my friends complain that these boys are puritanical. I think they're just polite and trying to ignore certain activity taking place around them. At times I feel like I'm part of an alternate world, semi-invisible but occupying the same space.

In this other world some of us are older and some are still students. It is a world of fleeting encounters in stairwells or steaming shower rooms, appointments to meet again outside.

Here men walk to the showers wearing nothing but the towels around their necks, whistle Sondheim, check each other out. In this other world when one catches a glimpse of a bare ass, one turns casually to see more, meets a gaze with eyes wide open.

I was looking for some other guys who had been around for a while. I found Ben and walked the treadmill next to his. Kenny was there too. The last time I'd noticed, they were an item. Now, I seemed it wasn't so.

Just after eleven, we were drying off from the shower. Ben is about my age, a tenured professor in the School of the Arts. Kenneth is much younger, a poet, working on a doctorate and teaching freshman composition.

In the distance someone yelled, "Closing time."

"Today on the phone, a friend mentioned the King of the Big Night Hours," I said.

"Oh my," said Ben. "Your friend must be so old. I barely remember the King."

"Who?" Kenneth asked.

"Once upon a time when this was a sweeter scene and everyone was hot and available, there was this incredible guy," I said.

"Some security guard who managed to get himself assigned here on the evening shift," Ben said in a bored tone. He pulled on white briefs and black trousers, ducked his shaven head into a Hermes sweater. "He was the one who cleared out the men's locker rooms and the showers at closing time and he did it slowly and very . . . selectively. He had this smug little smile like this was his game preserve."

It bothered me that Ben was so dismissive. I remembered the King holding me and how comforting he was.

"You called him the King of the Big Night Hours," Kenneth said. Why?"

"It was his joke. One to four were the wee small hours in Sinatra territory. Around here, when the King ran things, nine to twelve were the big night hours." As I said this, I realized that nothing about this scene now evoked the King.

Just then a youngish man, a Russian experimental film director with piercing eyes and several days' worth of facial stubble glanced our way.

Ben who lives right around the corner said, "Excuse me, I see my ride." He stepped into Gucci loafers and followed the Russian.

Kenneth looked a little lost but not surprised. "I heard what happened in the library today," he said. "I taught the kid who jumped."

We sat for some time in an all-night coffeehouse on MacDougal Street. Two years before Kenneth had taught the suicide freshman English. He said the boy was straight, a little withdrawn, and quite smart.

"I suppose I should have been able to spot something," he said.

"His friends, people who saw him earlier this afternoon, had no idea," I said. But I was getting tired of being reassuring. I wanted someone to try to make me feel better. When I got home, the caffeine meant I couldn't sleep much. But considering my dreams, it was also a bit of a plus.

Saturday was a work day for me and I was mildly stupefied as I crossed the atrium the next morning. The whole floor had been cleaned. I couldn't pick out the exact spot where the kid had landed.

The place was quite empty. The students were staying away. Various administrators were on hand to greet the staff as we arrived and ask us if we were okay. I told them Hector was very upset about having to mop up the blood and that they needed to be nice to him.

When I got up to the ninth floor, I went over to the balcony and looked down. Great long windows cover the front side of the building. The light that morning was soft. The patterned floor stayed where it was.

I remembered an old European woman, a Jungian psychiatrist whom I'd gone to back even before I started working for the university. When I talked about suicide, which I sometimes did back then, she said, "My dear, there's no future in it."

When the library was being built in the early seventies, the university was still poor. Construction went on for years: funding problems interfered; the quarry that provided the sandstone exterior went bankrupt and had to be purchased by the university.

I could remember being sent over to the building to measure out spaces for offices. I was young and adrift, one of those bad companions parents warned their kids about. Kind of expendable.

In the building I wore a hardhat. The stairs weren't finished; the passenger elevators hadn't been installed. Work elevators open on all four sides, rose and descended in the atrium, carried me up to balconies without railings where I'd hop off.

The building had no electricity. Sunlight came through the long windows, turned silver in the brass and marble atrium. Once I came into the building when a broken pipe on the sixth floor had created a sheet of water that poured down like a miniature Niagara Falls. The construction workers paused to admire the sight.

When the place first opened, I gave tours. Most of it was by rote: "The pattern on the ten thousand square foot floor is based on the design of the floor of a Renaissance church."

More often than not, when we were up on one of the top floors looking down, someone would ask if there had been any suicides. And I would say no and there had been no reported attempts. I'd point out the bronze horizontal railings all along the balconies. I'd mention the security guards on patrol on the upper floors and the fact that in the week, the month, the semester, the year since we had opened, there had been no trouble.

I wouldn't mention the university employees who were unable to work on the upper floors when we moved into the building. There were people who had vertigo each time they got off the elevators. They had to sidle along near the walls, careful not to look over the edge and see how the glass and brass interior swept down to the marble floor. Some got used to it. Some were unable to continue in their old jobs.

Among the tour groups, some thought the geometric marble patterns made the floor appear to come toward them. Others thought it seemed to retreat as they stared. I would retell the university approved legend of how the geometric patterns were intended to appear like spikes and pyramids and how this was supposed to dissuade anyone from wanting to jump.

I would not mention the campus folk tale, the one in which those same shapes would draw you in if you looked at them too long.

Giving tours was a task they could find for a long-haired young man with no academic background and a bad attendance record. It was known that I lead a tumultuous private life and packed a switchblade. I was granted many second chances.

Around me, things were changing. The dozens of little libraries and departments stuck in various spots around the campus had been consolidated into the main building when it opened. All of us who had worked in those small and idiosyncratic situations had to find new places for ourselves in this huge building.

After a false start or two I got my life into some kind of order and was sent up to the science library on the ninth floor. The staff was a librarian who stayed in her office, and me out at the information desk. Thirty years later the department had grown and I had an office, but my job was much the same.

By then I was a kind of anomaly, a clerical who had written books which were in the collection, someone who was said to have institutional memory. One use they had found for me over the years was as the token non-professional, the union member at the table of faculty and administrators.

The week after the suicide there were email memos reminding us of the grief counseling services the university offered and announcing the formation of various committees. I didn't go for counseling, but I was appointed to a panel examining what the library could do to improve student life.

On the committee were a serials cataloger and a programmer, an assistant administrator, a brand new paraprofessional from electronic resources, and a woman from the personnel office. We sat around and conjectured about student alienation and loneliness. I think I was the only one in the room who actually dealt with the patrons. I had even spoken to the one who killed himself, though I never guessed his intent.

A week or two after the suicide, Marie Rose came to see us at the reference desk. Marie Rose's last name was Italian. She was a pleasant young lady who told us how the Saturday after the suicide she had to go to the wedding of a cousin in New Jersey and be happy and cheerful when all the while she was seeing the guy hit the floor. She thanked us and said she thought she was okay now.

Exactly four weeks after the suicide, I was on my way back from lunch when I met library staff and patrons walking away from the building quickly, looking straight ahead, never glancing back. They told me someone else had jumped a few minutes before.

This time it went almost by rote, like everyone knew their part. The EMS and police were already rolling him through the front door on a gurney when I arrived. His face, what I could see of it behind the oxygen mask, had a dark flush like the skin was full of blood.

He, too, had jumped from the tenth floor. Just as with the first suicide, he was still alive when they took him out and died in the emergency room.

This time there was very little blood. And this time Hector's supervisor came along and helped him clean it up. Then the dean thanked them. An etiquette was being worked out.

Later in the day I saw the jumper's picture and stared at the face. He was very young. He had only been at the university for a few weeks and I doubted we'd met. But he looked like dozens of other students past and present whom I had known.

That night, the kid fell past me in my dreams, looked up with large doomed eyes as I stared over the balcony and he fell onto the marble patterns.

Saturday I went to a grief counseling group session held right in the library. Everyone said where they were and what they saw when the boy jumped. A very serious young woman from the Legal Council Office on the eleventh floor spoke in tears about hearing him scream as he fell. I told about my dreams of the floor coming up to smash him. The therapist led us in breathing exercises, tried to get us to let go of memories and images like the young woman's and mine.

The next week at the committee meeting, we read reports and safety protocols for suicide prevention at large universities around the country. It seemed to us that each jumper marked a failure on the part of our community.

Privately though, I began to wonder about the building itself. The architect, an American, had been a Nazi sympathizer and had lived in Germany in the thirties. Speaking about his past at the time the library opened, he said he had been young and foolish and had been fascinated by the uniforms.

The benefactor who had donated millions for the construction of the library bearing his name was a pharmaceutical tycoon, a self-made man. He had helped Nixon into the White House. The president himself was supposed to dedicate the building. But by the time of the official opening, he faced impeachment and was not making public appearances.

Many years later, one of the benefactor's granddaughters picketed in front of the library claiming he had molested her. Back and forth in all weather she went, carrying a sign. It was something everyone got used to. Then she was gone. Some said he had settled money on her, others that she had been hospitalized.

Recollecting things like these made it easy to spin stories of a building that killed kids. But the unease fueling my dreams involved personal and more elusive memories, ones on which I wasn't willing to dwell.

The students certainly stayed away as if they knew the place was accursed. It was half deserted in the middle of the day. Staff working the reference and circulation desks, hauling book trucks in the stacks, editing the computer records, cataloguing books, all listened for the screams and the muffled thump.

All the available security guards were in the building. They patrolled the upper floors, stood on the flying staircases warned students away from the rails and discouraged anyone from hanging around on the balconies.

Some of them were normally on duty in other parts of the university and I'd not seen them before. Others I'd gotten to know over the years. Guard Robins was up on my floor one day and I found a chance to talk to him.

He had been in the army and in hotel security in Jamaica. His youngest kids had worked on my floor as shelvers when they were in high school some years before and I had liked them a lot.

"Lots of overtime, but it all goes in taxes," said Robins. "I will not die rich, I am saddened to say."

Robins and the King of the Big Night Hours had been friendly. I'd seen them talking long ago.

He was older and liked a bit of formality so I still addressed him as we'd been told to do when I first started work.

"Guard Robins you knew someone from a while back. Fortnum was his name."

Campus Security in its own small way is a police unit and as such is closed and secretive. There was a distance between us now that I'd asked this. "Charles Fortnum?"

"Yes. Someone was asking what happened to him."

"We came from the same town in Jamaica, Fortnum and I. He was younger and I didn't much know him there. But his mother knew my family and when he came here, they asked me to recommend him for a job.

"When he got sick, he went home to his mother. My old aunt was a nurse and she told me when Fortnum died. It must be fifteen or twenty years ago."

So now I knew what had happened to the King and it wasn't unexpected. He was very much a part of my reaction to the young jumpers. But I was poking around the periphery of my memories, reluctant to think about the two of us and what had brought us close.

Something in my expression made Robins add, "Unless it's in my job, I do not meddle in what others do."

In the days after the second death, men and women in suits and with blueprints stood in the atrium and on the upper floors and talked to men in work clothes. Then it was announced that tall, clear plastic baffles were going to be put up on all the balconies and stairs. No one would ever again have access to railings.

While this work was happening, all the balconies were closed except for seven. The elevators operated by the guards went directly there. Patrons would then be escorted into the stacks by staff. From there they could go to the cement fire stairs buried inside the walls of the building and get to whatever floors they wanted.

The first Saturday this construction was underway, I sat almost alone in the science reference center. The doors out to the balconies were all locked. Muffled drilling and workers' shouts could be heard from the atrium. An occasional student would climb the fire stairs and emerge onto my floor.

Marie Rose was one. She made her way upstairs to tell me, "I wanted to say goodbye. I'm not coming into this place ever again. My friend Julie has agreed to come here and take out any books I need. I'm transferring out next semester."

It seemed to me Marie Rose might well have been one who had looked down from these balconies and thought of death.

What I said, though, was, "I'd be sorry to see you leave." And I realized how bound I was to this place and how it seemed that when I was gone nothing would remain but one or two people asking, "What happened to the white-haired guy who used to sit at this desk?"

"After the second death," she said, "I started seeing the first one go over the side again."

Looking for something to say, I told her, "Julie sounds like she must be a wonderful friend."

"She is," Marie Rose nodded

"You have that, you're solid," I said.

In the strange weeks following, crews worked twelve to eighteen hours six or seven days a week. Slowly metal frames and plastic baffles grew along the balconies.

On the seventh floor, the elevator doors would open and a guard would step out. Patrons would be herded off the elevator and into and the stacks where library staff would direct them.

Staff would also line up the patrons who wanted to go downstairs, and when an empty elevator was ready they were herded aboard. None of them got to walk unescorted out onto the balcony.

Because people weren't asking reference questions, I signed up for this duty and stood on the seventh floor for hours each day. Often, late in the evenings, it would be just one security guard and me. The trickle of patrons mostly looked unhappy and wanted to know why we were doing this.

Once in a while that autumn, in no pattern or rhythm I could discover, I would fall from an immense height and jerk myself awake as I smashed into the floor. The breathing exercises the counselor taught me helped. I refused the offer of sedatives.

Finally one day in my office, I talked to Alex on the phone. "What made you think of the King of the Big Night Hours?" I asked. "You were talking about him just moments before the first kid jumped."

"You brought it up out of nowhere as I recall," said Alex. "Suddenly asked me if I remembered him. I hadn't thought about the guy since, maybe, the last time I saw him. And that must be twenty years ago."

When he said this, I remembered sitting at this desk a couple of months before and feeling hands on my back. It had been so real I'd looked around and found no one else in my office. I was reminded of a time the King had done that and I had asked Alex if he remembered him.

Realizing all this brought back a memory of standing on a high balcony one night not long after the building had first opened. Everything had felt black. I was broke and strung out and saw no place for myself in the world.

I had fallen silent on the phone. Alex said, "Are you okay? Listen, I'm going to come into the city and we'll get together this weekend."

I didn't tell him not to bother. But I did think of myself as having survived for a long time and to no real purpose.

When I was young I read Graham Greene's account of playing Russian roulette as a kid. When he was in a black depression, he'd get the revolver out of his father's desk. Each time he spun the barrel and pulled the trigger and lived, the depression cleared.

It had seemed such a distinct and reasonable thing to do back then that I never even thought to wonder why.

The guard on duty with me for my stint on the seventh floor that night was young and seemed uncomfortable in his uniform. He told me he wasn't used to it. He took classes at the university and looked so much like one of the students that they mostly had him in plainclothes.

I was getting old and wasn't used to standing for hours on end. It had begun to catch up with me, and my legs ached. While he talked, I looked around the atrium at the places where they still didn't have the baffles up.

After work, I considered going to the gym. Instead I sat on a park bench in the big night hours and thought about the time I'd stood with my hands grasping the rails.

Then I went back to the library. It was after closing time and Guard Robins was on the front desk. I told him I had lost my keys and had a spare set in my office.

I know he watched me cross the atrium and go to the fire stairs. The climb up all the flights was brutal, but I didn't care. I went out onto the seventh floor balcony and then went up the stairs. Earlier, I'd spotted a place on the eighth floor where the railings were still exposed.

Work had halted for the night. No one even noticed me step out on the balcony. This might be the last time I could do this.

Once, thirty years before I had stood with my hands on the brass spikes just as I did now. Back then my life was a hopeless and humiliating shambles. At work they were tired of my absences and tardiness. I'd alienated anyone who'd ever taken up my cause.

Earlier in the day I'd given a tour and someone had asked whether anyone had jumped. I'd said no. That night I grasped two of the brass spikes and pulled my weight up. My palms would get slashed as I vaulted over the side but that wouldn't matter when the marble floor rushed up.

Right then I felt a tap on my back. Two huge hands grasped my shoulders and turned me a hundred and eighty degrees. When I focused my eyes, I saw the King step over to an open elevator door and beckon me.

THE KING OF THE BIG NIGHT HOURS   91

Decades later, remembering all this, I heard the elevator behind me, and felt as if my ritual had evoked the King. When the door flew open I turned and saw the familiar uniform.

"Get in here, you stupid bastard," said Guard Robins. "You know the kind of trouble you would get me in?" he said as the elevator descended. "You have no thought of that? What is it in you people that you all want to become dead?" I knew he meant the King and the jumpers and me and wanted to tell him I hadn't been going to jump, couldn't even have scrambled over the side.

I wondered if the ones who jumped had been enacting their own ritual. Had they tried to see how far they could go before hands reached out to hold them?

"At your age," Robins said, "You should know that it will happen soon enough that we don't need to hurry it."

He saw me out the door. I knew he wouldn't report this since it would implicate him. Walking home, I felt alive, revived. My legs didn't hurt.

I thought about when the King of the Big Night Hours had found me. Ben was right that the King always looked pleased with himself. But I felt he had reason.

He moved so quickly for a big man, kept his hand on my back guiding me along to a little empty office in the subcellar. The "throne room" he called it. He had a key. The place, I remember, smelled like spice. As did the King himself. He laughed once when I asked what cologne he used. "It is my essence," he said.

Without the uniform, he looked even larger than with it. There was a silver scimitar of a scar along his ribcage. "A mean old man did that when I was young," he told me once when I asked.

If I got naked now and screwed on an old wooden desk I'd be in traction for the rest of my life. But I was young and the seventies were a bacchanalia. Death avoided, or at least postponed, made everything vivid and exhilarating. When we were finished he stood over me and said, "If you do anything like this again, I will keep you locked bare ass in my throne room for good."

We got together other times but it lacked the intensity of that first encounter. In an era of abundant opportunity we faded out of each other's lives. Possibly neither of us wanted to drain all the magic from that moment.

When I noticed he was never around it was in the plague time. The ones I asked only said he was back in Jamaica and I followed it no further.

Maybe the King had come back to the university after death. Or some part of him had never left. Had he tried to reach me in time to save the jumper?

If so, he failed or I did. But enough of him got through that I had known to tap those shoulders and turn those kids around when they stared agape. Minor good deeds like those may have helped his soul and mine.

That weekend Alex came into the city and stayed with me. I was happy to see him but my crisis had passed. Later, Kenneth—the poet I'd known from the gym—called and we got together.

When the grief therapist contacted me, I said I felt fine and thanked her. I was glad to see them erect the baffles and seal off the atrium.

The job got finished early. One afternoon in late fall it was suddenly over. The elevators started to work again and we could walk safely on the balconies and stairs.

The sun now reflected off the plastic panels. This changed the light in the atrium, made it seem far duller. It felt as if the building had been tamed.

Remembering the King had reminded me that there was no need to hurry death. Kenneth and I were having a minor affair. By January when the new semester began I had decided I didn't need to die in this place. I set a date for early retirement.

It was a bright winter morning when I reached my decision. I was walking to work when I saw Marie Rose with a plump dark young lady.

Seeing my surprise, Marie said, "Julie and I decided it made no sense to run away."

"You're going to stay and I'm going to leave," I said and told her about my plans.

"I'll miss you," she said. "I'll remember you." And that's all one can hope for.

Guard Robins was on duty that day. Our eyes never met now and we hadn't spoken since the night he ordered me off the balcony. Each time he ignored me I felt bad about what had happened.

I think about the King a lot and I miss him, but I haven't felt his presence since that September afternoon. Maybe nothing has happened that would bring him back.

THOSE WHO WATCH

Ruthanna Emrys

On my third full day, the library marked me. I should have been holding down the desk—I'd been hired for reference—but instead I was shelving. After a year with an MLIS and no prospects, you don't whine. Deep in the narrow aisles of the back stacks, the air conditioning struggled against the sticky Louisiana heat outside. I gave up on my itchy suit jacket, draped it over the cart, and tucked *Cults and Sects of Eastern Bavaria* under my arm while I hooked a rolling stool with my ankle. And felt a piercing sting against the inside of my elbow.

I screamed, almost dropped the book, caught it but lost my balance. My ass is pretty well padded, but now I felt a nasty bruise start up to go along with whatever mutant mosquito had snuck in from the swamps to assault me. I set *Cults and Sects* gently on floor and examined my arm. The skin swelled, red and inflamed, around a tiny spiral galaxy of indigo and scarlet flame.

I've never so much as pierced my ears. I hate pain. A lot of days I hate my body too, but it's mine and I don't expect it'd improve anything to ink it up or poke extra holes in it. But I've got braver friends, so I could tell this was unmistakably a tattoo, right about the point some people take off the Band-Aid—a little too early—and send you close-up selfies to make you wince in sympathy. I touched it and shrieked again, a little muffled because I expected the pain this time.

I prodded the book, turned it carefully with the tip of my finger. No needles hidden between pages by urban legend psychopaths, or protruding from the spine like some literary assassin's poison ring. An ordinary book, cloth bound and stamped along the page ends with "Crique Foudre Community College."

"Elaine! Are you all right?" My boss hurried around the end of the row. I scrambled to my feet, nearly tripping again, left hand clapped over the evidence of whatever screw-up I'd managed.

"Sorry, Sherise," I managed. Sherise, she'd made clear when I started, not Sherry or Miss Nichols or any of the other variants people had tried—she liked her name and she used it.

"Let me see," she said. When I didn't move, she pried my fingers away from the offending spot. She hummed as she traced the swollen area. "Better get the first aid kit to be safe. Come on."

She strode confidently through the stacks, a maze I'd already gotten lost in twice that morning. Florescent light gleamed off her brown skin and the darker maps winding around her arms—hers were probably from an actual tattoo parlor. Her hair puffed over her ears; big gold rings strung with lapis beads dangled underneath. I struggled to keep up.

A few more turns, and we'd come all the way around the shelf-lined halls that surrounded the library's central reading room, back to the staff office with its institutional carpet and laminate desks. Sherise's, in the corner, stood out by being bigger and uglier than the others, and topped by sort of an old style wooden card catalog, dozens of tiny drawers with brass pulls. She opened one, pulled out a box of what looked like alcohol wipes. She tore open a sealed pack, labeled in an alphabet I didn't recognize. It smelled of wintergreen and ashes. She rubbed the cool pad over my arm, and stinging gave way to a softer tingle.

"There, that should keep it from spreading. Be careful with the religion books. Powers want respect, and so do the words around them."

"Okay." My last semester at Rutgers I'd applied to jobs all around the country—and the same for a year afterward. It was August now, and plenty of hungry new graduates would be glad to move to rural Louisiana if I didn't work out.

CFCC had been a miracle of double-scheduling, tacked onto a disastrous interview at the smallest and most obscure branch of Louisiana State University. The LSU staff started by asking whether I had any family in the area and what church I liked. Their library was a disaster too: a modern brick monstrosity that turned off the climate control at night to keep under budget, and never mind if mold ate away their skimpy collection. After that, just about anywhere would have been an easy sell. The CFCC library, endowed by an alumnus-made-good with distinctly non-modern architectural tastes, about made me cry with gratitude.

At CFCC, they didn't ask about my family. They threw a dozen weird-ass reference queries at me in rapid succession, and seemed pleased by my sample class on databases. They did ask my religion, but "sort of an agnostic Neopagan"—I was through being coy after LSU—seemed like an acceptable answer. By the time they brought out an old leather-bound tome from their rare books collection and wanted to know if the font gave me a headache, I didn't much care. I was past wanting a job, any job—I wanted to work somewhere that actually cared about being a good library for their visitors. I wanted a space that cared, and never mind if outside the doors waited mosquitoes and killing humidity and drive-through liquor stores.

Sherise didn't send me home, which I kind of thought might have been justified. On the other hand she didn't yell at me, which would probably have been justified too. I'd been disrespectful to Sects and Cults, after all, whatever that meant. I retreated to the reading room.

The circular, high-domed room at the library's heart was a legacy of the generous alumnus. According to Sherise, this benefactor had traveled the world collecting antiquities, and decided that American education neglected the values that had made the ancient world great. "By ancient he meant Greece," she'd said. "Maybe Baghdad if he was feeling really broad-minded. But still, you won't find another building this pretty closer than New Orleans." And she was right: in the middle of a campus of shoebox buildings, the library stood out like a dandelion breaking through a sidewalk.

Each door to the reading room was crowned by cherubim bearing a motto on a banner—in this case: "The temple of knowledge shapes the mind within." Actual cherubim, not putti; I had to look up the original descriptions before I believed it. Inside, the room went up three stories. The center held the shelves and work stations and computers you'd expect, but allegorical sculptures of Cosmology and Determination and Wisdom, Agriculture and Epiphany and Curiosity, gazed down from over the doors. Above them a bas relief ribbon detailed stories related to these virtues. Some I recognized: Oedipus and the sphinx, Archimedes in his bath. In others, humans and fabulous monsters played out less familiar myths. A tromp l'oeil thunderstorm stood over all, making the room feel dim and cool even with the lamps turned up bright. A few professors bent over oak desks, and I felt self-conscious as I craned my neck.

The sculptures had been a definite selling point for the school, one that helped me work up the guts to come out as Neopagan—though it's not always a trustworthy sign; a guy screamed at me one time for pointing out Minerva's owls atop the Chicago Public Library. People don't like admitting they're taking advantage of other people's temples, maybe even worshiping just by walking through.

It was Determination I wanted—to get through the day, to do my work right so I'd still have a job and an apartment and insurance when David's visiting professorship in Chicago ended. There was a little spot between two shelves where I could get near her with no one watching. I sat heavily on a stool, looked up. She wore armor, and aimed her spear down at my seat. In her other arm, she clasped a book protectively, and she gazed with narrowed eyes, daring anyone to come up and try something. But someone had: carven blood spilled from a wound in her side, the only spot of color on the white marble.

When I first saw her, I assumed she got that wound from some enemy's weapon. But it was awfully close to the book. I opened my mouth to whisper a prayer, and couldn't get anything out.

The advantage of being agnostic is that you can pray to whatever you like. A stream, a statue, an abstract concept, a fictional character—if it feels like it ought to be a god, if it does you some good to think about how it might see your problems, you can just go ahead and babble. But I couldn't doubt the muddy multichromatic swirl pressed into my skin. Some power, aware or otherwise, had decided that was a good idea.

I knew enough stories. Gods, if they actually exist and don't mind letting you see the evidence, are scary fucks. No damn way was I *praying* to one. My arms slipped up to wrap around my chest and I scooted to the side. I felt ridiculous, but I also felt like at any moment Determination might shift her spear. Maybe she wanted to make sure I didn't misuse another precious book. My heart sped, and I started to feel dizzy. I pushed the stool farther back, checked the aisle behind me and saw Epiphany, globe upheld in one hand and wings spread, other hand on her robe. But her eyes—like Determination's—focused on me, mocking. I scrambled up, kicking the stool against the shelf, flinching as it banged into the wood. Backed away, then fled through Wisdom's door to the staff room, not daring to look either at her or at the professors who might've noticed my outburst.

I shouldn't have taken the prayer break in any case. I should've gone to work the reference desk—in the middle of the reading room—or back to the pre-semester re-shelving. But I still didn't know what I'd done wrong, and after a few minutes trying to swallow a growing lump of nausea, knew that I couldn't face either today. Sherise had left the staff room and I'd only get lost looking for her. I scribbled a note: "I'm feeling sick and need to go home early—I'll make it up later in the week. Sorry for the short notice."

As I gathered up my things, I imagined her reading the note. I had no idea what rare sequelae might result from book tattoos—would she call an ambulance? I went back and added: "It's a problem with the dose on my medication; I'll get it fixed." She knew I was on meds; I'd deliberately let her see the sertraline when I took my morning pills. Another thing I didn't feel like being coy about. And it was true about the dosage problem. After a year with no insurance, my new doctor wanted to start slowly; the amount I was taking now might work for an anxious supermodel, but for a big girl like me it barely made a dent.

Outside, heat slammed my lungs. I squinted against the blinding afternoon sun, trying to catch my breath. Halfway to the parking lot, sweat soaked my shirt; just walking felt disgusting. Skin and cloth stuck to each other and peeled away, again and again. By the time I got to the car, my legs were shaking and my heart still hadn't slowed. I felt short of breath, and couldn't tell whether I was hyperventilating or just having trouble with the humidity.

The first blast of AC cleared my head enough for me to realize that no way in hell should I drive like this. After a minute of circling the need-to-get-home/can't-go-home paradox, I gave in and called David. Skyped, actually—still just in range of the campus wi-fi, I needed to see him more desperately than I needed him not to see me in sweat-stained dishabille.

The phone sang its reassuring trying-to-connect melody, less reassuring as it went on and I wondered if I'd misremembered his class schedule. Or he could be with a student, or in a meeting, or just too busy. But finally, with a satisfied plink, the video came through.

"Hey, gorgeous," he said. "Are you okay?"

"Hey, pretty boy." It was ritual exchange, but at least my end of it was true. My fiancé was a beautiful red-haired Nordic type who could rock a Viking helmet or a slinky dress with equal aplomb. What he saw in me was still a mystery. I tried to explain what was going on, managed only: "I hate Louisiana."

"I don't blame you." He leaned closer. "Are you having a panic attack?"

I shook my head, then nodded, then shook it again.

"Okay. Take a deep breath. I'm right here, I'm holding you. Let it out. Breathe in."

I imagined his arms around me, imagined lying together in the shitty little apartment we'd shared near Rutgers. It made me feel lonely, but it gave me something to think about besides the heat and the tattoo and my boss and the job that might be too weird for me to handle. The breathing helped. My head cleared further, and keeping the car on the right side of the road no longer seemed like an overwhelming prospect.

"Thanks, that helps." I wanted to show him the tattoo—but the thought made my mouth feel dry again. What if he demanded I quit my job and come to Chicago right away? Or worse, what if he couldn't see it at all? Hallucination isn't supposed to be a symptom of generalized anxiety disorder, but it was actually the most rational explanation I could think of. "What do you do when your job gets weird?" I asked him instead.

He leaned back, obviously pleased to have been of use. "Research, mostly. Or diagnose my colleagues' personality disorders on insufficient evidence, depending on the brand of weirdness. Is someone being nasty?"

"No. Just, um, trying to figure out campus culture."

"Lots of alcohol and not enough drugs, probably."

We chatted a little longer, and then he had to get back to course prep. I let him go, and didn't tell him I'd called in sick. Nothing bad happened on my drive home.

Outside my apartment complex, I found the heat still intense, but now that I was calmer (and before I hit the barricade of smokers by the door) I took a moment to breathe. I can't stand the way Louisiana looks or feels, but the smell is amazing. Silt and decay like endless autumn, overlain with orchids and citrus and cypress and a million other trees and vines and roots bursting from every available surface. I can't face the swamp in person. Giant bugs to bite you or leap in your face, mud to slip on, alligators just lying around hoping you're weak enough to be worth a sprint. But I love the smell.

I drowned my sorrows in chocolate and a *Criminal Minds* marathon, and it helped. Sherise sent an email to say she hoped I'd feel better, and I stared at it for five minutes trying to figure out whether she believed me before giving up and going back to the TV.

But calling out sick only works for so long, and I've learned the hard way that if I let myself do it two days in a row it's easy to get inertia and stretch it for a week. So the next morning, lying in bed, I tried to put my thoughts in order.

The tattoo remained, stubbornly, on my arm. It still felt tender, but the dim light filtering through the blinds showed that the swelling had gone down. So I would go with the assumption that I wasn't hallucinating, if nothing else because I wasn't checking into any hospital without David there to look respectable for the doctors.

If the tattoo was real . . . then I still wasn't sure about the statues. I'd been spiraling, and I couldn't even trust my judgment of live people when that happened. How the hell was I supposed to predict allegorical virtues? But the tattoo, all by itself, meant I didn't understand how books worked. Probably it meant I didn't understand how the world worked at all, but I'd always known that. Books, though, I thought I had down.

When his job got weird, David did research. For him that meant digging through sociology databases and endless stacks of journal articles. I didn't know what database covered this situation—but if the library had untrustworthy books, it ought to have resources to tell you about them.

"Imagine it's someone else's reference question," I said aloud. Talking to myself feels stupid, but never speaking aloud at home feels a lot worse. "Miss, I've got a report about book attacks due in three hours. Can you find everything for me? Yes, damn straight I can."

Sherise nodded when I dropped my lunch in the staff room, and asked casually after my health. I told her I was fine today, tried to parse what she was thinking. Probably I ought to have gone ahead and asked about the book. But she hadn't told me when she cleaned the tattoo, and maybe there was a reason for that. Either it wasn't the sort of thing she could explain properly, or she assumed I already knew.

One of David's psych grad friends, a year ahead of him, figured out—halfway through his postdoc—that they'd hired him thinking he'd studied under a different professor from the same department. They'd never asked, he'd never told them, and he'd struggled to keep up the whole year. But it wasn't exactly the kind of thing you could come out and say. Suppose one of the Rutgers library science professors was secretly a Predatory Books specialist? Or more plausibly, suppose Sherise assumed this was something Neopagans just knew about? Either way, I didn't want to make her feel stupid—or like hiring me had been a mistake. I'd just have to paw through the databases myself until I found what I needed.

Walking into the reading room was hard. My body believed, even if I wasn't sure, that I'd faced a threat here. Bodies like to preserve themselves; mine wanted me to go back to my cave where it was safe. I told my body that it was stupid, and went in. I couldn't help glancing at Determination. She didn't seem about to spear me, but I still sensed something watching. The sense of attention seemed to pervade the room, all the allegories judging our choices of study. I shivered, tried to ignore what was probably just my neurotic imagination, and turned on the ancient reference computer.

The library's generous funder wasn't nearly as fond of technology as of architecture or hard copy, so I had far too long to sit in the crossfire of allegorical gazes without the screen to distract me. When I finally got the browser running, I looked over the library's scant list of databases. Medline? Likely to support the hallucination hypothesis. PsycInfo? Worse. Maybe JSTOR or the always over-general Academic Search Premier? Eventually I decided to start with databases I'd never heard of—if a community college with a lousy budget for online services subscribed to something really obscure, there was probably a reason.

I found a few, in fact. Mostly the weird ones claimed space in world mythology and folklore, though there was one in biology and another in physics. MythINFO turned out to be perfectly pedestrian, though kind of awesome: it let you search by a drop-down menu of Stith Thompson Motif Index entries. Several looked relevant—various "transformation" archetypes, magical books—but turned up only articles on fairy tales, drowned in the deep jargon of literary analysis.

PYTHIAS, though, seemed more promising. Various combinations of "book" and "tattoo," suitably modified by "AND" one thing and "-" another, got me nowhere. But an exasperated "bibliogenic illness" turned up a long list of books in the Zs. I scribbled down call numbers for those available locally, took a deep breath, and fled the reading room for whatever lurked in the stacks.

My first few days in the library, I could get lost by blinking. The stacks wound back in all directions, and I could never quite figure out how straight rows added up to a circular building—except that the rows seemed to curve subtly, sometimes, and the turns weren't always right angles. Today for the first time, a map stretched out in my mind; I couldn't see the edges, but could feel the shape and logic of how the rows spread from where I stood. Beneath my skin, the tattoo pulsed with soft heat. I touched it, gingerly, but felt nothing from outside.

I hadn't been back to the Zs—the "index" section whose self-referential topic is books and libraries—since the whirlwind tour during my interview. But the warmth in my arm seemed to increase along what I vaguely recalled was the right path. I gave in and followed it, trying not to think too hard about what I was doing.

The AC was managing better today, at least as far as temperature. The stacks felt cool and shadowy. But in the corner of my eye fog seeped from below the shelves, never there when I turned to look though I felt it against my skin. It sometimes seemed about to coalesce into more solid form and draw me to a particular shelf, a particular volume—but it never did.

My map grew as I walked, and at last I saw that the stacks were not so much neat rows as a galactic spiral, linear only to the cursory glance. And at the far end of the western arm, I found an alcove lit by buzzing fluorescents and lined with tightly packed mahogany bookshelves. Tiny paperbacks pressed against oversized leather-bound tomes, and the half-imagined fog cleared in favor of archival dryness. A circular stained-glass window, wider than the span of my hands, filtered light through an abstract pattern of magenta and midnight blue. The colors shifted as shadows moved beyond—probably leaves from the grand row of hollies and live oaks between library and parking lot. My arm burned, pain flaring as I stepped into the coruscating illumination. I whimpered and bit my lip.

I wanted to move away from the window and get my books. Instead, unwilled, I knelt. As in the reading room, I felt again the attention of some presence. This one seemed less judgmental, more curious. Not friendly curiosity: a biologist examining a noisy DNA sequence, perhaps, or me with a particularly recalcitrant new database. The attention sharpened, and I felt uncomfortably aware of my body: not only fat ass and weak ankles, but heart thudding and guts clenching and nerves struggling to keep up. All pus and blood and static, acid and slime and brittle bone.

And I felt the examination grow more active, as whatever attended through the window started to prod at my flaws and cracks.

The tattoo had been quick, done before I knew what was happening. Not so, here. This thing wanted to change me, though it clearly didn't care about my opinion on the specifics—probably didn't even consider that I might have one. I gasped, but still couldn't rise from where it held me bent almost to the floor, stomach compressing uncomfortably and legs cramping and falling asleep. Worse, a part of me didn't want to. I've never liked my body, not the ass and ankles and skin and face I deal with every day, and not the inside bits now suddenly forced into my awareness. Any change might be for the better—at the very least wouldn't be anything I could be blamed for.

But the part that knelt willingly was all conscious. A wave of revulsion and fear surged up to overwhelm any other reaction. My whole body shook and my pulse came so fast it hurt. In the throes of the panic attack, my instincts broke through whatever held me down, as they did everything that might have intent about it. I threw myself from the illuminated circle and scuttled backward until my back pressed against the nearest shelf. If the books wanted to bite me, I'd be ink all over.

Slowly—no Sherise to interrupt my reactions, no David to talk me down—I started to think in words again. I stared at dust motes floating in the light from the window, made swirling nebulae by the colors. The light hadn't moved while I curled frozen beside it. I'd lost track of time, but sunlight ought to have shifted across the floor. Maybe there was another room beyond this one, even if my unlikely map told me otherwise.

If I got up and went closer, I might be able to glimpse whatever lay on window's other side. That seemed like a bad idea.

Maybe the books could tell me.

I pulled myself to my feet, terrified every moment of toppling back into the light. My arm still ached with heat. In the panic's aftermath I felt washed out emotionally, just numb enough to actually consider sticking around for what I'd come to get.

The Nature of the Word was bound in calfskin, fine yellow-edged pages typeset save for hand-illuminated letters at the start of chapters. I winced at the yellowing; this ought to be in the rare book room, not the ordinary stacks. *Palaces of History* was library bound but looked like a reprint of something much earlier, each page imaged from a neatly handwritten monograph with intricate—if disturbing— illustrations. The simply-named *Libris* looked like a Penguin Classics paperback, except that it came from Sarkomand Translations, a publisher and imprint I'd never heard of.

I found a library cart lurking in a back corner, odd reassurance that the alcove existed for other people too. Maybe they all knew to avoid the window, or maybe it liked them better. Or maybe I ought to report it—like telling someone when you spot a leaking pipe. I trundled the cart back toward the galactic core.

I ducked my head at Determination and her companions as I settled at my desk. Powers want respect, Sherise had said, and until I knew what I was doing it was probably safer to give them at least a little. Epiphany's gaze stood higher now, no longer focused on those of us below. I caught myself staring at her left hand, the one holding her robe. It wasn't just a pose, I realized: she stood ready to bare her chest to Determination's spear, and it was her opposite's eye that she sought to attract.

I shivered, and forced my attention back to the books. I started with The Nature of the Word: at any minute, I expected someone to come along and tell me it needed to go into protective storage until I could prove my need to touch its fragile pages. Selfish but not sociopathic, I did snag a pair of nitrile gloves from the check-out counter.

Those who believe the universe was created, believe it was created with words. Those who know it for an accident still understand that language, once created, becomes a force in its own right. Fifteen million years before humanity's birth, the Tay-yug claimed that miserly gods hid favored words in the hearts of stars, making them unstable and scouring life from worlds that spun too close.

I sat back, breathing hard. It was a story, of course it was a story, a myth I'd never heard before. A myth of gamma ray bursts, in a book that looked older than the phenomenon's discovery—but how much did I know about the history of physics? I ought to keep reading. Would, in a moment.

When I was a kid, for a while I got really into urban legends. Even though I knew better, I'd sit up late reading about chupacabras and the Loch Ness monster. The one that really got to me was the mothman. It was sort of a humanoid with big bug wings, and people would look out their windows and it would just be hovering there, staring at them. That was it—it never broke the window or hurt anyone, at least not who reported it later. But I'd pull my shades down tight, eyes squeezed shut so that if anything was out there, I wouldn't see it. Knowing that if I hadn't read about it, if I hadn't known it was out there to look for, the windows would have been perfectly safe.

Of course I already knew, now, that there was something outside.

I scanned, sampled, turning pages cautiously but skimming as quickly as I could, looking for what I needed—something that would explain what had happened to me. Instead, I learned about books that started plagues or imprisoned their readers, and others that, read in the right place and at the right time, would let you cast your mind out to travel the stars. Stories that could leave your mind a husk colonized by parasitic characters, single words that could rewrite memory.

I did not slam the book shut. I closed it, carefully, like the rare archival volume that it was. I could not give up reading, wouldn't blind myself to what it offered, just because there might be monsters inside.

I hadn't found anything about tattoos, or stained glass windows—maybe another book might be more relevant. You've got to focus when you're doing research, can't just let yourself get sucked in by whatever seems shiniest. And "terrifying" is a lot like "shiny." *Libris*, with its two-tone paper cover, looked reassuringly pragmatic.

"How did you get ahold of that?" Sherise's voice, sharp and angry, froze me with my hand on the cover. My eyes shifted toward *The Nature of the Word* and I felt my cheeks grow hot. But it was *Libris* that she snatched from my desk.

"I'm sorry," I said. "I found it in the Zs. I was trying to look up something about—" I pushed up my sleeve to show the galaxy tattoo. It was, I realized, the same shape as the stacks, the same colors as the window. And I'd just made my ignorance obvious, too. "I'm sorry," I repeated.

"I'm not mad at you." She ran a finger across the cover, frowning. "But this shouldn't have been shelved in the regular stacks. A bit past anything you need to be handling, right now."

"Does it eat your brain?" I felt my cheeks flare again, worse for the knowledge that it showed like a beacon.

She smiled. "Not this one, no. But it's not translated from any human language, and it's safer to know what to expect before you get into it." She tucked it under her arm, though not against bare skin.

At this point, she could tell anyway that I didn't know what I was doing. Still, it took a few dry swallows before I could get the words out. They were angrier than I'd intended. "Am I supposed to ask? Or am I supposed to figure it out all on my own and hope I don't unleash a plague on the whole Gulf Coast?"

She leaned against the edge of my desk, put *Libris* back down, patted the offending volume a couple of times as if to reassure herself that it was still closed. Then she pushed her cloud of hair away from one ear. The whole outer curve had been sculpted into tiny scallops, like waves of flesh, and faded to cheap newsprint gray. It stood like a scar against the warm brown of the rest of her skin. She let the hair spring back.

"Happened my first day at Crique Foudre. I can hear the books, and hear people and other things thinking when they mean to do harm. Prophecies, sometimes. And people arguing in whispers down the block when I'm trying to sleep. The gifts have sharp edges. There's no way to know beforehand who can handle it all and who can't, and we've learned the hard way that you have to find out most of it for yourself. If someone explains everything straight up, it always ends badly."

"Suppose I quit?" I swallowed, because again I hadn't meant to speak so bluntly, and because I knew the answer. I'd show up at David's studio, and he'd support me as best he could—no one in Chicago was hard up for librarians—and he wouldn't criticize me for not being able to cut it in the real world.

"You could do that. The lady before you left at two months—that's why we were hiring so late in the summer." Nothing about how I'd leave them in the lurch if I quit just before the semester started, though it didn't really need saying. "This is riskier than holding down a desk just about anywhere else. The best I can offer is that if you stick around, you'll become something special. We all do. Whether that special is more like yourself, or less, depends on luck. And on your own choices, at least a little."

I didn't know whether I ought to be tempted by the "more" or the "less"—or whether I was even crazier than usual to be tempted by either. "What *can* you tell me? Without things ending badly?"

She sighed, fidgeted the beads on her earring. I wondered if they drowned out the voices of the books. "That's always a gamble, but I'll give it a shot. You know about our patron."

"Yeah. Although no one's told me his name. Or her name. I'd think there'd be a plaque or something—is this one of the things it's dangerous to know?"

"No, he just likes to keep a low profile. You might meet him, one of these days." She closed her eyes and inhaled sharply. "Maybe that's not the place to start. I'm sorry. I don't feel like I've explained this right to anyone, yet. Maybe this'll be the time—unless you want me to shut up and let you track it all down for yourself."

I shook my head, a bit shaken by her uncertainty.

"Well. The universe is a dangerous place. It's not trying to be dangerous, and it's full of things that have never heard of humans and wouldn't much care if they did—but not caring can do at least as much harm as hatred, from things that can break you just passing by. The safest way, for a species that wants time to grow up, is to make a few places that can focus the strangeness, draw it away from everywhere else, and help keep it from getting out of control. People have been doing that on earth for millions of years, maybe longer, each learning from fragments left by those who came before, and doing just a little better as a result. This library is one of those places for humans."

"Out in—" I just stopped myself from asking what—if she wasn't just making this up—a vital shield against extinction was doing out in the middle of nowhere, in a state that most of the country couldn't even bother to protect from floods.

She smiled wryly, making me think I'd been pretty transparent. "Safer this way. Crique Foudre is heir to Zaluski Library in Warsaw. Our patron traveled there in the 1920s, and when the Nazis destroyed it during World War II knew we'd need another one. He thought, a place that isn't the capital of anywhere or the center of anything—it would be a lot safer from other humans."

"So we're the quiet heroes who protect the world from terrible cosmic monsters?" I'd seen that show; I would have been happier to leave it on the screen.

"You've been to the edge of the stacks. It's not that simple. Sometimes we just keep the monsters happy, or distract them, or find a use for them, or study them to learn what else is out there. Sometimes we're bait. Sometimes we can't do a damn thing other than watch. And eventually we'll lose the fight—either to other humans, like Zaluski, or altogether, like the three other species on this world that we know about before us."

I shivered. "One more thing to worry about."

"That's one way to handle it, sure."

"What do you do?" I asked.

"I go for distraction, personally. There are so many things to *learn* here, that you'll never find in another library that isn't doing the same work. Things to become. As long as you're doing your job, the larger cosmic picture kind of takes care of itself, whether or not you grieve over it."

"Do you ever worry about asteroids?" I asked David. I was home, curled up with my laptop on the couch, insufficiently distracted by my pretty boyfriend.

"Like the one that got the dinosaurs?" he asked. "Not really. It doesn't seem like something that happens very often, and I'm not in a position to do anything about it in any case."

"Very logical." I drew up my knees, watched him pass back and forth across the screen as he made French toast. "Suppose you *could* do something. Or thought you could?"

"You mean like a desperate space mission to steer a comet away from Earth? Yeah, I would worry about that. I worry when there's something I can try, and it matters if I screw up." He smiled gently. "You've got to pick your battles—there's only so much worry to go around."

"Unless you're me."

"Even for you, gorgeous."

Later, I realized that I hadn't asked if he'd rather be in a position to try something, even if he thought he'd screw up, or whether he'd rather do work he was better at, and not have to look.

On the first day of classes, humidity spilled over the banks of the sky into a spectacular thunderstorm. I eased my car around puddles half-grown into lakes, breathing slowly through the constant strobe of lightning. I arrived ten minutes late, suit soaked through in spite of my umbrella. The AC set me shivering, but Sherise and the other librarians were talking and laughing in the staff room and one of them tossed me a giant beach towel.

Sherise nodded at me and said, "We're gonna get slammed even with the rain, so you know. And there are still a dozen professors who need pinned to the wall 'til they hand over their reserve lists." By the time I got the last math professor to confess the identity of his textbook, and started on the English department, umbrellas filled the foyer and students swirled through the reading room.

Most of the morning's reference questions were about what I'd expected. Students wanted their course reserves and panicked about their first day's homework and didn't know how to manage the catalogue. But a lot of them seemed to realize they were in sacred space. I saw a dozen conflicting rituals. People blew kisses to the statues, or stood under the *trompe l'oeil* ceiling with arms raised. One student fussed at my desk for five minutes while I grew increasingly exasperated, then asked hesitantly if I could leave her offering "for the loa Epiphany" after the library closed. She slipped me a sandwich bag filled with cookies and tiny slips of calligraphed poetry, then wanted to know whether we'd fixed the PYTHIAS bugs over the summer.

After the students cleared out at last, I stayed at my desk for a few minutes trying to catch my breath. Even the allegories seemed tired. Determination's spear might have drooped a little, unless it just pointed at where some student had annoyed her. I got up and started to put the reference section back in order, then went to give Epiphany her cookies. In the wall below each statue, just above eye level, were little niches that I'd never noticed before. They were easier to spot now, as plenty of people hadn't bothered with an intermediary for their offerings. There were flowers and pebbles, photos, cupcakes, a thankfully unlit candle, tiny jars of liquor that I was just going to assume came from faculty. I stuck the baggie in the appropriate spot.

"Hey," I told Epiphany. I still wasn't sure about talking with them, but ignoring them didn't seem wise, and the students knew the place better than I did. "Long day. Keep safe, okay?" I felt her attention on me, and knew that safety didn't interest her at all—not to give, and not to receive. I trembled: equal parts awe and anxiety, both uncomfortable. Her companions seemed to perk up, their notice sharpening. The air brightened with storm-tinged ozone, and my ears ached as if I'd gone up too fast in an elevator. I felt again the urge to kneel. But I'd spent the day doing my job, and doing it mostly right.

I looked around, found myself alone in the reading room. "I'm not just going to do what you want," I said. No response. I shivered.

"I'm not ignoring you," I went on. Then, swallowing. "I'm not running away, yet. But we're going to work together on this, or it's all going to fall apart."

Still no response—maybe Sherise would have been able to hear one—but the pressure lifted a little. My ears popped, painfully.

"That's better," I said. I kept the shakes out of my voice, knowing I would pay later—if not through some screw-up here, then through breaking down when I got home and thought too hard about the whole thing. But then, I'd have paid that price anywhere. "All right. Was there something you wanted to show me?"

I left through Epiphany's door, and followed the pulse of my little galaxy out into the stacks.

SPECIAL COLLECTIONS

—◊—

Norman Partridge

I had this shrink one time. I didn't see her very long . . . well, only as long as I had to because of the probation deal. Anyway, she was the one who suggested that I get into library work. She said I led a highly compartmentalized life.

I thought everybody did, but the shrink disabused me of that notion. Her name was Rebecca. Of course, I could never call her that out loud. In our sessions she always insisted that I address her as Dr. Nakamura. But in my head it was always *Rebecca Rebecca Rebecca*. I guess you could say that I thought about her a lot.

Rebecca was tall. She liked to wear boots and long skirts and cowl-necked sweaters. Her hair was curly and a shade of blond that made you wonder what color it really was. And she wasn't Japanese, so I have no idea where the *Nakamura* came from. Your guess is as good as mine. Maybe that name was all that remained of an ex-husband or a misplaced father. I never did figure it out, even with all the internet stalking I did.

(And, yes, I know none of this really matters when it comes to the story I'm telling you—unless it's to say that there are just some questions you never can answer—but bear with me. I have an eye for detail, and I admit that I can be more than a little garrulous at times. It's just me.)

Anyway, Rebecca had firm viewpoints on compartmentalization. I didn't argue with her. Only an idiot argues with a court-appointed shrink. Besides, it's true that I like things neat and orderly. And, sure, as Rebecca pointed out you can get carried away with that approach to life . . . but then again, you can get carried away with almost anything, can't you?

Of course you can. That's only human.

But let's get back to keeping things neat and orderly. General topic: compartmentalized devices. Specific frame of reference: boxes. If you approach life the way I do, you probably use a wide variety of same without even thinking about it. There's a toolbox for your work behavior, and a toy box for behavior at home. There's an easy-to-open box that holds the public you, and a Japanese puzzle box that holds the unvarnished real deal. Maybe there's even a little glass dollhouse for your spouse, and a gone-to-seed Barbie playhouse where you can fool around with your lover while Trailer Park Ken's out back cooking meth. And last but not least: a big metal safe full of secrets you'll never ever face, and a nailed-down coffin where you keep dreams so dark you wouldn't want to see them even if you dared to yank nails and open the creaking lid.

That last kind of box . . . well, I guess the contents would look something like Dorian Gray's portrait, wouldn't they? Meaning: You don't go traipsing up to the attic and pull the curtain on that one unless you absolutely have to. If you dare bring along a light, it's just a flickering candle so you won't have to eyeball the entire Goyaesque mess in a hundred-plus-watt glow. And to be honest, it's probably a better idea to expose the naked guts of that thing in complete darkness. That way, the only sensory input you'll receive is auditory—like grave worms wriggling around on slick, oily canvas.

Just imagine that sound inches away in the darkness. Those little worms churning in a face that's as much rot as paint, burrowing into bloodstained canvas . . . digging and devouring, writhing and twisting . . .

Pretty creepy, right? I mean, you wouldn't go tactile, reach out blindly, and bury your fingers like five little corpses in those wriggling worms, would you? Uh-uh. No way. But that's exactly the way it is with the dark things we file away, in life and in libraries. If you want knowledge, you have to reach out and touch it. You have to take a chance, perhaps even suffer the consequences. Information—and secrets—aren't always pretty or pleasant. Sometimes they can be dangerous, like hungry worms crawling through the winding tunnels of your mind. That's why information management is so important . . . believe me, I know.

Think three Cs: codify, consign, and care. This is especially important with managing dangerous information. Libraries deal with lots of things like that. Often they're consigned to Special Collections. Such materials demand careful oversight and limited access—sometimes so limited that the items are almost forgotten . . . except by a select few, or (sometimes) only one.

And really, to close the circle, you might say that's the way things ended up with Dr. Nakamura, my court-appointed shrink.

She was consigned to Special Collections.

In other words: I put her in a box.

Actually, I put Rebecca in several of them.

All it took was a little foresight, and a few very sharp knives.

∽

I don't want you to get the wrong impression. I really made an effort to listen to Rebecca . . . at first, anyway. And I took her advice about libraries to heart. I'd actually worked in one when I was in college. So I started submitting applications, hoping they wouldn't be checked too carefully. This was the late nineties, and you could still manage that. In those days there was barely an internet, and the term "computer literacy" was cutting edge.

I had a few interviews. Nothing surprising about any of them. Sit through enough interviews and you'll realize that search committees end up settling way more than anyone would ever admit. Basically, they see who walks through the door and pick the best of the lot. In the end it's mostly about personalities.

I knew I wasn't much of a personality, so I developed a basic game plan to become one . . . at least long enough to get what I wanted. I built a box from good old-fashioned aromatic cedar and filled it with photocopied stories. I found them in library trade journals, and most of them were pretty funny. Then I looked up some articles about the basic interview questions, and I matched the stories to the questions. The whole exercise was *easy-peasy, lemon squeezy.*

In most library interviews—at least for public desk jobs—there's always a question about handling problem patrons. Which, of course, demands quick thinking and good people skills. I found a great answer for that one. It was about a homeless guy who sat in a library children's room, clucking just like a chicken. Different staffers talked to him, but no one could shut him up. He'd quiet down for a few minutes then start up again: *"Bawk bawk bawk!"* Finally one staffer tried a different approach. You know, very understanding: "Sir, I'm really sorry to bother you, but could I ask you to keep your pet chicken quiet in the library? It's disturbing the other patrons."

The way the story went, the homeless guy didn't make a peep after that. He just sat there pretending to pet his (equally quiet) chicken, every now and then telling it to *shush*. End result of this patron interaction: *You could have heard crickets.*

Anyway, you should have heard the search committee howl when I dropped in that last line. It set up the clincher, and that was this: "Working in libraries isn't just about reading books. It's about reading people, too . . . and I'm very good at that."

Boy, you should have seen their collective eyeballs light up when I said that.

If only it had been true.

I got the job. It was a night supervisor gig at a little college library. The campus had a reputation for social justice advocacy, and maybe that's why they overlooked the minimal stuff I included on my application concerning my criminal record. Or maybe it was because the dot-com boom was still going strong. With a good portion of the emerging workforce making big bucks moving jillions of pixels around millions of screens, pickings were slim in the non-virtual playground of real-world Joe jobs.

Anyway, the library was open late—you know how college students like to procrastinate. I didn't have much to do . . . not at first, anyway. Just make sure students didn't bring a six-pack into one of the group study rooms, keep the student workers busy at the desk, and lock things up at the end of the night.

My boss worked with me the first few weeks, then turned over the keys and the alarm system passcodes. After that, I could pretty much do things my own way. I liked hanging out in the old bindery in the basement. Part of my job was managing book repair, so spending time downstairs was expected. Besides, the student workers at the front desk could buzz the bindery if they needed me . . . but that never happened much.

Anyway, I built a big plywood box—long but not too deep, and not very high. One of the bindery work tables had a piece of base trim at the bottom, and it wasn't much of a problem to install a hinge in the trim plate so I could hide the box beneath the table. I kept my woodworking tools inside, and I decided I'd make a present for Rebecca during my downtime. My probation was almost over, and after landing the library job I was her star pupil. I figured a gift was the least she deserved for giving me such good advice.

That's what I told myself, anyway.

Rebecca was usually tight-lipped, but she let slip that she was attending a conference in a few months. She planned to present a paper that referenced my case as a positive example of her rehabilitation methods. I wasn't sure I liked that, because it was information I couldn't control. But I had a kind of unspoken attraction to it, too—because, in the end, Rebecca was the one in control.

For some reason that excited me. So did the present I built for Rebecca. It was a *himtsu-bako*, or Japanese puzzle box. I made it from Hinoki wood, decorating it with a classic Koyosegi pattern. Fifty moves were required to open it. Up to that point the box was probably the finest piece of woodworking I'd ever produced, and I was especially proud of the combination of dowel pegs and sliders which I installed. A few of those sliders were actually lead, should anyone ever decide to x-ray the box. Back then I thought that was pretty clever.

Put me to the test, and I'd have to admit that opening Rebecca's *himtsu-bako* was a challenge for me—and remember, I'd designed the thing. But make those fifty moves, and you'd find a real treasure inside—a duplicate key for one of my storage units. Talk about dangerous stuff, giving something like that to a person who could put me away with a single phone call. Looking back on it, I can't believe

I took such a risk. Not that I thought Rebecca was the kind of person who'd figure out how to open such a complicated puzzle box, let alone turn detective and search out my storage unit. In truth, I figured she'd probably just put the box up on a shelf in her office and let it collect dust. Certainly, that would have ensured a smug and tasty victory for me. And if I'm honest with myself, that's probably why I took a chance by giving Rebecca the box in the first place . . . after all, it was a pretty sizable thrill to put one over on the oh-so-brilliant Dr. Nakamura.

But you can't ever predict what people will do. Not really. The way things turned out I spent a lot of time worrying about the puzzle box, even after I decided to murder Rebecca. I suppose that added some spice to the whole exercise. All those worries were locked up in different places in my skull, in boxes large and small, and sometimes they'd get opened before I even realized it. That was scary. It was like some stranger breaking into your house and rummaging through your most personal possessions when you're not even there.

Or to put it another way: It was information that was way out of control.

I hate to admit it, but that kind of excited me, too.

It's crazy the way your mind works, isn't it?

You bet it is.

A few months into the library job, I found out the place was haunted. Everyone thought so, anyway. The Public Safety officers said they got weird vibes in the building after closing, and the motion detectors for the alarm system would indicate movement when the building was empty. There was even a story about a custodian quitting the job cold after she saw one of the second-floor statues move . . . just its head, as if its stone eyes were tracking the young woman as she worked above the dimly lit atrium. She claimed she heard laughter bubbling up from the old fountain on the first floor below, and the sound was like something that belonged down in a cave.

Weird, right? Of course, I didn't worry about those stories . . . not at first, anyway. When it comes to the supernatural, I rely on my own sensory input. And that usually means that in the end everything adds up to a big fat zero . . . . except this time.

The incidents that bothered me most happened when I was alone in the building. I could write off several of them pretty easily—like, the elevator running by itself. The cab would come down to the first floor, and the doors would open. I'd be sitting at the Circulation Desk after closing, and I'd stare across the darkened lobby into that empty box bathed in its internal halogen glow. It was like a king-sized *himtsu-bako* waiting just for me, and you can probably guess that the very idea gave me a pretty sizable shiver.

The elevator doors always seemed to remain open just a little too long before closing automatically, but I figured that was just my imagination. Even so, I could write off the elevator antics as some kind of electrical glitch. But I couldn't explain away other phenomena so easily. Like the elevator, these incidents only occurred when I was alone in the building. For instance, I'd hear doors slam upstairs when I knew no doors were open. Or I'd be shifting books on the second floor, and I'd hear footsteps coming from the Periodical stacks on the third.

One night I even heard drawers sliding open and slamming closed in some old microfilm cabinets stored on one of the third floor breezeways. When I went upstairs to check things out, I found a spool loaded on the oldest microfilm reader and the machine humming away. I knew that no one had been using that equipment before closing . . . but there it was. Of course, I looked at the screen. Someone had been reading an old LIFE magazine article about Jack the Ripper. That was a little too creepy for me. I put away the microfilm and turned off the equipment, then set the building alarm and called it a night.

When I came to work the next afternoon, I ran into one of my closers in the quad. Stephen worked a lot of late-night shifts, and he'd go for a run around the campus after we closed the library at midnight.

"Hey," he said, "were you in the building last night around one a.m.?

"No. I cut out about ten minutes after you did. I was already home by then."

"You sure?"

"Sure I'm sure."

Stephen paused, as if he was hesitant to say more. "That's weird."

"Weird how?"

"Well, I was running past the library around one o'clock. You know. Along the access road. And I had this weird feeling someone was watching me. I glanced up at those big windows overlooking the parking lot, and I could see that breezeway on the third floor where the old microfilm readers are. The lights were off, but someone was up there. I only saw his silhouette, but I got the feeling he was staring right at me."

"Spooky," I said. "Unless you're just yanking my chain to get out of working more night shifts."

"Not at all. You know I like nights the best. I just thought I should tell you."

"Thanks."

Stephen hesitated.

"Something else?" I asked.

"Yeah . . . but you'll think I'm crazy."

I laughed. "I'll let you know."

"Well . . . don't judge, but the guy I saw up there on the third floor?"

"Yeah?"

"He was wearing a top hat."

Ghost or man, I kind of forgot about the wearer of the top hat . . . at least for a while. There was a lot going on in my head, and some of it wouldn't shake loose no matter how hard I tried. Mostly I was hung up on Rebecca, the puzzle box, and the hidden key to that storage unit. I just couldn't stop thinking about it. And the worst thing was that no matter how much I thought, I couldn't decide what I should do about the whole mess . . . so I didn't do anything.

I hate inertia. Don't you?

Anyway, I knew I'd go crazy if I kept spinning on a (metaphorical) hamster wheel, so I went looking for distraction. The college archivist suggested that I ought to move up the food chain and get a masters in Library Science. It sounded like a good idea, and maybe an answer to the Rebecca problem, too—school would keep my mind occupied during the day, and work would keep me busy at night. At the time I figured it was best to think less and do more.

So that was the way I played it. I was accepted to a program at a state college just before the semester started. Remember, this was the nineties. There weren't a lot of online classes yet. So I spent a good chunk of time driving to the campus, which was about sixty miles south of my apartment. Three hours of class, and then I'd make the drive back to work and put in my eight hours. For the first semester, I barely spent any time in my apartment at all . . . and when I was there I was (almost invariably) sleeping.

Some classes were dull, some interesting. It was the same with the people in them. There was one girl in a couple of my classes. Her name was Daphne, which is one of those names that conjures two very disparate sources—either the seductive naiad from Greek mythology, or the hot chick from *Scooby-Doo*.

And maybe in the end Daphne was a little bit of both. In those days most people would have (mistakenly) called her a Goth, but she was really more of a fifties throwback with a rockabilly twist. She wore a lot of black, and had these tortoise-shell glasses and a Betty Page hairstyle. Residing on her left arm was a tattoo of Elvis with a raven perched on his shoulder. Just those three sentences were enough to tell me that she really didn't see life the way I did at all. Meaning: Forget secreting things away in compartmentalized boxes; Daphne seemed to wear her boxes on the outside.

That was a strange enough concept for a fellow like me, but it wasn't what— dare I say it?—sparked my attraction. Not really. What I liked most about Daphne was that she'd say whatever she felt like saying without worrying about stepping on someone else's blue suede shoes.

Ha ha. Just a little Elvis humor there.

What I mean to say is that Daphne didn't care what other people thought of her. Plus, she was really funny . . . if you got her jokes and references, anyway. Most people in the class didn't have a clue, but I did. Sometimes I'd laugh out loud at something she said. More often I'd just arch an eyebrow, or grin. Daphne didn't let on that she noticed, but she did . . . and pretty soon I'd catch her checking me out after she said something just to gauge my reaction.

Anyway, I'm getting ahead of myself. Before I knew it I was thinking about Daphne a lot, especially during those drives between school and work. I even bought some CDs with artists I knew she liked—Elvis (of course), but also Wanda Jackson, Robert Gordon, and The Collins Kids. Sometimes I'd get lost in those songs while driving, just thinking of Daphne. I even ran over a dog on the way home one Friday night, so wrapped up in Gordon's version of "Only Make Believe" that I barely even noticed.

Bow-wow.

Clunk clunk.

Daphne Daphne Daphne.

Pathetic, right? I know. But that's the way my world turned . . . for a while, anyway. Of course, I still thought about Rebecca, too. It wasn't the same. Not at all. And then one night while driving home from work, I realized that I'd finally decided what to do about the oh-so-troubling Dr. Nakamura, and the puzzle box, and the whole horrible mess.

The solution was simple, once I realized what had really changed between me and Rebecca. My brain had already moved on, along with the small little knot of muscle that passed for my heart. It was time for the rest of me to follow, and (metaphorically speaking, anyway) put Dr. Nakamura in the rear-view mirror.

There was only one way to do that.

I'd have to kill Rebecca.

And close her box for good.

I'm like most people. There are some things I'm proud of, and (if I'm honest with myself) more than a few that I'm not. Take my criminal record, for instance. It's embarrassing. I can't even bring myself to tell you some of the things I've been convicted for. Stupid stuff, and more than a little compulsive . . . which is even more embarrassing, because it's hard to admit that a compulsion can overcome your natural intelligence.

But that's the way it was with me. The only good thing about my rap sheet was that it didn't match the profile for the type of perp who committed the crimes that were actually my *forte*. In other words, I was very successful at not getting caught for anything that mattered. In a way, I imagine that was why things went as smoothly as they did for such a long time. My record created a kind of blind alley sure to send inquisitive cops on equally blind detours . . . until that last thing with Daphne, anyway.

But there I go again, getting ahead of myself. I warned you I'd do that occasionally. Back to the upside—the things I'm proud of. One of them is my woodworking, and the true shame of that is that very few people ever saw the things I made. Like the boxes I built for Rebecca. Not the Japanese puzzle box. The other ones—the custom-made caskets I built to put her in after she was dead. They were beautiful, especially the box I made for her head. It was made of Zelkova wood seasoned for twenty years, and it was as lustrously blonde as the highlights in Rebecca's hair. I worked with the Zelkova to bring out its glow and inlaid a dark forest of stained hemlock fir against it—the latter wood harvested from Aokiaghara, the Japanese forest at the base of Mount Fuji which was infamous for its suicides.

Of course, Aokiaghara was famous for its ghosts, too, but I didn't think about that then.

I think about it now, though . . . and often.

To this day I wish I'd never touched that wood.

It was a night in May, just before the Memorial Day weekend. I'd closed the library, and (now that Rebecca's boxes were finished) I'd been sitting in my office for hours planning her murder. From out of nowhere, a door slammed upstairs. A moment later, that sound was followed by a short burst of *down in the bottom of a cave* laughter.

That laughter didn't scare me. It made me mad. After all, I already had more than enough on my plate to keep me busy. The last thing I needed was a supernatural side-order of ghostly laughter crowding out the main entrée. I was just about to grab a mallet from my woodworking tools and head upstairs to see if I could pound ectoplasm into cobwebs when the office phone rang. I grabbed the handset, said my name and the name of the library, so off my game that I didn't even bother with "How can I help you?"

"Riddle me this, Batman."

"Huh?"

"Where do you find narrow houses that last until doomsday?"

"The graveyard, of course. Now who is this, and—"

"Well, my name isn't Ophelia."

"What?"

"C'mon, slowpoke. You must have guessed by now. It's Daphne, from cataloging class."

"How'd you figure out where I work? I never mentioned the name of the library in class."

Daphne only laughed. "I'm a librarian, Sherlock . . . or I'm going to be, anyway. Have you tried this new search engine called Google? It's pretty amazing what you can find."

"I'm more of an AlltheWeb guy," I said.

"That's a good one, too. I like the way you can search by specific dates."

"So what's up?"

"Well, you answered my riddle, so you're still in the game. And Memorial Day weekend is just around the corner, which means a certain destination is *de rigueur*."

"So we're back to graveyards?"

"Dig it. We should excavate and investigate. You can be Mr. Burke, and I'll be Ms. Hare."

"You're kidding, right?"

"Certainly, silly. After all, we're a couple of purely straight-up individuals, embarking on careers as library professionals. So no shovels, no holes in the ground . . . just a nice little picnic lunch among the tombstones."

"That sounds kind of morbid."

"Indeed it does, but I'm kind of a morbid girl. And you're not too far off the mark . . . if I read you right, anyway. Besides, the cemetery I'm thinking of has something special."

"What's that?"

"A library. You need to see it, and so do I."

A library in a cemetery—now I was curious. Really curious. We exchanged a few more words, and somehow they seemed heavier now, as if everything we said had some kind of double meaning. I couldn't even tell you what it was, only that it carried a particular edge . . . and a certain weight not unlike secrets or truth.

Whatever it was, it was unsettling. I was relieved to hang up the phone. But I'll be honest—any trepidation I'd had turned to (more than rabid) curiosity . . . and something much stronger. Something I'll have to let you name. I'll simply say that I didn't have to be in Daphne's presence to realize the power she had over me. It was there, even over the phone. Those lips of hers, painted black, smiling just a little bit. A simple arch of an eyebrow, and a gleaming pupil (nearly) dilated past the color of its iris. All of that a vision in my head, so strong that I had to close my eyes and hold my breath.

"*Daphne Daphne Daphne,*" I whispered.

Speaking her name to myself.

And no one else at all.

I don't like dreams. I've never trusted them. They don't fit well into compartments, and you can't control them. That means they're dangerous . . . and the one I had that night after talking to Daphne was the most dangerous dream I ever had in my life.

It began in the library, and things were just the way they had been a few hours before. Only Daphne didn't call me, and I wasn't sitting in my office. No. I was sitting at the Circulation Desk. The library was closed and the building was dark except for that particular square of workplace illumination, which was surrounded by three counters and several metal shelves.

A door slammed somewhere upstairs, and that sound was followed by a short chorus of (by now familiar) *bottom of a cave* laughter. The dual sounds spurred my anger, just as they had in real life. And just the same way, I was ready to grab one of my hammers and make a trip upstairs to see if it was possible to pound a hole in a ghost.

So I stood up, and quickly. The rolling chair shot out behind me as if launched from a cannon, banging into the Reserves shelves. But that didn't matter, because I didn't move an inch. Instead, I just stood there, my feet suddenly buried in cement, frozen in place by a man standing on the staircase landing on the other side of the lobby. He wore a top hat, and (from a distance) his face seemed as narrow as it was pale. The rest of him was black—frock coat with a strange twice-buckled collar, riding boots, trousers, leather gloves.

That the man had not been there on the landing a moment before was a certainty . . . I was sure of that. But he was here now, and that was just as certain. Only five stairs separated the landing from the main floor. The man glided down them the way a marionette does, as if he were an apparition pretending to descend a staircase to create an expected impression.

Soon he was halfway across the lobby. As he came closer to the desk, into the light, the pale face beneath his black top hat came clearly into view. Only it wasn't a face. It was a translucent mask, imprinted with a slight smile that didn't seem like a smile at all. And the voice that came from behind it betrayed nothing more than did the expression—it was neutral, and little more than a whisper, with just the slightest hint of a British accent.

The man said, "I'd like to place an item on Reserve."

"You're a faculty member?"

"No, but I am a teacher, and I do have pupils. And I would like to—"

"If you're not a faculty member at this institution, I can't help you."

"Oh, but I'm certain that you can. You might say I have specific knowledge of an item housed in Special Collections here, and that knowledge is accompanied by certain privileges. I wish to share those privileges . . . with you, to begin."

"Well, I'm not a student, so I don't quite understand your request. What's the item, anyway?"

"As I said, it's housed in Special Collections. It's an autopsy kit from the Victorian era, an item of some particular import. I'd like to make it available for your inspection . . . and use."

Now I laughed. The idea of an autopsy kit in the library was completely ridiculous. "We don't have anything like that here."

"You most certainly do have. If you doubt me, look on the prep shelf behind you."

I did, and there it was, on the shelf with the other items waiting to be added to the Reserves Collection—a long case with leather straps, similar to ones I'd seen in medical histories of the Victorian era.

"Who are you?" It was the only question I could ask, but the man in the top hat didn't reply. He simply stood there, not moving at all . . . as if waiting. And then, he did move. Or at least his lips did. Not the pair on that mask, but the lips barely visible beneath that translucent plastic seemed to writhe, and curve, and—

Quite suddenly, the man reached up with one black-gloved hand and removed the mask from his face. Beneath, there wasn't a face at all. Just a mass of wriggling grave worms—pink, and gray, and blood red—balanced in a large horrible knot atop the twice-buckled collar of his heavy coat. The mass bulged and wobbled, and for a moment I was afraid it would topple and spill those horrid creatures across the desk. But it didn't topple at all. Instead it seemed to grow tighter, like a clenched fist. And then several bloated specimens twisted across the space where a mouth should have been, approximating lips . . . approximating a smile.

"You really want to know who I am?" the thing asked, its voice holding a horrible tenor of amusement.

I managed a nod.

"You're certain?"

"Yes . . . I am."

My words seemed to hang in the air. Those worms writhed and twisted, as if trying to snare them. The thing's smile became larger, the lips becoming a thick woven hole that widened over a patch of blackness. Soon enough, other words came from within that hole.

"Then you must do as I say—slip your fingers into my mouth like a good lad, and I'll tell you my name."

If I'd had any control, it was gone now. I closed my eyes and reached out as if hypnotized. My fingers slid inside that hole rimmed with worms, and the thing's mouth closed around them. Suddenly everything around me, and everything I heard, was a whisper. I was inside it, in a very small space no larger than the *himtsu-bako box* I'd built for Dr. Nakamura.

And, then, for a moment, I was nowhere at all.

The next thing I knew, I woke up in my apartment.

Screaming.

For a smart lady, Rebecca did some really stupid things. Like most people, she was a creature of habit. That was lucky for me. It was also lucky that the conference where she was presenting her paper took place on Memorial Day Weekend, just far enough north so it'd be a tough drive to make in a single day. Which (of course) meant I'd have to do just that, kill Dr. Nakamura, then make it back home in time to set up a solid alibi.

So pedal to the metal all the way up Highway 5 and across the Oregon border, cutting over to the coast and hitting the little resort town just as twilight fell. A long spike of beach jutted into the Pacific just south of the place, and I didn't park anywhere near it. No. I parked a mile away at a rocky beach unpopular with tourists, and I grabbed the backpack that contained my murder kit and humped it double-time down a state park trail that connected the two.

You wouldn't have recognized me. I was wearing an army-surplus jacket and had greased my hair so it looked a lot darker than it was. If you didn't look twice—and why would you?—you'd take me for a grad student who'd just finished finals and was hitting the Pacific Northwest trail for a summer adventure. And that was the story (exactly) I would have told had I run into a park ranger.

But I didn't run into a ranger. I didn't encounter anyone at all, except the person I was looking for. The one who liked to go for a run every night after dinner, no matter where she happened to be.

"Hi Rebecca," I said as I stepped out of the trees.

Rebecca's Nikes were new and expensive—electric blue with coral stripes, probably fresh out of the box. Her back was to me, but her little Nike stutter-step told me she recognized my voice. Just that fast her toes dug firmly into the sand, and she stopped cold.

"Don't turn around," I said. "It'll be easier that way."

Even as I spoke, I knew Rebecca wouldn't heed my warning. Her sharp inhalation cut the silence, and then a big wave broke across the beach and slapped the sound away. The sea wind caught Rebecca's blond hair, masking her face as she turned. She just couldn't help herself—I'm certain she already had a few persuasive paragraphs worked up to lob my way.

"I warned you," I said, and I fired the Taser before she could say a single word.

That was that. Dr. Nakamura hit the sand face-first. I dragged her into the forest. An hour later I was back on the road. Several hours beyond that, I was home. Rebecca's corpse was tucked away in one of my storage units, wrapped up nice and neat in a GE freezer. I'd finish with her later. After all, I had a date with Daphne the next day at noon, and it was already long past midnight.

I needed to get my rest.

If I shared it, you'd recognize the name of the cemetery where Daphne and I had our first date. It's famous. But I think I'll keep that information to myself. I suppose I'm a little sensitive about the place after the way things turned out. You'll have a better understanding of why later.

Anyway, as prominent as the place was, I'll bet no one had ever picnicked there. That's exactly what Daphne and I did on an afternoon that was as still as it was sunny—May light filtering through the trees, chill patches of shadow not quite ready to warm despite the change of seasons, the scent of pine and cut grass, the cool appraisal in Daphne's guarded glances.

Daphne (of course) had done her research. She said that cemeteries had been akin to city parks in Victorian times, when families would spread tablecloths on the grass and share memories of their dear departed along with roast squab and pickled eggs on sunny Sunday afternoons.

I can't speak for Daphne, but I certainly had no one to mourn with that level of sincerity. What I did have was Daphne's company and the picnic lunch she prepared. A pleasant Pinot gris, nicely chilled. Fried chicken, a loaf of sourdough with wedges of Irish butter, and an apple and grape salad with sour cream dressing. Cherries and chocolate cake.

Unfortunately, the conversation didn't match the food. The words that passed between us were simple chit-chat, with none of the electricity of our phone call. Just some mundane gossip about classmates and instructors, with a few conversational detours concerning the cemetery's more infamous residents. All that was entertaining enough as far as it went, but it wasn't the kind of conversation I'd hoped for . . . and I'm sure Daphne felt the same way.

All that changed as soon as we emptied the bottle of wine and packed the picnic basket.

"Ready to check out the library, Mr. Burke?"

"Definitely, Ms. Hare."

"I should warn you—it's a library with spirits."

"As in: distilled?"

The exchange passed so quickly it seemed we had rehearsed it, as chipper and quippy as dialogue in an old William Powell/Myrna Loy movie that was about to get much more twisted than Warner Brothers would have ever allowed. But neither of us laughed when it was over. For the truth was that we had simply progressed to the next point on the agenda, as in: I followed Daphne down a path that led to the edge of the cemetery grounds.

A cathedral stood at the end of the path . . . or at least a building I took for a cathedral. Inside was something else entirely. Instead of a large room with a vaulted ceiling, the building was a tangle of twisting corridors and oddly shaped rooms. The walls of each were lined with golden books that weren't books at all, but instead boxes bearing the cremains of the deceased with their names etched on the spines. The correct term for the place (I knew) was *columbarium*, but indeed it was a library, and it felt like one. For just as books do, each of these boxes held a particular story.

Of course, I never would have believed those stories could be shared. Daphne, I soon discovered, thought otherwise. Even her walk through the place was a lesson in that, for she brought with her the percussion of coffin nails. Her heels clicked along the empty corridor, each step a seeming precursor for a small ending, and as she walked she ran one black-nailed finger along those golden spines, as if searching for the beginning of a tale that struck her particular fancy.

I followed her down the corridor, listening to the scrape of that nail. Without turning to face me, Daphne asked: "So . . . do you believe in spooky stuff?"

"What do you mean?"

"You know—001.64."

"We're talking paranormal phenomenon?"

"You can close down the parameters a little: spectral manifestations . . . shades and revenants . . . your basic things that go bump in the night."

"Well, I suppose I'm the kind of person who believes what he can see."

"You mean, you're a *proof is in the pudding* kind of guy?"

"I suppose so."

"Then let's see what we can see, Stagger Lee . . . or maybe what we can feel."

Daphne turned and smiled at me, and that same finger she'd run across a hundred etched spines brushed my lips and crossed my chin. Only for a moment. Then she turned away, advancing down a narrow hallway. Her hips swayed beneath her skirt, and her fingers arched into claws, a fistful of nails scrapping over spines now.

The briefest moment later her fingers stopped, very quickly, index finger poised on one particular spine. "Ohhhh," she said, and it was the kind of sound I'd never heard from Daphne before. It echoed through the columbarium hallway like a sound from a cave.

"They say some people are mediums," Daphne said. "They stir shadows, raise the past and the dead, hold them in their grasp. For a while, for a time . . . and then that time is gone. In that regard they're like imperfect vessels, I suppose. But they're something more, too."

"People say all kinds of things."

"So—no verdict on that particular form of perception?"

"Uh-uh."

"Let's conduct a little experiment then. For example, it's my perception that this particular box is filled with firecrackers, psychically speaking. I'd like you to touch it and see what happens."

"I don't know."

"C'mon. Take a chance." Daphne smiled. "Do it and I'll guarantee a reward . . . later."

"Not my thing, really."

"Well there's a surprise."

"Uh." I stammered. "Well . . . maybe it is. Sometimes."

"Okay. You're the boss, applesauce . . . but just one other thing—our date's over."

Daphne turned away. From me. From the columbarium book. She started walking and didn't look back, heels clicking down the hallway, those little nail-driving steps marking percussion to my thoughts. Quite literally, she was disappearing into the shadows, and before my very eyes.

My hand reached out before I even knew it, fingers touching that yellow spine. But it wasn't a spine at all . . . at least not one you'd find on a book, or a box. No, it was too cold and slick, its ridges mimicking movement like those grave-worms knotted across that horrible face in my dreams. And then there were words, and they weren't Daphne's. *You see, my friend. We meet again.*

And now that face hung before me, above a buckled collar cinched from dead whore's nightmares. The thing wore a top hat, and it leered with that knotted-worm smile. One whiff of its breath and a wave of dizziness hit me so hard that for a moment I imagined I was back on that beach with Rebecca, cold Pacific tides pounding me to the ground as she escaped down the beach in her blue-and-coral Nikes. And even in the moment I realized that was only a fantasy, one shorn of every notion of personal power possible. I tried to focus, managed just for a moment to read the name on the spine of the box, and then the letters were lost in a wet, smeared sheen.

So was everything else. My knees buckled. I was about to pass out.

I started to fall. Daphne didn't allow that. Suddenly she was very close, holding me up. "I've been coming here for a few years," she said. "Touching a spine here, a spine there—collecting impressions. I still remember the first time I touched that book, and he told me who he was. I couldn't believe it, not at first. Later, I couldn't deny it. And now he's my special friend, one of a kind, no one like him anywhere. At least, I always thought so . . . until I met you."

Daphne's wine-dark lips drew closer, close to my ear. But her voice was far away, as if deep inside a seashell . . . or a memory boxed away. "Remember that day in class? When you loaned me a pencil? It started then. I got my first little tingle of you. And now there's nothing I don't know about you. I've been inside your storage units. Those are nice boxes you built for Dr. Nakamura . . . they should be a good fit. I've even held your knives. In fact, I borrowed one a few weeks ago, the night we took our final for AARC2. Remember that little dweeb who always sat in the front row? The one who asked the same question three different ways in every class? Well, his questioning days are over."

"I need to sit down," I said. "I think I'm going to pass out."

"Don't get fried, Mr. Hyde," Daphne said. "Not during our very first dance. He wouldn't like that."

I said something, but I can't imagine what it was. Moments had passed . . . perhaps minutes. The next thing I knew, Daphne was already moving away. I toppled sideways, leaning against the wall, trying to steady myself. Daphne's heels clicked over the tile floor. I tried to measure time by her footfalls. I still couldn't move. I was buried in a dream—her dream or mine, I couldn't be sure—and those coffin-nail footfalls were driving deeply . . . over and over and over again.

Daphne was further away now . . . very far. And then she was gone.

A door swung open, and a breath of wind washed over my back.

Outside the door Daphne voice rose over the marble forest ahead, and lingered behind.

"Come along now," she said. "After all, I keep my promises."

I don't know how I managed it, but I began to follow.

The darkness followed behind me.

No doubt Daphne had made promises to it, as well.

No one had ever been in my apartment before. Except the landlord, and a plumber when I had to have the toilet replaced. But now that we were there the rooms seemed too small and the things they contained even smaller. And the bed, well . . . it was only a single bed, but Daphne said it wouldn't matter because our real bed was darkness itself, and without borders. That was fine with me. I welcomed darkness wherever I found it.

That night, I hoped the shadows would deliver my mind to other places . . . alone. But you can't be alone with lovers, even in the dark. And so it was with us and the thing from the columbarium. Daphne and I, alive on a hideous canvas, our little hearts pounding, the two of us writhing in the night as worms that twist and couple in a ripe grave. That thing an oozing mess around and under and over and in, free of its buckles and clothes, ripe and corrupt.

Whether it was climax or prelude was a matter of perspective. As act or ceremony, the grave was the grit of it, and blood was its heart. Still Daphne burrowed in and so did I, like hungry little grave worms seeking the choicest morsel. There was no other choice, but any pleasure found was quickly lost between lips and belly in the manner of a ghoul's meal.

Or, to put it more succinctly:

"A nightmare?" you ask.

"Of course," I reply.

What else could I call it? For in truth or imaginings, nightmares must be endured. And as I drifted off to sleep, I thought it would have been better if we were all past enduring. If (on this night) we'd all worn knives for fingers instead of flesh and shadow. Make that simple adjustment, and the three of us would have slashed the darkness to ribbons and left nothing for the coming dawn but a puddle of gore fit only for the coroner's pail.

It would have been better that way, I think.

For in the end, the worms indeed had their way.

When I awoke in the morning, Daphne was already gone. She had a waitress job not far from the college where we attended library school, so she'd probably put my apartment in her rear-view mirror long before the sun came up. The only thing she left behind was a lipstick message on the bathroom mirror:

> *Stay loose, Dr. Mabuse.*
> *We'll see you soon.*
> *Xoxoxo,*
> *364.1523*[3]

Of course, I knew that Dewey Decimal number by heart long before I ever picked up a knife.

Amping it up to the third power was a nice touch, though.

Then again, I've never been much of a joiner.

I left my apartment not long after that, grabbing coffee, then waiting for the cemetery gates to open. Once inside, I made my way to the library . . . or the building that passed for one.

No one was there, of course. At least, no one living . . . not at this early hour. That was fine with me. There was only one thing I was after—I wanted another look at the name on the columbarium box I'd touched the day before, and I wanted to write down the dates of birth and death. That seemed as good a place as any to begin my research.

I hurried down the hallway, retracing my steps. Of course, I remembered the spot, and for a moment it was as if I walked in my own shadow, and the echo of my footsteps was an echo of Daphne's from the day before.

I shook those impressions away. All I wanted was that book, and the information on the spine.

My hand traveled upward, fingers spreading.

The nail of my index finger traveled spines, as Daphne's had the day before.

And then it came to a gap.

To the place a book had been.

In its place was another box—the Japanese puzzle box I'd built for Rebecca. It sat on the shelf, as open as open could be and just as empty. There was no storage-unit key inside.

I grabbed the box and hurried away from the chapel and the cemetery.

Feeling, with good reason, like an exorcised spirit.

It would have been a relief to go to work the next day, except for the eight a.m. phone call from the library director requesting that I come in early for a meeting. A few hours of uncomfortable tension passed before the appointed time arrived and I dropped my backpack on a chair in his outer office. His administrative assistant led me inside.

"I know you're a creature of the night, working the shift you do," the director said. "Thanks for coming out in the light of day."

"I wore my six-six-six sunblock," I said, "just to be safe."

"Good one." He laughed. "Now let's get to it. Looks like you really knocked out all the repair work we've been throwing at you. I think it's time you put the scrapper and glue away for a while. Now that you're getting your masters, we'll give you something really interesting to work on."

"Such as?"

"Let's take a walk, and I'll show you."

I followed the director, waiting for the other shoe to drop. We took the three flights to the Archives office, my suspicions mounting with every step, just waiting for him to say something about my hidden toolbox or some other troubling evidence. But the only things the director talked about were his doctor and his cholesterol numbers. Needless to say, he wasn't happy with either.

By the time we reached the third floor, I'd begun to relax. Obviously, this wasn't about me. The Archives itself was empty at this time of day. The main office adjoined several workrooms, and the director used his master key to make the trip down a narrow hallway leading to the very last one.

"You really won't believe this stuff," he said. "It's been in a warehouse over in Oakland for close to a hundred years. The place is changing hands, so the college had to relocate a ton of material that's been stored there since Moses was a baby. Mostly papers that belonged to a doctor who left his entire estate to the college years ago. He was a Brit expat who did pretty well for himself after immigrating in the 1890s, and he didn't have any relations . . . at least on this side of the pond. After his death, the college got his money and the library was stuck with rest of it—you know, the usual story. Who knows what the collection amounts to, but I think you're the man to give it a look and decide what's what. There's a ton of books on esoteric religions and cults—but I have a feeling a lot of that's just landfill waiting to happen. Seems the silverfish got to it long ago . . . or something that was hungry, anyway."

"And the rest of the collection?" I asked.

"Well, who knows? Turn-of-the-century scuttlebutt was that our doctor friend might have been the abortionist of choice for the privileged class of his day, so there might be something interesting. Buddy up with someone in the Women's Studies department, you might even get a juicy paper out of it."

The director unlocked the door. Even before it swung open, I had an idea what I'd see . . . and my gut told me it was something I knew I'd recognize.

"First off, here's your full box of *morbid*," the director said, pointing at an object on a table in the center of the room. "That's a Victorian autopsy kit. Saws and knives and the whole nine yards. Can you believe it?"

"Yes," I said. "I certainly can." It was a true statement, because (of course) I'd seen the box before, in a dream, and I recognized it down to every strap and buckle, ones that matched the buckles on a certain walking nightmare's collar.

Next to the autopsy kit was another box. This one was wooden. I'd never seen it before, but it was definitely a style with which I was familiar.

The director picked it up. "Judging from what I've found on the internet, this is a Japanese puzzle box—well-crafted, practically a museum piece. I believe it's in the Koyosegi style. No idea what's inside it, however. Who knows . . . maybe it's a diary or something. They say our friend the doctor spent a few years in Japan before immigrating to the States. Could be a find. Maybe he hung out with Lafcadio Hearn and took notes." He sighed. "Anyway, want to give it a look and see if you have any luck opening it? From what the students tell me, puzzles are your thing. Stephen told me you can knock out a Rubik's cube in less than thirty seconds."

"Actually, I'm not very good at puzzles," I said, realizing quite suddenly that I spoke the absolute truth. "Not at all."

There were a million things I should have done that night, but I suppose the only one that matters is the one I did. I paid a visit to my main storage unit, where I butchered Rebecca's frozen corpse and placed the parts in individual caskets. This itself was an exhausting process, and afterwards I embarked upon my usual ceremonies for secreting the caskets that held my victims. But in truth that was little better than indulging an avoidance mechanism. There were far more pressing matters at hand, most of them involving Mr. 364.1523 and/or Daphne.

I should have called Daphne . . . or perhaps kidnapped her. I should have found out if the game we were playing was of her design, or Mr. 364.1523's, or perhaps both. I should have found out if she opened Dr. Nakamura's puzzle box, or if it was opened by ghostly hands. And then we should have had a frank discussion about statistical improbabilities of certain coincidences involving serial killers both dead and alive, and the dangerous course (and absolute, incontrovertible outcomes) of certain obsessions. Namely those that fell within the parameters of 364.1523.

Or I could have done research about the infamous killer who dominated that particular number, and plugged the dead doctor's name into any number of search engines along with "Jack the Ripper." A little history lesson, if you please. And perhaps a lesson in connect-the-dates, because I was more than familiar with the timetable of Jack the Ripper's crimes. If the doctor were indeed a suspect, dates and places would not be hard to match.

Perhaps I could have even gone to the college and opened the doctor's puzzle box, still waiting for me in the Archives on the third floor. Perhaps there really was a diary inside. If that were true, it no doubt held answers.

In short, there were many things I could have done.

Many questions I might have answered with just a little effort.

But none of that was to be. As a result, many of those questions still haunt me today. Perhaps I could never have answered them, but I would have liked to say that I tried. I didn't. For one night, at least, I had hit my limit. So I washed Rebecca's blood off my hands, and I locked the caskets in my storage unit and drove home.

Then (in the manner of Mr. Poe) I quaffed Nepenthe and slept the sleep of the dead.

But not the dreamless.

This time the dream didn't take place in the library. Instead it was in the graveyard, outside the columbarium. Mr. 364.1523 stood there among the tombstones, his double-buckled collar cinched tight, his top hat perched above the little mountain of worms that masqueraded as his head.

"So, you're beginning to understand now?" he asked.

"I'm beginning to see a larger picture," I said. "I'll admit that. But I'm not sure I understand much at all."

"Come, come. You're a bright lad, and it's all very simple. I won't have to draw you a diagram, will I?"

"No. I'm perfectly capable of adding to three."

"Bravo. So nice to hear."

"Then you'll like this even better: I make my own choices, and I always have."

He laughed, as if highly amused by my audacity. The sound shook him from within. The worms ringing that familiar black hole in his face circled it the way gore-flecked water circles an autopsy table drain.

"It's funny, is it?" I said.

"Oh, yes. Dreadfully, so."

"I'm not so sure I see the humor in the situation."

"Perhaps not. But you must realize there's much I can teach you. And we obviously share common ground—a very nice patch of it. On that subject: Did you like it? The three of us? I suppose that is the primary question, simply put."

"I can't say as I did."

"Oh, now you're lying, sir. Shame, shame. Or perhaps you're simply not the kind to admit the particulars of your pleasures. Perhaps, in the end, that evening's work put you exactly where you belong. You're simply not accustomed to tucking your tail between your legs as of yet, but this too will come. You'll learn your place in the new order quickly enough . . . just as a well-used knife finds a new home in the barnyard when a sharp new blade arrives for the china cabinet."

"The fact is I've always seen myself as a lone wolf."

"You're not a wolf, my friend. That is my particular purview. But perhaps you're a dog. Yes, I think that's the role that would suit you best. An obedient and loyal servant. After all, you learned all the tricks, just as a good dog does. You learned from books, from histories of true wolves like myself. Not a lot of originality in your methods, but you're quite the talented imitator. In that role, I can use you."

"You're asking me to fetch and carry?"

"No. I'm saying you already are." Again, those worms were twisting where his lips should have been. "Would you like me to show you?"

"I wish you would."

The dream-wind was higher now, scoring my skin, brushing the worms across Mr. 364.1523's brow. He removed his top hat and held it aloft . . . just for a moment. And then his fingers set it free and it tumbled on the wind.

"There's a good dog," he said. "Fetch and carry."

I stood there for a moment, not believing the words he'd spoken. The top hat tumbled through the air, traveling between wind-twisted boughs, and then it touched down between the tombstones. Before I knew it I was chasing after it, running through the graveyard. For a moment, I even dropped to all fours, charging ahead without a care for whatever came afterward . . . without a care, forevermore.

And then I stopped, quite suddenly. I knew what had happened . . . what was happening. Mr. 364.1523's laughter whipped me like the wind and rang in my head. That sound chilled me as nothing ever had. And suddenly I understood just how it would be if things stayed that way . . . just how it would be, forevermore.

I couldn't allow that to happen. So I fought the dream. I started to awaken. I know I did. I tried to swim up from deep black water, the way you do when you rouse yourself from a nightmare.

But something held me back. Or someone. At first I thought it was Daphne. She stood at the edge of the graveyard, in shadows that hung from the trees. Her pale face was flushed with excitement. "Can you imagine what it will be like?" she asked. "Using that kit? Carving up a victim with his knives? It's time to get started. Hurry and join me . . . I'm ready. Let's go to the library. Let's get that case—"

I wanted to warn her. I wanted to tell Daphne what Mr. 364.1523 had asked. I wanted to tell her what life would be like as a hunting hound, and say that I'd never spend my life in a dead man's kennel. I opened my mouth, ready to tell her everything. I ran my tongue over my lips, for that graveyard wind had dried them. But all I tasted on my lips were the slick excretions of carrion worms, and the words that came from my mouth were not my own.

"It's time to make a new start," he said, his voice coming from a hollow place inside me. "A red parade—that's what it will be. Meet me at the library. We don't need him at all. Tonight it will be just the two of us. That's all we really need. . . . "

When I awoke, I found myself standing in the kitchen of my apartment. The handset of the wall phone was wrapped in my fingers, and my mouth was open. But the words he'd spoken were gone and it was too late to replace them with others.

A dial tone buzzed from the receiver.

Daphne was gone.

I dropped the phone, grabbed my keys, and left my apartment in a rush. I was barely awake when I started the car and headed for the library. But soon my mind was ticking away, running different scenarios the way it always did, searching for a way to come out on top in the confrontation that lay ahead.

Of course, in truth I was still running like a dog in a dream.

I just didn't know it yet.

I have wondered if I was the one responsible for everything that happened that night. I mean, if I was the real murderer. Certainly, I might have been. Certainly, my brain didn't function the way other brains function, and I was clearly capable of the acts which occurred. So I won't blame you if you read this and think: "That's it, exactly. He was crazy. He imagined half the coincidences that led up to that night. He probably imagined half of everything. Hell, he was probably alone when he ate that picnic lunch in the graveyard. And I'll bet he barely spoke to that Daphne chick at all, just stalked her like a creepy little mouse. Just listen to what he says, do the math, and it all adds up to *beyond batshit*. Even if you go best-case scenario, that Ripper stuff was already hard-wired in his head . . . and if Daphne really was tuned in to all that supernatural jazz the way he said she was then she was probably a couple cans short of a six pack, too. And when they bumped up against each other it was dead-on destiny that it'd end up badly . . . in no uncertain terms."

And who knows? If that's the way you read the cards, maybe you're right. I can't convince you otherwise. After all, they say that perception is everything. But so is honesty. And while I understand there's no real reason that you would accept the latter quality as part of my makeup, I can assure you that it is.

Or was.

I can also assure you of a few other facts of which I'm absolutely certain.

First: When I arrived at the library that night, the front doors were already open.

Two: Daphne was already on the second floor, screaming bloody murder.

I wish this were another kind of story. If it were, I could provide you with a more satisfying ending. One that involved pulp heroics, or noirish anti-heroics, or perhaps a Hitchcockian twist or two. One with full measures of shadow and darkness and a triple-play of bad business and murderous intent. Or, to put it simply for those who appreciate the classics, I'd love to be able to provide you with a twisted version of "The Most Dangerous Game" times three.

But doing that with the facts at hand would be just as impossible as making a butcher shop display case seem exciting. No matter how hard you try, you can't do it. In the end, it's just dead meat. And that's the kind of ending I found at the library. I didn't have to see what the man in the top hat left upstairs to know that was true, for I'd studied his methods for years. I could imagine well enough what remained of Daphne after he finished with his knives and assorted autopsy instruments. To paraphrase a comment from my dream: I didn't need him to draw me a diagram.

Not that he would have. Not that he needed to. Not anymore. If I'd been useful to him at all, the time had passed. At that moment we'd circled back to the beginning. Meaning I was frozen in place when he descended the library staircase—I had been for several minutes as Daphne screamed her last—frozen just the way I had been that first night he appeared on the landing after the library was closed. He wore no leather apron, just the black clothes he'd worn that very first night. And for a ghost he seemed to handle material objects just fine. In one hand he held the old puzzle box that might have contained a diary, and with the other he carried the autopsy kit. It was buckled and secure the same way his collar was buckled, and it swung in his gloved hand the way a pendulum swings in a funeral home, marking time that no longer matters.

He spoke as he approached me, his head writhing and alive now, no longer approximating anything human at all. "You don't realize what I offered you. The secrets I know, the things I was willing to teach. The nightmares we might have shared, the three of us. The boxes we might have opened, together. But now they're shut, forevermore. For you, for her . . . for eternity. I will always walk alone."

The words washed over me. I stood there like a statue as the Ripper's smile writhed across those lips one last time. It was almost wistful. I couldn't say a single word. Not as he patted my cheek with a bloody hand. Not as he crossed the lobby to the Circulation Desk. Not as he picked up the phone and dialed the extension for Public Safety. Not as he reported a murder using my voice.

In a moment, he was gone.

The darkness closed in—for seconds, for minutes—and then sirens rose in the distance. And soon I was running. Just as I had in my dream, like a starving dog in a cemetery, charging over bones that lay buried much too deep to be noticed.

I ran farther than you'd expect, and finally the sirens and lights closed in on me. The light was followed by bullets.

In some measure, that was another ending.

And a beginning, as well.

Of course, you can probably guess how the remainder of my journey progressed. Autopsy table, crime lab, a long blast of crematorium fire. All of it leading to a final destination that is a given: the cemetery where I picnicked with Daphne, and a box in that very same columbarium chapel where hallways led one to another, and the rooms did the same . . . all of them (given the circumstances) ultimately leading nowhere at all.

Who knows about Daphne. Perhaps she's here, too. If she is, I haven't found her yet. I've checked the shelves at least a hundred times, scoured every room searching for a golden box which bears her name. But perhaps that isn't the kind of box I should be looking for. Perhaps I should look for a puzzle box made of laurel. In a perfect world (or a perfect myth), I'm sure that's exactly where Daphne would be.

As for my own box, it's really no different than all the others here. That may surprise you, but it really doesn't matter to me. There have always been boxes hidden away, in my life and in my mind. But I have never really inhabited a single one of them. I have never shut myself in. I won't change by doing that now.

Instead, I think of the boxes here as books. Each one holds a story, and I've come to know many of them. I am their curator. Of course, if you asked anyone on staff, they'll tell you there is no librarian here. But there is. It's me. I walk the halls, and I know the stories.

And I listen carefully, searching for another story that will inform my own. One that will tell me more about Daphne, or answer the questions that remain in the Ripper's wake. Was he ghost or demon or something stranger, I don't know. Maybe I never will. But you can never tell where an answer might be hidden, just as you can never know the unexpected places a tale might lead. In life and in stories there's always another panel to slide, another puzzle box to open.

Perhaps it's that way in death, too.

For here, in this place, there are always more boxes, always more stories.

They arrive every day.

Maybe someday I'll find the one I need to finish my own.

EXCHANGE

Ray Bradbury

There were too many cards in the file, too many books on the shelves, too many children laughing in the children's room, too many newspapers to fold and stash on the racks . . .

All in all, too much. Miss Adams pushed her gray hair back over her lined brow, adjusted her gold-rimmed pince-nez, and rang the small silver bell on the library desk, at the same time switching off and on all the lights. The exodus of adults and children was exhausting. Miss Ingraham, the assistant librarian, had gone home early because her father was sick, so it left the burden of stamping, filing, and checking books squarely on Miss Adams' shoulders.

Finally the last book was stamped, the last child fed through the great brass doors, the doors locked, and with immense weariness, Miss Adams moved back up through a silence of forty years of books and being keeper of the books, stood for a long moment by the main desk.

She laid her glasses down on the green blotter, and pressed the bridge of her small-boned nose between thumb and forefinger and held it, eyes shut. What a racket! Children who fingerpainted or cartooned frontispieces or rattled their roller skates. High school students arriving with laughters, departing with mindless songs!

Taking up her rubber stamp, she probed the files, weeding out errors, her fingers whispering between Dante and Darwin.

A moment later she heard the rapping on the front-door glass and saw a man's shadow outside, wanting in. She shook her head. The figure pleaded silently, making gestures.

Sighing, Miss Adams opened the door, saw a young man in uniform, and said, "It's late. We're closed." She glanced at his insignia and added, "Captain."

"Hold on!" said the captain. "Remember me?" And repeated it, as she hesitated.

"*Remember?*"

She studied his face, trying to bring light out of shadow. "Yes, I think I do," she said at last. "You once borrowed books here."

"Right."

"Many years ago," she added. "Now I almost have you placed."

As he stood waiting she tried to see him in those other years, but his younger face did not come clear, or a name with it, and his hand reached out now to take hers.

"May I come in?"

"Well." She hesitated. "Yes."

She led the way up the steps into the immense twilight of books. The young officer looked around and let his breath out slowly, then reached to take a book and hold it to his nose, inhaling, then almost laughing.

"Don't mind me, Miss Adams. You ever smell new books? Binding, pages, print. Like fresh bread when you're hungry." He glanced around. "I'm hungry now, but don't even know what for."

There was a moment of silence, so she asked him how long he might stay.

"Just a few hours. I'm on the train from New York to L.A., so I came up from Chicago to see old places, old friends." His eyes were troubled and he fretted his cap, turning it in his long, slender fingers.

She said gently, "Is anything wrong? Anything I can help you with?"

He glanced out the window at the dark town, with just a few lights in the windows of the small houses across the way.

"I was surprised," he said.

"By what?"

"I don't know what I expected. Pretty damn dumb," he said, looking from her to the windows, "to expect that when I went away, everyone froze in place waiting for me to come home. That when I stepped off the train, all my old pals would unfreeze, run down, meet me at the station. Silly."

"No," she said, more easily now. "I think we all imagine that. I visited Paris as a young girl, went back to France when I was forty, and was outraged that no one had waited, buildings had vanished, and all the hotel staff where I had once lived had died, retired, or traveled."

He nodded at this, but could not seem to go on.

"Did anyone know you were coming?" she asked.

"I wrote a few, but no answers. I figured, hell, they're busy, but they'll be *there.* They weren't."

She felt the next words come off her lips and was faintly surprised. "I'm still here," she said.

"You *are*," he said with a quick smile. "And I can't tell you how glad I am."

He was gazing at her now with such intensity that she had to look away. "You know," she said, "I must confess you look familiar, but I don't quite fit your face with the boy who came here—"

"Twenty years ago! And as for what *he* looked like, that other one, me, well—"

He brought out a smallish wallet which held a dozen pictures and handed over a photograph of a boy perhaps twelve years old, with an impish smile and wild blond hair, looking as if he might catapult out of the frame.

"Ah, yes." Miss Adams adjusted her pince-nez and closed her eyes to remember. "That one. Spaulding. William Henry Spaulding?"

He nodded and peered at the picture in her hands anxiously.

"Was I a lot of trouble?"

"Yes." She nodded and held the picture closer and glanced up at him. "A fiend." She handed the picture back, "But I loved you."

"Did you?" he said and smiled more broadly.

"In spite of you, yes."

He waited a moment and then said, "Do you *still* love me?"

She looked to left and right as if the dark stacks held the answer.

"It's a little early to know, isn't it?"

"Forgive."

"No, no, a good question. Time will tell. Let's not stand like your frozen friends who didn't move. Come along. I've just had some late-night coffee. There may be some left. Give me your cap. Take off that coat. The file index is there. Go look up your old library cards for the hell—heck—of it."

"Are they still *there*?" In amazement.

"Librarians save everything. You never know who's coming in on the next train. Go."

When she came back with the coffee, he stood staring down into the index file like a bird fixing its gaze on a half-empty nest. He handed her one of the old purple-stamped cards.

"Migawd," he said, "I took out a lot of books."

"Ten at a time. I said no, but you took them. And," she added, "*read* them! Here." She put his cup on top of the file and waited while he drew out canceled card after card and laughed quietly.

"I can't believe it. I must not have lived anywhere else but here. May I take this with me, to sit?"

He showed her the cards. She nodded. "Can you show me around? I mean, maybe I've forgotten something.'

She shook her head and took his elbow. "I doubt that. Come on. Over here, of course, is the adult section."

"I begged you to let me cross over when I was thirteen. 'You're not ready,' you said. But—"

"I let you cross over anyway?"

"You did. And much thanks."

Another thought came to him as he looked down at her.

"You used to be taller than me," he said.

She looked up at him, amused.

"I've noticed that happens quite often in my life, but I can still do *this*."

Before he could move, she grabbed his chin in her thumb and forefinger and held tight. His eyes rolled.

He said: "I remember. When I was really bad you'd hold on and put your face down close and scowl. The scowl did it. After ten seconds of your holding my chin very tight, I behaved for days."

She nodded, released his chin. He rubbed it and as they moved on he ducked his head, not looking at her.

"Forgive, I hope you won't be upset, but when I was a boy I used to look up and see you behind your desk, so near but far away, and, how can I say this, I used to think that you were Mrs. God, and that the library was a whole world, and that no matter what part of the world or what people or thing I wanted to see and read, you'd find and give it to me." He stopped, his face coloring. "You *did*, too. You had the world ready for me every time I asked. There was always a place I hadn't seen, a country I hadn't visited where you took me. I've never forgotten."

She looked around, slowly, at the thousands of books. She felt her heart move quietly. "Did you really call me what you just said?"

"Mrs. God? Oh, yes. Often. Always."

"Come along," she said at last.

They walked around the rooms together and then downstairs to the newspaper files, and coming back up, he suddenly leaned against the banister, holding tight.

"Miss Adams," he said.

"What is it, Captain?"

He exhaled. "I'm scared. I don't want to leave. I'm afraid."

Her hand, all by itself, took his arm and she finally said, there in the shadows, "Sometimes—I'm afraid, too. What frightens you?"

"I don't want to go away without saying goodbye. If I never return, I want to see all my friends, shake hands, slap them on the back, I don't know, make jokes."

He stopped and waited, then went on. "But I walk around town and nobody knows me. Everyone's gone."

The pendulum on the wall clock slid back and forth, shining, with the merest of sounds.

Hardly knowing where she was going, Miss Adams took his arm and guided him up the last steps, away from the marble vaults below, to a final, brightly decorated room, where he glanced around and shook his head.

"There's no one here, either."

"Do you believe that?"

"Well, where are they? Do any of my old pals ever come visit, borrow books, bring them back late?"

"Not often," she said. "But listen. Do you realize Thomas Wolfe was wrong?"

"Wolfe? The great literary beast? Wrong?"

"The *title* of one of his books."

"*You Can't Go Home Again*?" he guessed.

"That's it. He was wrong. *This* is home. Your friends are still here. This was your summer place."

"Yes. Myths. Legends. Mummies. Aztec kings. Wicked sisters who spat toads. Where I really lived. But I don't see my people."

"Well."

And before he could speak, she switched on a green-shaded lamp that shed a private light on a small table.

"Isn't this nice?" she said. "Most libraries today, too much light. There should be shadows, don't you think? Some mystery, yes? So that late nights the beasts can prowl out of the stacks and crouch by this jungle light to turn the pages with their breath. Am I crazy?"

"Not that I noticed."

"Good. Sit. Now that I know who you are, it all comes back."

"It couldn't possibly."

"No? You'll see."

She vanished into the stacks and came out with ten books that she placed upright, their pages a trifle spread so they could stand and he could read the titles.

"The summer of 1930, when you were, what? ten, you read all of these in one week."

"Oz? Dorothy? The Wizard? Oh, *yes*."

She placed still others nearby. "*Alice in Wonderland. Through the Looking-Glass.* A month later you reborrowed both. 'But,' I said, 'you've already read them!' 'But,' you said, 'not enough so I can speak. I want to be able to tell them out loud.'

"My God," he said quietly, "did I say that?"

"You did. Here's more you read a dozen times. Greek myths, Roman, Egyptian. Norse myths, Chinese. You were *ravenous.*"

"King Tut arrived from the tomb when I was three. His picture in the Rotogravure started me. What else have you there?"

"*Tarzan of the Apes.* You borrowed it . . . "

"Three dozen times! *John Carter, Warlord of Mars*, four dozen. My God, dear lady, how come you remember all this?"

"You never left. Summertimes you were here when I unlocked the doors. You went home for lunch but sometimes brought sandwiches and sat out by the stone lion at noon. Your father pulled you home by your ear some nights when you stayed late. How could I forget a boy like that?"

"But still—"

"You never played, never ran out in baseball weather, or football, I imagine. Why?"

He glanced toward the front door. *They* were waiting for me."

"They?"

"You know. The ones who never borrowed books, never read. They. Them. *Those.*"

She looked and remembered. "Ah, yes. The bullies. Why did they chase you?"

"Because they knew I loved books and didn't much care for them."

"It's a wonder you survived. I used to watch you getting, reading hunchbacked, late afternoons. You looked so lonely."

"No. I had these. Company."

"Here's more."

She put down *Ivanhoe*, *Robin Hood*, and *Treasure Island*.

"Oh," he said, "and dear and strange Mr. Poe. How I loved his Red Death."

"You took it so often I told you to keep it on permanent loan unless someone else asked. Someone did, six months later, and when you brought it in I could see it was a terrible blow. A few days later I let you have Poe for another year. I don't recall, did you ever—?"

"It's out in California. Shall I—"

"No, no. Please. Well, here are *your* books. Let me bring others."

She came out not carrying many books but one at a time, as if each one were, indeed, special.

She began to make a circle inside the other Stonehenge circle and as she placed the books, in lonely splendor, he said their names and then the names of the authors who had written them and then the names of those who had sat across from him so many years ago and read the books quietly or sometimes whispered the finest parts aloud, so beautifully that no one said *Quiet* or *Silence* or even *Shh!*

She placed the first book and there was a wild field of broom and a wind blowing a young woman across that field as it began to snow and someone, far away, called "Kathy" and as the snows fell he saw a girl he had walked to school in the sixth grade seated across the table, her eyes fixed to the windblown field and the snow and the lost woman in another time of winter.

A second book was set in place and a black and beauteous horse raced across a summer field of green and on that horse was another girl, who hid behind the book and dared to pass him notes when he was twelve.

And then there was the fair ghost with a snowmaiden face whose hair was a long golden harp played by the summer airs; she who was always sailing to Byzantium where emperors were drowsed by golden birds that sang in clockwork cages at sunset and dawn. She who always skirted the outer rim of school and went to swim in the deep lake ten thousand afternoons ago and never came out, so was never found, but suddenly now she made landfall here in the green-shaded light and opened Yeats to at last sail home from Byzantium.

And on her right: John Huff, whose name came clearer than the rest, who claimed to have climbed every tree in town and fallen from none, who had raced through watermelon patches treading melons, never touching earth, to knock down rainfalls of chestnuts with one blow, who yodeled at your sun-up window and wrote the same Mark Twain book report in four different grades before the teachers caught on, at which he said, vanishing, "Just call me Huck."

And to *his* right, the pale son of the town hotel owner who looked as if he had gone sleepless forever, who swore every empty house was haunted and took you there to prove it, with a juicy tongue, compressed nose, and throat garglings that sounded the long October demise, the terrible and unutterable fall of the House of Usher.

And next to him was yet another girl.

And next to her . . .

And just beyond . . .

Miss Adams placed a final book and he recalled the fair creature, long ago, when such things were left unsaid, glancing up at him one day when he was an unknowing twelve and she was a wise thirteen to quietly say: "I am Beauty. And you, are *you* the Beast?"

Now, late in time, he wanted to answer that small and wondrous ghost: "No. He hides in the stacks and when the clock strikes three, will prowl forth to drink."

And it was finished, all the books were placed, the outer ring of his selves and the inner ring of remembered faces, deathless, with summer and autumn names.

He sat for a long moment and then another long moment and then, one by one, reached for and took all of the books that had been his, and still were, and opened them and read and shut them and took another until he reached the end of the outer circle and then went to touch and turn and find the raft on the river, the field of broom where the storms lived, and the pasture with the black and beauteous horse and its lovely rider. Behind him, he heard the lady librarian quietly back away to leave him with words . . .

A long while later he sat back, rubbed his eyes, and looked around at the fortress, the encirclement, the Roman encampment of books, and nodded, his eyes wet.

"Yes."

He heard her move behind him.

"Yes, *what*?"

"What you said, Thomas Wolfe, the title of that book of his. Wrong. Everything's *here*. Nothing's changed."

"Nothing will as long as I can help it," she said.

"Don't ever go away."

"I won't if you'll come back more often."

Just then, from below the town, not so very far off, a train whistle blew. She said:

"Is that *yours*?"

"No, but the one soon after," he said and got up and moved around the small monuments that stood very tall and, one by one, shut the covers, his lips moving to sound the old titles and the old, dear names.

"Do we *have* to put them back on the shelves?" he said.

She looked at him and at the double circle and after a long moment said, "Tomorrow will do. Why?"

"Maybe," he said, "during the night, because of the color of those lamps, green, the jungle, maybe those creatures you mentioned will come out and turn the pages with their breath. And maybe—"

"What else?"

"Maybe my friends, who've hid in the stacks all these years, will come out, too."

"They're already here," she said quietly.

"Yes." He nodded. "They are."

And still he could not move.

She backed off across the room without making any sound, and when she reached her desk she called back, the last call of the night.

"Closing time. Closing time, children." And turned the lights quickly off and then on and then halfway between; a library twilight.

He moved from the table with the double circle of books and came to her and said, "I can go now."

"Yes," she said. "William Henry Spaulding. You can."

They walked together as she turned out the lights, turned out the lights, one by one. She helped him into his coat and then, hardly thinking to do so, he took her hand and kissed her fingers.

It was so abrupt, she almost laughed, but then she said, "Remember what Edith Wharton said when Henry James did what you just did?"

"What?"

" 'The flavor starts at the elbow.' "

They broke into laughter together and he turned and went down the marble steps toward the stained-glass entry. At the bottom of the stairs he looked up at her and said:

"Tonight, when you're going to sleep, remember what I called you when I was twelve, and say it out loud."

"I don't remember," she said.

"Yes, you do."

Below the town, a train whistle blew again. He opened the front door, stepped out, and he was gone.

Her hand on the last light switch, looking in at the double circle of books on the far table, she thought: What was it he called me?

"Oh, yes," she said a moment later.

And switched off the light.

Paper Cuts Scissors

Holly Black

000 — *Generalities*

When Justin started graduate school in library science, he tried to sit next to the older women who now needed a degree as media specialists to keep the same job they'd done for years. He avoided the hipster girls, fresh from undergrad, wearing black turtlenecks with silver jewelry molded in menacing shapes and planning careers in public libraries. Those girls seemed as dangerous as books that unexpectedly killed their protagonists.

He wasn't used to being around people anymore. He fidgeted with his freshly cut hair and ran shaking fingers over the razor burn on his pale skin. He didn't meet anyone's eyes as he dutifully learned about new user interfaces and how to conduct a reference interview. He wrote papers with pages of citations. He read pile after pile of genre novels to understand what people saw in inspirational romance or forensic mysteries, but he was careful to read the ends before the beginnings. He told himself that he could hold it together.

At night, when all his reading was done and he'd printed all the papers he needed for the next day, he tried not to open Linda's book.

He'd read it so many times that he should know it by heart, but the words kept changing. She was always in danger. She'd nearly got run over by a train and frozen on a long march to Moscow while Justin had sat on his parent's pullout couch in the den and forgotten to eat. While his hair had grown long and his fingernails jagged. Until his friends had stopped coming over. Until he'd remembered the one thing he could do to get her out.

One afternoon, Justin checked the notice board and saw a sign:

*Looking for library student to organize
private collection: 555-2164. $10/hour.*

His heart sped. Finally. It had to be. He punched the number into his cell phone and a man answered.

"Please," Justin said. He had practiced a convincing speech, but he couldn't remember a word of it. His voice shook. "I need this job. I'm very dedicated, very conscientio—"

"You're hired," said the man.

Relief made him lightheaded. He sagged against the painted cinderblock wall of the hallway.

After, in Classification Theory, Sarah Peet turned half around in her chair. Her earrings swung like daggers. "Rock, paper, scissors for who buys coffee at the break."

"Coffee?" His voice came out louder than he'd intended.

"From the vending machine," she said and made a fist.

One. Two. Three. Rock breaks scissors. Justin lost.

"I take it black," said Sarah.

100 — *Philosophy and Psychology*

The private collection that Justin was supposed to organize was located in the basement of a large Victorian house outside New Brunswick. He drove there in his beat-up Altima and parked in the driveway. He didn't see another car and wondered if Mr. Sandlin—the man he was sure he'd spoken with on the phone— had forgotten that he was coming. According to his watch, it was quarter to seven in the evening. He was fifteen minutes early.

When Justin knocked on the door, he was met by a gentleman in a waistcoat. He had a slight paunch and long hair tied back in a ponytail.

"Excellent," the man said. "Eager. I'm Sandlin."

"Justin," said Justin. He hoped his palms weren't sweating.

"Each year I hire a new library student—you'll pick up where the last one left off. Dewey decimal. No Library of Congress, got it?"

"I understand perfectly," Justin said.

Sandlin led Justin through a house shrouded in white sheeting, down a dusty staircase to a cavernous basement. Masses of bookshelves formed a maze beneath swaying chandeliers. Justin sucked in his breath.

"There's a desk somewhere that way," Sandlin said. "A computer. Some books still in boxes. I used to run a bookshop, but I found that I wasn't suited for it. I didn't like when people bought things. I like to have all my books with me."

It was a vast, amazing collection. Justin could feel his pulse speed and a smile creep onto his face.

"Best to get started," said Sandlin, turning and walking back up the stairs. "You have to leave before midnight. I have guests."

Justin couldn't imagine that there'd been many visitors entering through the front door, considering how thick the dust was upstairs. The wooden planks under his feet, however, were swept clean.

Sandlin stopped at the landing, gesturing grandly as he called down. "It is my belief that books are living things."

That sent a shiver up Justin's spine as he thought of Linda.

"And as living things, they need to be protected." Sandlin walked the rest of the way up the stairs.

Justin rubbed his arms and bit back what he wanted to say. It was readers that needed to be protected, he thought. Books were something that happened to readers. Readers were the victims of books.

He'd considered this a lot at the bookstore, once Linda was gone and before he'd lost the job altogether. Grim-faced women would come in, dressed sensibly, pleading for a sequel like they were pleading for a lover's life. Children would sit on the rug and cry inconsolably over picture books where rabbits lost their mothers.

The desk—when he found it—was ordinary, gray metal rusted at the corners and the PC sitting on top was old enough that it had a floppy drive. The keyboard felt sticky under his fingers. Justin opened his backpack and looked in at Linda's book; when packing the night before, he found that he couldn't bring himself to leave it behind.

200 — *Religion*

Justin had always opened new books with a sense of dread, but no dread could compare with opening Linda's book. Sometimes the *militsiya* were arresting a member of her new family, or she was swallowing priceless rubies so that she could smuggle them out of Russia. Occasionally she was in love. Or drinking strong tea out of a samovar. Or dancing.

He remembered her with ink-stained fingers and a messy apartment full of paperbacks. He'd lived there with her when they both worked in the bookstore. She was allergic to cats, but she couldn't resist petting the stray that the owner kept and her nose was always red from sneezing. She made spaghetti with olives when she was depressed.

He remembered the way they'd curled up together on the futon and read to one another. He remembered his laughing confession that he opened new books with a sense of dread akin to jumping off a cliff with a bungee on. He knew he probably wouldn't hit the rocks, but he was never really sure. Linda didn't understand. She read fearlessly, without care for how things turned out.

Things, she said, could always be changed.

She told him that she knew how to fold stuff up and put it in books. *In* the books, inside the stories themselves. She'd proven it to him. She put a single playing card into a paperback edition of *Robin Hood*. The Ace of Spades. Little John had found it. He'd become convinced it was a sign that they would be defeated by the Sheriff of Nottingham and hanged himself. The Merry Men were less merry after they found his body. Justin had looked at other editions of Robin Hood, but they were unchanged.

After that, he'd believed her. He'd wanted her to alter other books—like fix *Macbeth* so that no one died. She said that *Macbeth* was unlucky enough without her tampering.

They'd fought a lot in their third year together. Linda had heard that there was a man named Mr. Sandlin who could take things out of books as well as putting them in. She wanted them to give up the lease on their apartment and their jobs at the bookstore. She wanted them to enroll in library school. Early one morning, after fighting all night—a fight that had started out about moving and wound up about every hateful thing they'd ever thought about one another—she folded herself up and put herself into a fat Russian novel.

"Ohgodohgodohgod," Justin had said. "Please. No. Please. Oh God. Please." He'd opened the cover to see an illustration of her in pen and ink, sitting in a group of unsmiling characters.

After that, he couldn't tell her that he was sorry or that her bolshie-sympathizing uncle was going to expose her in the next chapter or that she was going to regret leaving him now that she was stuck in an ice storm with only a mink cloak and muff to protect her. He was just a reader and readers can't do anything to make the story stop—except close the book.

300 — *Social Sciences*

The next time that Sandlin opened the door, he was dressed less impressively, in pajamas with blue stripes. He greeted Justin with a huge yawn.

"Am I early?" Justin asked, although he knew he wasn't.

Sandlin shook his head and waved Justin in. "Time I got up anyway."

"Right. I'll be downstairs," said Justin as Sandlin dumped out the coffeepot and filled it with water from the tap.

The collection, which had looked so grand at first sight, was, on closer inspection, quite odd. None of the books seemed to be first editions. Many were not even hardcover. Tattered paperbacks nestled up against reprinted hardcover editions of classics with their spines cracked. Some books even appeared to be galleys from publishers, marked, "for review purposes only—not for resale."

Most of the books were easy to classify. They were almost all 800s, mostly 810s or 820s.

He glanced at the backs of their covers and the copyright pages and then typed their titles into the database. On the spines of each, he taped a label printed in marker.

After he finished a dozen, Justin decided that he should start shelving. He lifted the stack, inhaling book dust, and headed into the aisles.

The problem with everything being in the 800s is that the markers on the ends of the shelves blurred together. Justin took a few turns and then wasn't sure he knew where he was going or where he could find the places for the books in his arms.

"Sandlin?" he called, but although his voice echoed in the vast room, he doubted it was loud enough to carry all the way upstairs.

He turned again. A plastic drink stirrer rested on the floor. Bending to pick it up, he felt panic rise. Where was he? He'd thought he was retracing his steps.

By the time he found his way back to the desk, he felt a faintly ridiculous but almost overwhelming sense of relief.

Sarah leaned back in her seat and sat a roll of twine in front of him.

"I heard you got the Sandlin job," Sarah said. "My friend used to work there, said it was like a maze. This is his Theseus trick."

"That's smart," Justin said, thinking of Theseus picking his way through the Minotaur's lair, unwinding Ariadne's string behind him. Thinking of how his heart had pounded when he was lost in the stacks. It wasn't just smart, it was clever, even classical. He wished he'd thought of it.

"Rock, paper, scissors to see if I can come with you."

"No way," Justin said. "I could lose my job."

"My friend said some other stuff—about what happens after midnight. Come on. If you win, I'll tell you everything I know. If I win, I get to come."

"Fine." Justin scowled, but Sarah didn't seem cowed. She raised a brow studded with tiny silver bars.

Rock. Paper. Scissors. Her rock smashed his scissors.

"Best two out of three," Justin said, but he knew he was already defeated.

"Tomorrow night," said Sarah, with a smile that he couldn't interpret. In fact, the more he thought about it, the less he knew about why she'd started talking to him at all.

400 — *Language*

That night, Justin tucked the string and Linda's book into his backpack and drove to Sandlin's house. He worked his way through cataloging an entire box of books, when, on impulse, he flipped a thin volume open.

The spine of the book read *Pride and Prejudice* so Justin was surprised to find Indiana Jones in the text. Apparently, he'd been sleeping his way through all the Jane Austen books and had seduced both Kitty and Lydia Bennett. Justin discovered this fact when Eleanor Tilney from *Northanger Abbey* showed up to confront Indy with his illegitimate child.

He looked at the page and read it twice just to be sure:

> *To Catherine and Lydia, neither Miss Tilney nor her claims were in any degree interesting. It was next to impossible that Miss Tilney had told the truth, and although it was now some weeks since they had received pleasure from the society of Mr. Jones, they had every confidence in him. As for their mother, she was weathering the blow with a degree of composure which astonished her husband and daughters.*

He closed the book, set it back on the shelf, and opened another. *Peter Pan.* In it, Sherlock Holmes deduced that Tinkerbell had poisoned Wendy while Watson complained to the mermaids that no one understood his torrid romance with one of the shepherdesses from a poem. Wendy's ghost flitted around quoting lines from *Macbeth*. Peter wasn't in the book at all. He'd left to be a valet to Lord Rochester in a play of which no one had ever heard.

Justin shut *Peter Pan* so quickly that one of the pages cut a thin line in his index finger. He stuck his bleeding finger in his mouth and tasted ink and sweat. It made him feel vaguely nauseous.

500 — *Natural Sciences & Mathematics*

Scrambling over to his backpack, Justin started unrolling the string. It dragged across the floors, through the aisles as he wound his way though the maze of shelves. At first, it was just books, but as he moved deeper into the stacks, he discovered a statue of a black-haired man in a long blue robe and eyes that glittered like they were set with glass, a velvet fainting couch, and a forgotten collection of champagne flutes containing the dregs of a greenish liquid beside a single jet button.

He glanced at the shelves, thinking of Sandlin's pajamas and Sarah's words: *My friend said some other stuff—about what happens after midnight*. A party happened here, a party with guests that never disturbed the dust upstairs, that never entered or exited through the front hall.

A party with guests that were already in the house. Guests that were *inside the books*.

He shuddered then laughed a little at himself. This was what he'd been hoping for, after all. Now he had to just count

on the fact that Sandlin wouldn't notice one more book.

That night Justin called out his usual farewell to Mr. Sandlin, before sneaking back down the library stairs. He climbed one of the old ladders along the far wall and cracked open a high, thin window. Then he rolled onto the very top of the bookshelf and flattened himself against the wood. Something banged against the glass.

"Wow. We're pretty high up," said Sarah as she slid inside. Her foot knocked a stack of papers and a bookend shaped like a nymph crashed to the floor. "Shit!"

"Careful," whispered Justin. He knew he sounded prissy as soon as it came out of his mouth, but Sarah didn't seem like a very careful person.

"So," she said. She wore a tattered black coat covered in paint stains and a new hoop gleamed in her eyebrow. The skin around it was puffy and red. "Here we are. This is it."

"What's it?"

"This is where Richard hid. My friend. Pretty genius, right? He could see everything from up here. And who ever looks up?" She answered her own question with a nod. "Nobody."

"Did he say what happens now?"

"*The books come to life!*" Her voice was filled with awe, like she was about to take a sacrament from the Holy Church of Literature.

Justin looked at his bag where Linda's Russian novel rested. He had a sudden urge to pitch it out the window. "How do you think that happens? There are so many . . ." He wasn't sure how to end that sentence. Characters? Settings? Books?

A footfall kept him from finding out.

"*Shhhh*," said Sarah, completely unnecessarily.

Sandlin appeared, walking down the stairs with a crate. Justin crawled forward to see him begin to set up bottles and a cheese platter. He removed red grapes from their plastic-covered package and set them carefully on one end of the tray, then stepped back to look at his arrangement.

He appeared to be satisfied because when he turned around, he made a motion with his hands and a ripple went through the shelves. The books shuddered and then, one by one, the room began to fill with people.

They climbed out of the stacks, brushing themselves off, sometimes hopping from a high place, sometimes crawling out of what seemed like a very cramped low shelf.

Justin looked over at his backpack in time to see women in high-necked dresses and men in uniforms scamper down. He looked for Linda, but from the back, he wasn't sure which one she was. He started to follow, but Sarah grabbed his arm.

"What are you doing?" she hissed. "You said to be careful—remember?"

He leaned over the side, scanning all the faces for Lindas. He tried to remember what she looked like; he kept thinking of lines of description instead. Her hair was "thick chestnut curls like the shining mane of a horse" in the book. He was pretty sure he'd read a passage about her eyes being "amber as the pin at her throat," but he remembered them as brown.

Women with powdered cones of hair and black masks on sticks swept past knights decked out for jousting and comic book heroes in slinky, rubbery suits. A wolf in a top hat and tails conversed with a wizard in a robe of moons and stars as faeries flew over their heads.

He thought he saw Linda near the grapes, whispering behind a fan. He strained to hear what she said, but all he heard were other conversations. Without quite meaning to, he realized what he was hearing.

"Sarah." Justin pointed to a large-shouldered man decked out in lace, with a slim sword at his hip and a small reddish flower in his hands. He was lazily chatting up a skinny, red-headed young woman in jeans and a T-shirt.

"Demmed smart you are," said the man. "Pretty, too. I've been assured my taste is unerring so there's no need to protest."

"Sarah," said Justin. "That's the Scarlet Pimpernel!"

"Oh my god," Sarah whispered back, wriggling closer. "I think you're right. Percy Blakeney. I had such a crush on him."

"I think he's hitting on that girl."

"Isn't that?" She paused. "It can't be . . . but I think the girl is Anne of Green Gables."

Justin squinted. "I never read it."

"I heard her say something about there being no one like him in Avonlea," said Sarah. "What's she doing in jeans? Anne! Anne! Don't do it!"

"*Shhh!*" Justin said.

"He's married! Marguerite will kick your ass!"

Justin tried to put his hand over her mouth. "You can't just—"

Sarah pulled away, but she seemed a little bit embarrassed. "Chill out. She couldn't hear me anyway. And I wasn't the one who almost climbed down there."

He looked back into the crowd, tamping down both rising panic and chaotic glee. Characters shouldn't be able to meet like this, to mix and converse anachronistically and anarchically in the basement of a house in jersey. It seemed profane, perverse, and yet it was the perversion itself that tempted him to dangerous joy.

"Okay. Jeesh," said Sarah, mistaking the reason for his silence. "I'm sorry I got carried away—hey, who's that in the gold armor? Standing near. Oh." She stopped. "Is that Wolverine talking to a wolverine? In a dress?"

"Which one's wearing the dress?" Justin asked, but the grin slid off his face when he saw Linda move away from the refreshments. She was talking to a man in a doublet.

Sarah put her hand on his arm. "Who are you staring at? You look really weird."

"That's my girlfriend," said Justin.

"A character in a book is your girlfriend?"

"She put herself there. We had an argument—it's not important. I'm just trying to get her out again."

Sarah stared at him, but her expression said: *I don't believe you. You did something bad to your girlfriend to make her put herself in a book.* Her earrings swung like pendulums, dowsing for guilty secrets. "You knew what was going on when you applied for this job, didn't you?"

"So?" Justin asked. "Oh, you wanted it too, didn't you? I just called first."

"Well, she's out from the book now. You don't look too happy."

Justin scowled and they said little to each other after that. They just rested on their stomachs on the dusty bookshelves and watched the crowd swirl and eddy beneath them, watched Little Lord Fauntleroy piss in a corner and an albino in armor mutter to the black sword in his hands as he headed for one of the more private and shadowed parts of the library.

And Justin watched as Linda flitted among them, laughing with pleasure.

"Oh, you doth teach the torches to burn bright," the man in the doublet told her.

What a line, Justin thought ruefully. *I hope she knows he's quoting Shakespeare.* Then an unpleasant thought occurred to him. *Who was Linda talking to?*

"Lo, John Galt hath eaten all the salsa," said a knight in green armor adorned with leaves.

"Oh, how awful," said Dolly Alexandrovna from Anna Karenina. She smoothed her gown, looking exactly like a painting of her Justin had seen. "I won't forgive him and I can't forgive him. He persists in doing this every night."

Justin wondered why none of them spoke in Russian or French or whatever, but then it occurred to him that all the books were in translation. The logic made him dizzy.

"Who's John Galt?" growled Wolverine around the cigar in his mouth.

Anne of Green Gables danced a waltz with a man that Justin failed to recognize and wasn't going to ask Sarah about. Stephen Daedalus got into a fistfight with Werther. Hamlet shouted at them to stop, yelling, "It is but foolery," but they didn't stop until Werther got hit hard enough that his nose bled.

Justin thought that after being punched, he looked weirdly like the guy on the cover of the Modern Library reprint edition of *Werther*, where his whole face is wet with tears.

"How can I, how can you, be annihilated?" Werther spat. "We exist. What is annihilation? A mere word, an unmeaning sound that fixes no impression on the mind."

Stephen's knuckles looked bruised. "Whatever," he said.

Linda sunk down beside Werther, silky skirts billowing around her, and dabbed at the blood on his face with a handkerchief. What was she doing? It made no sense! She didn't even like Goethe! She'd complained that Werther was a coward and whiny, besides.

Justin started to climb down the bookshelf.

Sandlin shouted something at that moment and then a great gust of wind blew through the library and when it had gone, so had all the party guests.

Gone. Linda was gone. Justin looked out the small window and, sure enough, the sky was beginning to lighten outside. Reaching for his pack, he opened Linda's book and flipped frantically, scanning each page for her name.

Nothing.

Gone.

600 — *Technology (Applied Sciences)*

The next day at the break, Sarah brought a cup of coffee from the machine and set it on the desk in front of him without resorting to rock, paper, or scissors. He still wore the same clothes from the night before and when he looked down at his notebook, all he had written was "faceted classification" with several lines drawn under the words. He had no idea what that meant.

"I should be mad at you," she said, "but you're just too pathetic."

He picked up the coffee and took a sip. He was glad it was warm.

She sat on the edge of his desk. "Okay, so tell me about your girlfriend. What happened?"

"I don't know. We just started fighting. She wanted to meet Sandlin, but I wanted to stay at the bookstore. Then this."

"And by *this*, you mean that instead of locking herself in the bathroom or throwing a vase at you, she put herself in a book and didn't come out."

"Yeah," Justin said, looking at the desk.

"You might seriously consider that that translates to breaking up with you."

He scrubbed his hand over his face. His skin felt rougher than his stubble. "I don't think she knew how to get out." But, as he thought back on it, he couldn't recall reading that she wanted to; characters in Russian novels are big on bemoaning their personal tragedy. It seemed that wouldn't have been left out.

Sarah shrugged. "You said that she wanted to meet Sandlin. You brought her to him. You're done."

"I never got to say I was sorry."

"Are you?" Sarah took a sip from her cup and made a face.

Justin scowled. "What kind of question is that?"

"Well, you don't even seem to know what you did, or if you did anything."

He looked down at the laces of his sneakers, the dirty knots that he hated untangling so much that he'd just pulled the things off and on. Now they were hopeless. The knots would never come out. He sighed.

"Do you even like books?" Sarah asked. She waved her hand around. "Was all of this for her?"

"Of course I like books!" Justin said, looking up. He didn't know how to explain. He'd started library school to get Linda to Sandlin, but he actually liked it. It felt good to carefully organize the books so that other people would know what they were getting themselves into. "I've always liked books. I just don't *trust* them."

"What about people?" Sarah asked.

He looked at her blankly.

"Do you trust people?"

"I guess. I mean, sure. Within reason. I don't think people usually have terrible secrets the way characters do, but people often aren't as amazing, either. Were watered down."

"I have a secret," Sarah said. "I compete in rock, paper, scissors tournaments."

He laughed.

"I'm serious," Sarah said.

"Wait a minute. You mean you cheated me out of all that coffee?" For a moment, Justin just looked at her. She seemed different now that he knew she had secrets, even if they were kind of lame ones.

"Hey," she said. "I won fairly!"

"But you're like a pool shark or something. You have strategies."

Sarah shook her head. "Okay, you want my RPS secret? It's about understanding people. Rock's basically a weapon. Like something an ogre might hurl. It's an angry throw. Some people shy away from it because it seems crude, but they'll use it if they're desperate."

"Okay," Justin said.

"Now, scissors. Scissors are shiny and sharp. Still dangerous, but more elegant, like a rapier. Lots of people make their first throw scissors because it seems like the clever throw. The rakish throw. The hipster throw."

"Really?" Justin frowned.

"You threw it the first time. And the second."

He thought back, but he couldn't recall. He wondered which play Sarah usually opened up with. Was it always rock?

"Now, paper. Paper's interesting. Some people consider it a wimpy throw and they use it very infrequently. Others consider it the most subtle throw. Words can, they say, be more dangerous than rocks or scissors."

"Of course, scissors still cut paper," Sarah said.

"Oh," said Justin suddenly, getting up. "They do. You're right." He could cut Linda out like a paper doll.

700 — The Arts

Justin pulled book after book from the shelves, not caring about their spines, not caring about the mess he made, scanning each one for a mention of Linda. They piled up around him and the dust coated his hands, ink smearing his fingers as he ran them down countless pages.

Heavy metal scissors weighed down the pocket of his coat and sometimes his hand would drop inside to touch their cool surface before emptying another shelf.

"What are you doing?" Sandlin asked.

Justin jumped up, hand still in his pocket.

Sandlin was dressed in another waistcoat. A single silver pin held a cravat in place at his neck. He sneezed.

"I'm looking for my girlfriend. She got out of her book, but I don't know which book she got into."

"The girl with all the piercings I saw you hiding with last night?"

"No," said Justin, trying not to seem as rattled as he felt.

If Sandlin knew . . . No, he couldn't dwell on that. "That's Sarah. Linda's my girlfriend, or she was, and she knew how to put things into books. She put herself in a Russian novel, but last night you took her out and I don't know what book she's in now."

Sandlin ran his hand over his short beard.

"You see," Justin said, his voice rising, "she could be anywhere, in danger. Novels are always putting characters in peril because it's exciting. Characters die."

"Your problem isn't with books, it's with girls," Sandlin said.

"What?" Justin demanded.

"Girls," said Sandlin. "You don't know why they do the things they do. Who does? I'm sure they feel the same about us. Hell, I'm sure they feel the same way about each other."

"But the books," said Justin.

"Fiction. I used to own a bookstore before I inherited a lot of money from my great aunt. The money went to a cat first, but when the cat died, I was loaded. Decided I'd shut my store down, sleep all day and do whatever I wanted. This is it."

"But . . . but what about what you said about books being alive? Needing our protection?"

Sandlin waved his hand vaguely. "Look, I love spending time with characters from books. I love the strange friendships that spring up, the romances. I don't want to lose any of them. Did you know that Naruto has become close to Edmond Dantes and a floating skull with glowing red eyes? I couldn't make that up if I tried! But it's still *fiction*. Even if it's happening in my basement. It's not real."

Justin looked at him in disbelief. "But books *feel* real. Surely they must seem more real to you than anyone. They can hurt you. They can break your heart."

"It wasn't a book," said Sandlin, "that broke your heart."

800 — *Literature & Rhetoric*

Justin went home and slept for the rest of the day and night. When he woke up too early to do much else, he opened a familiar paperback and re-read it. Then he went to a cafe and bought two cups of coffee to bring to class.

"Oh wow," said Sarah. "Double latte with a sprinkle of cinnamon. I think I just drooled on myself."

"You still have to win it," he said. "You made up the rules. Now be made miserable by them."

She made a fist. "You sure you don't want to pick some game you're good at?"

Her earrings swung and glittered. Justin wondered if she wore them to tournaments to distract her opponents. He wondered if it worked.

He wished he could raise an eyebrow, but he tried to give her the look that might accompany one.

"Your funeral," said Sarah.

Rock. Paper. Scissors. Scissors cut paper. Justin won. He gave her the coffee anyway.

"I didn't think you'd throw scissors again," she said. "Since I pointed out that you threw it the first two times."

"Exactly." *See*, he thought, *I don't have a problem figuring out girls.*

Just one girl.

And possibly himself.

900 — *Geography & History*

Later that week, Justin attended the midnight party at Sandlin's house. He walked through the front door, disturbing as much dust as he could, before heading down the stairs. He arrived fashionably late. Characters were making toasts.

"*Salut!*" a group shouted together.

"To absent friends, lost loves, old gods, and the—" started another before Justin walked out of earshot.

He touched the heavy scissors in his pocket. His plan had changed.

Linda sat on a stool in black robes embroidered with the Hogwarts emblem and talked earnestly to a frog in a crown. Imps, nearby, appeared to be sticking a lit match between the stitches on the sole of a boot belonging to a chain-smoking blond man with a thick British accent.

"Linda," said Justin, "I have to talk to you."

Linda turned and something like panic crossed her face. She stood. "Justin?"

"Don't bother thanking me for bringing you to Sandlin," he said. "I won't bother saying I'm sorry. You were right. I'm glad I moved, glad I started library school. But what you did—"

"I'd always wanted to," she said. "Put myself in a book. It wasn't you. It would have happened eventually."

"Look, what I came to say was that you have responsibilities in the real world. Your parents haven't heard from you in forever. What you're doing isn't safe. You have to come back."

"No," she said firmly. "I'm not ready yet. Not now, when I can visit any book I want. I'll come out when I'm ready."

"You should have stayed and fought with me," said Justin. "It wasn't fair."

"I could have put you in a book." She tilted her head. "I still could."

He took an involuntary step back and she laughed.

"You don't deserve it, though," she said. "You don't love books the way that I do."

He opened his mouth to protest and then closed it. It was true. He didn't know how she loved books, only that he loved them differently.

She turned away from him and he let her go. He stayed for the rest of the party and after all the characters were back in their books, he took *Harry Potter* off the shelf.

Justin nodded and took the scissors out of his pocket.

"What are you going to do?" Sandlin sounded nervous. Justin turned on the old computer. "I'm going to change the story. Just a little. No one will notice." He flipped to a page where Linda's name appeared and carefully cut her out. Sandlin winced.

"Don't worry," Justin said. "It's just fiction."

He typed a few words and printed out the page. Then he carefully taped Linda's name in place so that the sentence read: "Linda doesn't just know how to put things in books. She knows how to get things out again, including herself. Hopefully someday she will."

Folding the paper in half, he tucked it between the pages. When he left, he didn't take the book with him.

SUMMER READING

Ken Liu

On this summer day, with the air still cool after a thundershower, with sunlight slanting through the cracks in the roof and walls of the Library, dappling the floor strewn with vines and leaves, CN-344315 made his daily rounds.

The robot docent muttered to himself as he dragged his squat, filing-cabinet-sized body through the rubble. He turned his cubical head from side to side, expressionlessly surveying his domain. He had last seen a visitor to the Library over five thousand years ago, but he wasn't about to change his routine now.

After mankind had scattered to the stars like dandelion seeds, Earth was maintained as a museum overseen by robot curators. At first, new generations born in the far-flung colonies made pilgrimages to visit the cradle of civilization, to marvel at the Great Pyramids (really holographic re-creations), the Chrysler Building (plastinated against any further erosion), the Forbidden City (complete with the Starbucks logo, a late addition), the Space Elevator of Singapore (still featuring the quaint sign: "Please use the restroom before boarding"), and other cultural attractions.

But over a hundred millennia, the flow of tourists slowed to a trickle, then a drip, and finally, stopped.

CN-344315 passed rows and rows of empty racks that age and rust had turned into delicate filigree, as fragile and brittle as glass. Climbing vines draped over them, creating bowers whose shade provided homes for mushrooms, ferns, wildflowers, and the occasional hare. The robot seemed to see in them ghosts of the mighty servers that once preserved yottabytes of the human race's accumulated knowledge.

"You cannot take them!" CN-344315 had shouted at the Council of Curators. "The data on them—"

"—can no longer be read," the Head Curator had answered. "You have used up so much of our resources trying to keep them going, but these machines weren't designed to last. Whatever information humans found useful, they copied it onto their ships and took it away. Data only lives when it is constantly copied. What is left here is just digital detritus, bit rot, worthless."

"What is thought useless in one era may be treasured in another!"

But the servers, having rusted into useless hunks of metal, had been recycled. And CN-344315 had grieved for all the data that had no copies in the universe: digitized words, images, sounds that dissipated forever into the void.

The old robot continued to trundle down the well-worn path between the empty racks, the noise of grinding gears and antiquated treads like wheezing breath.

On the tenth floor of the Library is a tiny room about ten meters square.

CN-344315's joy was to enter this room at the end of a day. He would survey his collection, nestled on the shelves like rows of sleeping babies. He would extend a probe from his chassis through a slot in the airtight glass panes covering the shelves, so that the chemical detectors on the probe could process the fragrance of ancient paper and ink. The resulting electric patterns in his brain were pleasurable. Then, he would relax his motors and actuators, his pincers and wheels, and be as still as a piece of furniture.

When the Library was built, people had already stopped using books. The few hundred books that were left in the world were kept in this small room as a kind of shrine of relics. *Not unlike the Earth itself now is kept as a memento for all of humanity*, CN-344315 reflected.

Gears grinding with weariness, he pulled open the door to the room and ground to a halt at the sight within.

"Hello," the small child said. She wore a yellow dress, like a ray of sunlight in the gloom of the ruins of the Library. She stared at CN-344315 with large, dark eyes, as limpid as the first rain of fall. Her hands were placed against the glass covering the shelves, as though CN-344315 had found her peering into an aquarium.

She was about seven, CN-344315 guessed, dredging up ancient routines for interacting with visitors that hadn't been accessed for five thousand years.

"Hello," CN-344315 said. He had to reach up with his manipulators to dislodge his voice box, rusty from disuse. "Welcome . . . to the Library."

"What are these?"

"Books," CN-344315 said. He thought about how to explain them. "Very old, ancient data, preserved at ultra-low density."

Even a decent-sized book only held a few thousand kilobits of data. CN-344315 had calculated that to store even a tiny fraction of the data once held on the servers in the Library would have required a stack of books that reached to the Moon.

The girl examined the spines of the books. Her eyes suddenly lit up. "Can I see that one?" Unlike the other spines, which consisted of small letters against solid, dull backgrounds, the one she pointed at was bright yellow, just like her dress.

CN-344315 thought about the grease on her fingers, about the moisture in her warm breath, about rough, unsteady little hands against paper that has lasted a thousand centuries. The robot shuddered.

Because CN-344315 had been unable to save the severs, he poured all his energy into the preservation of the books.

And they were hard to preserve. The dead wooden fibers that made up the pages were subject to decay and tempted insects. The ink faded when exposed to direct sunlight and moisture. The glue and thread in the binding became brittle and fell apart with the passage of time. CN-344315 had to devise special cases, sealants, control every aspect of the environment inside the room: temperature, light, humidity, vibrations.

The girl looked at the robot expectantly. CN-344315 wanted to say no.

Though the books were so much trouble to keep alive, to maintain against decay, this only made him care more for them. In this, CN-344315 was simply learning the lesson that every parent knew: it is the effort given to protect and nourish the helpless that binds you to them with love, tighter and tighter. Each time that he had to rush to reinforce the small room against an oncoming storm, each time he had to labor to eliminate a fungal or entomological threat, each time he sat, patiently, and examined each page of a hundred books for signs of damage, he came to love them more.

But even with all his ceaseless struggles, the laws of entropy held sway, and every century, books were lost to rain, animals, plain age. He grieved the passing of each one as deeply as his circuits allowed.

"Please," the girl said. "There's nothing to do here. None of the machines work."

It was true, CN-344315 knew. The servers that had taken up most of the space in the Library were of course gone. The shelves of discs and cubes that had once fit the viewing kiosks downstairs no longer worked either. They were so fragile that even the smallest bit of damage, a slight warping caused by a change in temperature or a minuscule scratch, rendered the data on them inaccessible. The storage devices were designed to be thrown away. As the Council had said, data only lives when it is constantly copied. And humans did not seem to care to preserve the medium that data lived on.

But the books, even when the pages were torn or faded, dog-eared or written-over, could still be read.

Wanted to be read?

"All right," CN-344315 said, surprising even himself. He creaked over to the shelf, unlocked the sealed glass doors, and gingerly took out the book.

CN-344315 placed the volume gently on the small desk in the center of the room. The girl climbed onto the chair next to it. Together, the robot and the young child examined the book.

The hard cover showed a vivid drawing of a smiling tortoise with pink leg warmers and a matching pink hair bow. She was getting ready to start a road race against a cat (wearing headphones and a look of determination) and a dog (snarling to show his sharp teeth).

"Oh," she said. She placed her fingers against the letters on the cover, her voice trying to hide her disappointment. "I don't know how to read this."

"It's written in Archaic English," CN-344315 said, "one of the ancestors of the language we all speak now. Let me translate and read it to you: *The Adventures of Sophia, the Fastest Tortoise in Suburbia.*"

For ten minutes, they were not sitting in a decaying library on an ancient, forgotten planet. For ten minutes, they were in a place, at a time, where talking tortoises and caterpillars who tossed salads made sense. For ten minutes, they were not an old robot and a young girl, but readers, communing with an author across an ocean of one hundred thousand years.

An entire world rose, grew, and blossomed around them as they read.

The robot turned the last page. "The end."

They were silent for a while.

"I liked that," the girl said. "It wasn't like a sim, but it was better than a sim. I couldn't touch anything, but I could feel everything in my head. If I close my eyes, I can still see Sophia. I think she's having more adventures. We'll be great friends."

The old robot smiled. He didn't have the right words for the electrical patterns in his brain at this moment.

"Read it again!"

CN-344315 turned the book back to the first page.

"Erin!" a man's voice called. The robot and the girl looked up.

"Mom! Dad!" Erin leapt off the chair and ran over to the door, where a man and a woman were standing.

"We've been looking all over for you," the woman said. "We told you not to wander off by yourself. Good thing that our tracking beacon still works in this primitive dump."

"I think 'dump' is a bit strong—" the man began.

"This is the *last* time you pick where we go for vacation! We could have had all the 'culture' we wanted just through a sim back home. Now let's get back to our ship and go somewhere civilized."

CN-344315 stayed out of their way. He knew that for some visitors, the past was simply the past, as alien and as irrelevant as a planet on the other side of the galaxy.

Erin lingered at the door of the small room. "I had fun here," she said to CN-344315.

"Me too," CN-344315 said.

The girl looked longingly at the other books on the shelves around the room, as her parents turned to leave.

"Wait," CN-344315 said. He picked up T*he Adventures of Sophia, the Fastest Tortoise in Suburbia* and handed it to Erin.

"Thank you." She clutched it to her chest tightly and beamed.

CN-344315 knew that the book would not last. The child's hands were rough. She might leave it out in the rain, might spill juice on it, might tear its ancient pages out of carelessness. She might tire of the book and lose it like a cheap toy.

Yet CN-344315 had no regrets as he handed the book to Erin. The Council was right about one thing: books are only alive when they're read. For books are seeds, and they grow in minds.

"Goodbye," the old robot said, and watched as the little girl walked away with her book.

He remained where he was as the ruined Library fell into silence, and the summer birds began to chitter again.

MAGIC FOR BEGINNERS

Kelly Link

Fox is a television character, and she isn't dead yet. But she will be, soon. She's a character on a television show called *The Library*. You've never seen *The Library* on TV but I bet you wish you had.

In one episode of *The Library*, a boy named Jeremy Mars, fifteen years old, sits on the roof of his house in Plantagenet, Vermont. It's eight o'clock at night, a school night, and he and his friend Elizabeth should be studying for the math quiz that their teacher, Mr. Cliff, has been hinting at all week long. Instead they've sneaked out onto the roof. It's cold. They don't know everything they should know about X, when X is the square root of Y. They don't even know Y. They ought to go in.

But there's nothing good on TV and the sky is very beautiful. They have jackets on, and up in the corners where the sky begins are patches of white in the darkness, still, where there's snow, up on the mountains. Down in the trees around the house, some animal is making a small, anxious sound: "Why cry? Why cry?"

"What's that one?" Elizabeth says, pointing at a squarish configuration of stars.

"That's The Parking Structure," Jeremy says. "And right next to that is The Big Shopping Mall and The Lesser Shopping Mall."

"And that's Orion, right? Orion the Bargain Hunter?"

Jeremy squints up. "No, Orion is over there. That's The Austrian Bodybuilder. That thing that's sort of wrapped around his lower leg is The Amorous Cephalopod. The Hungry, Hungry Octopus. It can't make up its mind whether it should eat him or make crazy, eight-legged love to him. You know that myth, right?"

"Of course," Elizabeth says. "Is Karl going to be pissed off that we didn't invite him over to study?"

"Karl's always pissed off about something," Jeremy says. Jeremy is resolutely resisting a notion about Elizabeth. Why are they sitting up here? Was it his idea or was it hers? Are they friends, are they just two friends sitting on the roof and talking? Or is Jeremy supposed to try to kiss her? He thinks maybe he's supposed to kiss her. If he kisses her, will they still be friends? He can't ask Karl about this. Karl doesn't believe in being helpful. Karl believes in mocking.

Jeremy doesn't even know if he wants to kiss Elizabeth. He's never thought about it until right now.

"I should go home," Elizabeth says. "There could be a new episode on right now, and we wouldn't even know."

"Someone would call and tell us," Jeremy says. "My mom would come up and yell for us." His mother is something else Jeremy doesn't want to worry about, but he does, he does.

Jeremy Mars knows a lot about the planet Mars, although he's never been there. He knows some girls, and yet he doesn't know much about them. He wishes there were books about girls, the way there are books about Mars, that you could observe the orbits and brightness of girls through telescopes without appearing to be perverted. Once Jeremy read a book about Mars out loud to Karl, except he kept replacing the word Mars with the word "girls." Karl cracked up every time.

Jeremy's mother is a librarian. His father writes books. Jeremy reads biographies. He plays trombone in a marching band. He jumps hurdles while wearing a school tracksuit. Jeremy is also passionately addicted to a television show in which a renegade librarian and magician named Fox is trying to save her world from thieves, murderers, cabalists, and pirates. Jeremy is a geek, although he's a telegenic geek. Somebody should make a TV show about him.

Jeremy's friends call him Germ, although he would rather be called Mars. His parents haven't spoken to each other in a week.

Jeremy doesn't kiss Elizabeth. The stars don't fall out of the sky, and Jeremy and Elizabeth don't fall off the roof either. They go inside and finish their homework. Someone who Jeremy has never met, never even heard of—a woman named Cleo Baldrick—has died. Lots of people, so far, have managed to live and die without making the acquaintance of Jeremy Mars, but Cleo Baldrick has left Jeremy Mars and his mother something strange in her will: a phone booth on a state highway, some forty miles outside of Las Vegas, and a Las Vegas wedding chapel. The wedding chapel is called Hell's Bells. Jeremy isn't sure what kind of people get married there. Bikers, maybe. Supervillains, freaks, and Satanists.

Jeremy's mother wants to tell him something. It's probably something about Las Vegas and about Cleo Baldrick, who—it turns out—was his mother's great-aunt. (Jeremy never knew his mother had a great-aunt. His mother is a mysterious person.) But it may be, on the other hand, something concerning

Jeremy's father. For a week and a half now, Jeremy has managed to avoid finding out what his mother is worrying about. It's easy not to find out things, if you try hard enough. There's band practice. He has overslept on weekdays in order to rule out conversations at breakfast, and at night he climbs up on the roof with his telescope to look at stars, to look at Mars. His mother is afraid of heights. She grew up in L.A.

It's clear that whatever it is she has to tell Jeremy is not something she wants to tell him. As long as he avoids being alone with her, he's safe.

But it's hard to keep your guard up at all times. Jeremy comes home from school, feeling as if he has passed the math test after all. Jeremy is an optimist. Maybe there's something good on TV. He settles down with the remote control on one of his father's pet couches: oversized and re-upholstered in an orange-juice-colored corduroy that makes it appear as if the couch has just escaped from a maximum security prison for criminally insane furniture. This couch looks as if its hobby is devouring interior decorators. Jeremy's father is a horror writer, so no one should be surprised if some of the couches he reupholsters are hideous and eldritch.

Jeremy's mother comes into the room and stands above the couch, looking down at him. "Germ?" she says. She looks absolutely miserable, which is more or less how she has looked all week.

The phone rings and Jeremy jumps up.

As soon as he hears Elizabeth's voice, he knows. She says, "Germ, it's on. Channel forty-two. I'm taping it." She hangs up.

"It's on!" Jeremy says. "Channel forty-two! Now!"

His mother has the television on by the time he sits down. Being a librarian, she has a particular fondness for *The Library*. "I should go tell your dad," she says, but instead she sits down beside Jeremy. And of course it's now all the more clear something is wrong between Jeremy's parents. But *The Library* is on and Fox is about to rescue Prince Wing.

When the episode ends, he can tell without looking over that his mother is crying. "Don't mind me," she says and wipes her nose on her sleeve. "Do you think she's really dead?"

But Jeremy can't stay around and talk.

Jeremy has wondered about what kind of television shows the characters in television shows watch. Television characters almost always have better haircuts, funnier friends, simpler attitudes toward sex. They marry magicians, win lotteries, have affairs with women who carry guns in their purses. Curious things happen to them on an hourly basis. Jeremy and I can forgive their haircuts. We just want to ask them about their television shows.

Just like always, it's Elizabeth who worked out in the nick of time that the new episode was on. Everyone will show up at Elizabeth's house afterward, for the postmortem. This time, it really is a postmortem. Why did Prince Wing kill Fox? How could Fox let him do it? Fox is ten times stronger.

Jeremy runs all the way, slapping his old track shoes against the sidewalk for the pleasure of the jar, for the sweetness of the sting. He likes the rough, cottony ache in his lungs. His coach says you have to be part-masochist to enjoy something like running. It's nothing to be ashamed of. It's something to exploit.

Talis opens the door. She grins at him, although he can tell that she's been crying, too. She's wearing a T-shirt that says *I'm So Goth I Shit Tiny Vampires*.

"Hey," Jeremy says. Talis nods. Talis isn't so Goth, at least not as far as Jeremy or anyone else knows. Talis just has a lot of T-shirts. She's an enigma wrapped in a mysterious T-shirt. A woman once said to Calvin Coolidge, "Mr. President, I bet my husband that I could get you to say more than two words." Coolidge said, "You lose." Jeremy can imagine Talis as Calvin Coolidge in a former life. Or maybe she was one of those dogs that don't bark. A basenji. Or a rock. A dolmen. There was an episode of *The Library*, once, with some sinister dancing dolmens in it.

Elizabeth comes up behind Talis. If Talis is unGoth, then Elizabeth is Ballerina Goth. She likes hearts and skulls and black pen-ink tattoos, pink tulle, and Hello Kitty. When the woman who invented Hello Kitty was asked why Hello Kitty was so popular, she said, "Because she has no mouth." Elizabeth's mouth is small. Her lips are chapped.

"That was the most horrible episode ever! I cried and cried," she says. "Hey, Germ, so I was telling Talis about how you inherited a gas station."

"A phone booth," Jeremy says. "In Las Vegas. This great-great-aunt died. And there's a wedding chapel, too."

"Hey! Germ!" Karl says, yelling from the living room. "Shut up and get in here! The commercial with the talking cats is on—"

"Shut it, Karl," Jeremy says. He goes in and sits on Karl's head. You have to show Karl who's boss once in a while.

Amy turns up last. She was in the next town over, buying comics. She hasn't seen the new episode and so they all shut it (except for Talis, who has not been saying anything at all) and Elizabeth puts on the tape.

In the previous episode of *The Library*, masked pirate-magicians said they would sell Prince Wing a cure for the spell that infested Faithful Margaret's hair with miniature, wicked, fire-breathing golems. (Faithful Margaret's hair keeps catching fire, but she refuses to shave it off. Her hair is the source of all her magic.)

The pirate-magicians lured Prince Wing into a trap so obvious that it seemed impossible it could really be a trap, on the one-hundred-and-fortieth floor of The Free People's World-Tree Library. The pirate-magicians used finger magic to turn Prince Wing into a porcelain teapot, put two Earl Grey tea bags into the teapot, and poured in boiling water, toasted the Eternally Postponed and Overdue Reign of the Forbidden Books, drained their tea in one gulp, belched, hurled their souvenir pirate mugs to the ground, and then shattered the teapot, which had been Prince Wing, into hundreds of pieces. Then the wicked pirate-magicians swept the pieces of both Prince Wing and collectible mugs carelessly into a wooden cigar box, buried the box in the Angela Carter Memorial Park on the seventeenth floor of The World-Tree Library, and erected a statue of George Washington above it.

So then Fox had to go looking for Prince Wing. When she finally discovered the park on the seventeenth floor of the Library, the George Washington statue stepped down off his plinth and fought her tooth and nail. Literally tooth and nail, and they'd all agreed that there was something especially nightmarish about a biting, scratching, life-sized statue of George Washington with long, pointed metal fangs that threw off sparks when he gnashed them. The statue of George Washington bit Fox's pinky finger right off, just like Gollum biting Frodo's finger off on the top of Mount Doom. But of course, once the statue tasted Fox's magical blood, it fell in love with Fox. It would be her ally from now on.

In the new episode, the actor playing Fox is a young Latina actress whom Jeremy Mars thinks he recognizes. She has been a snotty but well-intentioned fourth-floor librarian in an episode about an epidemic of food-poisoning that triggered bouts of invisibility and/or levitation, and she was also a lovelorn, suicidal Bear Cult priestess in the episode where Prince Wing discovered his mother was one of the Forbidden Books.

This is one of the best things about *The Library*, the way the cast swaps parts, all except for Faithful Margaret and Prince Wing, who are only ever themselves. Faithful Margaret and Prince Wing are the love interests and the main characters, and therefore, inevitably, the most boring characters, although Amy has a crush on Prince Wing.

Fox and the dashing-but-treacherous pirate-magician Two Devils are never played by the same actor twice, although in the twenty-third episode of *The Library*, the same woman played them both. Jeremy supposes that the casting could be perpetually confusing, but instead it makes your brain catch on fire. It's magical.

You always know Fox by her costume (the too-small green T-shirt, the long, full skirts she wears to hide her tail), by her dramatic hand gestures and body language, by the soft, breathy-squeaky voice the actors use when they are Fox. Fox is funny, dangerous, bad-tempered, flirtatious, greedy, untidy, accident-prone, graceful, and has a mysterious past. In some episodes, Fox is played by male actors, but she always sounds like Fox. And she's always beautiful. Every episode you think that this Fox, surely, is the most beautiful Fox there could ever be, and yet the Fox of the next episode will be even more heartbreakingly beautiful.

On television, it's night in The Free People's World-Tree Library. All the librarians are asleep, tucked into their coffins, their scabbards, priest-holes, buttonholes, pockets, hidden cupboards, between the pages of their enchanted novels. Moonlight pours through the high, arched windows of the Library and between the aisles of shelves, into the park. Fox is on her knees, clawing at the muddy ground with her bare hands. The statue of George Washington kneels beside her, helping.

"So that's Fox, right?" Amy says. Nobody tells her to shut up. It would be pointless. Amy has a large heart and an even larger mouth. When it rains, Amy rescues worms off the sidewalk. When you get tired of having a secret, you tell Amy.

Understand: Amy isn't that much stupider than anyone else in this story. It's just that she thinks out loud.

Elizabeth's mother comes into the living room. "Hey guys," she says. "Hi, Jeremy. Did I hear something about your mother inheriting a wedding chapel?"

"Yes, ma'am," Jeremy says. "In Las Vegas."

"Las Vegas," Elizabeth's mom says. "I won three hundred bucks once in Las Vegas. Spent it on a helicopter ride over the Grand Canyon. So how many times can you guys watch the same episode in one day?" But she sits down to watch, too. "Do you think she's really dead?"

"Who's dead?" Amy says. Nobody says anything.

Jeremy isn't sure he's ready to see this episode again so soon, anyway, especially not with Amy. He goes upstairs and takes a shower. Elizabeth's family have a large and distracting selection of shampoos. They don't mind when Jeremy uses their bathroom.

Jeremy and Karl and Elizabeth have known each other since the first day of kindergarten. Amy and Talis are a year younger. The five have not always been friends, except for Jeremy and Karl, who have. Talis is, famously, a loner. She doesn't listen to music as far as anyone knows, she doesn't wear significant amounts of black, she isn't particularly good (or bad) at math or English, and she doesn't drink, debate, knit or refuse to eat meat. If she keeps a blog, she's never admitted it to anyone.

The Library made Jeremy and Karl and Talis and Elizabeth and Amy friends. No one else in school is as passionately devoted. Besides, they are all the children of former hippies, and the town is small. They all live within a few blocks of each other, in run-down Victorians with high ceilings and ranch houses with sunken living rooms. And although they have not always been friends, growing up, they've gone skinny-dipping in lakes on summer nights, and broken bones on each others' trampolines. Once, during an argument about dog names, Elizabeth, who is hot-tempered, tried to run Jeremy over with her ten-speed bicycle, and once, a year ago, Karl got drunk on green-apple schnapps at a party and tried to kiss Talis, and once, for five months in the seventh grade, Karl and Jeremy communicated only through angry e-mails written in all caps. I'm not allowed to tell you what they fought about.

Now the five are inseparable; invincible. They imagine that life will always be like this—like a television show in eternal syndication—that they will always have each other. They use the same vocabulary. They borrow each other's books and music. They share lunches, and they never say anything when Jeremy comes over and takes a shower. They all know Jeremy's father is eccentric. He's supposed to be eccentric. He's a novelist.

When Jeremy comes back downstairs, Amy is saying, "I've always thought there was something wicked about Prince Wing. He's a dork and he looks like he has bad breath. I never really liked him."

Karl says, "We don't know the whole story yet. Maybe he found out something about Fox while he was a teapot." Elizabeth's mom says, "He's under a spell. I bet you anything." They'll be talking about it all week.

Talis is in the kitchen, making a Velveeta-and-pickle sandwich.

"So what did you think?" Jeremy says. It's like having a hobby, only more pointless, trying to get Talis to talk. "Is Fox really dead?"

"Don't know," Talis says. Then she says, "I had a dream."

Jeremy waits. Talis seems to be waiting, too. She says, "About you." Then she's silent again. There is something dreamlike about the way that she makes a sandwich. As if she is really making something that isn't a sandwich at all; as if she's making something far more meaningful and mysterious. Or as if soon he will wake up and realize that there are no such things as sandwiches.

"You and Fox," Talis says. "The dream was about the two of you. She told me. To tell you. To call her. She gave me a phone number. She was in trouble. She said you were in trouble. She said to keep in touch."

"Weird," Jeremy says, mulling this over. He's never had a dream about *The Library*. He wonders who was playing Fox in Talis's dream. He had a dream about Talis, once, but it isn't the kind of dream that you'd ever tell anybody about. They were just sitting together, not saying anything. Even Talis's T-shirt hadn't said anything. Talis was holding his hand.

"It didn't feel like a dream," Talis says.

"So what was the phone number?" Jeremy says.

"I forgot," Talis says. "When I woke up, I forgot."

Kurt's mother works in a bank. Talis's father has a karaoke machine in his basement, and he knows all the lyrics to "Like a Virgin" and "Holiday" as well as the lyrics to all the songs from *Godspell* and *Cabaret*. Talis's mother is a licensed therapist who composes multiple-choice personality tests for women's magazines. "Discover Which Television Character You Resemble Most." Etc. Amy's parents met in a commune in Ithaca: her name was Galadriel Moon Shuyler before her parents came to their senses and had it changed legally. Everyone is sworn to secrecy about this, which is ironic, considering that this is Amy.

But Jeremy's father is Gordon Strangle Mars. He writes novels about giant spiders, giant leeches, giant moths, and once, notably, a giant carnivorous rosebush who lives in a mansion in upstate New York, and falls in love with a plucky, teenaged girl with a heart murmur. Saint Bernard–sized spiders chase his characters' cars down dark, bumpy country roads. They fight the spiders off with badminton rackets, lawn tools, and fireworks. The novels with spiders are all bestsellers.

Once a Gordon Strangle Mars fan broke into the Mars's house. The fan stole several German first editions of Gordon Strangle's novels, a hairbrush, and a used mug in which there were two ancient, dehydrated tea bags. The fan left behind a betrayed and abusive letter on a series of Post-It Notes, and the manuscript of his own novel, told from the point of view of the iceberg that sank the Titanic. Jeremy and his mother read the manuscript out loud to each other. It begins: "The iceberg knew it had a destiny." Jeremy's favorite bit happens when the iceberg sees the doomed ship drawing nearer, and remarks plaintively, "Oh my, does not the Captain know about my large and impenetrable bottom?"

Jeremy discovered, later, that the novel-writing fan had put Gordon Strangle Mars's used tea bags and hairbrush up for sale on eBay, where someone paid forty-two dollars and sixty-eight cents, which was not only deeply creepy, but, Jeremy still feels, somewhat cheap. But of course this is appropriate, as Jeremy's father is famously stingy and just plain weird about money.

Gordon Strangle Mars once spent eight thousand dollars on a Japanese singing toilet. Jeremy's friends love that toilet. Jeremy's mother has a painting of a woman wearing a red dress by some artist, Jeremy can never remember who. Jeremy's father gave her that painting. The woman is beautiful, and she looks right at you as if you're the painting, not her. As if you're beautiful. The woman has an apple in one hand and a knife in the other. When Jeremy was little, he used to dream about eating that apple. Apparently the painting is worth more than the whole house and everything else in the house, including the singing toilet. But art and toilets aside, the Marses buy most of their clothes at thrift stores.

Jeremy's father clips coupons.

On the other hand, when Jeremy was twelve and begged his parents to send him to baseball camp in Florida, his father ponied up. And on Jeremy's last birthday, his father gave him a couch reupholstered in several dozen yards of heavy-duty *Star Wars*-themed fabric. That was a good birthday.

When his writing is going well, Gordon Strangle Mars likes to wake up at 6 AM and go out driving. He works out new plot lines about giant spiders and keeps an eye out for abandoned couches, which he wrestles into the back of his pickup truck. Then he writes for the rest of the day. On weekends he reupholsters the thrown-away couches in remaindered, discount fabrics. A few years ago, Jeremy went through his house, counting up fourteen couches, eight love seats, and one rickety chaise lounge. That was a few years ago. Once Jeremy had a dream that his father combined his two careers and began reupholstering giant spiders.

All lights in all rooms of the Mars house are on fifteen-minute timers, in case Jeremy or his mother leave a room and forget to turn off a lamp. This has caused confusion—and sometimes panic—on the rare occasions that the Marses throw dinner parties.

Everyone thinks that writers are rich, but it seems to Jeremy that his family is only rich some of the time. Some of the time they aren't.

Whenever Gordon Mars gets stuck in a Gordon Strangle Mars novel, he worries about money. He worries that he won't, in fact, manage to finish the current novel. He worries that it will be terrible. He worries that no one will buy it and no one will read it, and that the readers who do read it will demand to be refunded the cost of the book. He's told Jeremy that he imagines these angry readers marching on the Mars house, carrying torches and crowbars.

It would be easier on Jeremy and his mother if Gordon Mars did not work at home. It's difficult to shower when you know your father is timing you, and thinking dark thoughts about the water bill, instead of concentrating on the scene in the current Gordon Strangle Mars novel, in which the giant spiders have returned to their old haunts in the trees surrounding the ninth hole of the accursed golf course, where they sullenly feast on the pulped entrail juices of a brace of unlucky poodles and their owner.

During these periods, Jeremy showers at school, after gym, or at his friends' houses, even though it makes his mother unhappy. She says that sometimes you just need to ignore Jeremy's father. She takes especially long showers, lots of baths. She claims that baths are even nicer when you know that Jeremy's father is worried about the water bill. Jeremy's mother has a cruel streak.

What Jeremy likes about showers is the way you can stand there, surrounded by water and yet in absolutely no danger of drowning, and not think about things like whether you screwed up on the Spanish assignment, or why your mother is looking so worried. Instead you can think about things like if there's water on Mars, and whether or not Karl is shaving, and if so, who is he trying to fool, and what the statue of George Washington meant when it said to Fox, during their desperate, bloody fight, "You have a long journey ahead of you," and, "Everything depends on this." And is Fox really dead?

After she dug up the cigar box, and after George Washington helped her carefully separate out the pieces of tea mug from the pieces of teapot, after they glued back together the hundreds of pieces of porcelain, when Fox turned the ramshackle teapot back into Prince Wing, Prince Wing looked about a hundred years old, and as if maybe there were still a few pieces missing. He looked pale. When he saw Fox, he turned even paler, as if he hadn't expected her to be standing there in front of him. He picked up his leviathan sword, which Fox had been keeping safe for him—the one which faithful viewers know was carved out of the tooth of a giant, ancient sea creature that lived happily and peacefully (before Prince Wing was tricked into killing it) in the enchanted underground sea on the third floor—and skewered the statue of George Washington like a kebab, pinning it to a tree. He kicked Fox in the head, knocked her down, and tied her to a card catalog. He stuffed a handful of moss and dirt into her mouth so she couldn't say anything, and then he accused her of plotting to murder Faithful Margaret by magic. He said Fox was more deceitful than a Forbidden Book. He cut off Fox's tail and her ears and he ran her through with the poison-edged, dog-headed knife that he and Fox had stolen from his mother's secret house. Then he left Fox there, tied to the card catalog, limp and bloody, her beautiful head hanging down. He sneezed (Prince Wing is allergic to swordplay) and walked off into the stacks. The librarians crept out of their hiding places. They untied Fox and cleaned off her face. They held a mirror to her mouth, but the mirror stayed clear and unclouded.

When the librarians pulled Prince Wing's leviathan sword out of the tree, the statue of George Washington staggered over and picked up Fox in his arms. He tucked her ears and tail into the capacious pockets of his bird-shit-stained, verdigris riding coat. He carried Fox down seventeen flights of stairs, past the enchanted-and-disagreeable Sphinx on the eighth floor, past the enchanted-and-stormy underground sea on the third floor, past the even-more-enchanted checkout desk on the first floor, and through the hammered-brass doors of the Free People's World Tree Library. Nobody in *The Library*, not in one single episode, has ever gone outside. *The Library* is full of all the sorts of things that one usually has to go outside to enjoy: trees and lakes and grottoes and fields and mountains and precipices (and full of indoors things as well, like books, of course). Outside *The Library*, everything is dusty and red and alien, as if George Washington has carried Fox out of *The Library* and onto the surface of Mars.

"I could really go for a nice cold Euphoria right now," Jeremy says. He and Karl are walking home.

Euphoria is: *The Librarian's Tonic—When Watchfulness Is Not Enough*. There are frequently commercials for Euphoria on *The Library*. Although no one is exactly sure what Euphoria is for, whether it is alcoholic or caffeinated, what it tastes like, if it is poisonous or delightful, or even whether or not it's carbonated, everyone, including Jeremy, pines for a glass of Euphoria once in a while.

"Can I ask you a question?" Karl says.

"Why do you always say that?" Jeremy says. "What am I going to say? 'No, you can't ask me a question?'"

"What's up with you and Talis?" Karl says. "What were you talking about in the kitchen?" Jeremy sees that Karl has been Watchful.

"She had this dream about me," he says, uneasily.

"So do you like her?" Karl says. His chin looks raw. Jeremy is sure now that Karl has tried to shave. "Because, remember how I liked her first?"

"We were just talking," Jeremy says. "So did you shave? Because I didn't know you had facial hair. The idea of you shaving is pathetic, Karl. It's like voting Republican if we were old enough to vote. Or farting in Music Appreciation."

"Don't try to change the subject," Karl says. "When have you and Talis ever had a conversation before?"

"One time we talked about a Diana Wynne Jones book that she'd checked out from the library. She dropped it in the bath accidentally. She wanted to know if I could tell my mother," Jeremy says. "Once we talked about recycling."

"Shut up, Germ," Karl says. "Besides, what about Elizabeth? I thought you liked Elizabeth!"

"Who said that?" Jeremy says. Karl is glaring at him.

"Amy told me," Karl says.

"I never told Amy I liked Elizabeth," Jeremy says. So now Amy is a mind-reader as well as a blabbermouth? What a terrible, deadly combination!

"No," Karl says, grudgingly. "Elizabeth told Amy that she likes you. So I just figured you liked her back."

"Elizabeth likes me?" Jeremy says.

"Apparently everybody likes you," Karl says. He sounds sorry for himself. "What is it about you? It's not like you're all that special. Your nose is funny looking and you have stupid hair."

"Thanks, Karl." Jeremy changes the subject. "Do you think Fox is really dead?" he says. "For good?" He walks faster, so that Karl has to almost-jog to keep up. Presently Jeremy is much taller than Karl, and he intends to enjoy this as long as it lasts. Knowing Karl, he'll either get tall, too, or else chop Jeremy off at the knees.

"They'll use magic," Karl says. "Or maybe it was all a dream. They'll make her alive again. I'll never forgive them if they've killed Fox. And if you like Talis, I'll never forgive you, either. And I know what you're thinking. You're thinking that I think I mean what I say, but if push came to shove, eventually I'd forgive you, and we'd be friends again, like in seventh grade. But I wouldn't, and you're wrong, and we wouldn't be. We wouldn't ever be friends again."

Jeremy doesn't say anything. Of course he likes Talis. He just hasn't realized how much he likes her, until recently. Until today. Until Karl opened his mouth. Jeremy likes Elizabeth too, but how can you compare Elizabeth and Talis? You can't. Elizabeth is Elizabeth and Talis is Talis.

"When you tried to kiss Talis, she hit you with a boa constrictor," he says. It had been Amy's boa constrictor. It had probably been an accident. Karl shouldn't have tried to kiss someone while they were holding a boa constrictor.

"Just try to remember what I just said," Karl says. "You're free to like anyone you want to. Anyone except for Talis."

The Library has been on television for two years now. It isn't a regularly scheduled program. Sometimes it's on two times in the same week, and then not on again for another couple of weeks. Often new episodes debut in the middle of the night.

There is a large online community who spend hours scanning channels; sending out alarms and false alarms; fans swap theories, tapes, files; write fanfic. Elizabeth has rigged up her computer to shout "Wake up, Elizabeth! The television is on fire!" when reliable *Library* watch-sites discover a new episode.

The Library is a pirate TV show. It's shown up once or twice on most network channels, but usually it's on the kind of channels that Jeremy thinks of as ghost channels. The ones that are just static, unless you're paying for several hundred channels of cable. There are commercial breaks, but the products being advertised are like Euphoria. They never seem to be real brands, or things that you can actually buy. Often the commercials aren't even in English, or in any other identifiable language, although the jingles are catchy, nonsense or not. They get stuck in your head.

Episodes of *The Library* have no regular schedule, no credits, and sometimes not even dialogue. One episode of *The Library* takes place inside the top drawer of a card catalog, in pitch dark, and it's all in Morse code with subtitles. Nothing else. No one has ever claimed responsibility for inventing *The Library*. No one has ever interviewed one of the actors, or stumbled across a set, film crew, or script, although in one documentary-style episode, the actors filmed the crew, who all wore paper bags on their heads.

When Jeremy gets home, his father is making upside-down pizza in a casserole dish for dinner.

Meeting writers is usually disappointing at best. Writers who write sexy thrillers aren't necessarily sexy or thrilling in person. Children's book writers might look more like accountants, or axe murderers for that matter. Horror writers are very rarely scary looking, although they are frequently good cooks.

Though Gordon Strangle Mars is scary looking. He has long, thin fingers—currently slimy with pizza sauce—which are why he chose "Strangle" for his fake middle name. He has white-blond hair that he tugs on while he writes until it stands straight up. He has a bad habit of suddenly appearing beside you, when you haven't even realized he was in the same part of the house. His eyes are deep-set and he doesn't blink very often. Karl says that when you meet Jeremy's father, he looks at you as if he were imagining you bundled up and stuck away in some giant spider's larder. Which is probably true.

People who read books probably never bother to wonder if their favorite writers are also good parents. Why would they?

Gordon Strangle Mars is a recreational shoplifter. He has a special, complicated, and unspoken arrangement with the local bookstore, where, in exchange for autographing as many Gordon Strangle Mars novels as they can possibly sell, the store allows Jeremy's father to shoplift books without comment. Jeremy's mother shows up sooner or later and writes a check.

Jeremy's feelings about his father are complicated. His father is a cheapskate and a petty thief, and yet Jeremy likes his father. His father hardly ever loses his temper with Jeremy, he is always interested in Jeremy's life, and he gives interesting (if confusing) advice when Jeremy asks for it. For example, if Jeremy asked his father about kissing Elizabeth, his father might suggest that Jeremy not worry about giant spiders when he kisses Elizabeth. Jeremy's father's advice usually has something to do with giant spiders.

When Jeremy and Karl weren't speaking to each other, it was Jeremy's father who straightened them out. He lured Karl over, and then locked them both into his study. He didn't let them out again until they were on speaking terms.

"I thought of a great idea for your book," Jeremy says. "What if one of the spiders builds a web on a soccer field, across a goal? And what if the goalie doesn't notice until the middle of the game? Could somebody kill one of the spiders with a soccer ball, if they kicked it hard enough? Would it explode? Or even better, the spider could puncture the soccer ball with its massive fangs. That would be cool, too."

"Your mother's out in the garage," Gordon Strangle Mars says to Jeremy. "She wants to talk to you."

"Oh," Jeremy says. All of a sudden, he thinks of Fox in Talis's dream, trying to phone him. Trying to warn him. Unreasonably, he feels that it's his parents' fault that Fox is dead now, as if they have killed her. "Is it about you? Are you getting divorced?"

"I don't know," his father says. He hunches his shoulders. He makes a face. It's a face that Jeremy's father makes frequently, and yet this face is even more pitiful and guilty than usual.

"What did you do?" Jeremy says. "Did you get caught shoplifting at Wal-Mart?"

"No," his father says.

"Did you have an affair?"

"No!" his father says, again. Now he looks disgusted, either with himself or with Jeremy for asking such a horrible question. "I screwed up. Let's leave it at that."

"How's the book coming?" Jeremy says. There is something in his father's voice that makes him feel like kicking something, but there are never giant spiders around when you need them.

"I don't want to talk about that, either," his father says, looking, if possible, even more ashamed. "Go tell your mother dinner will be ready in five minutes. Maybe you and I can watch the new episode of *The Library* after dinner, if you haven't already seen it a thousand times."

"Do you know the end? Did Mom tell you that Fox is—"

"Oh jeez," his father interrupts. "They killed Fox?"

That's the problem with being a writer, Jeremy knows. Even the biggest and most startling twists are rarely twists for you. You know how every story goes.

Jeremy's mother is an orphan. Jeremy's father claims that she was raised by feral silent-film stars, and it's true, she looks like a heroine out of a Harold Lloyd movie. She has an appealingly disheveled look to her, as if someone has either just tied or untied her from a set of train tracks. She met Gordon Mars (before he added the Strangle and sold his first novel) in the food court of a mall in New Jersey, and fell in love with him before realizing that he was a writer and a recreational shoplifter. She didn't read anything he'd written until after they were married, which was a typically cunning move on Jeremy's father's part.

Jeremy's mother doesn't read horror novels. She doesn't like ghost stories or unexplained phenomena or even the kind of phenomena that require excessively technical explanations. For example: microwaves, airplanes. She doesn't like Halloween, not even Halloween candy. Jeremy's father gives her special editions of his novels, where the scary pages have been glued together.

Jeremy's mother is quiet more often than not. Her name is Alice and some-times Jeremy thinks about how the two quietest people he knows are named Alice and Talis. But his mother and Talis are quiet in different ways. Jeremy's mother is the kind of person who seems to be keeping something hidden, something secret. Whereas Talis just is a secret. Jeremy's mother could easily turn out to be a secret agent. But Talis is the death ray or the key to immortality or whatever it is that secret agents have to keep secret. Hanging out with Talis is like hanging out with a teenage black hole.

Jeremy's mother is sitting on the floor of the garage, beside a large cardboard box. She has a photo album in her hands. Jeremy sits down beside her.

There are photographs of a cat on a wall, and something blurry that looks like a whale or a zeppelin or a loaf of bread. There's a photograph of a small girl sitting beside a woman. The woman wears a fur collar with a sharp little muzzle, four legs, a tail, and Jeremy feels a sudden pang. Fox is the first dead person that he's ever cared about, but she's not real. The little girl in the photograph looks utterly blank, as if someone has just hit her with a hammer. Like the person behind the camera has just said, "Smile! Your parents are dead!"

"Cleo," Jeremy's mother says, pointing to the woman. "That's Cleo. She was my mother's aunt. She lived in Los Angeles. I went to live with her when my parents died. I was four. I know I've never talked about her. I've never really known what to say about her."

Jeremy says, "Was she nice?"

His mother says, "She tried to be nice. She didn't expect to be saddled with a little girl. What an odd word. Saddled. As if she were a horse. As if somebody put me on her back and I never got off again. She liked to buy clothes for me. She liked clothes. She hadn't had a happy life. She drank a lot. She liked to go to movies in the afternoon and to séances in the evenings. She had boyfriends. Some of them were jerks. The love of her life was a small-time gangster. He died and she never married. She always said marriage was a joke and that life was a bigger joke, and it was just her bad luck that she didn't have a sense of humor. So it's strange to think that all these years she was running a wedding chapel."

Jeremy looks at his mother. She's half-smiling, half-grimacing, as if her stomach hurts. "I ran away when I was sixteen. And I never saw her again. Once she sent me a letter, care of your father's publishers. She said she'd read all his books, and that was how she found me, I guess, because he kept dedicating them to me. She said she hoped I was happy and that she thought about me. I wrote back. I sent a photograph of you. But she never wrote again. Sounds like an episode of *The Library*, doesn't it?"

Jeremy says, "Is that what you wanted to tell me? Dad said you wanted to tell me something."

"That's part of it," his mother says. "I have to go out to Las Vegas, to find out some things about this wedding chapel. Hell's Bells. I want you to come with me."

"Is that what you wanted to ask me?" Jeremy says, although he knows there's something else. His mother still has that sad half-smile on her face.

"Germ," his mother says. "You know I love your father, right?"

"Why?" Jeremy says. "What did he do?"

His mother flips through the photo album. "Look," she says. "This was when you were born." In the picture, his father holds Jeremy as if someone has just handed him an enchanted porcelain teapot. Jeremy's father grins, but he looks terrified, too. He looks like a kid. A scary, scared kid.

"He wouldn't tell me either," Jeremy says. "So it has to be pretty bad. If you're getting divorced, I think you should go ahead and tell me."

"We're not getting divorced," his mother says, "but it might be a good thing if you and I went out to Las Vegas. We could stay there for a few months while I sort out this inheritance. Take care of Cleo's estate. I'm going to talk to your teachers. I've given notice at the library. Think of it as an adventure."

She sees the look on Jeremy's face. "No, I'm sorry. That was a stupid, stupid thing to say. I know this isn't an adventure."

"I don't want to go," Jeremy says. "All my friends are here! I can't just go away and leave them. That would be terrible!" All this time, he's been preparing himself for the most terrible thing he can imagine. He's imagined a conversation with his mother, in which his mother reveals her terrible secret, and in his imagination, he's been calm and reasonable. His imaginary parents have wept and asked for his understanding. The imaginary Jeremy has understood. He has imagined himself understanding everything. But now, as his mother talks, Jeremy's heartbeat speeds up, and his lungs fill with air, as if he is running. He starts to sweat, although the floor of the garage is cold. He wishes he were sitting up on top of the roof with his telescope. There could be meteors, invisible to the naked eye, careening through the sky, hurtling toward Earth. Fox is dead. Everyone he knows is doomed. Even as he thinks this, he knows he's overreacting. But it doesn't help to know this.

"I know it's terrible," his mother says. His mother knows something about terrible.

"So why can't I stay here?" Jeremy says. "You go sort things out in Las Vegas, and I'll stay here with Dad. Why can't I stay here?"

"Because he put you in a book!" his mother says. She spits the words out. He has never heard her sound so angry. His mother never gets angry. "He put you in one of his books! I was in his office, and the manuscript was on his desk. I saw your name, and so I picked it up and started reading."

"So what?" Jeremy says. "He's put me in his books before. Like, stuff I've said. Like when I was eight and I was running a fever and told him the trees were full of dead people wearing party hats. Like when I accidentally set fire to his office."

"It isn't like that," his mother says. "It's you. It's *you*. He hasn't even changed your name. The boy in the book, he jumps hurdles and he wants to be a rocket scientist and go to Mars, and he's cute and funny and sweet and his best friend Elizabeth is in love with him and he talks like you and he looks like you and then he dies, Jeremy. He has a brain tumor and he dies. He dies. There aren't any giant spiders. There's just you, and you die."

Jeremy is silent. He imagines his father writing the scene in his book where the kid named Jeremy dies, and crying, just a little. He imagines this Jeremy kid, Jeremy the character who dies. Poor messed-up kid. Now Jeremy and Fox have something in common. They're both made-up people. They're both dead.

"Elizabeth is in love with me?" he says. Just on principle, he never believes anything that Karl says. But if it's in a book, maybe it's true.

"Oh, whoops," his mother says. "I really didn't want to say that. I'm just so angry at him. We've been married for seventeen years. I was just four years older than you when I met him, Jeremy. I was nineteen. He was only twenty. We were babies. Can you imagine that? I can put up with the singing toilet and the shoplifting and the couches and I can put up with him being so weird about money. But he killed you, Jeremy. He wrote you into a book and he killed you off. And he knows it was wrong, too. He's ashamed of himself. He didn't want me to tell you. I didn't mean to tell you."

Jeremy sits and thinks. "I still don't want to go to Las Vegas," he says to his mother. "Maybe we could send Dad there instead."

His mother says, "Not a bad idea." But he can tell she's already planning their itinerary.

In one episode of *The Library*, everyone was invisible. You couldn't see the actors: you could only see the books and the bookshelves and the study carrels on the fifth floor where the coin-operated wizards come to flirt and practice their spells. Invisible Forbidden Books were fighting invisible pirate-magicians and the pirate-magicians were fighting Fox and her friends, who were also invisible. The fight was clumsy and full of deadly accidents. You could hear them fighting. Shelves were overturned. Books were thrown. Invisible people tripped over invisible dead bodies, but you didn't find out who'd died until the next episode. Several of the characters—The Accidental Sword, Hairy Pete, and Ptolemy Krill (who, much like the Vogons in Douglas Adams's *The Hitchhiker's Guide to the Galaxy*, wrote poetry so bad it killed anyone who read it)—disappeared for good, and nobody is sure whether they're dead or not.

In another episode, Fox stole a magical drug from The Norns, a prophetic girl band who headline at a cabaret on the mezzanine of The Free People's World-Tree Library. She accidentally injected it, became pregnant, and gave birth to a bunch of snakes who led her to the exact shelf where renegade librarians had misshelved an ancient and terrible book of magic which had never been translated, until Fox asked the snakes for help. The snakes writhed and curled on the ground, spelling out words, letter by letter, with their bodies. As they translated the book for Fox, they hissed and steamed. They became fiery lines on the ground, and then they burnt away entirely. Fox cried. That's the only time anyone has ever seen Fox cry, ever. She isn't like Prince Wing. Prince Wing is a crybaby.

The thing about *The Library* is that characters don't come back when they die. It's as if death is for real. So maybe Fox really is dead and she really isn't coming back. There are a couple of ghosts who hang around the Library looking for blood libations, but they've always been ghosts, all the way back to the beginning of the show. There aren't any evil twins or vampires, either. Although someday, hopefully, there will be evil twins. Who doesn't love evil twins?

"Mom told me about how you wrote about me," Jeremy says. His mother is still in the garage. He feels like a tennis ball in a game where the tennis players love him very, very much, even while they lob and smash and send him back and forth, back and forth.

His father says, "She said she wasn't going to tell you, but I guess I'm glad she did. I'm sorry, Germ. Are you hungry?"

"She's going out to Las Vegas next week. She wants me to go with her," Jeremy says.

"I know," his father says, still holding out a bowl of upside-down pizza. "Try not to worry about all of this, if you can. Think of it as an adventure."

"Mom says that's a stupid thing to say. Are you going to let me read the book with me in it?" Jeremy says.

"No," his father says, looking straight at Jeremy. "I burned it."

"Really?" Jeremy says. "Did you set fire to your computer too?"

"Well, no," his father says. "But you can't read it. It wasn't any good, anyway. Want to watch *The Library* with me? And will you eat some damn pizza, please? I may be a lousy father, but I'm a good cook. And if you love me, you'll eat the damn pizza and be grateful."

So they go sit on the orange couch and Jeremy eats pizza and watches *The Library* for the second-and-a-half time with his father. The lights on the timer in the living room go off, and Prince Wing kills Fox again. And then Jeremy goes to bed. His father goes away to write or to burn stuff. Whatever. His mother is still out in the garage.

On Jeremy's desk is a scrap of paper with a phone number on it. If he wanted to, he could call his phone booth. When he dials the number, it rings for a long time. Jeremy sits on his bed in the dark and listens to it ringing and ringing. When someone picks it up, he almost hangs up. Someone doesn't say anything, so Jeremy says, "Hello? Hello?"

Someone breathes into the phone on the other end of the line. Someone says in a soft, musical, squeaky voice, "Can't talk now, kid. Call back later." Then someone hangs up.

Jeremy dreams that he's sitting beside Fox on a sofa that his father has reuphol-stered in spider silk. His father has been stealing spider webs from the giant-spider superstores. From his own books. Is that shoplifting or is it self-plagiarism? The sofa is soft and gray and a little bit sticky. Fox sits on either side of him. The right-hand-side Fox is being played by Talis. Elizabeth plays the Fox on his left. Both Foxes look at him with enormous compassion.

"Are you dead?" Jeremy says.

"Are you?" the Fox who is being played by Elizabeth says, in that unmistakable Fox voice which, Jeremy's father once said, sounds like a sexy and demented helium balloon. It makes Jeremy's brain hurt, to hear Fox's voice coming out of Elizabeth's mouth.

The Fox who looks like Talis doesn't say anything at all. The writing on her T-shirt is so small and so foreign that Jeremy can't read it without feeling as if he's staring at Fox-Talis's breasts. It's probably something he needs to know, but he'll never be able to read it. He's too polite, and besides he's terrible at foreign languages.

"Hey look," Jeremy says. "We're on TV!" There he is on television, sitting between two Foxes on a sticky gray couch in a field of red poppies. "Are we in Las Vegas?"

"We're not in Kansas," Fox-Elizabeth says. "There's something I need you to do for me."

"What's that?" Jeremy says.

"If I tell you in the dream," Fox-Elizabeth says, "you won't remember. You have to remember to call me when you're awake. Keep on calling until you get me."

"How will I remember to call you," Jeremy says, "if I don't remember what you tell me in this dream? Why do you need me to help you? Why is Talis here? What does her T-shirt say? Why are you both Fox? Is this Mars?"

Fox-Talis goes on watching TV. Fox-Elizabeth opens her kind and beautiful un-Hello-Kitty-like mouth again. She tells Jeremy the whole story. She explains everything. She translates Fox-Talis's T-shirt, which turns out to explain everything about Talis that Jeremy has ever wondered about. It answers every single question that Jeremy has ever had about girls. And then Jeremy wakes up—

It's dark. Jeremy flips on the light. The dream is moving away from him. There was something about Mars. Elizabeth was asking who he thought was prettier, Talis or Elizabeth. They were laughing. They both had pointy fox ears. They wanted him to do something. There was a telephone number he was supposed to call. There was something he was supposed to do.

In two weeks, on the fifteenth of April, Jeremy and his mother will get in her van and start driving out to Las Vegas. Every morning before school, Jeremy takes long showers and his father doesn't say anything at all. One day it's as if nothing is wrong between his parents. The next day they won't even look at each other. Jeremy's father won't come out of his study. And then the day after that, Jeremy comes home and finds his mother sitting on his father's lap. They're smiling as if they know something stupid and secret. They don't even notice Jeremy when he walks through the room. Even this is preferable, though, to the way they behave when they do notice him. They act guilty and strange and as if they are about to ruin his life. Gordon Mars makes pancakes every morning, and Jeremy's favorite dinner, macaroni and cheese, every night. Jeremy's mother plans out an itinerary for their trip. They will be stopping at libraries across the country, because his mother loves libraries. But she's also bought a new two-man tent and two sleeping bags and a portable stove, so that they can camp, if Jeremy wants to camp. Even though Jeremy's mother hates the outdoors.

Right after she does this, Gordon Mars spends all weekend in the garage. He won't let either of them see what he's doing, and when he does let them in, it turns out that he's removed the seating in the back of the van and bolted down two of his couches, one on each side, both upholstered in electric-blue fake fur.

They have to climb in through the cargo door at the back because one of the couches is blocking the sliding door. Jeremy's father says, looking very pleased with himself, "So now you don't have to camp outside, unless you want to. You can sleep inside. There's space underneath for suitcases. The sofas even have seat belts."

Over the sofas, Jeremy's father has rigged up small wooden shelves that fold down on chains from the walls of the van and become table tops. There's a travel-sized disco ball dangling from the ceiling, and a wooden panel—with Velcro straps and a black, quilted pad—behind the driver's seat, where Jeremy's father explains they can hang up the painting of the woman with the apple and the knife.

The van looks like something out of an episode of *The Library*. Jeremy's mother bursts into tears. She runs back inside the house. Jeremy's father says, helplessly, "I just wanted to make her laugh."

Jeremy wants to say, "I hate both of you." But he doesn't say it, and he doesn't. It would be easier if he did.

When Jeremy told Karl about Las Vegas, Karl punched him in the stomach. Then he said, "Have you told Talis?"

Jeremy said, "You're supposed to be nice to me! You're supposed to tell me not to go and that this sucks and you're not supposed to punch me. Why did you punch me? Is Talis all you ever think about?"

"Kind of," Karl said. "Most of the time. Sorry, Germ, of course I wish you weren't going and yeah, it also pisses me off. We're supposed to be best friends, but you do stuff all the time and I never get to. I've never driven across the country or been to Las Vegas, even though I'd really, really like to. I can't feel sorry for you when I bet you anything that while you're there, you'll sneak into some casino and play slot machines and win like a million bucks. You should feel sorry for me. I'm the one that has to stay here. Can I borrow your dirt bike while you're gone?"

"Sure," Jeremy said.

"How about your telescope?" Karl said.

"I'm taking it with me," Jeremy said.

"Fine. You have to call me every day," Karl said. "You have to e-mail. You have to tell me about Las Vegas show girls. I want to know how tall they really are. Whose phone number is this?"

Karl was holding the scrap of paper with the number of Jeremy's phone booth.

"Mine," Jeremy said. "That's my phone booth. The one I inherited."

"Have you called it?" Karl said.

"No," Jeremy said. He'd called the phone booth a few times. But it wasn't a game. Karl would think it was a game.

"Cool," Karl said and he went ahead and dialed the number. "Hello?" Karl said, "I'd like to speak to the person in charge of Jeremy's life. This is Jeremy's best friend Karl."

"Not funny," Jeremy said.

"My life is boring," Karl said, into the phone. "I've never inherited anything. This girl I like won't talk to me. So is someone there? Does anybody want to talk to me? Does anyone want to talk to my friend, the Lord of the Phone Booth? Jeremy, they're demanding that you liberate the phone booth from yourself."

"Still not funny," Jeremy said and Karl hung up the phone.

Jeremy told Elizabeth. They were up on the roof of Jeremy's house and he told her the whole thing. Not just the part about Las Vegas, but also the part about his father and how he put Jeremy in a book with no giant spiders in it.

"Have you read it?" Elizabeth said.

"No," Jeremy said. "He won't let me. Don't tell Karl. All I told him is that my mom and I have to go out for a few months to check out the wedding chapel."

"I won't tell Karl," Elizabeth said. She leaned forward and kissed Jeremy and then she wasn't kissing him. It was all very fast and surprising, but they didn't fall off the roof. Nobody falls off the roof in this story. "Talis likes you," Elizabeth said. "That's what Amy says. Maybe you like her back. I don't know. But I thought I should go ahead and kiss you now. Just in case I don't get to kiss you again."

"You can kiss me again," Jeremy said. "Talis probably doesn't like me."

"No," Elizabeth said. "I mean, let's not. I want to stay friends and it's hard enough to be friends, Germ. Look at you and Karl."

"I would never kiss Karl," Jeremy said.

"Funny, Germ. We should have a surprise party for you before you go," Elizabeth said.

"It won't be a surprise party now," Jeremy said. Maybe kissing him once was enough.

"Well, once I tell Amy it can't really be a surprise party," Elizabeth said. "She would explode into a million pieces and all the little pieces would start yelling, 'Guess what? Guess what? We're having a surprise party for you, Jeremy!' But just because I'm letting you in on the surprise doesn't mean there won't be surprises."

"I don't actually like surprises," Jeremy said.

"Who does?" Elizabeth said. "Only the people who do the surprising. Can we have the party at your house? I think it should be like Halloween, and it always feels like Halloween here. We could all show up in costumes and watch lots of old episodes of *The Library* and eat ice cream."

"Sure," Jeremy said. And then: "This is terrible! What if there's a new episode of *The Library* while I'm gone? Who am I going to watch it with?"

And he'd said the perfect thing. Elizabeth felt so bad about Jeremy having to watch *The Library* all by himself that she kissed him again.

There has never been a giant spider in any episode of *The Library*, although once Fox got really small and Ptolemy Krill carried her around in his pocket. She had to rip up one of Krill's handkerchiefs and blindfold herself, just in case she accidentally read a draft of Krill's terrible poetry. And then it turned out that, as well as the poetry, Krill had also stashed a rare, horned Anubis earwig in his pocket which hadn't been properly preserved. Ptolemy Krill, it turned out, was careless with his kill jar. The earwig almost ate Fox, but instead it became her friend. It still sends her Christmas cards.

These are the two most important things that Jeremy and his friends have in common: a geographical location, and love of a television show about a library. Jeremy turns on the television as soon as he comes home from school. He flips through the channels, watching reruns of *Star Trek* and *Law & Order*. If there's a new episode of *The Library* before he and his mother leave for Las Vegas, then everything will be fine. Everything will work out. His mother says, "You watch too much television, Jeremy." But he goes on flipping through channels. Then he goes up to his room and makes phone calls.

"The new episode needs to be soon, because we're getting ready to leave. Tonight would be good. You'd tell me if there was going to be a new episode tonight, right?"

Silence.

"Can I take that as a yes? It would be easier if I had a brother," Jeremy tells his telephone booth. "Hello? Are you there? Or a sister. I'm tired of being good all the time. If I had a sibling, then we could take turns being good. If I had an older brother, I might be better at being bad, better at being angry. Karl is really good at being angry. He learned how from his brothers. I wouldn't want brothers like Karl's brothers, of course, but it sucks having to figure out everything all by myself. And the more normal I try to be, the more my parents think that I'm acting out. They think it's a phase that I'll grow out of. They think it isn't normal to be normal. Because there's no such thing as normal.

"And this whole book thing. The whole shoplifting thing, how my dad steals things, it figures that he went and stole my life. It isn't just me being melodramatic, to say that. That's exactly what he did! Did I tell you that once he stole a ferret from a pet store because he felt bad for it, and then he let it loose in our house and it turned out that it was pregnant? There was this woman who came to interview Dad and she sat down on one of the—"

Someone knocks on his bedroom door. "Jeremy," his mother says. "Is Karl here? Am I interrupting?"

"No," Jeremy says, and hangs up the phone. He's gotten into the habit of calling his phone booth every day. When he calls, it rings and rings and then it stops ringing, as if someone has picked up. There's just silence on the other end, no squeaky pretend-Fox voice, but it's a peaceful, interested silence. Jeremy complains about all the things there are to complain about, and the silent person on the other end listens and listens. Maybe it is Fox standing there in his phone booth and listening patiently. He wonders what incarnation of Fox is listening. One thing about Fox: she's never sorry for herself. She's always too busy. If it were really Fox, she'd hang up on him.

Jeremy opens his door. "I was on the phone," he says. His mother comes in and sits down on his bed. She's wearing one of his father's old flannel shirts. "So have you packed?"

Jeremy shrugs. "I guess," he says. "Why did you cry when you saw what Dad did to the van? Don't you like it?"

"It's that damn painting," his mother says. "It was the first nice thing he ever gave me. We should have spent the money on health insurance and a new roof and groceries and instead he bought a painting. So I got angry. I left him. I took the painting and I moved into a hotel and I stayed there for a few days. I was going to sell the painting, but instead I fell in love with it, so I came home and apologized for running away. I got pregnant with you and I used to get hungry and dream that someone was going to give me a beautiful apple, like the one she's holding. When I told your father, he said he didn't trust her, that she was holding out the apple like that as a trick and if you went to take it from her, she'd stab you with the peeling knife. He says that she's a tough old broad and she'll take care of us while we're on the road."

"Do we really have to go?" Jeremy says. "If we go to Las Vegas I might get into trouble. I might start using drugs or gambling or something."

"Oh, Germ. You try so hard to be a good kid," his mother says. "You try so hard to be normal. Sometimes I'd like to be normal, too. Maybe Vegas will be good for us. Are these the books that you're bringing?"

Jeremy shrugs. "Not all of them. I can't decide which ones I should take and which ones I can leave. It feels like whatever I leave behind, I'm leaving behind for good."

"That's silly," his mother says. "We're coming back. I promise. Your father and I will work things out. If you leave something behind that you need, he can mail it to you. Do you think there are slot machines in the libraries in Las Vegas? I talked to a woman at the Hell's Bells chapel and there's something called The Arts and Lovecraft Library where they keep Cleo's special collection of horror novels and gothic romances and fake copies of The Necronomicon. You go in and out through a secret, swinging-bookcase door. People get married in it. There's a Dr. Frankenstein's LoveLab, the Masque of the Red Death Ballroom, and also something just called The Crypt. Oh yeah, and there's also The Vampire's Patio and The Black Lagoon Grotto, where you can get married by moonlight."

"You hate all this stuff," Jeremy says.

"It's not my cup of tea," his mother says. "When does everyone show up tonight?"

"Around eight," Jeremy says. "Are you going to get dressed up?"

"I don't have to dress up," his mother says. "I'm a librarian, remember?"

Jeremy's father's office is above the garage. In theory, no one is meant to interrupt him while he's working, but in practice Jeremy's father loves nothing better than to be interrupted, as long as the person who interrupts him brings him something to eat. When Jeremy and his mother are gone, who will bring Jeremy's father food? Jeremy hardens his heart.

The floor is covered with books and bolts and samples of upholstering fabrics. Jeremy's father is lying facedown on the floor with his feet propped up on a bolt of fabric, which means that he is thinking and also that his back hurts. He claims to think best when he is on the verge of falling asleep.

"I brought you a bowl of Froot Loops," Jeremy says.

His father rolls over and looks up. "Thanks," he says. "What time is it? Is everyone here? Is that your costume? Is that my tuxedo jacket?"

"It's five-ish. Nobody's here yet. Do you like it?" Jeremy says. He's dressed as a Forbidden Book. His father's jacket is too big, but he still feels very elegant. Very sinister. His mother lent him the lipstick and the feathers and the platform heels.

"It's interesting," his father allows. "And a little frightening."

Jeremy feels obscurely pleased, even though he knows that his father is more amused than frightened. "Everyone else will probably come as Fox or Prince Wing. Except for Karl. He's coming as Ptolemy Krill. He even wrote some really bad poetry. I wanted to ask you something, before we leave tomorrow."

"Shoot," his father says.

"Did you really get rid of the novel with me in it?"

"No," his father says. "It felt unlucky. Unlucky to keep it, unlucky not to keep it. I don't know what to do with it."

Jeremy says, "I'm glad you didn't get rid of it."

"It's not any good, you know," his father says. "Which makes all this even worse. At first it was because I was bored with giant spiders. It was going to be something funny to show you. But then I wrote that you had a brain tumor and it wasn't funny anymore. I figured I could save you—I'm the author, after all—but you got sicker and sicker. You were going through a rebellious phase. You were sneaking out of the house a lot and you hit your mother. You were a real jerk. But it turned out you had a brain tumor and that was making you behave strangely."

"Can I ask another question?" Jeremy says. "You know how you like to steal things? You know how you're really, really good at it?"

"Yeah," says his father.

"Could you not steal things for a while, if I asked you to?" Jeremy says. "Mom isn't going to be around to pay for the books and stuff that you steal. I don't want you to end up in jail because we went to Las Vegas."

His father closes his eyes as if he hopes Jeremy will forget that he asked a question, and go away.

Jeremy says nothing.

"All right," his father says finally. "I won't shoplift anything until you get home again."

Jeremy's mother runs around taking photos of everyone. Talis and Elizabeth have both showed up as Fox, although Talis is dead Fox. She carries her fake fur ears and tail around in a little see-through plastic purse and she also has a sword, which she leaves in the umbrella stand in the kitchen. Jeremy and Talis haven't talked much since she had a dream about him and since he told her that he's going to Las Vegas. She didn't say anything about that. Which is perfectly normal for Talis.

Karl makes an excellent Ptolemy Krill. Jeremy's Forbidden Book disguise is admired.

Amy's Faithful Margaret costume is almost as good as anything Faithful Margaret wears on TV. There are even special effects: Amy has rigged up her hair with red ribbons and wire and spray color and egg whites so that it looks as if it's on fire, and there are tiny papier-mâché golems in it, making horrible faces. She dances a polka with Jeremy's father. Faithful Margaret is mad for polka dancing.

No one has dressed up as Prince Wing.

They watch the episode with the possessed chicken and they watch the episode with the Salt Wife and they watch the episode where Prince Wing and Faithful Margaret fall under a spell and swap bodies and have sex for the first time. They watch the episode where Fox saves Prince Wing's life for the first time.

Jeremy's father makes chocolate/mango/espresso milk shakes for everyone. None of Jeremy's friends, except for Elizabeth, know about the novel. Everyone thinks Jeremy and his mother are just having an adventure. Everyone thinks Jeremy will be back at the end of the summer.

"I wonder how they find the actors," Elizabeth says. "They aren't real actors. They must be regular people. But you'd think that somewhere there would be someone who knows them. That somebody online would say, hey, that's my sister! Or that's the kid I went to school with who threw up in P.E. You know, sometimes someone says something like that or sometimes someone pretends that they know something about *The Library*, but it always turns out to be a hoax. Just somebody wanting to be somebody."

"What about the guy who's writing it?" Karl says.

Talis says, "Who says it's a guy?" and Amy says, "Yeah, Karl, why do you always assume it's a guy writing it?"

"Maybe nobody's writing it," Elizabeth says. "Maybe it's magic or it's broadcast from outer space. Maybe it's real. Wouldn't that be cool?"

"No," Jeremy says. "Because then Fox would really be dead. That would suck."

"I don't care," Elizabeth says. "I wish it were real, anyway. Maybe it all really happened somewhere, like King Arthur or Robin Hood, and this is just one version of how it happened. Like a magical After School Special."

"Even if it isn't real," Amy says, "parts of it could be real. Like maybe the World-Tree Library is real. Or maybe *The Library* is made up, but Fox is based on somebody that the writer knew. Writers do that all the time, right? Jeremy, I think your dad should write a book about me. I could be eaten by giant spiders. Or have sex with giant spiders and have spider babies. I think that would be so great."

So Amy does have psychic abilities, after all, although hopefully she will never know this. When Jeremy tests his own potential psychic abilities, he can almost sense his father, hovering somewhere just outside the living room, listening to this conversation and maybe even taking notes. Which is what writers do. But Jeremy isn't really psychic. It's just that lurking and hovering and appearing suddenly when you weren't expecting him are what his father does, just like shoplifting and cooking. Jeremy prays to all the dark gods that he never receives the gift of knowing what people are thinking. It's a dark road and it ends up with you trapped on late night television in front of an invisible audience of depressed insomniacs wearing hats made out of tinfoil and they all want to pay you nine-ninety-nine per minute to hear you describe in minute, terrible detail what their deceased cat is thinking about, right now. What kind of future is that? He wants to go to Mars. And when will Elizabeth kiss him again? You can't just kiss someone twice and then never kiss them again. He tries not to think about Elizabeth and kissing, just in case Amy reads his mind. He realizes that he's been staring at Talis's breasts, glares instead at Elizabeth, who is watching TV. Meanwhile, Karl is glaring at him.

On television, Fox is dancing in the Invisible Nightclub with Faithful Margaret, whose hair is about to catch fire again. The Norns are playing their screechy cover of "Come On, Eileen." The Norns only know two songs: "Come On, Eileen," and "Everybody Wants to Rule the World." They don't play real instruments. They play squeaky dog toys and also a bathtub, which is enchanted, although nobody knows who by, or why, or what it was enchanted for.

"If you had to chose one," Jeremy says, "invisibility or the ability to fly, which would you choose?"

Everybody looks at him. "Only perverts would want to be invisible," Elizabeth says.

"You'd have to be naked if you were invisible," Karl says. "Because otherwise people would see your clothes."

"If you could fly, you'd have to wear thermal underwear because it's cold up there. So it just depends on whether you like to wear long underwear or no underwear at all," Amy says.

It's the kind of conversation that they have all the time. It makes Jeremy feel homesick even though he hasn't left yet.

"Maybe I'll go make brownies," Jeremy says. "Elizabeth, do you want to help me make brownies?"

"Shhh," Elizabeth says. "This is a good part."

On television, Fox and Faithful Margaret are making out. The Faithful part is kind of a joke.

Jeremy's parents go to bed at one. By three, Amy and Elizabeth are passed out on the couch and Karl has gone upstairs to check his e-mail on Jeremy's iBook. On TV, wolves are roaming the tundra of The Free People's World-Tree Library's fortieth floor. Snow is falling heavily and librarians are burning books to keep warm, but only the most dull and improving works of literature.

Jeremy isn't sure where Talis has gone, so he goes to look for her. She hasn't gone far. She's on the landing, looking at the space on the wall where Alice Mars's painting should be hanging. Talis is carrying her sword with her, and her little plastic purse. In the bathroom off the landing, the singing toilet is still singing away in German. "We're taking the painting with us," Jeremy says. "My dad insisted, just in case he accidentally burns down the house while we're gone. Do you want to go see it? I was going to show everybody, but everybody's asleep right now."

"Sure," Talis says.

So Jeremy gets a flashlight and takes her out to the garage and shows her the van. She climbs right inside and sits down on one of the blue-fur couches. She looks around and he wonders what she's thinking. He wonders if the toilet song is stuck in her head.

"My dad did all of this," Jeremy says. He turns on the flashlight and shines it on the disco ball. Light spatters off in anxious, slippery orbits. Jeremy shows Talis how his father has hung up the painting. It looks truly wrong in the van, as if someone demented put it there. Especially with the light reflecting off the disco ball. The woman in the painting looks confused and embarrassed as if Jeremy's father has accidentally canceled out her protective powers. Maybe the disco ball is her Kryptonite.

"So remember how you had a dream about me?" Jeremy says. Talis nods. "I think I had a dream about you, that you were Fox."

Talis opens up her arms, encompassing her costume, her sword, her plastic purse with poor Fox's ears and tail inside.

"There was something you wanted me to do," Jeremy says. "I was supposed to save you, somehow."

Talis just looks at him.

"How come you never talk?" Jeremy says. All of this is irritating. How he used to feel normal around Elizabeth, like friends, and now everything is peculiar and uncomfortable. How he used to enjoy feeling uncomfortable around Talis, and now, suddenly, he doesn't. This must be what sex is about. Stop thinking about sex, he thinks.

Talis opens her mouth and closes it again. Then she says, "I don't know. Amy talks so much. You all talk a lot. Somebody has to be the person who doesn't. The person who listens."

"Oh," Jeremy says. "I thought maybe you had a tragic secret. Like maybe you used to stutter." Except secrets can't have secrets, they just *are*.

"Nope," Talis says. "It's like being invisible, you know. Not talking. I like it."

"But you're not invisible," Jeremy says. "Not to me. Not to Karl. Karl really likes you. Did you hit him with a boa constrictor on purpose?"

But Talis says, "I wish you weren't leaving." The disco ball spins and spins. It makes Jeremy feel kind of carsick and also as if he has sparkly, disco leprosy. He doesn't say anything back to Talis, just to see how it feels. Except maybe that's rude. Or maybe it's rude the way everybody always talks and doesn't leave any space for Talis to say anything.

"At least you get to miss school," Talis says, at last.

"Yeah," he says. He leaves another space, but Talis doesn't say anything this time. "We're going to stop at all these museums and things on the way across the country. I'm supposed to keep a blog for school and describe stuff in it. I'm going to make a lot of stuff up. So it will be like Creative Writing and not so much like homework."

"You should make a list of all the towns with weird names you drive through," Talis says. "Town of Horseheads. That's a real place."

"Plantagenet," Jeremy says. "That's a real place too. I had something really weird to tell you."

Talis waits, like she always does.

Jeremy says, "I called my phone booth, the one that I inherited, and someone answered. She sounded just like Fox when she talked. They told me to call back later. So I've called a few more times, but I don't ever get her."

"Fox isn't a real person," Talis says. "*The Library* is just TV." But she sounds uncertain. That's the thing about *The Library*. Nobody knows for sure. Everyone who watches it wishes and hopes that it's not just acting. That it's magic, real magic.

"I know," Jeremy says.

"I wish Fox was real," Fox-Talis says.

They've been sitting in the van for a long time. If Karl looks for them and can't find them, he's going to think that they've been making out. He'll kill Jeremy. Once Karl tried to strangle another kid for accidentally peeing on his shoes. Jeremy might as well kiss Talis. So he does, even though she's still holding her sword. She doesn't hit him with it. It's dark and he has his eyes closed and he can almost imagine that he's kissing Elizabeth.

Karl has fallen asleep on Jeremy's bed. Talis is downstairs, fast-forwarding through the episode where some librarians drink too much Euphoria and decide to abolish Story Hour. Not just the practice of having a Story Hour, but the whole Hour. Amy and Elizabeth are still sacked out on the couch. It's weird to watch Amy sleep. She doesn't talk in her sleep.

Karl is snoring. Jeremy could go up on the roof and look at stars, except he's already packed up his telescope. He could try to wake up Elizabeth and they could go up on the roof, but Talis is down there. He and Talis could go sit on the roof, but he doesn't want to kiss Talis on the roof. He makes a solemn oath to only ever kiss Elizabeth on the roof.

He picks up his phone. Maybe he can call his phone booth and complain just a little and not wake Karl up. His dad is going to freak out about the phone bill. All these calls to Nevada. It's 4:00 a.m. Jeremy's plan is not to go to sleep at all. His friends are lame.

The phone rings and rings and rings and then someone picks up. Jeremy recognizes the silence on the other end. "Everybody came over and fell asleep," he whispers. "That's why I'm whispering. I don't even think they care that I'm leaving. And my feet hurt. Remember how I was going to dress up as a Forbidden Book? Platform shoes aren't comfortable. Karl thinks I did it on purpose, to be even taller than him than usual. And I forgot that I was wearing lipstick and I kissed Talis and got lipstick all over her face, so it's a good thing everyone was asleep because otherwise someone would have seen. And my dad says that he won't shoplift at all while Mom and I are gone, but you can't trust him. And that fake-fur upholstery sheds like—"

"Jeremy," that strangely familiar, sweet-and-rusty door-hinge voice says softly. "Shut up, Jeremy. I need your help."

"Wow!" Jeremy says, not in a whisper. "Wow, wow, wow! Is this Fox? Are you really Fox? Is this a joke? Are you real? Are you dead? What are you doing in my phone booth?"

"You know who I am," Fox says, and Jeremy knows with all his heart that it's really Fox. "I need you to do something for me."

"What?" Jeremy says. Karl, on the bed, laughs in his sleep as if the idea of Jeremy doing something is funny to him. "What could I do?"

"I need you to steal three books," Fox says. "From a library in a place called Iowa."

"I know Iowa," Jeremy says. "I mean, I've never been there, but it's a real place. I could go there."

"I'm going to tell you the books you need to steal," Fox says. "Author, title, and the jewelly festival number—"

"Dewey Decimal," Jeremy says. "It's actually called the Dewey Decimal number in real libraries."

"Real," Fox says, sounding amused. "You need to write this all down and also how to get to the library. You need to steal the three books and bring them to me. It's very important."

"Is it dangerous?" Jeremy says. "Are the Forbidden Books up to something? Are the Forbidden Books real, too? What if I get caught stealing?"

"It's not dangerous to you," Fox says. "Just don't get caught. Remember the episode of *The Library* when I was the little old lady with the beehive and I stole the Bishop of Tweedle's false teeth while he was reading the banns for the wedding of Faithful Margaret and Sir Petronella the Younger? Remember how he didn't even notice?"

"I've never seen that episode," Jeremy says, although as far as he knows he's never missed a single episode of *The Library*. He's never even heard of Sir Petronella.

"Oh," Fox says. "Maybe that's a flashback in a later episode or something. That's a great episode. We're depending on you, Jeremy. You have got to steal these books. They contain dreadful secrets. I can't say the titles out loud. I'm going to spell them instead."

So Jeremy gets a pad of paper and Fox spells out the titles of each book twice. (They aren't titles that can be written down here. It's safer not to even think about some books.) "Can I ask you something?" Jeremy says. "Can I tell anybody about this? Not Amy. But could I tell Karl or Elizabeth? Or Talis? Can I tell my mom? If I woke up Karl right now, would you talk to him for a minute?"

"I don't have a lot of time," Fox says. "I have to go now. Please don't tell anyone, Jeremy. I'm sorry."

"Is it the Forbidden Books?" Jeremy says again. What would Fox think if she saw the costume he's still wearing, all except for the platform heels? "Do you think I shouldn't trust my friends? But I've known them my whole life!"

Fox makes a noise, a kind of pained *whuff*.

"What is it?" Jeremy says. "Are you okay?"

"I have to go," Fox says. "Nobody can know about this. Don't give anybody this number. Don't tell anyone about your phone booth. Or me. Promise, Germ?"

"Only if you promise you won't call me Germ," Jeremy says, feeling really stupid. "I hate when people call me that. Call me Mars instead."

"Mars," Fox says, and it sounds exotic and strange and brave, as if Jeremy has just become a new person, a person named after a whole planet, a person who kisses girls and talks to Foxes.

"I've never stolen anything," Jeremy says.

But Fox has hung up.

Maybe out there, somewhere, is someone who enjoys having to say good-bye, but it isn't anyone that Jeremy knows. All of his friends are grumpy and red-eyed, although not from crying. From lack of sleep. From too much television. There are still faint red stains around Talis's mouth and if everyone weren't so tired, they would realize it's Jeremy's lipstick. Karl gives Jeremy a handful of quarters, dimes, nickels, and pennies. "For the slot machines," Karl says. "If you win anything, you can keep a third of what you win."

"Half," Jeremy says, automatically.

"Fine," Karl says. "It's all from your dad's sofas, anyway. Just one more thing. Stop getting taller. Don't get taller while you're gone. Okay." He hugs Jeremy hard: so hard that it's almost like getting punched again. No wonder Talis threw the boa constrictor at Karl.

Talis and Elizabeth both hug Jeremy good-bye. Talis looks even more mysterious now that he's sat with her under a disco ball and made out. Later on, Jeremy will discover that Talis has left her sword under the blue fur couch and he'll wonder if she left it on purpose.

Talis doesn't say anything and Amy, of course, doesn't shut up, not even when she kisses him. It feels weird to be kissed by someone who goes right on talking while they kiss you and yet it shouldn't be a surprise that Amy kisses him. He imagines that later Amy and Talis and Elizabeth will all compare notes.

Elizabeth says, "I promise I'll tape every episode of *The Library* while you're gone so we can all watch them together when you get back. I promise I'll call you in Vegas, no matter what time it is there, when there's a new episode."

Her hair is a mess and her breath is faintly sour. Jeremy wishes he could tell her how beautiful she looks. "I'll write bad poetry and send it to you," he says.

Jeremy's mother is looking hideously cheerful as she goes in and out of the house, making sure that she hasn't left anything behind. She loves long car trips. It doesn't bother her one bit that she and her son are abandoning their entire lives. She passes Jeremy a folder full of maps. "You're in charge of not getting lost," she says. "Put these somewhere safe."

Jeremy says, "I found a library online that I want to go visit. Out in Iowa. They have a corn mosaic on the façade of the building, with a lot of naked goddesses and gods dancing around in a field of corn. Someone wants to take it down. Can we go see it first?"

"Sure," his mother says.

Jeremy's father has filled a whole grocery bag with sandwiches. His hair is drooping and he looks even more like an axe murderer than usual. If this were a movie, you'd think that Jeremy and his mother were escaping in the nick of time. "You take care of your mother," he says to Jeremy.

"Sure," Jeremy says. "You take care of yourself."

His dad sags. "You take care of yourself, too." So it's settled. They're all supposed to take care of themselves. Why can't they stay home and take care of each other, until Jeremy is good and ready to go off to college? "I've got another bag of sandwiches in the kitchen," his dad says. "I should go get them."

"Wait," Jeremy says. "I have to ask you something before we take off. Suppose I had to steal something. I mean, I don't have to steal anything, of course, and I know stealing is wrong, even when *you* do it, and I would never steal anything. But what if I did? How do you do it? How do you do it and not get caught?"

His father shrugs. He's probably wondering if Jeremy is really his son. Gordon Mars inherited his mutant, long-fingered, ambidextrous hands from a long line of shoplifters and money launderers and petty criminals. They're all deeply ashamed of Jeremy's father. Gordon Mars had a gift and he threw it away to become a writer. "I don't know," he says. He picks up Jeremy's hand and looks at it as if he's never noticed before that Jeremy had something hanging off the end of his wrist. "You just do it. You do it like you're not really doing anything at all. You do it while you're thinking about something else and you forget that you're doing it."

"Oh, Jeremy says, taking his hand back. "I'm not planning on stealing anything. I was just curious."

His father looks at him. "Take care of yourself," he says again, as if he really means it, and hugs Jeremy hard.

Then he goes and gets the sandwiches (so many sandwiches that Jeremy and his mother will eat sandwiches for the first three days, and still have to throw half of them away). Everyone waves. Jeremy and his mother climb in the van. Jeremy's mother turns on the CD player. Bob Dylan is singing about monkeys. His mother loves Bob Dylan. They drive away.

~

Do you know how, sometimes, during a commercial break in your favorite television shows, your best friend calls and wants to talk about one of her boyfriends, and when you try to hang up, she starts crying and you try to cheer her up and end up missing about half of the episode? And so when you go to work the next day, you have to get the guy who sits next to you to explain what happened? That's the good thing about a book. You can mark your place in a book. But this isn't really a book. It's a television show.

In one episode of *The Library*, an adolescent boy drives across the country with his mother. They have to change a tire. The boy practices taking things out of his mother's purse and putting them back again. He steals a sixteen-ounce bottle of Coke from one convenience market and leaves it at another convenience market. The boy and his mother stop at a lot of libraries, and the boy keeps a blog, but he skips the bit about the library in Iowa. He writes in his blog about what he's reading, but he doesn't read the books he stole in Iowa, because Fox told him not to, and because he has to hide them from his mother. Well, he reads just a few pages. Skims, really. He hides them under the blue-fur sofa. They go camping in Utah, and the boy sets up his telescope. He sees three shooting stars and a coyote. He never sees anyone who looks like a Forbidden Book, although he sees a transvestite go into the woman's rest room at a rest stop in Indiana. He calls a phone booth just outside Las Vegas twice, but no one ever answers. He has short conversations with his father. He wonders what his father is up to. He wishes he could tell his father about Fox and the books. Once the boy's mother finds a giant spider the size of an Oreo in their tent. She starts laughing hysterically. She takes a picture of it with her digital camera, and the boy puts the picture on his blog. Sometimes the boy asks questions and his mother talks about her parents. Once she cries. The boy doesn't know what to say. They talk about their favorite episodes of *The Library* and the episodes that they really hated, and the mother asks if the boy thinks Fox is really dead. He says he doesn't think so.

Once a man tries to break into the van while they are sleeping in it. But then he goes away. Maybe the painting of the woman with the peeling knife is protecting them.

But you've seen this episode before.

It's Cinco de Mayo. It's almost seven o'clock at night, and the sun is beginning to go down. Jeremy and his mother are in the desert and Las Vegas is somewhere in front of them. Every time they pass a driver coming the other way, Jeremy tries to figure out if that person has just won or lost a lot of money. Everything is flat and sort of tilted here, except off in the distance, where the land goes up abruptly, as if someone has started to fold up a map. Somewhere around here is the Grand Canyon, which must have been a surprise when people first saw it.

Jeremy's mother says, "Are you sure we have to do this first? Couldn't we go find your phone booth later?"

"Can we do it now?" Jeremy says. "I said I was going to do it on my blog. It's like a quest that I have to complete."

"Okay," his mother says. "It should be around here somewhere. It's supposed to be four point five miles after the turnoff, and here's the turnoff."

It isn't hard to find the phone booth. There isn't much else around. Jeremy should feel excited when he sees it, but it's a disappointment, really. He's seen phone booths before. He was expecting something to be different. Mostly he just feels tired of road trips and tired of roads and just tired, tired, tired. He looks around to see if Fox is somewhere nearby, but there's just a hiker off in the distance. Some kid.

"Okay, Germ," his mother says. "Make this quick."

"I need to get my backpack out of the back," Jeremy says.

"Do you want me to come too?" his mother says.

"No," Jeremy says. "This is kind of personal."

His mother looks like she's trying not to laugh. "Just hurry up. I have to pee."

When Jeremy gets to the phone booth, he turns around. His mother has the light on in the van. It looks like she's singing along to the radio. His mother has a terrible voice.

When he steps inside the phone booth, it isn't magical. The phone booth smells rank, as if an animal has been living in it. The windows are smudgy. He takes the stolen books out of his backpack and puts them in the little shelf where someone has stolen a phone book. Then he waits. Maybe Fox is going to call him. Maybe he's supposed to wait until she calls. But she doesn't call. He feels lonely. There's no one he can tell about this. He feels like an idiot and he also feels kind of proud. Because he did it. He drove cross-country with his mother and saved an imaginary person.

"So how's your phone booth?" his mother says.

"Great!" he says, and they're both silent again. Las Vegas is in front of them and then all around them and everything is lit up like they're inside a pinball game. All of the trees look fake. Like someone read too much Dr. Seuss and got ideas. People are walking up and down the sidewalks. Some of them look normal.

Others look like they just escaped from a fancy-dress ball at a lunatic asylum. Jeremy hopes they've just won lots of money and that's why they look so startled, so strange. Or maybe they're all vampires.

"Left," he tells his mother. "Go left here. Look out for the vampires on the crosswalk. And then it's an immediate right." Four times his mother let him drive the van: once in Utah, twice in South Dakota, once in Pennsylvania. The van smells like old burger wrappers and fake fur, and it doesn't help that Jeremy's gotten used to the smell. The woman in the painting has had a pained expression on her face for the last few nights, and the disco ball has lost some of its pieces of mirror because Jeremy kept knocking his head on it in the morning. Jeremy and his mother haven't showered in three days.

Here is the wedding chapel, in front of them, at the end of a long driveway. Electric purple light shines on a sign that spells out HELL'S BELLS. There's a wrought-iron fence and a yard full of trees dripping Spanish moss. Under the trees, tombstones and miniature mausoleums.

"Do you think those are real?" his mother says. She sounds slightly worried.

"'Harry East, Recently Deceased,'" Jeremy says. "No, I don't."

There's a hearse in the driveway with a little plaque on the back. RECENTLY BURIED MARRIED. The chapel is a Victorian house with a bell tower. Perhaps it's full of bats. Or giant spiders. Jeremy's father would love this place. His mother is going to hate it.

Someone stands at the threshold of the chapel, door open, looking out at them. But as Jeremy and his mother get out of the van, he turns and goes inside and shuts the door. "Look out," his mother says. "They've probably gone to put the boiling oil in the microwave."

She rings the doorbell determinedly. Instead of ringing, there's a recording of a crow. *Caw, caw, caw*. All the lights in the Victorian house go out. Then they turn on again. The door swings open and Jeremy tightens his grip on his backpack, just in case. "Good evening, Madam. Young man," a man says and Jeremy looks up and up and up. The man at the door has to lower his head to look out. His hands are large as toaster ovens. He looks like he's wearing Chihuahua coffins on his feet. Two realistic-looking bolts stick out on either side of his head. He wears green pancake makeup, glittery green eye shadow, and his lashes are as long and thick and green as AstroTurf. "We weren't expecting you so soon."

"We should have called ahead," Jeremy's mother says. "I'm real sorry."

"Great costume," Jeremy says.

The Frankenstein curls his lip in a somber way. "Thank you," he says. "Call me Miss Thing, please."

"I'm Jeremy," Jeremy says. "This is my mother."

"Oh please," Miss Thing says. Even his wink is somber. "You tease me. She isn't old enough to be your mother."

"Oh please, yourself," Jeremy's mother says.

"Quick, the two of you," someone yells from somewhere inside Hell's Bells. "While you zthtand there gabbing, the devil ithz prowling around like a lion, looking for a way to get in. Are you juthzt going to zthtand there and hold the door wide open for him?"

So they all step inside. "Is that Jeremy Marthz at lathzt?" the voice says. "Earth to Marthz, Earth to Marthz. Marthzzz, Jeremy Marthzzz, there'thz zthomeone on the phone for Jeremy Marthz. She'thz called three timethz in the lathzt ten minutethz, Jeremy Marthzzzz."

It's Fox, Jeremy knows. Of course, it's Fox! She's in the phone booth. She's got the books and she's going to tell me that I saved whatever it is that I was saving. He walks toward the buzzing voice while Miss Thing and his mother go back out to the van.

He walks past a room full of artfully draped spider webs and candelabras drooping with drippy candles. Someone is playing the organ behind a wooden screen. He goes down the hall and up a long staircase. The banisters are carved with little faces. Owls and foxes and ugly children. The voice goes on talking. "Yoohoo, Jeremy, up the stairthz, that'thz right. Now, come along, come right in! Not in there, in here, in here! Don't mind the dark, we *like* the dark, just watch your step." Jeremy puts his hand out. He touches something and there's a click and the bookcase in front of him slowly slides back. Now the room is three times as large and there are more bookshelves and there's a young woman wearing dark sunglasses, sitting on a couch. She has a megaphone in one hand and a phone in the other. "For you, Jeremy Marth," she says. She's the palest person Jeremy has ever seen and her two canine teeth are so pointed that she lisps a little when she talks. On the megaphone the lisp was sinister, but now it just makes her sound irritable.

She hands him the phone. "Hello?" he says. He keeps an eye on the vampire.

"Jeremy!" Elizabeth says. "It's on, it's on, it's on! It's just started! We're all just sitting here. Everybody's here. What happened to your cell phone? We kept calling."

"Mom left it in the visitor's center at Zion," Jeremy says.

"Well, you're there. We figured out from your blog that you must be near Vegas. Amy says she had a feeling that you were going to get there in time. She made us keep calling. Stay on the phone, Jeremy. We can all watch it together, okay? Hold on."

Karl grabs the phone. "Hey, Germ, I didn't get any postcards," he says. "You forget how to write or something? Wait a minute. Somebody wants to say something to you." Then he laughs and laughs and passes the phone on to someone else who doesn't say anything at all.

"Talis?" Jeremy says.

Maybe it isn't Talis. Maybe it's Elizabeth again. He thinks about how his mouth is right next to Elizabeth's ear. Or maybe it's Talis's ear.

The vampire on the couch is already flipping through the channels. Jeremy would like to grab the remote away from her, but it's not a good idea to try to take things away from a vampire. His mother and Miss Thing come up the stairs and into the room and suddenly the room seems absolutely full of people, as if Karl and Amy and Elizabeth and Talis have come into the room, too. His hand is getting sweaty around the phone. Miss Thing is holding Jeremy's mother's painting firmly, as if it might try to escape. Jeremy's mother looks tired. For the past three days her hair has been braided into two long fat pigtails. She looks younger to Jeremy, as if they've been traveling backward in time instead of just across the country. She smiles at Jeremy, a giddy, exhausted smile. Jeremy smiles back.

"Is it *The Library*?" Miss Thing says. "Is a new episode on?"

Jeremy sits down on the couch beside the vampire, still holding the phone to his ear. His arm is getting tired.

"I'm here," he says to Talis or Elizabeth or whoever it is on the other end of the phone. "I'm here." And then he sits and doesn't say anything and waits with everyone else for the vampire to find the right channel so they can all find out if he's saved Fox, if Fox is alive, if Fox is still alive.

THE INHERITANCE OF BARNABAS WILCOX

Sarah Monette

Some four months after I attended the fifteen-year reunion at Brockstone School, I received a letter from Barnabas Wilcox. I was puzzled, for there was no love lost between Wilcox and me, but instead of doing the sensible thing and throwing the letter unopened on the fire, I read it.

> *Dear Booth* (Wilcox wrote)*:*
> *I'm writing to you because you know all about old books. The case is that I have recently inherited a house in the country from my Uncle Lucius, and there's a stipulation in his will that his library catalogue should be made up-to-date. Would you care to come down with me this weekend and take a look at it? I don't know anyone else who would even know where to begin.*
>
> *Yrs,*

And then an involved squiggle in which a "B" and a "W" were dimly perceptible.

It took no great leap of intuition to guess that Wilcox's "Uncle Lucius" had to be the noted antiquary Lucius Preston Wilcox, and that lure overcame my dislike of Wilcox. Friday I took a half-day, packed my bag, and met Wilcox on the platform at quarter of three. He was a big, square, red-faced man, with thick, blunt-fingered hands and smallish, squinty hazel eyes. Despite my white hair, he looked easily ten years older than I; when we shook hands, I smelled liquor on his breath.

"How are you, Booth?" he said when we were settled in our compartment. "It's good of you to come."

"I, er," I said. " . . . I like libraries."

"Well, old Uncle Loosh should keep you happy then. I remember, my brother and I used to think the books had to be fake, he had so many."

I recollected in time that Wilcox's brother had died in the war, and asked instead, "When did your uncle die? I don't remember reading an obituary."

"Daft old coot. He wouldn't have one written. It was the first stipulation in his will, and he'd told his lawyer and his housekeeper and everybody about it. And, after all, there's no law that says you have to publish one. It's just that people usually do. But Uncle Loosh was crazy."

" . . . Crazy?"

"He got into some weird things. He used to write me these long letters saying he'd figured out how to cheat death and was going to live forever. I couldn't understand half of what he said."

"That's not a very pleasant occupation."

"Uncle Loosh wasn't a very pleasant person. I can't think why he left everything to me. We didn't get along."

The train began to move. With a muttered apology, Wilcox dug some papers out of his attaché case and settled in to work. I stared out the window and watched as the train left the city behind.

The estate of Wilcox's uncle was called Hollyhill and was accurately named in both respects. The house stood on a prominence among the farms and woods of the gently rolling countryside, and was surrounded by as thriving a stand of holly trees as I had ever seen.

"I shall have those cut down first thing," Wilcox said as we turned through the gates. "I don't know what Uncle Loosh was thinking of, letting them grow like that."

In the rear-view mirror, I caught the eyes of the driver; his name was Esau Flood, and he had been Mr. Preston Wilcox's groundskeeper. He was small, very tan, with a head of thick white hair. His eyes were gray and reminded me strongly of the sort of smooth, round pebbles one finds in a swiftly-moving stream. He said, "Mr. Preston Wilcox was very fond of the holly, sir."

"That doesn't surprise me," Wilcox said disagreeably. "I'm not."

"I'm sure not, sir," said Flood, too politely.

The house itself was remarkably unattractive, with an aggressively square façade and windows that seemed too small for the proportions. Inside, I was oppressed to discover that the entire house was paneled with dark-varnished oak, and that the windows gave as little light as one would expect. They had uncommonly thick curtains. Wilcox seemed uncomfortable as well; he said several times over dinner that he did not know why his uncle had left him the place, and he was not sure but that the best thing to do would be to sell it—"not that I could find a buyer," he added.

"It might be more pleasant without the, er, the paneling."

"Oh, but that paneling's valuable. They don't make stuff like that any more."

"Yes, but it's quite dark."

"Better lights would solve that," he said, staring up at the chandelier with disapprobation. "Well, *that* I can take care of tomorrow. I fancy I'll have to leave you on your own most of the day, Booth. There's quite a list of things that need buying, and for some reason Flood hasn't done any of it."

"Perhaps," I said, because I did not want to be a witness to what already seemed like an alarming escalation of hostilities between Wilcox and Flood, "perhaps he didn't like to do anything without . . . that is, without asking you first."

"Good God, it takes no more than common sense to see that I shan't kick over buying enough plaster to repair a great gaping hole in the cellar wall!" Wilcox stared at me; for a moment he was the bully I remembered from Brockstone. Then he said, more mildly, "I daresay you're right. Flood and I have rubbed each other the wrong way a bit, but we'll get along all right soon enough. I know Uncle Loosh couldn't speak highly enough of him."

I managed to mutter something about "time," and Wilcox turned the conversation to bridge, of which he appeared to be an addict. I do not play myself, disliking any form of activity which requires a partner, but Wilcox needed no encouragement to discourse at length.

After dinner, he said, "D'you want to look at the library now?"

"I, er . . . yes, while you're here to . . . "

He rolled his eyes. "Come on, then."

The doors to the library—vast, carved things like cathedral doors—were locked. While Wilcox, grumbling, sorted through his key-ring, I examined the carvings. They were crude, almost primitive, in design and execution, and their crudeness bothered me because I could not quite tell what the reliefs were meant to represent. There were trees—I was sure of that—and there was one figure, always holding a box and thus easy to identify, that seemed quite reliably to be human, but the rest of it was disturbingly muddled, so that I could not determine whether the other shapes were persecuting the human shape or obeying its commands.

"Ha!" said Wilcox and unlocked the doors.

In the library, at last, we found a well-lit and comfortably appointed room. It was quite large, large enough that it disrupted the severely square proportions of the house by jutting out into the back garden. Although the windows were still small and mean, in the library it seemed almost reasonable that they should be so, since every inch of wall space, including both above and below the windows, was taken up with bookshelves, themselves crammed with books. Where the shelves were deep enough and the books small enough, the books had been double-stacked; everywhere, books had been shoved sideways on top of the rows, and there were stacks on the floor in front of the bookcases, stacks on the desk, stacks on the two small tables—so that the impression was less of a collection and more of an explosion of books.

"Good God," Wilcox said faintly.

After a moment, I said, "You mentioned a catalogue. Do you know . . . er, can you find it?"

"I don't know," Wilcox said, staring around helplessly. "I just know it's mentioned in the will."

"Flood might . . . "

"Or the lawyer, Dropcloth or whatever his name is. But I'll ask Flood." There was a bell-pull, conveniently situated by the desk; Wilcox pulled it briskly.

Flood appeared in the doorway, and I thought again how round and flat his eyes seemed. Wilcox put his question, and Flood said, "Oh, yes, sir. I believe you'll find the catalogue in Mr. Preston Wilcox's desk. He was making notes just before his last illness." Flood did not come into the library; it struck me, perhaps unjustly, that he regarded the massed books with some distaste. Wilcox started opening desk drawers and said, "Thank you, Flood, that was all I wanted," without looking up.

"Yes, sir. Good night, sir," said Flood, and I did not like the expression in those round, flat eyes. He vanished as silently as he had appeared.

"How long was he, er, with your uncle?"

"Flood? Ages and ages. I remember him from when I was a boy, looking just as he does now. Why?"

" . . . No reason. He just . . . that is, I don't . . . "

"He gives you the creeps," Wilcox said, resorting to the lowest and deepest desk drawer, which seemed to be crammed to the brim with paper. "He does me, too. I don't expect I'll keep him on. Get my own people in. New blood and all that."

" . . . Yes," I said, although I found myself wishing he had not used the word "blood," and then did not know why it bothered me.

"This must be it," Wilcox said; he dragged a leather-bound ledger from the bottom of the drawer, sending sheets of paper flying in a kind of fountain. "Blast. Here, you take a look at this, and I'll get this stuff back in the drawer." He shoved the catalogue into my hands.

Lucius Preston Wilcox's rigidly legible handwriting marched across the pages of his catalogue like a conquering army. I noted the careful descriptions of the books, including provenances and conditions, and then, obedient to the signs of Wilcox's growing impatience, allowed myself to be herded out of the library and up to bed.

～

I slept badly that night. In itself, that was not surprising. I am an insomniac—I rarely sleep more than six hours a night, frequently no more than four, sometimes not at all—and I am always nervous in strange bedrooms.

I had not expected to sleep at all, had come prepared with a book on forgers' techniques. But my eyes grew heavy, and finally the book slipped out of my fingers entirely, and I found myself in a dream.

Even at the time, I knew it was a dream, which was some comfort. I was dreaming of being a boy again, thirteen or fourteen, the age at which I had most hated Barnabas Wilcox. I was standing on a staircase; in the dream, it was the main staircase at Brockstone School, but I recognized it as the staircase here at Hollyhill, the one I had just climbed in Wilcox's company on the way to our respective rooms. I was on the landing, by the newel-post, and two boys came running past me down the stairs. I recognized one as Wilcox and tensed, clutching the banister. But they did not notice me; I wondered hopefully if I was invisible.

I followed them downstairs, where they had been caught by a master and were being scolded for something. He was an old man, with bright, piercing eyes. The dream insisted that he was Dr. Smayle, the Greek master, but I kept thinking that he was really someone else, although I did not know whom.

"Useless the both of you!" he was saying. "Senseless as stones. Can't lift your heads above the animal reek of the world, can you, lads?"

"But, sir," said Wilcox, "Tony's dead."

At that I recognized the other boy as Wilcox's older brother, the one who had died in the war.

"Makes no difference," said the old man. "Alive or dead, you just can't see. Your friend would be more use than you are. What's your name, boy?"

Then I'm not invisible, I thought sadly, and said, "Booth."

"Booth?" said Wilcox, twisting around to look at me, his face sneering. "What are *you* doing here?"

"You brought him, you lunk," the old man said. He wasn't Dr. Smayle now, and he never had been. "Brought him right into the middle of something you don't have the motherwit to understand." I fell back a pace under the hammerfall of his eyes. They were not Dr. Smayle's kind blue eyes; they were black and hard. "Booth, you said your name is. Stay in the library, Booth. Don't let Barney drag you out."

"That's right," said Wilcox. "Don't come out of the library, or I'll make you sorry."

The dream changed then, became a different dream, a dream of Wilcox chasing me through Brockstone School, Wilcox and his thuggish friends. I ran until I woke up.

～

At breakfast, Wilcox looked as haggard as I felt. He did not look like the Wilcox of my dream, but I still felt edgy, as if the fourteen-year-old boys we had been were watching us, each horrified at the perceived betrayal in our eating breakfast together. I was grateful that he did not speak.

He disappeared promptly after breakfast, with a mutter about "business." I went into the library and settled down to work.

There was no great difficulty. The catalogue was carefully kept and accurate in all its details. My worst trouble was in finding each volume; the shelves looked to have undergone at least two partial reorganizations, so that the volumes wedged in sideways might as easily be among Mr. Preston Wilcox's first purchases as among his last. I ended up making stacks of my own on his desk, and it was inevitable that around two o'clock that afternoon I knocked one stack over, sending books sliding across the desk and onto the floor.

I gave a yelp of dismay and dove after them. Happily, none had been damaged; it was as I was crawling out from beneath the desk, having retrieved the last of them (*Life Among the Anthropophagi of the South Pacific*), that the corner of a piece of paper caught my eye.

I realized that it had to be one of the papers Wilcox had dropped the night before. It had slid all the way under the bottom drawer, so that no one who did not crawl entirely beneath the desk, as I had done, would ever see it. I put *Life Among the Anthropophagi* on the desk and went back after the paper.

It was a page of notes, clearly belonging to Mr. Preston Wilcox. I recognized the handwriting from the catalogue, and the contents matched up with Wilcox's description of his uncle's obsessions. Elliptical and oblique, they were notes to jog the old man's memory, not to enlighten anyone else. There were references to the holly trees, and to something he called "the Guide" and something else he called "the Vessel." It did not make sense to me, but I was troubled by a feeling that it *ought* to, that I had seen something like this somewhere before. But every time I tried to track that feeling down, I found myself remembering my dream of the previous night— Wilcox chasing me through endless hallways, calling me "freak" and "coward" and worse things. In the end, I put the paper on the desk and returned to the catalogue.

When Wilcox returned, he came to the library and apologized for being so late. Startled, I looked at my watch and saw that it was past eight o'clock.

Wilcox laughed, not pleasantly to my ear. "Same old Booth. Come on and eat."

I went to turn the lamp off before I followed him, and the paper on the desk caught my eye. "Oh! I found this under the desk."

I handed it to him. He glanced at it, said, "More of Uncle Loosh's nonsense, looks like to me. Thanks." He stuffed it in his pocket, and we left the room.

Dinner consisted of sandwiches and soup. Wilcox was restless, fidgeting even as he ate, getting up periodically to stride over to the windows and stare out at the darkness. Finally, I said, "Is something the matter?"

"I'm having those damn trees down tomorrow!"

"Oh," I said, not usefully.

"I'm sorry. They get on my nerves, and it seems like every time I turn around, there's Flood telling me how much Uncle Loosh loved the hollies. All the more reason they should go."

"There was, er . . . there was something about them on that paper I found."

He raised his eyebrows in a disagreeable sneer, but did not comment.

"It looks like . . . however he thought he was going to, er, cheat death, it looks like the hollies . . . "

Wilcox stared at me, his brows drawing down in an ugly, brooding expression. Then, all at once, he burst out laughing. "My God, Booth, don't tell me you believe in that nonsense!"

I felt my face flood red; I could not answer him.

"I bet you do!" Wilcox hooted with laughter. "You're as crazy as Uncle Loosh!"

I stood up, said, "Good night, Wilcox," with what vestiges of dignity I could, and walked out of the room. I would have liked to return to work in the library, but I was afraid Wilcox would find me there. I went up to my bedroom and locked the door. I could leave tomorrow afternoon—maybe even tomorrow morning. I could ask Flood about trains before breakfast.

I did not expect to sleep at all, but I changed into my pajamas and climbed into bed. If nothing else, I could read comfortably. About half an hour later, I heard Wilcox come upstairs. His footsteps stopped outside my door, but he did not knock or speak. I was just as glad.

I read long enough to quiet my nerves. When I looked at the clock, it was five minutes past midnight, and the house was perfectly still. No one would notice or care if I went back down to the library for a couple of hours. I would feel better about leaving—less like I was running away—if I had at least completed the task Wilcox had asked me here to perform.

I got up, put my book carefully back in my valise, and put on my dressing gown, already rehearsing my story should I run into Flood or Wilcox. I needed something to read—what better reason to be found creeping downstairs to the library in the middle of the night?

But the house might as well have been deserted, for all the signs of life it showed. I made it to the library without incident and shut the doors carefully behind me before I turned on the light. In that single moment of darkness, I suffered the horrible conviction that there was someone sitting behind the desk, but when I turned on the light, no one was there.

I worked peacefully for almost five hours, slowly restoring order to the chaos of Mr. Preston Wilcox's library. The darkness beyond the windows was softening to gray, the sun's first rays reaching up above the brooding hollies, when I pulled a book out of the lowest shelf of the bookcase behind the desk and with it fell a second book, which flipped itself open to its title page.

I stared at that second book for a long time, perfectly still, just as I would have stared at a tarantula that might or might not have been dead. The book was not listed in Mr. Preston Wilcox's catalogue. I had only ever seen a copy once before. But now I knew why those notes referring to "the Guide" and "the Vessel" had looked familiar. It was *The Book of Whispers*—not the nineteenth-century fake, but the genuine edition from 1605. I could not bring myself to touch it.

And while I was standing there, staring at that small, fragile volume, I heard Wilcox coming down the stairs. I clutched my dressing gown closed at the neck. I could not let him see me like this: in my pajamas with my hair uncombed and my face stubbled. He would never believe me then, and the matter had suddenly become much larger than our enmity, preserved like an ant in amber, and my wounded pride.

Then I thought, He'll go in to breakfast. I can get upstairs and get decent without him seeing me.

At the same moment at which I remembered it was only a quarter after five, far too early for breakfast, I heard the front door slam. I knew then, and the knowledge made me cold. He intended to have those hollies down today; he was going out to look at them, to plan his attack.

I had seen *The Book of Whispers*; I knew what was waiting for him among the holly trees.

"Wilcox!" I shouted uselessly and plunged for the door.

The door would not open. I tugged and rattled, but the latch stayed jammed. The first part of my dream from Friday night came back; I remembered the old man saying, "Stay in the library."

But whether I liked Wilcox or not, I could not leave him to his fate, to the terrible thing Lucius Preston Wilcox intended.

"Flood!" I shouted and then caught myself; Flood had his own role to play among the holly trees. I shouted for the housekeeper instead, Mrs. Grant, and pounded on the door in between my frantic assaults on the doorknob. I could feel the old man's black eyes watching me from behind the desk. I did not turn around, afraid that I would find the feeling to be more than just nerves.

The library was not far from the kitchen, and Mrs. Grant got up at dawn to bake the day's bread. Although it felt like hours, it was no more than ten minutes—maybe only five—before I heard her on the other side of the door, saying, "What on Earth—?"

"The door's stuck!"

"Stuck? It's never been stuck before."

For her, the door swung smoothly open. I wasted no time in explanations, apologies, or curses, but bolted past her. The front door did not resist me; I threw it open just in time to see Wilcox disappear into the close-serried ranks of holly.

"Wilcox!" I shouted and started running.

I lost both my carpet slippers within ten feet, but ran on regardless. Stones and sticks and shed holly leaves hurt my feet, but there was still a chance. If I could get to the hollies, get Wilcox out of the hollies . . .

I reached the trees, ducked between them as Wilcox had, and came face to face with Flood.

"Where's Mr. Wilcox?"

"Mr. Wilcox has met with an accident," he said smoothly, well-rehearsed, "but I think—"

"Let it go, Flood."

Those smooth, perfect pebbles stared at me.

"Let him go."

"I don't understand you, Mr. Booth."

"You're the Guide, aren't you? And poor Wilcox is the Vessel. I found the book."

His face twisted; I remembered how he had stood in the doorway of the library, refusing to come in. And I remembered the carvings on the library doors; that thing I had taken for a box could just as easily be a book. I wondered, distractedly, my hackles rising, just what Flood had been before Mr. Preston Wilcox had used the book to command him.

"I'm sorry, Mr. Booth," he said. "I think you misunderstood me. Mr. Wilcox—"

"What on Earth are you doing out here, Booth?"

I whipped around, my heart hammering in my throat. Wilcox was approaching through the trees.

"Wilcox?" I said weakly.

"Good God, man, you look like you've seen a ghost. What's the matter?"

"N-nothing." I could not stop staring at him, his ruddy face and aggressively square body, his rumpled hair and— "What happened to your hand?"

Flood said, "I was trying to tell you, Mr. Booth. Mr. Wilcox met with an accident."

"Bumping around like a bull in a china shop," Wilcox said cheerfully. "Fell over and bashed my hand on some damn rock. I was just going back to the house for some Mercurochrome. Come on, and we'll get Mrs. Grant to make you some tea."

"All right," I said, numb and bewildered, and we started back toward Hollyhill. I could feel embarrassment rising, washing over me like a tide. "I'm done in the library, and I, er . . . that is, is there a morning train?"

"Ten o'clock," Wilcox said. "Capital work, old man. I'll have Flood drive you. Oh, and Flood!"

As he glanced over his shoulder at Flood, I saw his eyes plainly in the clarifying dawn light. They were Wilcox's little, sandy-lashed eyes, but surely Wilcox's eyes had been hazel, not that obsidian-hard black.

"Tell the men not to bother about the hollies," Wilcox said. "They're starting to grow on me."

I left by the ten o'clock train. Flood and I said nothing to each other. What could we say? We both knew what had happened; we both knew that no one would believe me if I tried to tell them the truth, and even if I were believed, there was nothing that anyone could do. After he let me out at the station, I saw him hiss at me like a cat through the windshield before the car pulled away.

I have not heard from Wilcox since.

The Midbury Lake Incident

—⁓—

Kristine Kathryn Rusch

Mary Beth Wilkins had the most perfect library, until one day, in the middle of June, the library burned down.

She arrived at the two-hundred-year-old structure to find the roof collapsed, the walls blackened, and the books . . . well, let's just say the books were gone, floating away in the clouds of smoke that darkened the early morning sky.

No one had called her, even though she had always thought of the Midbury Lake Public Library as her library. She was the only librarian, and even though she didn't own the building—the Town of Midbury Lake did—she treated it like her own, defended it like a precious child, and managed to find funding, even in the dark years of dwindling government support.

She sat in her ancient Subaru, too shocked to move, not just because the firefighters were still poking out of the smoking building as if they were posing for the cover of next year's Fire Fighters Calendar, but because of all of the emotions that rose within her.

Grief wasn't one of them. Grief would come, she knew. Grief always came, whether you wanted it or not. She had learned that in her previous life—a much more adventurous life, a life *lived*, her mother would say (and why, *why* was she thinking of her mother? Mary Beth had banned thoughts of her mother for nearly ten years). No one could avoid grief, but grief came in its own sweet time.

No, the dominant emotion she was feeling was fury. Fury that no one had called her. Fury that the library—her sanctuary—was gone. Fury that her day— her life—had been utterly destroyed.

She gripped the leather cover she had placed on the Subaru's steering wheel, so that her hands would never touch metal or hard plastic, and she made herself take a deep breath.

Her routines were shattered. Every morning she arrived before six, made coffee, put out the fresh-baked donuts whose tantalizing aroma was, even now, wafting out of the back seat.

Her assistant, Lynda Sue, would arrive shortly, and then Mary Beth would have to comfort her, since Lynda Sue was prone to dramatics—she had been a theatah majah once, you knoow, deah—and then it would become all about Lynda Sue and the Patrons and the Library and the Funding, and oh, dear, Mary Beth would find herself in the middle of a mainstream maelstrom.

Too many emotions, including her own.

She had made a serious mistake, because her morning routine hadn't been in her control. That meditative hour, before anyone arrived, would happen at the library, in what everyone called the Great Room, which was—had been—a wall of windows overlooking Midbury Lake and the hills beyond.

Midbury Lake changed with the seasons and sometimes, Mary Beth thought, with her moods. This morning, the lake itself seemed to be ablaze, the reds and oranges reflecting on the rippling water.

Then she realized that the colors were coming from the sunrise, not from the fire at the library, and she bowed her head.

When she opened the car door, a new phase of her life would begin, and she would have to make choices.

It had been so nice not to make choices any more.

It had been wonderful to be Mary Beth Wilkins, small town librarian.

She would miss Mary Beth.

She could never rebuild Mary Beth.

She would have to become someone new, and becoming someone new always took way too much work.

She drove back to her apartment, and parked near the secluded wooded area near the two-story block-long building. She often parked there—at least she had kept up that old habit—and knew all the ways to the building's back entrance that couldn't be seen from the street.

Then she glanced over the back seat of the car. The donuts. That little incompetent clerk at the local donut shop probably wouldn't remember her, and as usual, Mary Beth had paid cash. She hoped if anyone saw her, they would think they'd seen her earlier than they had or maybe they would confuse the days.

She hoped. Because she had stopped thinking defensively three years ago. Somehow, she had thought Midbury Lake was too remote, too obscure, too off-the-beaten path for anyone to find her.

Better yet, she had thought no one remembered her. She had done everything she could to scour herself from the records, and she hadn't used magic in what seemed like forever, so she wouldn't leave a trail.

The donut aroma was too much for her, or maybe she had just become one of those middle-aged women who ate whenever they were stressed. She didn't care. She reached into the back seat, nudged up the top of the donut box, and took a donut, covering her fingers with granules of sugar.

She couldn't fix the library, not without someone noticing.

She bit into the donut, savoring the mix of sugar and grease and soft, perfect cake. She would miss these donuts. They were special.

At least she had already picked a new name. She needed to adopt it. Not Mary Beth Wilkins any longer. Now, Victoria Dowspot. Her identification for the new identity was in the apartment. She should have been carrying it. Yet another mistake.

She also should have been practicing the name in her own mind. She hadn't done that either. Victoria. Victoria Marie Dowspot.

Another librarian. The kind of single middle-aged woman no one noticed, even, apparently, when her library burned.

She swallowed the fury. That was Mary Beth's fury, not Victoria's. She needed to keep that in mind.

Victoria finished the donut, wiped the sugar off her mouth, then sighed. The donuts, comfortable in their box, were just one symbol of all she had to do, how lax she had become.

She stepped out of the Subaru, then pulled out the donut box, and put it in the trunk. No one would accidentally see them there. And there was nothing else in the car that would directly tie it to her, at least from the perspective of someone who didn't know her.

She had learned, three identities ago, to be as cautious about strange little details as possible. Too bad she had gotten so relaxed here in Midbury Lake. She had already made half a dozen mistakes.

She hoped they weren't fatal.

She snuck up the back stairs, stepping around the creaks and groans, and quietly turned the key in her apartment door's deadbolt. She pushed the door open and slipped inside. Magoo greeted her, concern on his feline face. He was a big orange male, battered when she found him, or, rather, when he found her.

He had lived through two different identity changes, the only consistent part of her life. She always thanked the universe that librarians and cats went together like hands and gloves. No one thought anything of a librarian who had cat.

Victoria was just glad she hadn't brought him to the library of late. That had actually been his idea. He hadn't liked one of the new patrons, a middle-aged man with an overloaded face—big forehead, small piggy eyes, heavy cheekbones.

She hadn't like him either, but unlike Magoo, she couldn't bail on her job.

Until today, that is. And she would bail because they would think her dead in that fire.

She just had to do a few things first.

She had a go-bag in the van she kept in the apartment's parking area. She paid for the extra space, telling the management the van belonged to her cousin, whom she'd pretended to be more than once. She would use that disguise again today, after she grabbed some food and water for Magoo. Everything else would stay here.

She wouldn't mind leaving this apartment. It was dark, especially in the winter, but it was heavily soundproofed and, unlike the library, made of stone.

Magoo looked at her, his tail drooping. He knew. He hated what was going to come next, but at least he didn't run away from her.

She scooped him under one arm and put him in the special cat carrier she had made. It was solid on the inside, but on the outside, it looked like a canvas carryall. And she had spelled it so no one could see a cat inside.

Magoo made one soft sound of protest, but he went in willingly enough. She put one bag of his dry food in her real carryall, along with two extra cans of his wet food. Then she grabbed two of his toys, the ones he played with the most, and packed them as well.

Her eyes filled with tears as she looked at the remaining cat toys, scattered on the hard wood floor. The toys were battered and well-loved, and she had to leave them behind.

Funny, how the emotion rose over Magoo's things, and not her own. She had worked on staying unattached for so long that she didn't mind leaving her possessions behind. She minded leaving his.

She stood. She had hoped she could stay in Midbury Lake. After so many years, she had thought she could. But she should have known that disaster would follow her.

It always did.

She made herself take a deep breath, then ran a hand over her forehead. She went into the bedroom, smoothed the coverlet on the bed because she didn't want anyone to think she was a slob, not that it mattered. It wasn't her after all; it was Mary Beth.

Then she peered out the bedroom window, with its view of the parking lot. She couldn't see the Subaru, but the van looked just fine.

No one else stood in the lot either. So, it was now or never.

She clenched a fist and focused her ears on the Subaru. Then she slid her right fingernails along her thumb, mimicking the slow opening of a trunk lid. She heard it unlock, and squeal open.

For the first time, she was happy she had never used rust remover. Sometimes it was the little things that allowed success.

Always, it was the little things.

Then she scooped her left hand downward. She could feel the donut box, even though it was far away. She levitated it, seeing it in her mind's eye, and waited until it was over the trees before igniting it. Then she sent it to the library, as fast as the breeze could take it.

If anyone saw the burning box, they'd think it sparks or debris from the library fire, or a figment of their imaginations.

The box arrived, and she lowered it into one of the still burning sections, careful to keep it away from firefighters.

Then she closed the trunk lid, and leaned on the window sill.

Her heart was pounding as if she had run five miles. She had trouble catching her breath. Sweat dripped from her forehead.

She was out of practice on everything, and that wasn't good. She really had become complacent.

And she still had some magic to go before she could quit.

She wiped off her forehead with the back of her hand, then crouched beside the bed. She removed a locked box with her many identities and two dental models of her mouth.

Her hand was shaking as she removed one of the dental models. This was the tricky spell, and she was tired from the easy one. She had to make real human teeth out of one of the models. Then she had to send it to the library, and lower it into one of the still burning sections. If there were still-burning sections.

She had been moving awfully slowly.

She grabbed the glass of water beside her bed. The glass was smudged. Magoo had probably stuck his little face in it, just so he could touch the water with his tongue.

Even so, she needed the refreshment, so she drank. The water was warm and stale, and she thought she could taste cat saliva. Probably her overactive imagination.

She drank the entire glass, then set it down, and squared her shoulders. She held the dental model, squinched her eyes closed, and imagined it as bone, yellowed with age and tarnished with plaque.

She opened her eyes. She was now holding a mandible instead of a model. It actually looked like someone had ripped teeth from her mouth.

She shuddered just a little, opened the window six inches and stuck her hand—and the teeth—outside. Then she sent them to the burning library.

Her mind's eye showed her that one section still burned. She lowered the teeth there, snapped the mandible in half, and let it fall. It didn't matter if it hit someone. They wouldn't know what it was. They would think it was just debris.

She shut off her mind's eye for the second time, leaned back, and felt her legs wobble.

If only she could sit for twenty minutes. But she couldn't. She had to get out of here before someone remembered her, before someone decided to check up on her.

That fury rose a third time—no one was thinking of her at *all*—and then she remembered that it played to her advantage.

She wiped a shaking hand over her forehead, and turned around.

That hideous man with the overloaded face was standing in the doorway, holding Magoo with one hand. If anything, the man looked even more menacing than he had in the library.

And Magoo seemed remarkably calm. He hated being held without having someone support his back feet.

And he hated this man.

She held her position, as if she were frozen in fear. Her heart was pounding too hard. She hated it when someone snuck up on her, but that was her fault. She hadn't retuned her ears.

Even when she was trying not to be careless, she was being very careless indeed.

"Making your escape?" the man asked. "You're a little slow this time, Darcy, aren't you? Complacent. It trips up escapees every single time."

Her heart pounded harder. He used her real name. She stared at Magoo, whose ears were flat.

Then she made herself swallow against a dry throat.

"Put him down," she said, careful not to use Magoo's name. She didn't even have to work at making her voice quaver. "He didn't do anything."

"True enough," the man said. "He isn't even a real familiar. And even though he's lived in close proximity to you for—what? a year?—your magic hasn't rubbed off on him."

The caveman's numbers were wrong. She wasn't sure if that was deliberate. She wasn't sure if he had said that to get her to correct him. She wasn't going to correct him.

Because Magoo *was* a familiar, but she had cloaked him long ago. And he had clearly practiced his itty bitty magic more than she had. He had made a doppel-gänger, and that doppelgänger was at least a year old. How often had Magoo used that doppelgänger with her, so that he could do whatever it was he did when he didn't want her to catch him? Enough so that this doppelgänger had some heft and a tiny bit of catlike life.

Good for Magoo, sending the doppelgänger out when he heard the caveman come through the door.

Or was the creature that the man held actually Magoo?

Her heart rate spiked.

She was going to have to use her mind's eye to check, which meant magic, which meant even more doors opening, more people coming for her. Those tears pricked her eyes again.

"What do you want?" she asked the man, even though she knew.

"We need you back in Alexandria," he said.

How many times had she heard that answer in her nightmares? And for how many years? Ever since she had inherited the library. The *real* library and all of its knowledge, once thought lost.

Her stomach twisted. "And if I don't go?"

He raised Magoo—or the Magoo doppelgänger—and shook him slightly. The cat made a mew of protest. Unless the man had magicked Magoo, that really was the doppelgänger. The actual Magoo would've bitten the man's fingers off.

"Do you really want to test it?" the man asked.

She clenched her fists. No, she didn't want to test it. And no, she didn't want to deal with the man either, because that would mean fire, and if she somehow set this place on fire, and the library was already burning, then that would draw attention to Mary Beth Wilkins, and Darcy (no, Victoria. She had to think of herself as Victoria) didn't want any attention ever falling on Mary Beth.

"What do you get paid if you bring me to Alexandria?" she asked, not willing to say, *Bring me back*, because that would imply that she had left, and in actuality, she had never been to Alexandria. The library had. The library was born there, and parts of the library died there. Her ancestors managed to save some of it— much of it—during the four different times it burned.

But they had learned to never, ever put the books back on the shelves, because doing so brought out men like this one. And sometimes started fires.

She took a deep silent breath, then flashed her mind's eye for a half second, looking past the man, seeing what his powers were, and seeing if that creature he held was the real Magoo.

The man had less power than he thought he did, and the creature wasn't Magoo. Magoo was crouching motionlessly in his carryall.

She retracted her mind's eye, but the man had noticed.

So she stood taller, and let her power thread up. Without planning it, she extended one hand and sent a ball of flame to the man so quickly that he didn't have time to scream before it engulfed him.

His mouth opened, then his face melted as his entire body incinerated.

She stopped the fire before it destroyed him completely. The stench of burning meat and grease filled the air.

Magoo sneezed.

The man's body had toppled to the hardwood floor, and the flames had left a serious scorch mark. She walked over to the body, and poked it with her foot.

She had needed a body. Actually having one would be so much better than those stupid teeth had been.

She bent over him, and separated the top of the skull from the jawbone. She left the top of the skull to float just above the body. Then she removed some small bones from the feet and the hands, not enough to show that the hands were bigger than hers, but enough to show that the hands were human. She took a small portion of a rib as well.

She compiled them into a little ball, covered them with a cloak, and sent them, still steaming, through the still-open window. She monitored them as she sent them to the library, and let them tumble into the section where she had sent the teeth.

Then she uncloaked them. Their steam mixed with the smoke of the still-smoldering section.

She shut off her mind's eye and took a shuddering breath, then wished she hadn't. It tasted foul, like rotting meat. She licked her lips.

Her neighbors would notice that odor.

She used the last of her energy to cremate the remains into little bits of nothing, careful to contain the fire. Then she put it all out, staggered into her kitchen, and took out a broom and dustpan. She swept up the ash, and dumped it into the toilet in small sections, flushing several times so that it wouldn't clog up the system.

By the time she was done, she was woozy with exhaustion. She hadn't used that much magical power in years and years. And using it had opened the door to more interlopers like the man who had just died.

She ran a hand through her hair and looked in the mirror. Shadows under her eyes, and a face smudged with ash. She washed off her skin, then staggered into the kitchen and drank an ancient bottle of Ice Blue Gatorade. It helped, a little.

In the living room, Magoo mewed. It was probably a get-me-out-of-here mew, but she took it as a move-your-ass mew. Because she had to.

She really had been careless. Not just here, but at the Midbury Lake Public Library.

That fire. It had to be her fault. Not because she set it, but because she hadn't monitored the books. With all the interest in the history of the ancient world these days, particularly the history of religion as it pertained to modern times, someone had probably ordered a book through interlibrary loan that she hadn't seen.

A paper book, one that shouldn't be on the shelf of an library where she worked. A paper book about paganism or magic spells or showing ancient scrolls. The kind of book that had actually been in the Library of Alexandria in its heyday or in the Serapeum just before it was destroyed.

The kind of book stored inside her memory, in a locked area, where she couldn't touch it. Like the women before her, all of them, from the same family. She likened that locked area to a computer chip. It contained knowledge and power, but only tapped that knowledge and power when something demanded them.

She had put herself in a position where nothing would tap the knowledge, or she thought she had. But she hadn't done enough. She should have kept an active inventory on the books that her family guarded. She hadn't, and it had caused this.

Because, whenever one of the old books hit a shelf, or a facsimile of one of the old books hit a shelf near a library repositorian (like her), the ancient spells revived, the ones that had actually destroyed the library. If the books from the Library of Alexandria reappeared on shelves, those shelves were supposed to burn.

Her family, one of the sixteen ancient families that guarded the library's knowledge, had never been able to counter those spells. Her grandmother had died trying, so her mother simply avoided libraries, bookstores, and any other place where books gathered.

Darcy had embraced libraries, but she had been cautious.

Not cautious enough though, since that horrid man had found her. And she had destroyed her favorite little library by not monitoring what crossed its shelves.

She went back into the living room. The carryall was inching its way across the floor. Apparently Magoo had had enough.

She crouched beside him and put her hand on his back through the soft side of the carryall.

"I'm sorry," she said. "We still have to go."

Before someone caught her again. Before someone took her back to Alexandria. Before someone tried to take that chip of library knowledge out of her brain, and destroy it entirely. Or, worse in her opinion, tried to revive it all at once, and use it for the wrong purpose—whatever that purpose might be.

She put on the wig and hoodie that marked her as Mary Beth's cousin, then grabbed both carryalls and walked to the door. The apartment still smelled faintly of greasy meat, and there was a lingering bit of smoke.

That was on her. It was always on her.

The magic inside her wasn't her own. It wasn't even the library's. It was an ancient evil spell, designed to destroy the very things she loved.

Books.

Maybe the next time she stopped somewhere, she wouldn't become a librarian. Maybe she would run a movie theater or open a donut shop. Or maybe she would spend her days in genteel poverty, sitting in a coffee shop and watching the world go by.

She had a lot of time to think about it, and a long way to drive. Where to, she didn't know. She would wait until she deemed herself as far from this place as possible, in a location that seemed as far from Alexandria as possible.

Then she let herself out and walked down the stairs, quietly, so as not to disturb the neighbors, who were already gathering around the front of the building. She could hear the conversation: they thought the stench was coming from the burning library.

Let them.

People always misunderstood why libraries burned. They blamed old paper or faulty wiring. They never blamed the ignorant, who deemed some knowledge worthy and some too frightening to know.

She wished she could defend that knowledge, but all she could do was protect it, and hold it, until someone else came up with a solution. And when the time came, she would pass that little kernel on to some other member of her family, who would adopt the burden and treasure it.

Like she had adopted Magoo.

"Come on, kiddo," she said to him as they headed to the van. "Adventures await."

And she hoped those adventures would be of the gentle, placid kind. Like summer mornings staring at a still Midbury Lake.

One could always hope. Because hope was what kept the bits of the library alive. Hope that one day the spells would lift, one day the library would be reunited, and one day the books would return to the shelves.

And she would never ever have to grieve again.

With Tales in Their Teeth, from the Mountain They Came

A.C. Wise

She woke with the words *I love you* on her tongue, speaking them aloud to an empty room.

They tasted of smoke and ash drifting over a far-distant, muddy field. The War that had taken her lover had lost him. She knew he was dead, because she'd never spoken the words aloud before.

He'd whispered them in her ear countless times—lying side-by-side in the furrows of their sheets, offered on summer days, spoken in the midst of roof-drumming rainstorms keeping her from her dreams. She'd smiled in return, meaning to answer every time. But she found her teeth locked, her lips stitched closed. He would squeeze her hand, echo her smile with sad patience, and say, *Some day. When you're ready.*

Ten years passed in a single, conjoined heartbeat. Then news came from beyond the Mountain. The papers were full of men and women dying in rain-battered fields. Her lover read them, and every day carved deeper lines around his mouth, and between his eyes.

Over breakfasts of buttered toast, his untouched, he read to her of mud-spattered corpses, of bright poppies trampled beneath heavy-soled boots, and children crushed the same way, until their skin no longer hid their bones. He read of mass graves, of torture, and atrocities, and leaving grew in his eyes. When she wanted to ask him to stay, fear once more stitched her lips closed.

She held him as long as she could in their house by the sea. But hands pressed to his skin, and stubborn lips and teeth refusing to shape words, could only hold him so long. His love was vast; it encompassed strangers, dying in fields he'd never seen. He went to War. Her love was small, and encompassed only him. She stayed behind.

I love you.

Now she could say the words until her throat bled with them; he would never hear.

Moonlight streamed through the window, illuminating soft-rumpled sheets. She wrapped arms around her body, surveying furniture and knick-knacks that would never mean as much, absent of his hands. She retraced his footsteps; she fit the whorls of her fingertips into the ghost of his touch.

There was nothing to hold her here anymore. No hands pressed to her skin, no words waited to be spoken.

She packed, and left at dawn. The absence of words had lost him, but there was a place she'd heard of in tales where she could drown herself in them. Abandoning the house by the sea, she set out for the Library on the Mountain.

The librarians shaved her head. They called her acolyte. They gave her a new name, Alba, which they told her meant dawn. And they assigned her the duty of dusting and caring for the books in the Main Hall.

She never saw the librarians, only their shapes, buried in deep-hooded robes the color of the sky just before sunrise. They wrote words on slips of paper, and dropped them into her hands. Their instructions given, the librarians hid their fingers in their voluminous sleeves again, and turned away.

"Wait!" Alba called after them.

The word echoed, vast and terrible, shocking the Library's silence. She put a hand over her mouth, expecting a hood to drop, baleful eyes to fix her, and a hand to point her back the way she'd come. Instead, a single finger emerged, brief, thin, and pressed to invisible lips inside a hood.

"Shh."

Footsteps made arcane patterns in the dust. The Librarians withdrew, leaving her alone.

Alba memorized the librarians' slips of paper—directions to the Main Hall, to a small cell she could call her own, to the Refectory where acolytes and novices took their meals. There were other scraps, telling her where she could and could not go. Acolytes were not allowed beyond the Main Hall, the Primary Stacks, or the First Archives. The Reading Rooms, the Second Archives, the Restricted Section, and the Vaults, were for novices, apprentices, and librarians alone.

"Why?" Alba asked her neighbor at one meal.

The dour man, his skin the color of his porridge, glared at her with sunken eyes. He snatched his bowl, and scuttled away, as though Alba's single word bore the seeds of a plague to infect the Library's stillness and bring it crashing down. After that meal, Alba never saw him again.

Alba tried to be content with what she was allowed; after all, it wasn't without wonder. The Main Hall was vast, filled with floor to ceiling shelves, wooden leviathans lit by tall, narrow windows. They held volumes, packed tight, their spines of every color and texture—cloth-bound, leather-bound, and clapped between boards of thin wood tied with rough twine.

Alba dusted, striving to lose herself in repetitive motion, telling herself it was everything she could desire. Still, when she paused to wipe sweat from her brow, she would remember the particular scent of her lover, like sharp spice and incense. She would feel his shirt—heat-damp from a day in the garden—as he put his arms around her. When she ran a hand over the stubble of her hair, she would remember the back of his neck, fresh from a haircut. Once, when she bit her tongue, she remembered the way his would flick out between his teeth at the beginning of a laugh.

Ten years, and never once, and always, always, his patient response: *When you're ready.*

She counted books, making her own patterns regardless of the librarians' arcane system. She used dust to stop tears. Trailing her fingers across the alternating textures and shades, Alba came to know the books, *her* books—calf-skin green from linen mauve. Day in and day out, she greeted them as old friends.

And for a while, Alba *was* content. Until one of her books went missing.

Perhaps she'd miscounted? But, no, more books disappeared each day. The loss tugged at her. She'd come here to sate herself on words, and now they piled up behind her teeth, question on question. This last, the question of where her books had gone, broke the dam.

At the long Refectory tables, scattered with multi-hued light from the stained glass windows, Alba leaned close to the nearest Acolyte. "Have you noticed books missing?"

After so long in silence, the words scraped her throat, but it was a relief to speak. Not even the horror in her dining companion's eyes could make her regret it.

"No." The Acolyte pressed his lips tight, returning to his porridge to contemplate the transit of his spoon around the circumference of his bowl.

"Who understands librarians?" Another Acolyte said; it was the longest reply Alba received.

Mostly the acolytes and novices cast their eyes down, and pretended they hadn't heard. Frustrated, Alba pushed away from the table, leaving her meal half-finished. She glared at the assembled novices and acolytes. Didn't they understand War raged on the other side of the mountain? Hadn't they lost loved ones, too?

She wanted to shout, wanted to shake the Library's foundations, and felt a hypocrite for even thinking it. What right did she have to call words to her defense now? Alba turned on her heel, and stalked away. At the Refectory door, a woman, a novice by the particular gray of her robe—smoke, rather than dust, as Alba's, or pre-dawn light, as the Librarians—stopped her.

The novice's fingers touched the bones of Alba's wrist just below her sleeve. Her lips emitted the barest whisper.

Alba leaned close, "What?"

The novices had perfected the trick of not moving their lips when they spoke. The apprentices, as Alba understood it, were worse, with a system of code tapped on errant desks and shelves, mouse-foot soft. The librarians had their scrolls.

"What?" she said again.

She spoke louder this time, reveling in the sound, and the pained look it drew from the Novice's face. She knew the price of silence, and they would, too.

"Come." The novice jerked her head, a frightened fish, startled by a diver cutting the deep.

The novice's fingers withdrew from Alba's skin, and Alba regretted the harshness of her word. The novice tucked her hands into her sleeves, making a seamless continuum of smoke-gray cloth. She led Alba past the First Archives and the Primary Stacks.

At a plain, wooden door, the novice put a finger to her lips. Alba's tongue stuck to the roof of her mouth; she couldn't have spoken if she had wanted to. The door opened on a garden.

In the middle of winter mountains, no snow touched delicate branches heavy with blossom and slick, green leaves. Birds, jewel-bright, stitched the air above the courtyard, silent as the rest of the Library. The air smelled of honey-suckle.

"One day, the Library will burn," the Novice said.

Her voice was hoarse, as though she hadn't used it in years. She caught Alba's hands, a touch in place of a plea, and closed her lips tight over her teeth. Alba looked at the long fingers holding hers, and the wrists, almost visible beneath the sleeves. The novice snatched her hands back, hiding them in smoke-gray again.

"I don't understand," Alba said.

"The Library. It will burn. The Library always burns."

With a tilt of her head, the novice indicated a bench. They sat.

"Can I trust you?" The novice glanced at Alba side-wise.

Like a thaw, Alba heard the melt in the novice's voice. How many years of silence had she borne? Alba's pulse thudded, the beat of her heart reaching toward this woman, so afraid of words.

"Don't you want to know my name, first?" Alba tried a smile.

"Eleuthere," the novice said.

"Alba." Alba touched the novice's hand, warm skin against warm skin.

"You asked about the books," Eleuthere said.

She ducked when she spoke. It was more than fear of words. The novice hid her hands, and kept her lips over her teeth, everything about her careful. It wasn't the care of fear, though; it was the care of a woman holding eggshells in her hands, not wanting to break them.

"The Librarians steal the books to save them." Eleuthere raised her sleeve. Black text, tiny and dense, crowded her skin up to her elbow.

"I found out what the Librarians were doing, and asked them to use me. I wasn't supposed to tell."

Alba touched a finger to the words. They shivered, a tiny storm beneath her touch.

"What is it?" she asked.

"The Fifth Song of Solomon. It's a book." Eleuthere lowered her sleeve. "They're all books, the Librarians. They're making me one, too. The Library will burn, but this way, the books will go on."

Since arriving here, Alba hadn't heard so many words, piled one on top of each other. Lightning traced her veins.

"Who would burn a Library?"

"Soldiers." Eleuthere lowered her gaze, ducking her head again.

The word thudded against Alba's heart. Her lover, the scent of him, his hands rattling the paper as he read to her the latest horrors of the war. Alba realized she was standing when Eleuthere spoke, standing, too.

"I've upset you, I'm sorry."

"You didn't." Alba shook her head, wishing for dust now against rising tears.

Eleuthere reached for her shoulder, but Alba stepped out from under it. "I have to go."

Her footsteps clattered, clumsy and un-schooled to silence. She ran, paused at the door, and glanced over her shoulder at her.

Words piled up, but once again her lips stitched themselves closed.

I'm sorry.

Such a simple phrase, but it turned her tongue to lead. Eleuthere opened her mouth, but Alba didn't dare wait to hear what she had to say.

Eyes stinging, she fled the garden.

Alba counted her sorrow with her books. She ran fingers over multi-colored spines; there were more missing every day. She breathed dust, and let it fill the corners of her eyes. Silence squeezed the breath from her lungs, and threatened to break her bones.

After three days, she sent a note to Eleuthere, passing it hand to hand along the Refectory table under the leaf-scatter light: *I'm sorry.*

She hoped Eleuthere would give her the chance to say it aloud. The panic that had sent her running from the garden had faded, and she felt foolish. Silence had cost her everything once. She needed words, needed to give them voice, and let them fill the raw corners of her being, leaving no room for regret.

Eleuthere came to her past dusk, past dust, pressing a hand flat to Alba's door. She didn't knock. Alba let her into the stone space just big enough to hold a narrow cot. There was nothing else, no mirror to show Alba how gray she'd become, taking on the Library's hues. There was only a high window, arched, and a fading candle wax-stuck to the sill.

"There's more," Eleuthere said.

She pressed her lips against her teeth. The now familiar gesture made Alba realize she'd never seen Eleuthere smile. Alba closed the door. She sat on the bed, leaving space for the novice. Eleuthere joined her; their knees touched, because there wasn't room for anything else.

"It's okay," Alba said. "It's safe here."

"I shouldn't have come." Eleuthere started to rise, but Alba caught her hands.

"Stay." She gripped bony, warm fingers, asking Eleuthere, asking her vanished lover.

Asking him not to go to war, asking the world not to change.

The tension left Eleuthere, and Alba freed one hand, pushing back Eleuthere's sleeve. She brushed the words with her thumb, reading of mermaids, damned sailors, and shipwrecks.

"There's more," Eleuthere said again.

Alba looked up, lips stilling on salty words. Echoes of bird-cry sounded in the stone room, chased by crashing waves. Sea-spray touched her cheek. Eleuthere skinned back her lips. There were minute words carved onto the novice's teeth.

"And more."

Eleuthere stood, and in a smooth motion, pulled smoke-gray robes over her head. She turned, revealing words on naked flesh—here a paragraph on her lower back, there a scroll around her ankle. A sestina spiraling around her breast, a hymn, trailing down her spine, all as full of taste, smell, sound, as the ocean written on her arm.

"It's beautiful." Alba breathed out.

"I wanted someone to know."

With a pained look in her eyes, Eleuthere reached for her robe. Alba caught her inked wrist. Words, so many words, one could never keep silent faced with them. Where Alba's fingers touched Eleuthere, her skin tingled. Alba traced the text with her gaze, following each line spiraling around Eleuthere's body until she reached the Novice's face.

There were words enough to fill the empty spaces, and chase the ache from between her bones. She met Eleuthere's eyes—black as ink. Eleuthere didn't pull away; Alba kissed her.

Her tongue traced teeth, gathering the tale of a witch who spent all winter stitching shapes out of skin, and by summer had three fine children. She trailed fingers down spine, learning a dozen names for god. Her palm sweat-slicked the skin on Eleuthere's lower back, and a poem about drowned children, and little black dogs, and yellow rain boots soaked through her.

Hungry. No, thirsty. She drowned.

She fixed ravenous lips to Eleuthere's skin. Tales, verse, song—the Library itself—pounded through her, filling her years of not speaking with words sounding of forgiveness.

Alba's bones reverberated—each rib a shelf, her skin vellum, her blood ink. It built inside her, shivering, humming, until she couldn't hold it in anymore, and it poured from her in perfect harmony. She sang the Library, sang with volume upon volume of soon-to-be-burned lore.

As the sun rose beyond the high, arched window, Alba laid her head in the hollow between Eleuthere's shoulder and throat, cheeks wet with tears. "We have to save the Library."

Alba took Eleuthere's hand to feel the song of words written on the novice's skin. It wasn't love; that word was gone and done for her. That word was too small, and there were other words to take its place.

"I want to go deeper," Alba said as they walked the Library's silent halls. "I want to find the librarians."

Eleuthere stopped, Alba's hand slipping from hers. In this light, Eleuthere's eyes were the same dust gray as her robe.

"Why?"

"They shouldn't keep this secret." Her fingers traced the words on Eleuthere's arm. "I want to help. If others knew, I'm sure they'd want to help, too."

Doubt moved like clouds through the Novice's eyes, but after a moment, she nodded. Whatever conviction had brought Eleuthere here, Alba saw a hint of it now, as the Novice straightened her spine.

"Here." She led Alba to a wooden door, arched like the one leading into the garden courtyard.

"Is there a key?" Alba asked.

Eleuthere made a sound, almost a sigh, reminding Alba of turning pages.

"Recite a verse."

A moment of panic seized her. Alba closed her eyes, and tasted Eleuthere's skin—not the salt of it, but an inky bitterness that made her think of deep sea creatures in lightless places, and stone ground so fine it became like water. The words flooded her tongue, her lips, and Alba spoke them to the lock.

She pushed open the door. Shadows crowded beyond the arch, and stairs went . . . Alba couldn't tell the direction. Vertigo swept her. She stood on the edge of a precipice, poised to fall; she stood at the base of a mountain, waiting to climb.

Alba put a foot on the first step, fighting the sensation of flying and falling. Eleuthere followed. The steps ended in a room as vast as the Main Hall. Light came from globes—starlight soft—drifting in mid-air, suspended from nothing.

Eleuthere touched Alba's arm, making her pause. Light caught in the novice's eyes, and traced the curve of her mouth. Both were unutterably sad. Eleuthere had forgotten to hide her hands in her sleeves. The words on her skin shone.

"Are you sure you want this?" The empty spaces took Eleuthere's voice, swallowing it.

Alba could see how years in the Library might take someone's voice completely. The words here, the words she'd gathered from Eleuthere's skin, they were too beautiful for all this silence.

"Why?" Alba said.

"You might not like what you see."

Alba brushed Eleuthere's arm. Words shivered beneath her palm. Alba imagined the pain of them, carved into the novice's flesh.

"Were you sure?" Alba asked.

Eleuthere shook her head. The ink of her eyes, dark again in the room's soft glow, seemed on the verge of spilling over.

"Are you sure now?"

Eleuthere looked down, lips pressed tight over her teeth, so Alba barely heard her words. "It's worth it."

Alba gripped the novice's hand. "Show me."

Eleuthere led her past shelves holding tablets, scrolls, past shelves of etched, delicate glass, and carved blocks of wood. Shadows piled behind and before them; they could never see more than one shelf ahead.

Alba resisted the urge to peer beyond the cluster of globes, searching the shadows for gray-robed Librarians, sleeping upside down like bats.

"How did you find this place?" Alba said.

She glanced at Eleuthere, sidelong. The globes turned the novice's head into a moonlit field of stubble.

"I got curious. I explored." Eleuthere shrugged.

The motion seemed designed to slip her from beneath Alba's gaze. More silence to regret—Alba had never asked what brought Eleuthere to the Library.

"When I found what the Librarians were doing, I asked them to make me like them."

"What exactly are they doing?" Alba hadn't taken her eyes from the Novice, watching her as they passed by shelf after shelf, deeper into twilight reaches. Something in Eleuthere's voice made her think there was more to the story than the novice had yet told.

"Saving the books." Eleuthere pointed. "Any way they can."

Alba stopped in her tracks, stopped her breath, and nearly her heart. Dead men and women, packed shoulder to shoulder, filled the shelves. They were naked, skin inked-dense. Their eyes were stitched closed, their mouths, too. There were words in the thread.

Some looked ancient, flesh cured as though by ages of desert sand. Others appeared fresh. If not for the stitches binding them, they might open their eyes. Alba's fingers slipped from Eleuthere's. She moved closer, wonder-caught, then her heart skittered, missing a beat.

Her lover. Her lover, gone and lost to the war. Her lover, with words inked onto his skin, crowded among the Library's dead.

His eyes were stitched closed, his hair shorn. Words covered his scalp, circled his throat, dripped down his chest and erased the memory of her palm resting over his heart. He'd become tome, volume. In death, he'd become the Library's lifeblood—flesh for paper, ink for bones.

"Alba!"

Eleuthere's voice was behind her, a million miles away. Alba had pulled away, running. She skidded to a halt, and stared open-mouthed at her lover. She expected his lips to part, breathe her name, or speak patient-sad as always.

One day. When you're ready.

Tears blurred her vision. Alba's palm slapped his feet, her foot finding the shelf below him. She climbed. Eleuthere's hand caught her ankle. Alba twisted around, kicking out as hard as she could. Eleuthere dodged the blow, and refused to let go.

"They killed him!"

"No." Eleuthere pulled; Alba slipped.

Her palms, slick with sweat, lost their grip, and she tumbled backward. Eleuthere broke her fall, and they both crashed to the ground in a tangle of limbs.

Alba struggled, trying to rise, climb to him again and rip the thread from his lips, kiss them, tell him she was sorry.

Eleuthere wrapped her arms around Alba, pinning her, grip unshakable.

"Stop." Eleuthere's lips next to Alba's ear stilled her.

She sagged in the Novice's arms, weeping. "They killed him."

"No, they collect the dead. The soldiers won't burn other soldier's bodies. They're afraid of vengeful ghosts. The Librarians bring them here, mark them as they mark themselves to keep the books safe."

Eleuthere rocked Alba as she spoke, smoothing prose-dense palms over Alba's scalp, her back, her trembling shoulders.

"We can't just leave him there. We have to get him down."

Alba's breath hitched. She couldn't draw in enough air. There wasn't enough space beside the grief, beside the guilt. She'd tried to fill herself with words, and it wasn't enough.

"Who was he?" Eleuthere asked.

"He ... I loved him."

The words ripped her open all over again, leaving the wound of him fresh and bleeding.

"He wouldn't burn a Library." Alba scrubbed tears from her eyes.

"War changes people." Eleuthere's etched teeth showed fierce in the globes' moon-colored light, her ink black eyes hard.

"You go to war for an ideal, an idea, and it breaks you. You come back a ghost, haunted, dreaming of flame. You come back sick, hating ideas. What are books but ideas? You start to believe if you burn them, it will stop the pain."

Alba stared at the novice. The ghost of flames lay deep in the blackest part of Eleuthere's eyes, ink-drowned, but still there. The novice lifted her sleeve, bringing the words on her wrist inches from Alba's face.

"There are scars under the ink," she said. "I came to the Library to burn it, years ago."

"You were a soldier."

"The books, the words, saved me."

"Show me how?" The words slipped, small and pleading into the space around them.

Eleuthere's gaze didn't waver. She lowered her sleeve, unpitying. "I already did."

Alba caught her breath. Words, singing through her skin, words filling her, burning her to ash, and building her anew. She tried to hold onto the sensation, tried to remember love was small, and these words were vast enough to swallow her whole.

Her heart tripped on memory, regret. She could scale the shelf, pull her lover down, run. She could hide deep in the mountains.

And live on what? Words never spoken?

The words here lived—shouted onto paper and skin, pressed into her bones with Eleuthere's hands, with her sweat, with her teeth and tongue. Alba's books in the Main Hall were crowded with words. Her dead lover was wrapped in them. They were worth speaking; they were worth saving.

"Show me again," Alba said.

The hardness in Eleuthere's eyes faded, the fire dimming to smoke again. The corner of her mouth lifted in a smile. She held out a hand, and Alba took it, enfolding herself in Eleuthere's arms. The novice's words sang against her skin.

There is a story they tell, of the day the Library burned, and the day the Library was born. An acolyte and a novice became librarians in the deepest, most secret reaches of the old Library. They returned from those reaches, dust-soaked, sweat-streaked, and shouted into the Library's silence. They shocked the old librarians' hoods from their heads, revealing ink dense skin.

"Look," they said. "Listen. We will tell you how to save the Library. No more secrets. No more silence. No more fear. These words are for everyone."

And so they wrote on skin. They carved in teeth. They inked burial shrouds, and mummy wrappings. Where flesh had decayed, they etched in bone. They scrawled on living flesh, too, recorded prose and poetry in the beat of heart and blood.

Not just librarians, but novices, apprentices, and acolytes. They gathered the living and dead, working feverishly, scorning sleep to breathe poetry, shout verse. They pulled books from the shelves—ancient scrolls, fat leather tomes, skinny cloth-bound volumes, and wooden panels. They piled them high in the Main Hall. They smashed glass globes and clay tablets, breathing in dust. It wasn't a funeral, but a wake; not a murder, but a celebration.

Hand in hand, inked skin to inked skin, the new head librarians stood by the pile they had made. Together, Alba and Eleuthere threw the first match. Not a holocaust, but a pyre—a joyous blaze sending the books spiraling up to the stars. Each librarian, novice, apprentice, and acolyte threw a match in turn. The books roared; they wept. They laughed. And they sang.

Words danced on sweat-slick skin and flashed from carved teeth. Shedding their robes, naked, the librarians, novices, apprentices, and acolytes, marched out into the snow, carrying the dead on their backs. Alba's lover lay draped across her shoulders, his legs bound around her waist, his arms about her chest in a last embrace. Eleuthere walked beside her, holding Alba's hand. The other denizens of the Library followed behind them.

Laughing, shouting, crying, singing, living and dead, they streamed down the Mountain to meet the soldiers climbing up with torches in their hands.

Wild and fierce, they were librarians all. Flame lit, they were beautiful. With the dead strapped to their backs, with love and madness in their eyes, they met the soldiers, who stopped, and stood aghast to find the Library already in flame.

The librarians, who were also books, who were a library of blood and skin and bones, embraced the stunned soldiers. They touched lip to lip, and breathed tales. They quieted ghosts with song, with fairy stories, with ancient histories, and new philosophies. They poured words from skin to skin; they crowded the empty spaces inside the war-haunted women and men until the ghosts had no choice but to flee.

They lay together in the snow, and their burning skin melted it around them. When the soldiers rose again, they were weeping, and laughing. They were Librarians, too. They joined the parade of mad women and men flowing down the mountain, carrying words, an unstoppable tide to drown in beauty the world.

That is the legend of the old Library, written in the stones of the new Library, built into the side of a cliff overlooking the sea. The halls there echo with the crash of waves. No one is forbidden to speak in the new Library. There is laughter. The words of the books lining the walls are shouted aloud—Alba and Eleuthere, the head librarians, encourage it.

The walls are white stone. The librarians' eyes and robes are sea-glass green. The pages of the books taste of salt. They taste of sweat and ink, printed on a lover's skin. Gathering words on the tongue, straight from the source, is encouraged here, too.

One day, men and women may come with torches in their hands to burn this Library down. But the books, the words, will go on and on.

WHAT BOOKS SURVIVE

Tansy Rayner Roberts

Books are the carriers of civilization. Without books, history is silent, literature is dumb, science is crippled, thought and speculation at a standstill. They are engines of change, windows on the world, lighthouses erected in the sea of time.—Barbara W. Tuchman.

My ~~Chronicle~~ ~~Diary~~ Historical Account of What Happened After The Invaders Came, by Katie Scarlett Marsden, Age 16? (and yes, that is a deliberate Adrian Mole reference, so there)

My brother Otis caught me, the first time I tried to sneak out through the barricade. I remember when he wasn't such a boy scout, but we're all different now.

"Don't be thick, tadpole," he said to me. I hated that nickname. It reminded me of the river we had lost; of the muddy, happy weekends before everything ended. "There's nothing out there any more."

"Nothing that you care about," I snapped, and went straight home so he would think he had won.

Everyone in town acted like the barricade was it; the thing that would save us from the invaders who had come crashing in from the skies. I guess it made them feel better. But how could the barricade be good when it cut us off from everyone and everything else?

Our family was lucky. At least our house was on the right side of the eight-foot wall they built of broken things and piled earth and dead cars. We didn't even have to take in guests from the abandoned houses, because there were already five of us: Mum, me, Otis, his girlfriend Frances, and the baby.

Everyone's so busy being frightened, pretending that the barricade will fix everything, that no one ever talks about what was left behind. The stuff that's smaller than houses and roads and the river, anyway. The really important stuff.

They talk about how sensible it was to keep the town hall, so we have a central point for meetings, and we can use that for the school too, when there aren't town meetings (our town likes meetings, twice a week—as good as the barricade for making people feel safe).

No one talks about the fact that when we built the barricade, drawing the line along Wharton Street and Mansfield Avenue, we didn't just leave the school on the other side, and half the shops, and the river.

We left the library.

My house is full of books that don't work. That's the worst thing about the invasion. Well, okay. Not the worst thing. But it's not like people were shot out of the sky, bodies lying in the street or anything like that. The invaders don't care about us, as long as we stay behind our walls.

Meanwhile, nothing electronic functions. Computers, TV, phones. Our shelves are full of DVD cases full of shiny silver discs we can't watch. Everyone's acting like the world we knew is going to come back any minute.

What if it doesn't come back? We have a dozen actual paper books in our house, and I've read all of them. Most people have less. When they drew those big red lines in the map, they thought about space to hold school lessons once things are back to normal, but no one thought about what they were going to hold lessons with. Slate and chalk? What happens when all the ink runs out of the biros?

Anyway. That's not my problem. Not like I'm trying for a uni place now.

I just want to read the second half of *Wuthering Heights*.

There was a scream. Three weeks ago. Not a person screaming. It was like the sky filled with scream, from edge to edge. I was lying on my bed with some stupid soap blaring at me, and music drilling into half my brain through a single earbud, with my Kindle resting against my knees. One more book to go. I'd figured, reading all the Brontës, that was an easy project for my class reading assignment. There were only three of them, right?

Should have guessed from the smirk on Ms. Hopkinson's face, what I was getting myself into. *The Tenant of Wildfell Hall* went okay, and then Jane Eyre basically kicked my arse six ways from Sunday, and then it turned out that Charlotte (officially my LEAST favorite Brontë) had written tons of books. Screw that. One book per sister, I decided.

And I only had three days left, before the assignment was due. But *Wuthering Heights* was brilliant. It was spooky and weird and kept changing voices. I hated everyone in it, and I wasn't sure what a moor actually was, but I couldn't stop reading.

Catherine died. Like, she actually died, and it was only halfway through the story. What the hell was that about? Was she going to come back as a zombie or something for the second act? I wouldn't put it past Em and her nasty sense of humor (me and Emily Brontë were on first name terms by now).

Then the sky screamed, and my TV flickered, and my iPod went silent. I saw something, on the screen of my Kindle, and then reflected in the TV screen too. A face. At least, I think it was a face. Whatever it was, it sure as hell was not human.

Wuthering Heights turned into a mess of pixels as the Kindle shut down, and then there was nothing there but one of those weird line drawings of dead authors. Only, it wasn't a dead author at all, was it? It was the same face that had stared out from the TV screen. The same face that stared out from every electronic screen, it turned out, when the sky screamed. Before the world stopped working.

The second time I sneaked through the barricade, Otis didn't stop me.

I felt like a criminal at first. I tried to walk really softly on the pavement, even though I was already wearing sneakers, and not exactly clomping around. I walked close to the side, near the fences of abandoned houses, so my shadow wouldn't give me away.

It was night, but there was a decent sized moon, enough for me to see the world. I was wearing dark jeans, the pair that already has a rip in them (and where am I going to get new ones?).

I used to walk this way every day. From home to school. It takes maybe seven minutes, unless I stop to chat or hover around the corner shop for too long.

There it was, the old corner shop. The windows were broken and the door half bashed in, from the embarrassing half-riot that had gone on during the building of the barricades, before everyone came over. The whole town went crazy for about ten minutes, then regretted it. I could see cans of food on the floor of the shop where they had been dropped in the panic. There was still a display of chocolate bars by the counter. They wouldn't be too gross, right? Not after only four weeks. But I couldn't bring myself to step inside.

It felt like they'd know. The invaders. Bad enough I was out on the wrong side of the barricade. They'd know as soon as I touched the chocolate. If I was going to get in trouble for stealing (rescuing!) something, it wasn't going to be junk food. It was going to be for a book.

My backpack hung loosely from my shoulders. I hadn't brought anything in it, not even water. I didn't want to waste an inch of space. My mouth was dry and yuck already, though, and I couldn't help thinking about the closed fridges in the shop, full of bottles of Coke. Sure, it would be room temperature, but it would still be Coke.

Later. Maybe. Books first.

The school looked undamaged at first. Empty, like on the first day of the holidays. But the thought of crossing that wide asphalt yard to get to it was too much. I already felt exposed, and there was moonlight sweeping across the black space. So I kept to the wall, following it around until I got to the front gate, with all the scrubby bushes and the gum trees. The windows were broken on this side, and the school looked a whole lot less okay.

Maybe this wasn't a good idea. Maybe there wasn't anything left worth saving inside.

But I had to try.

I scurried up the little path to the doors. They were locked, and barred. Of course they were. The adults might have been making some pretty dumb decisions lately, but they weren't completely stupid.

One of the windows had most of the glass missing, and I found a loose brick in the corner I could use to knock the rest of the pieces through, one by one. With every small crunch of glass, my stomach twisted hard, and I checked behind me a million and twelve times.

Finally, I clambered in over the windowsill and landed on the glass-strewn lino.

Inside was safer. It had to be. The invaders didn't come within our walls. It was one of their rules, right? So I was okay. I was alone in my old school, only one staircase and a couple of corridors away from where I needed to go.

That was when I heard the music.

It was so quiet I wasn't sure at first, but as I got closer to the library . . . oh. It was coming from there.

The music didn't sound right. It was uneven and sort of scratchy, and one of those old fashioned tunes that they wouldn't even cover on *Glee*, something that lived in a black and white movie.

The music hit me full in the face as I opened the doors. It felt heavier than I was used to, from mp3s and e-videos. It vibrated through the carpet into my feet.

I want to be loved by you, just you and nobody else but you . . .

It was a record. I could see it now. An actual record playing on an actual record player. I'd seen them in the tip shop from time to time, but never actually seen one working. Even Nan has a CD player, and iTunes.

(I haven't heard from her since the invaders came. She lives in Newcastle, and it's just too far to hear from. I hope she's okay.)

The needle reached the end of the track and sort of jerked for a moment. Then a hand snaked out, and lifted it off the record.

I froze, but didn't yell or anything. I just backed up, towards the doors.

"You don't have to run anywhere," said a lazy male voice. "Safer in here."

"Oh, you think?" I said back, like I wasn't freaking out.

"Safest place in the world, libraries." There was a squeak as a chair spun around. I sidled around the desk, to get a look at him. Oh.

He was younger than I'd thought from his voice, but still older than me. Definitely out of high school. Not old enough to be a teacher. And I'd never seen him before, not ever. He wasn't one of us. "What's your name?" he asked, leaning back in the chair, spinning it slowly around. He had a ponytail, and battered jeans. A jacket that had taken some damage, with charred marks around one sleeve. But maybe he just wore it to look cool, like he was all dangerous.

He didn't look cool, incidentally, scorched leather aside. He looked thirty or more years out of date.

"Ka— Amy," I said, too late realizing that I didn't want to give him my name.

He raised his eyebrows, like I'd said something funny. "Nice to meet you, Kay-amy. Welcome to my castle."

"It's not yours," I said, angrier than I had expected to be, now I wasn't afraid of him. He looked like too much of a slacker to be dangerous.

"I bet you went to school here. Good girl, were you? Popped in to pick up your homework?"

"I came for a book," I said crossly.

He leaned forward, suddenly intent. "You came through the hole in the barricade on the far end of Mansfield, yeah? Walked down Susann Street to come in the front entrance of the school?"

That was creepy. Really creepy. "How did you know that?"

"Because," he said, shrugging back into his chair like my confirming his guess made me uninteresting all over again. "The other obvious way is around Mitchell Lane, and if you'd come that way, the Observers would have wiped you out."

What was a girl supposed to say to a line like that? "I don't believe you," I said, though I sort of did. I didn't want to think about it. How stupid was I? I'd heard the rumors, even without radio and TV. There was a reason all the adults were so hot on barricades, and a reason that the invaders hadn't just blown our new walls apart.

Observers, everyone called them. I wasn't even sure what they were—cameras, I guess, or mines, or something in between.

No one who ever saw one survived it.

244   TANSY RAYNER ROBERTS

The rule was, if we didn't move around, if we stayed inside the barricades, we stayed alive. I knew that. And I'd risked everything for a stupid book.

Well, not a stupid book. A really good book.

"Help yourself," he said, waving one hand. "Plenty of books here. Grab an e-reader while you're at it. Maybe you can trade it on the black market for some bubble gum."

"Funny," I said, glaring at him.

He put another record on, another stupid old song that I remembered from some Saturday afternoon old movie, and lost interest in me altogether.

I stomped off to the Classics section. What else was there to do? My plan was to save the books. There were a good number of real books floating around of recent releases, if not in our town then in general, around the world. But classics . . . ever since they started loading hundreds of famous old books on to every e-reader they sold, I don't know anyone who bothered to buy the Brontës or Shakespeare in hard copy.

My mum used to have a whole lot of them, battered paperbacks and a few nice hardcovers. I hadn't read most of them, but I loved the bright covers all lined up unevenly on the shelves. My favorites were the Penguins, spine after spine in brilliant orange. So many books I was planning to read, when I got a chance.

One holiday, when I was staying at Nan's, Mum cleared off half her shelves, boxed up the books and took them off to the tip shop. "I've got them all on the Kindle," she said impatiently, when I yelled at her. "We needed the space."

2

I spent my whole allowance at the tip shop that week, buying back *The Three Musketeers* and *Playing Beatie Bow* and a whole row of Agatha Christies. She thought I was mad, but I liked looking at them, rearranging them on my shelves.

In the library, now, I stashed a handful of Jane Austens in my backpack. I wasn't a particular fan of Lizzy Bennet and that crowd, but they were my Mum's favorites, and she was going to need them.

I picked books out carefully. I wasn't sure if I was coming back here again, not after what the creep had said. Maybe he was lying and maybe he wasn't but . . .

Should I pick books because of posterity and shit like that, or should I just be selfish and save the ones I wanted to read? It wasn't like anyone else was coming to salvage anything from this library.

No one but me and him.

I stomped back to the main area of the library. He was still there, swinging his foot and listening to his stupid old record player. Where had he even got that from? He must have stolen it from the antique store or something. They wouldn't have one here in the school.

"How do you know about the Observers?" I snapped. "Or were you just trying to sound impressive?"

"Impressed you, did I?"

"Don't try so hard. No one's ever seen them. Not and survived."

"Maybe no one in your hick town. I know people. I hear things. I know what to look for."

I glared at him. "Fine. If you're so smart. Where's *Wuthering Heights*?"

He laughed at me. "Is that what you came all this way for? Emily Brontë? That's so earnest of you. If I was going to risk my life for an author, I'd stick to one who'd bothered to write more than one book."

"She died of consumption!" I yelled at him.

He shrugged and looked away. "Try to leave the Asterix comics when you make off with your backpack of contraband, yeah? I don't want to be left here completely without culture."

The school library had six copies of *Wuthering Heights*. I remember that. I remember looking at them on the shelf a month earlier and thinking it was kind of dumb, really, because there were so many e-readers and they all pretty much had it on there as a freebie. Why would they not be on the shelf now?

I didn't have time for this. I was going to get into so much trouble if I was caught. I whirled back and grabbed books quickly, filling my backpack. I grabbed history books, and poetry, and a bunch of Dorothy Sayers novels. I left some space at the top, just in case Emily Bronte turned up, and finally found what I wanted, several battered paperback copies of *Wuthering Heights*, hidden on the lower shelf of the Recent Returns (ha!) trolley. I picked the one in best shape and hugged it to my chest like it was a treasure map.

"I can tell you how it ends," said the creep as I walked past him, on my way out.

"Don't."

"If you really want to know . . . "

"I'm going to report you, when I get back."

"No, you're not," he said lightly.

"You could be a spy. I sneaked out, but that doesn't mean I'm not . . . "

"A patriot? A good girl? A law-abiding citizen?"

I stared at him for a moment. "Stupid. I'm not stupid."

"When you report me," he called after me as I left. "Call me Heathcliff. With two fs."

I gave him the middle finger, and went home. Slowly. By the safe route.

I hid the books under the bed for a month. I didn't realize it at first, but *Wuthering Heights* hadn't made it home with me. I searched my backpack three times, and asked if anyone had been in my room, but they all ignored me.

So much for my rescue mission. So much for Emily Brontë.

When they finally got around to setting up school lessons in the town hall, I volunteered to make a database of all the hard copy books owned by people in the town, as an independent project.

My teacher was delighted with the idea. We had three teachers. Which is odd, because the school had at least fifteen, and I'm pretty sure none of them died in the invasion. I would have heard. Maybe some of them didn't come inside the barricade. Maybe they were off somewhere selling black market copies of Gothic novels for food and medicine.

Maybe they didn't want to be teachers any more. A lot of people refused to do their old jobs, now that the world was different, and our town was stuck behind a wall.

My brother Otis used to have an apprenticeship as a mechanic, but he stopped bothering when the invaders came. He didn't help Frances with the baby much either. He hung out with the other men who called themselves the town militia, and marched up and down the inside of the barricade, acting like tools.

He didn't care about books. Lots of people didn't care about books. They acted like I was crazy, most of them. My mum even got angry at me once, like collecting the books and keeping track of who owned what was somehow—admitting that the electricity was never coming back.

Then they moved the barricade.

I didn't realize at first, but Otis and Dad were gone for lunch, and I overheard them talking when they came back. "What do you mean, Martin Avenue is gone?"

"Town business," my dad muttered.

"That means it's everyone's business," I said sharply. "What happened?"

My dad shuffled off into the house, leaving Otis to tell me. "No one's heard from the Jacksons in three days. One of our patrols evacuated the rest of the families this morning. New barricade is more defensible."

I wanted to argue, to scream. Defensible against what? Either we're safe inside the barricade, or we're not.

"Are the Steeles okay?" I asked finally. "And the Hopkinsons?" I didn't want to think about the Jacksons, about what might have happened to them. Now they were on the other side of the barricade, so if they were okay, they wouldn't be for long.

"They had to leave a lot of their stuff behind, but they're alive. We're sorting out accommodation now."

Their stuff. I looked at him, stricken. "Their stuff? But forty percent of the town's Mills and Boons were archived with Mrs. Hopkinson. We're already running short!"

"Katie, when are you going to stop with all this book crap?" he roared at me. "We're trying to stay alive here. Survival doesn't have time to stop for a cup of tea and a nice bedtime story."

"Then what are we surviving FOR?" I retorted, and walked away from him.

So yeah, I went back. You saw that coming, right? Maybe I was crazy, maybe it was post-invasion syndrome or whatever they'd be calling it on TV if we still had working TVs.

But *Wuthering Heights* had vanished, and I knew there were more copies in that library. And. And the book supplies were getting smaller, and.

And. And.

We weren't safe behind the barricade. We all knew that, now. I didn't know how to deal with that knowledge. I didn't even know how to deal with all the adults around me, pretending they weren't freaking out just as much as I was.

So after I sneaked through the barricade, on a night with barely a sliver of moon in the sky, I didn't go to the school by the same route I had used last time. I went the Mitchell Lane way.

People all said something different, about what observers looked like. They were CCTV cameras, they were spiky silver balls that hovered in the air, they were actual people, they were robots, they were . . .

I didn't see any of those things, that night. I walked slowly, keeping to the shadows, step after step, looking up at every window, the line of every roof.

Maybe he had just been screwing with me. That was a distinct possibility, right? It was the dickheadiest thing he could possibly have done, and I had no doubt he was capable of a lie like that, just to see what my reaction would be.

Then I saw it. A small, bright white smudge in the darkness. A pool of light that moved slowly across the road ahead of me, only there was nowhere for it to come from. It wasn't moonlight, or streetlight. It was something else.

It was growing. The whiteness spread like psychedelic milk spilled from a plastic bottle, out and out and out.

I turned and ran, and had no doubt that it was following me.

～

A few minutes later, I slammed the front door of the school behind me and leaned against it, gasping for breath. I had come here. Why had I come here?

Oh. Because an observer was following me, and I didn't want to lead it—them—it through the barricade. It made some sort of sense at the time, or maybe that was the adrenalin talking.

My chest hurt.

He was playing Elvis this time. Of course he was.

I knew these songs. I walked slowly, from the front door and up the stairs and along the corridors towards the library, and in that time I heard "Loving You," and "Got a Lot of Living To Do," and the stupid one about the teddy bear.

My dad used to sing that to my mum, when he thought we weren't listening. Which is weird, right? They're both far too young for Elvis. It was some kind of parent joke, that made them giggly and flirty in a way that made me and Otis want to stick our fingers in our ears and go, *Lalalalala*.

I couldn't remember the last time I saw my mum smile.

Also, wasn't the front door of the school supposed to be locked? I didn't remember walking through it, but I must have done. I definitely didn't climb in through the window.

I stopped outside the library doors and thought about it.

The needle scratched its way along the record, and "Lonesome Cowboy" started up. It seemed appropriate enough music as I pushed open the doors and made my entrance.

He was sitting in the same place, with his feet up, as the last time I'd been here. Which was weeks ago. Also, there was no way I was going to call him Heathcliff. Even if he was as much of a douche as the original.

"Someone stole my *Wuthering Heights*," I said, though I didn't really think that was what had happened.

"Damn those post-apocalyptic book clubs," 'Heathcliff' drawled without looking up. "Cut-throat to the last."

"I saw one of them," I blurted, and wondered why. I hadn't been planning to tell him. "An Observer."

He looked sharply at me, and then grinned. "Scary fuckers, yeah? Even though they don't look like anything at all."

"It might have followed me."

I expected him to be angry at my confession, but instead he laughed. "Yeah, no. Not in here. This is the one place that's completely safe from them."

That unsettled me. "You mean the one place outside the barricade," I corrected him.

He didn't flinch. "Do I?"

"You could come back to the town with me," I said, not sure why I was even offering this much. "They let in travelers, you know. At least, they did once." Hitchhikers who had been stranded in the middle of the electromagnetic pulse, and walked for weeks before they found us. They had been carrying two well-thumbed Harlequin romances, a ripped Archie comic, and a copy of Jack Kerouac's *On the Road* that didn't even have a crease in its spine.

His face closed over. "Didn't I make it clear? This is the only place that's safe. You're cute and all, with your mission to rescue the world's reading material, but I don't fancy the rest of your town moving in here with me."

I didn't know what to say to that, so I went back to the Recent Returns trolley, and fished out another copy of *Wuthering Heights*. If I was really superstitious, I'd sit here and read the whole thing, from beginning to end, just in case the next one I took got lost too.

There were three left. I took one, thought about it, then took the other two, then put one back. In case my backpack had some kind of *Wuthering Heights* eating vortex in it.

I didn't only pick fiction this time. I loaded up on some practical books about farming and making your own butter and shit like that. I thought about Frances, my brother's girlfriend, and how hard it was to get an appointment with the few health professionals left in our town, but sadly high school libraries aren't great on maternity and early childhood books. Not many picture books, either. When do babies start to read?

"We value your custom," drawled the creep as I walked past him. My backpack felt lighter. Without a word, I sat down on the library floor and started unpacking it, book after book. The practical books had gone. So had *Wuthering Heights*. All I had left was the fiction, more Agatha Christies, a few familiar romances and the Sherlock Holmes novels I had added in at the last minute because if the baby didn't have picture books we were just going to have to start him on the classics early.

"What the hell?" I said, and then glared up at him. "Did you do this?"

He—whatever his name was—not Heathcliff, leaned over the desk. He looked kind of sad. "Nothing to do with me."

"I put the books in here."

"You can't take them with you."

"Why not?"

He sank back on to his chair, spinning it slowly around. "Figure it out, Kay-amy. What do they have in common, the books that you're allowed to take?"

I looked down at what looked like a pretty ordinary selection. Then it clicked. "I've read them before. All of these. I've read them before."

It felt like the library was pressing in on me, and the books were sucking all the air from the room. I was very small, in this giant space of bookshelves and Elvis music on a scratchy record player. "What did they do to the library, the invaders?" I asked, in a tiny voice.

"Absolutely nothing," he said. "I was asleep in the basement of the school, the night they came. My dad had kicked me out, and I was going to hitch across to the big city, but I didn't get farther than two towns over. This was the easiest building to break into. So I was asleep when it hit, you know."

"The electromagnetic pulse." The thing that stopped everything working, every electronic device, every television, every . . . every . . . every . . .

Something I was forgetting, on the tip of my tongue. Brain. Finger. "It's funny," he said, in a tone that made it very clear that it wasn't, actually. "I figured it out later. The bit of basement I was dossing in was right here, beneath the library. It was like . . . the books protected me, when everyone else . . . "

"What happened to everyone else?" I whispered.

He looked so sad, so hollowed out, and I didn't even know what his name was. Maybe I should call him Heathcliff after all. It was the only name he'd ever given me.

"The wave—the pulse—whatever you want to call it. It killed them all. I walked out of the school into a ghost town. The buildings were dust, most of them. And the ones that weren't—some houses, a few shops. The antique shop, the newsagency. I figured it out, eventually. It was the buildings that had books in them. Real, paper books. All the rest of them were gone to dust. And all the people were dead. Dust and shadows."

"But that's not true," I argued. "Not this town. All the buildings are still standing. And everything behind the barricade is just fine."

"No," he said with a small smile. "It's really not, Kay-amy."

"Katie. My name is Katie."

"Huh," he said. "Did you know that's Scarlett O'Hara's real name, in *Gone with the Wind*? It's Katie Scarlett O'Hara."

"Yes," I said impatiently. "What's that got to do with anything?"

"Books are important."

"Not if we're all dead, they're not." I leaned in and tweaked his nose.

"Ow."

"See? I'm not dead. None of us are. You're just being stupid."

"I know what I saw," he said. "I saw a town full of people, gone to dust. And then—they all stood up again. They kept themselves busy, building a wall of air and imaginary things. I could walk right through them, and they never saw me. Whatever it is that pulse did to our electronics, it did something to people, too. We're not real any more. We're just memories that won't lie down."

I thought about Otis, and my Mum, and Frances and the baby. I didn't know what to think about them. All I knew was that they were going about their lives as they always had, only everything was smaller and fading and . . . maybe it was true.

"You were so worried about preserving the books, weren't you?" he said now. "But you didn't have to be. The invaders like books. Paper ones, especially. They have a reverence for them. They want to keep the books, store them and tend to them. It's human beings they don't plan on cataloguing."

His skin looked paler than before, almost a bright white. His skin shimmered like moonlight in the darkness. Like a spreading pool of milk.

"You're an Observer," I said, stepping backwards, tripping over my empty backpack and landing hard against the scattered pile of books I had already read.

He moved through the desk like he was a ghost, the milky whiteness of him parting and then reforming. "They made us," he said. "I don't think they meant to kill all the humans, with that first wave. But the bodies were so fragile. The thing that's left, the memory of humans, they're trying to figure out how to make a record of them, but they can only change a handful into something . . . permanent. They chose me because I was here. They thought I was a librarian, can you believe that? I promised them I would bring them someone who cared about the books, who could explain to them how they work. And here you are. You're the only one who came, while the rest of them were building that fucking wall. You're the only one who thought about the books."

I could hardly keep myself together. The tiny pieces of me were all clinging tightly, but I could burst apart at any moment.

"I won't get to read any new ones," I said.

"A small price to pay. You're the chosen one, Katie Scarlett. You're going to survive."

The fluorescent lights flicked off, and the only light in the room was the bright whiteness of him, and of me.

My arms looked like glowing moonlight, like milk, like crisp printing paper fresh from the packet.

I couldn't remember the baby's name. If I was real, if I was alive, I would remember his name, right? If all this was a lie, I should be able to remember something about my nephew. Something other than the yellow blanket they wrapped him in when he was born, and the book I bought him as a present, the touchy feely one made of plastic and crinkles and soft, soft felt.

His name was . . .

"Heathcliff," I said in a very small voice, knowing it wasn't the answer.

The Observer held a hand out to me. "We'll be the ones who save humanity. Who remember what being human was like. We'll make them remember, too. We'll save the books. There will be a record, at least, that we were here, that we had this history. They'll read about who we were. Once we teach them to read."

I stared up at him, and his outstretched, bone bright hand. I inhaled, and exhaled, though I no longer had any reason to do either of those things. The library breathed with me.

The Librarian's Dilemma

E. Saxey

Jas's job was to bring libraries into the twenty-first century. Saint Simon's library hadn't left the seventeenth, yet.

Jas stood in a university quad, surrounded by stone buildings. In the center was a huge yew whose branches brushed the walls. The wooden library door, ahead, was studded with nails.

The house Jas shared with his mother in Bradford would have fitted comfortably into this quad. Jas felt his principles—the anti-elitist, democratic ones that drew him to work in libraries—should have soured the sight. But they didn't. He felt out of place (too brown, too poor, too queer) but was still attracted.

The oak door opened. An older woman appeared in its shadow, straight-backed in dark clothes that swung about her like robes.

"Jaswinder? I'm the librarian for the Harrad Collection. You've brought a lot of luggage."

Jas was smuggling the future, in big suitcases. Digitization equipment: expensive and unique, and terribly heavy. They'd been hell to drag around on the long train journey (although had probably done wonders for developing his arm muscles). *The librarian hasn't asked for them*, his boss had said. *But you can change her mind. Just don't tell her you brought them with you.* "I wasn't sure what the weather would be like," Jas said.

"I'll send Fred to help."

She slipped back inside, and from the same door rocketed a figure in a suit, thin as a stick with thick-framed glasses and a mane of hair tossing around. "Hand 'em over. I'm stronger than I look." A Scots accent. "I do all the shelving. Up and down the stairs, too—no lifts, the place is too old." He grabbed a case, swung it over his shoulder, staggered a little. "Follow me."

Up a stone staircase, into a room overlooking the quad. The yew tree pressed its fingers on the leaded glass window.

"Do I sleep here?"

"Yep. Student rooms. I'm down the corridor."

"Aren't you a librarian?"

"God, no. Who'd want to do that?"

"I do." His holiday job was a decent start, but Jas planned (when he'd finished his degree) to get properly chartered.

"You're young. You'll grow out of it."

Fred led Jas back to the library. A dim room, as long as one side of the huge quad. When the door opened, a knife of light stabbed across the floorboards. Tweedy readers clustered around the windows. Academics were strange. Any sane person would take a book outside, sit under the tree.

The librarian looked up from her desk near the door, shook back her bobbed gray hair.

"Jas. Call me Moira. Now, we have you for eight weeks?"

"Yes." *Or longer, if they need you*, Michelle-the-boss had said.

"You're going to tag our rare books, and connect each book to our catalogue record. You've had experience?"

"I tagged the incunabula in the founders' library in Lampeter." A miserable wet fortnight in Wales, but useful for the CV.

Moira laid a book on her desk. "Show me."

Jas eyed the book, conscious of being auditioned. Nice leather binding, useful crescent-moon gap between the sewn pages and the spine. He took from his bag a small plastic box and a slim long tool, like a sparkler. *Talk them through it*, Michelle reminded him.

"So these are the seeds." The box was full of flat beads, like white lentils. "And I pick one up . . . "

Dipping the sparkler in the box, giving it a theatrical stir, then tapping to dislodge all but one seed.

"Then we . . . " He slid the sparkler into the spine-gap of the book. Good: no knots of glue, no tearing threads. You wanted the invisible worm, from Blake's poem, to wriggle into the book and hide the seed there, in the spine or the cover. The benevolent reader would never notice, the malevolent reader would never be able to find the seed and remove it.

"And now you can never lose it." It was part of the sales patter, but heartfelt. In a traditional library, books got lost, not just in a prosaic sense (like lost keys) but in a profound way (like lost souls)—misplaced, they became inert, never again to be useful.

This was a great time for a quick demonstration. *Find an excuse*, Michelle had said. *It'll hook them.*

"Can I show you . . ." Jas moved around the room, sprinkling seeds at different heights on the shelves. (They were fiddly, but you couldn't, *ipso facto*, lose them.)

This was the fun part. "Now, if you want to find something . . ."

Jas held his device up to the room. The screen showed dots of light sprinkled all around. Constellations. Jas knew why it worked: because librarians thought of themselves as being Gods of a miniature cosmos.

"Each light is a book. And when you know which book you want . . ." Jas turned off all the seed-lights except for the one he'd just installed. A single light remained, the star over Bethlehem.

"Hmm. I suppose it could be useful," said the librarian.

Jas felt his smile congeal on his face.

"Okay, let's do philosophers," said Fred.

"Plato."

"Ooh, a toughie. Ockham! William of Ockham. Your turn."

"Morris. William Morris."

"Sartre!"

At Moira's instruction, Fred was helping Jas to seed the books. He was beaky, frenzied, seemed likely to jab a seed tool straight through a book cover. "I'm only working in this library until I get a post-doc job," he'd announced. Jas resented this slur on the profession, but Fred did help to pass the time with whispered word games. Without Fred, it would have been dull work; Jas never read the books he seeded, to avoid getting sucked in.

By lunch on the first day, they'd seeded a huge stack of texts.

"We need the catalogue," Jas whispered. "To match the seeds to records. How do I access it?"

Fred pointed to a beige terminal.

Jas read a peeling sticker announcing it had been inspected for safety. "Ten years ago?"

"Well, it passed!" Fred said. "What more do you want?"

When consulted, Moira searched under her desk and dragged out a laptop, maybe only five years old. "Don't take it out of the library."

It was ridiculously slow. The ancient kit was inexplicable, given that Saint Simon's was so well endowed. The library catalogue wasn't complex, you could run it on anything. Jas could load it on his phone, for goodness' sake.

After an hour of wrestling with the ancient laptop, he did just that, and the work went so much quicker he nearly cried with relief. He kept the laptop open in case anyone was watching.

On the dot of five o'clock Fred stood and clapped his hands. Every tweedy reader looked up, and half of them closed their books and donned their jackets. Fred the pied piper led them towards a pub on the seafront.

"Why do you want to be a librarian, then?" Fred asked Jas as they walked. "Isn't it a wee bit boring?"

Jas wondered if he was being tested. "There are radical librarians."

"Really?"

"Yeah, fighting restrictions. Freeing information." Jas admired them for all those things. What stole his heart was also the multicolored hair, the facial piercings, and the fact that half of them seemed to be trans or queer. "Mostly in America," he admitted.

"If you say so. I'll get the drinks in. Connell, tell Jas about your research!"

Connell was a squat black professor from Los Angeles. He nodded his bald head sharply at Jas. "Trauma! War, civil conflict, interpersonal violence."

"Oh. Goodness."

One by one, the other researchers named their expertise.

"Italian Fascism."

"Madness. Sorry, I wouldn't say 'madness' normally, of course. But I'm eighteenth century, it's all *madness*, *lunacy*, all that outdated terminology."

"Medical ethics. Well, mostly when it goes wrong." That was a woman from Sweden.

"I suppose you could say . . . the occult?" A younger man wearing a pentagram necklace.

"Mass graves."

There was nobody else to speak. Say something! thought Jas. Anything! "Nazis?"

"Not really."

With a clunk, Fred set down his tray of pints.

Ritual grumbling commenced. Jas knew it had all been said before, because people took up one another's refrains.

"If I could take books back to my room . . . "

"And you're only working on early twentieth century, aren't you? They're not fragile . . . "

". . . not fragile at all."

"And the chairs!"

"No back support! I have to do stretches . . . "

Professor Connell murmured to Jas. "Hey, you're doing something technological with the library, Jas?"

"Yeah."

"Fantastic. Now, this place needs to open up a little, you know? An amazing collection. Should be available to the best people, 24/7. No offense to these guys! Are you going to shake things up?"

Jas nodded weakly.

When he next saw Professor Connell, the professor was reading a book while sitting in the yew tree.

"Stop this at once." Moira's voice ricocheted off the walls of the quad.

"Okay, okay. Tell me which part I can't do. Is the tree the problem? Can I sit on the grass?"

Jas grinned, then un-grinned. Better not to appear partisan. Better not to be seen at all. He'd just arrived in the quad, and hung back.

"You've removed a book from the library. You signed a contract."

"Yeah, I'm not sure that contract's legal. Forgive me. Two months in a dark room could make anyone a little wild. Cabin fever. Jas?" He'd been spotted. "Take this book while I climb down?"

The professor leaned down from the branches to pass Jas the book: a slim gum-bound paperback from the 1970s. Then the professor dropped neatly onto the grass, and walked back into the library.

"Good morning, Jas." Moira fell into step beside him. "You've done counter work, haven't you?"

"Sorry?"

"You've worked on library counters."

"Oh, yeah."

"You've probably had moments like this."

"Mm." Students hiding books down their trousers. Tossing them in the air as they walked through the security sensor. "I reckoned it was their job to push it as far as they could, and my job to bat it back."

"It's not symmetrical, though, is it? If half the time the thieves win, and half the time we win, soon there's no library." Moira held the door. "Jas, I want all the books seeded. Not just the old ones."

"Yes." That doubled the project. Michelle would be delighted. "I mean—I'm studying, I start my course again in October."

"What are your grades like? You could study here at Saint Simon's, perhaps, and work in the Collection."

The casual offer, in the chill of the dark room, sent a shiver up Jas's neck. To *go to University*—to indulge in that old, expensive rite of passage. To use a real library, rather than downloading ebooks.

Then there was the added appeal of starting in a new place. His friends, his mother, had been a life support. But to begin again, where people had always known him as Jas, was tempting.

Fred had been eavesdropping. "So, she said you could study here? Will you go for it?"

To distract him, Jas asked: "What are you researching?"

"The Gothic." Fred widened his eyes, tossed his hair.

"Isn't that old-fashioned?"

"It won't die! It's big in America right now. I'm working on getting myself a stateside post-doc. Going to become a genius."

"Can you—I mean, you can't *plan* to be a genius."

"You need more than brains. You need funding."

Moira was clearly embracing technology, so Jas decided to give her another demonstration.

"University of Salisbury—special collections. My boss designed this for them."

Moira prodded Jas's device, bringing up related lecture notes, an audio clip of two students debating.

"You could have something like this," Jas said. "Use work from the visiting researchers. Showcase what the library does."

Moira shook her head without taking her eyes off the device.

"This modernity," she said. Jas thought she was referring to something on the screen, until she continued: "This *modernization*."

"Yes?"

"It happens, of course, but it's not inevitable. This project you're leading. It's incredibly useful. But it's not the leading wave of an unavoidable rising tide."

"Of course!" Jas tried to sound sympathetic. "Not every innovation suits every library."

"I hope you don't feel you're here under false pretenses."

"No, no. I'm happy just tagging," Jas lied. "I just—I liked this." He pointed at the device, at the University of Salisbury's shining showcase.

"I like it too." Moira was faking regret. Dishonesty was contagious. "Perhaps if things were different." Then, sincere again, she held out a Post-it note. "Here's the number for Saint Simon's admissions. I told them you'd be in touch."

"... your fatuous little dictatorship ..."

Professor Connell had been shouting for a couple of minutes. Jas's hands had started to shake—he hated arguments—so he put down the seeding wand.

"What harm does it do anyone?" The professor was playing to the gallery, but getting no response. The madness expert shook her head regretfully, the occultist pursed his lips. "So that's it? No second chance?"

"You used your second chance weeks ago, professor," replied Moira.

The professor scooped up his notebooks. Everyone found somewhere else to look as he stomped down the aisle, slammed the oak door behind him.

Jas scribbled on a piece of paper: *What was that about?* Pushed it towards Fred.

Fred mimed holding a box, squeezing: a camera. Except the Professor wouldn't have made that gesture—he'd have taken his snap with a discrete tap on his phone.

Back to America, Fred wrote. *Utterly expelled.*

"So photographs aren't allowed at all?" Later, in the pub, Jas was still keeping his voice down.

"Nothing's allowed." Fred pulled out a sheet of crumpled paper. "Here's the contract researchers sign. Check which ones you've already broken."

No stealing, no smoking. Fair enough. No photocopying, no scanning. Well, it might damage the books. But for every three reasonable requests, there was a big ask.

The researcher will not discuss the Harrad Collection in person or on social media.

Texts from the Collection will not be added to referencing apps or software including (but not limited to) Zotero, EndNote, RefMe . . .

Modernity isn't inevitable, the librarian had said. She knew about social media and referencing software, but had decided to ban them. She wasn't an aging dusty stereotype. She was well informed, and gatekeeping.

"I don't like it either," Fred said. "But I'm not going to climb a tree with a book up my arse to prove a point."

"I don't think anyone could expect you to do that."

"I'm out of here, anyway." Fred's exodus predictions had taken on a personal, insulting note for Jas. *This place that you want to get into?* Fred seemed to be saying. *I shun it. I'm better. I'm gone.*

"So you said."

"You should read up on the founder, Lady Harrad. She had some interesting principles."

Lady Harrad had been born in 1890, Jas remembered vaguely. Victorian Values didn't seem relevant here.

Jas felt Fred's hand fumbling with his own under the pub table. He felt a flush of embarrassment, then realized Fred was trying to slip a tiny object into his palm.

"Have a look at that."

"What—"

"There are more discreet ways to take photographs."

Jas remembered the thick-rimmed glasses Fred wore for reading.

In his bedroom that evening, Jas phoned his boss.

"Jas! Great work so far."

"Michelle, did I sign a contract to work here?"

"The company signed one."

"Could you send me a copy? I want to make sure I'm sticking to it."

"Sure. Probably common sense, though."

But there was nothing common, or sensible, about the Harrad Collection.

Jas held Fred's gift. The sliver of plastic was almost weightless. He knew he shouldn't examine it. He'd lose his job, and any chance of studying here.

But a radical librarian had to be brave. Jas opened up Fred's gift.

The memory card held a dozen files, all photos of pages. Jas read a header at random: *Unlike Other Women*. Intrigued, Jas read on.

The woman was Unlike Other Women because she wasn't a woman at all.

The page was from a transsexual autobiography. Jas knew the label was anachronistic, but the story felt so familiar. I rarely found myself drawn to feminine ways, and as a child threw myself into games with hoops and trains. The voice bubbled off the page. By the end of the first page, the narrator had become engaged but could not rest while betrothed to Daniel, having no wifely feelings for him. I then lived ten years in Clacton under the name of Donald.

Lived under the name of Donald. What a world of activity that sentence glossed over. How had she—he—earned his keep, bought his clothes . . .

Jas checked the title of the book. *Accounts from the Patients at Woburn Sands.* Fred had also photographed the contents page, and there were twenty names: *Constance, Jack, Alicia, Robert, JC.* Were they all trans?

Published in 1878. A voice from history, a miracle.

Michelle, in Jas's mind, said, *Slow down, hold back.* But Jas still cornered Moira the following morning for another demonstration. There were things in this collection too precious to stay boxed up. He'd known it objectively, but Fred's illicit snaps—Donald's story—had brought it home.

He needed to know where Moira stood.

Jas opened some images from the Lampeter website. "This was incredibly fragile, a Vulgate Bible from the twelfth century." Everyone liked illuminated manuscripts. "We scanned it without even opening it."

Moira didn't dismiss it out of hand. "How?"

"Michelle's inventions." He showed Moira pictures of the scanners. Sheets of graphene that slid in between pages, ultra-fast book flippers for the most robust texts, or ultrasound devices for the most fragile. "So now that book can never be lost, or destroyed, even if it's stolen or water-damaged . . . "

"Or burnt."

It felt wrong to mention fire, to a librarian. Like saying *Macbeth* to an actor. "Yes."

"Interesting."

He would pitch hard, now, while he had her attention. "And with a collection like this, it seems such a waste for only the readers who are physically present to see it. I'm not saying you should throw it open . . . " He wanted that with all his untrained anarchist librarian heart, but he could haggle. "You would still absolutely be able to control exactly who has access to the texts." She'd like that.

"So you see digitization as a way to circulate the texts."

It was such a basic question that it confused Jas completely. "Yes." Of course, why else?

Moira sighed. "Jas, you are a very diligent young man. That's why I hope you'll work here for a long while, perhaps study here. But please understand, I will invest in any technology that means *I know where my books are*." Tapping her desktop with a bloodless fingernail. "And which means they cannot be destroyed. Anything that makes it harder to steal them, to photograph them, to gain access to them without my knowledge—I want that."

She wasn't interested in opening the library up. She wanted to close it down. Maybe she'd misunderstood.

"We live in such an amazingly connected world, now," Jas said. "It's such a part of scholarship, and learning, and . . . " Vainly throwing keywords at the librarian.

"You're right. In fact, I've been speaking to Michelle. She's agreed that you can advise me on this."

"Really?" A bloom of optimism.

"Building a security net, for a connected world. I'll tell you about some of the worst offenders of the last five years." Her eyes were bright at the thought of book thieves. Worse than that: library thieves. "You can tell me how you would have caught them."

"Yeats," said Jas. They were using famous writers for the game, today.

Each touch they give / love is nearer death . . . Jas had read that Yeats poem when he was learning about the librarian's dilemma. It applied more to books than to lovers.

There were always two impulses in any librarian, any library, any collection: the desire to preserve a text, and the desire to make it available. Those two impulses were always at war. Each finger on a book lessened its lifespan.

But that was the marvelous thing about Jas's scanning work: now the whole world could read a book without damaging it, without even touching it. How many other professions built around a central paradox could say: we solved it?

"Wallace Stevens. Hey. Sleepyhead. Stevens."

Moira didn't seem to be conflicted at all about her collection. Preservation trumped access, for her, every time. She was committing an act of enclosure: taking things which could easily be in the public domain and building a wall round them.

There was a dark side to collecting books. A hoarding, acquisitive desire. To keep the books away from other people and their sticky fingers. You had to temper that desire, and use your knowledge to increase the knowledge of others. Without that, you weren't a librarian. You were just a hoarder.

"Stoker," said Jas. "Bram Stoker."

"Hey, not fair. That's my turf. Anything Gothic—mine. Anyway. Ayn Rand."

And now she wanted to put Jas's diligent young brain to keeping people out. Poacher turned gamekeeper.

"You coming to the pub?"

"Already?" The whole day gone, and he hadn't even tried to find the Woburn Sands book.

"All librarians are evil," Fred announced, as they crossed the dark quad on the way home that night. "You want to be a librarian, Jas. It's because they *make a difference*, right?"

Jas shrugged. There was still a light burning in the library. At lunchtime he'd emailed his best essays to an admissions tutor at Saint Simon's, and he wouldn't let Fred's ramblings damage his chances.

Fred rolled on. "But librarians are supposed to be neutral, right? You want a book about raising Satan, the librarian's supposed to give it to you. So how can you be moral and neutral? They want to make a difference, but they don't say what difference they actually make."

"But you gave me that book."

Jas hadn't intended to say it. He was tipsy. He wanted to check if he had someone on his side. "That made a difference, to me."

"Oh, that was just queer solidarity. Hope you didn't mind. I mean, I'm not assuming . . . Y'know."

"I thought you were agreeing with me. Showing me something that should be shared—released."

"Nah. None of that hippy stuff. Just a present."

They climbed the stairs to Jas's room, and at the door, Fred said: "Hold on a moment." He reached behind Jas's head, speaking and moving so casually that Jas thought Fred was brushing fluff off his coat collar.

Fred laid his hand across the nape of Jas's neck and kissed him. His beer-tasting tongue parted Jas's lips and moved in a slow circle inside Jas's mouth. It was a bit much, but not unpleasant.

"Can I come in?" Fred asked.

"You're drunk."

"Have you met me? I'm always drunk."

They were both laughing. He could feel the upwards curve of Fred's lips, wished he could remember what Fred's face looked like, if he'd been attracted to him at all before this ambush.

"Look, come in, but maybe not ... "

"Not for that."

"Maybe not."

"But maybe."

After all Fred's threats to leave, his sudden attempt to move closer was sexy. Sexier than his musty suit jacket. "Perhaps."

It was hard to plan the theft.

Jas found *Woburn Sands* the following day and read more of it in the library. It was too intense to read it in a dark public room during his lunch hour. It needed to be read on a windy beach, in a cafe in a city, on a bed, being charmed and buffeted by the voices from the past.

More importantly, it should be shared with the people who would be cheered by it, who were trying in the face of hostility to construct a history.

Jas checked the perimeter first: no door, no hatches. No means whereby he could slip the book into another bit of the building.

He argued with himself while he patrolled: I could get sacked.

I probably wouldn't.

This would be a ridiculous way to remove all hope of studying at Saint Simon's.

It's really important. It's the principle.

I'm a thief. When you steal from a library, you steal from everyone in the world.

That's such a pre-digital idea. A childish idea. I'm not a thief. I'll bring it back.

You'll keep it.

Shut up.

Jas looked at the windows. In most libraries, the windows were sealed. If you didn't have a central courtyard, you were condemned to swelter. Here, at least, they were open.

Jas set his book on a wide windowsill.

Then he worked for another half hour, to make it less suspicious.

"I'm going for lunch."

"Mind if I join you?" said Fred.

"Oh, I need to do some things."

Fred's pokerface rebuked Jas. It would be tactless, after last night, to fob him off.

"Sorry. We could meet later?"

Fred shrugged, all bony shoulders and nonchalance. "If you like."

Jas forced a smile. His footsteps down the library aisle had never sounded louder.

Moira was in her office. His heart slapped insistently, *Something is wrong, something is wrong.*

Jas opened the library door, turned hard right along the wall, to the window where, on the sill, his prize waited for him. He scooped it up silently, slipped it into his bag and kept walking.

In his room, Jas slid the book under his mattress. No, that was the first place people would look.

He turned round and round, eying every crevice and seeing no hiding place. What had he done? A sackable offense, definitely a sackable offense.

Better to scan it, and take it back straight away. He popped the book into one of the slower flicker-scanners and watched it deftly turn the pages.

The door opened.

Jas tried to stand in front of the device.

Fred stood in the doorway.

"Cheeky," he observed. "Oh, no, don't faint on me . . . "

Jas sat on the edge of the bed and waited for the room to stop spinning.

"It's not enough," Jas said, when he was calmer. "I mean, it's not fair for me just to borrow a book that I want to read. There must be other books, useful to other people . . . "

"Aye."

"What should I do?"

"Well, what can you do? You can't take snapshots of everything."

"I've got these scanners. Really good scanners."

Fred raised his eyebrows. "Moira wouldn't like that."

"Do you think we could talk to the Vice Chancellor of the University?"

" 'We'? Leave me out of it."

For the next fortnight, Jas was remarkably productive in both halves of his double life.

He set up the online security net Moira had requested. First, he cross-referenced the Harrad Collection catalogue against other library catalogues to find the really unusual books. Then he set up alerts, triggered if anyone mentioned one of these rare books online.

"That'll catch them," Moira said. It was the most satisfied he'd ever heard her.

After work, Jas smuggled texts out of the library. Ones that seemed to him to relate to queer history, a couple every day. He scanned them and returned them, too nervous even to read them. They went no further; he couldn't work out how to share them. It was a futile, minuscule act of rebellion.

Most evenings he ate dinner in the pub while Fred drank, and they slept in Fred's room together. And while Jas worked and stole and slept, he waited for an offer from Saint Simon's.

He woke up in Fred's room, colder than usual. Fred's warm weight was absent.

Jas wondered if he should go back to his own bed. It was weird to be here on his own. The pillows smelled of cigarette smoke—it had seemed exotic and sexy as he'd fallen asleep, but now he didn't want to rest his face in it.

Jas walked as softly as he could to his own room.

There was a light shining under the closed door. He flung open the door, hoping to startle whoever was in there.

The surprises came in quick waves.

To find Fred in his room, when he'd just come from Fred's bed.

To see Fred juggling very competently one of the graphene scanners, clearly having used the slippery and delicate thing before. A flicker-scanner fanned a stack of five books in one corner of the room, and the ultrasound machine hummed in another.

But mainly, Jas was startled by the scale of it. There had to be a hundred books stacked on the carpet. Fred alone had clearly carried them from the library, intending to scan and replace them tonight. Up and down the stairs, and no lifts. Fred was enthusiastic, manic at times, but Jas had never seen him so industrious.

Jas realized that Fred and Moira both scared him. But at least he knew what Moira wanted.

Fred sprung towards him. Wrapped his pajama-clad arms round him.

"You were right. Information wants to be free," said Fred.

"Fred, why . . . ?" Fred had been awake for hours, Jas for only minutes. He couldn't think straight, and Fred talked over him.

"You've opened my eyes," said Fred.

"You've nicked my scanners."

"Borrowed. Just for tonight. But something's better than nothing, eh? Send a few books out into the world, like doves after the flood." Fred tightened his hold.

Jas spoke into Fred's mop of smoky hair. "You need to promise—swear—you'll never do this again."

"Okay, okay."

"Have you shared any of it?"

"No."

"You have to wipe your memory cards, wipe everything. I'll help you put the books back."

Up and down the stairs in the dark. Barefoot on stone, so as to make as little noise as possible, so that each step was painful—like the little mermaid, he thought, as sleeplessness sent his brain off on strange tangents.

He was so bone-cold and bone-weary at the end of it that he never wanted to see Fred again. But so much of both that he let him creep into his bed and hold him.

"Promise. Never again." Jas knew his own lesser transgressions would have to end, too. Even though they was hardly comparable to Fred's efforts. No more scanning for either of them.

"I promise," said Fred.

An alert was triggered the next morning; something caught in the new security net. An academic in America boasting about working on a "lost" Gothic novel. It could be a coincidence. Jas didn't report it to Moira.

Fred didn't turn up to work. Catching up on sleep, Jas guessed.

An email at midday from Saint Simon's made Jas an offer: a place on an undergraduate degree, starting that autumn.

Jas prayed they'd never find out about the scanned books.

During the afternoon, a different fear crept over him. If he took up the offer, would he be tied to Moira and the library indefinitely?

As Jas was leaving the library, that evening, Moira spoke. "Wait, Jas."

She'd found out. About the alert Jas hadn't reported, or his thefts, or Fred's misdeeds. She was going to sack him, prosecute him, have him barred for life from all libraries.

Or she knew about his offer, and he was trapped.

"I've not been fair to you. Come with me."

Moira led Jas a long way into the library. Unlocked doors, revealed a dusty room. On a table lay metal guillotines, a pin-cushion stuck with three-inch needles. Moira was going to torture him. No, don't be daft.

"I do some small repairs, here. Have a seat."

She laid a book in front of him. Published in the 1940s, maroon cloth binding. He picked it up, automatically looking for the crevice in which to insert the tracking seed.

"The founder of the Collection."

Jas shifted his attention from the binding to the content. *A Life of Lady Harrad*. The contents page described the founder campaigning for women's suffrage; then for pacifism and the League of Nations; then against fascism, and in favor of self-government for India. An all-round good egg, Jas thought.

"Lady Harrad saw the book burnings in Berlin. Including the archives of the Hirschfeld Institute." Did Moira know that Hirschfeld would strike a chord with him? Did everyone know he was queer? "She started the Collection after that."

Surely, then, she'd want the world to use the damn Collection. Not for it to sit and moulder in a stone room in an odd corner of a small country. He phrased it as mildly as he knew how. "So she knew it was important to—preserve ideas."

"She collected books to get them out of circulation."

Jas stared in disbelief at the frontispiece photograph of an Edwardian teenager, big eyes and swept-up hair.

"Anti-suffragette materials, fascist tracts," said Moira. "She boxed them up and sent them home to her mother and kept collecting."

Moira laid other books on the desk. Jas opened the covers carefully.

The Segregated City.

Motherhood in the Lower Classes.

Disordered Desire: Deportation as Solution.

"And the Collection kept collecting, after she died."

More volumes were added to the desk, modern ones. *Virology, Anthropology, Economics.*

It was horrible because the books wore all the trappings of legitimacy: smart typefaces, cloth-bound covers, a familiar formal layout. Like a polite voice saying terrible things. And because Jas loved books, totally bloody loved books—it was like the voice of a friend in a nightmare.

Were all the texts in the Collection similarly awful? Had he been surrounded by walls crawling with malice, for weeks? But the book Jas had found, the book from Woburn Sands—had Lady Harrad disapproved of it? Why was it here?

"There are good things, too."

"I don't doubt it. She didn't have time to read everything herself. And fashions change, in politics, as in everything."

Jas took deep breaths, looked away from the books. "So why keep them all?" he asked.

"For the same reason that we preserve the smallpox virus. They could be useful to study. That's why we permit researchers to visit. But the books shouldn't be allowed to spread."

Jas's head was swimming with objections. Paternalistic. Patronizing.

"I suggest you take tomorrow," Moira offered, "*To look around*. Read the books. Talk to the researchers. Ask them about their work: the unethical medical experiments—the economists advocating enforced labor—the novels that are as beautiful as Proust but, oh, five times as anti-Semitic. See if they think *those* books should be available to the world."

She was defending herself heatedly against objections Jas hadn't even raised. "Okay. I will." He needed the conversation to stop.

Moira sighed. "It's expensive to keep people out. Distance is a great boon. That's why Lady Harrad lodged the Collection at Saint Simon's. It's rather far from everywhere."

Jas walked on the beach for an hour to get his head straight. He imagined the horrors of the Collection, and tried to reconcile that with the dark, orderly library room. He heard the shingle growl as the waves dragged it back, then saw the surf roil and crash.

When he was exhausted, he turned back towards the university. Across the beautiful quad, which his new knowledge still couldn't make ugly. Up the stone stair, opening the door to his room.

The sight was so much as it had been last night that Jas wondered if he'd become stuck in a loop of time. Fred, cross-legged on the bed, feeding books into scanners. More books, if anything, than before.

"Ah! Finally! You're back." Fred sprung up and moved from device to device, clicking out memory cards.

"You promised . . ."

"I lied."

"You've been here all day?"

"Yep."

"But you were up all night, as well. You can't have slept . . . "

"I've hardly slept for two weeks, Jas. I've been in here every night. I'm on uppers. Didn't you bloody notice?"

"What are you doing?" He definitely wasn't releasing books like doves after the flood.

"I'm taking everything relevant from the Collection and I'm going to America. Where I'm starting a post-doc. I'm not smart enough to get it on my own. No, no, Jas—I know my limits. I have to research a unique resource. And I have to bring that resource with me." Fred tucked the memory cards into his breast pocket. "Nobody's even heard of half these texts. They're nasty stuff. Turn your hair white."

"This is all for your research?"

"Of course. Oh, and because information, it wants to be free, apparently."

"You set off the alarm I set up."

"One of my future colleagues. Got overexcited about one particular book. Idiot."

Jas tried to breathe evenly. He should tell Moira. But it was his own bedroom stacked with books, his own equipment (smuggled into the building) which had pirated them.

"Anyway, I'm off tomorrow," Fred announced. "But first: the final step."

"What?"

Fred's eyes sparkled.

"I burn the originals." Fred reached into his inside pocket.

Jas had a sudden vision of the room on fire, bindings blazing, leaded windows cracking in the heat.

Jas hit Fred.

He'd never done it before, and he did it badly. His knuckles jarred against Fred's cheek, instantly aching like they were broken. But at least he'd stopped Fred reaching for a lighter, or a bottle of petrol.

Fred reeled back, clutching his face. Laughing. "Good God, Jas, I'm not going to do that! Why would I need to do that? You're so bloody gullible!"

The side of his face was red, a spreading blotch, horrifying Jas.

"I wouldn't *burn* them. They're too bloody valuable. I mean, I've *sold* a lot of them. To cover my relocation costs. You wouldn't believe how much a neo-Nazi will pay for a—"

Jas hit him again. No ticking clock as an excuse, this time.

Fred fell, and lay on the floor, gulping.

"Sorry," said Jas automatically.

"Help me up, then."

Jas couldn't move. He could have helped skinny, frenetic Fred, the friend who was reaching up a hand to him. But Fred had metamorphosed himself into something untouchable. Revulsion welled up in Jas so strongly that it became awe.

The man at his feet was a library-thief. He had stolen from everyone in the world.

THE GREEN BOOK

Amal El-Mohtar

MS. Orre. 1013A Miscellany of materials copied from within Master Leuwin Orrerel's (d. Lady Year 673, Bright Be the Edges) library by Dominic Merrowin (d. Lady Year 673, Bright Be the Edges). Contains Acts I and II of Aster's The Golden Boy's Last Ship, *Act III scene I of* The Rose Petal, *and the entirety of* The Blasted Oak. *Incomplete copy of item titled only* The Green Book, *authorship multiple and uncertain. Notable for extensive personal note by Merrowin, intended as correspondence with unknown recipient, detailing evidence of personal connection between Orrerel and the Sisterhood of Knives. Many leaves regrettably lost, especially within text of* The Green Book: *evidence of discussion of Lady Year religious and occult philosophies, traditions in the musical education of second daughters, and complex reception of Aster's poetry, all decayed beyond recovery. Markers placed at sites of likely omission.*

My dear friend,

I am copying this out while I can. Leuwin is away, has left me in charge of the library. He has been doing that more and more, lately—errands for the Sisterhood, he says, but I know it's mostly his own mad research. Now I know why.

His mind is disturbed. Twelve years of teaching me, and he never once denied me the reading of any book, but this–this thing has hold of him, I am certain plays with him. I thought it was his journal, at first; he used to write in it so often, closet himself with it for hours, and it seemed to bring him joy. Now I feel there is something fell and chanty about it, and beg your opinion of the whole, that we may work together to Leuwin's salvation.

The book I am copying out is small—only four inches by five. It is a vivid green, quite exactly the color of sunlight through the oak leaves in the arbor, and just as mottled; its cover is pulp wrapped in paper, and its pages are thick with needle-thorn and something that smells of thyme.

There are six different hands in evidence. The first, the invocation, is archaic:

large block letters with hardly any ornamentation. I place it during Journey Year 200-250, Long Did It Wind, and it is written almost in green paste: I observe a grainy texture to the letters, though I dare not touch them. Sometimes the green of them is obscured by rust-brown stains that I suppose to be blood, given the circumstances that produced the second hand.

The second hand is modern, as are the rest, though they vary significantly from each other.

The second hand shows evidence of fluency, practice, and ease in writing, though the context was no doubt grim. It is written in heavy charcoal, and is much faded, but still legible.

The third hand is a child's uncertain wobbling, where the letters are large and uneven; it is written in fine ink with a heavy implement. I find myself wondering if it was a knife.

The fourth is smooth, an agony of right-slanted whorls and loops, a gallows-cursive that nooses my throat with the thought of who must have written it.

The fifth hand is very similar to the second. It is dramatically improved, but there is no question that it was produced by the same individual, who claims to be named Cynthia. It is written in ink rather than charcoal—but the ink is strange. There is no trace of nib or quill in the letters. It is as if they welled up from within the page.

The sixth hand is Leuwin's.

I am trying to copy them as exactly as possible, and am bracketing my own additions.

Go in Gold,
Dominic Merrowin

[First Hand: invocation]
  Hail!
  To the Mistress of Crossroads, [blood stain to far right]
  The Fetch in the Forest
  The Witch of the Glen
  The Hue and Cry of mortal men
  Winsome and lissom and Fey!
  Hail to the [blood stain obscuring] Mother of Changelings
of doubled paths and trebled means
of troubled dreams and salt and ash
  Hail!

[Second Hand: charcoal smudging, two pages; dampened and stained]

Cold in here–death and shadows–funny there should be a book! the universe provides for last will and testament! [illegible]

[illegible] I cannot write, mustn't [illegible] they're coming I hear them they'll hear scratching [illegible] knives to tickle my throat oh please

They say they're kind. I think that's what we tell ourselves to be less afraid because how could anyone know? Do [blood stain] the dead speak?

Do the tongues blackening around their necks sing?

Why do I write? Save me, please, save me, stone and ivy and bone I want to live I want to breathe they have no right [illegible]

[Third Hand: block capitals. Implement uncertain—possibly a knife, ink-tipped.]

What a beautiful book this is. I wonder where she found it. I could write poems in it. This paper is so thick, so creamy, it puts me in mind of the bones in the ivy. Her bones were lovely! I cannot wait to see how they will sprout in it—I kept her zygomatic bone, but her lacrimal bits will make such pretty patterns in the leaves!

I could almost feel that any trace of ink against this paper would be a poem, would comfort my lack of skill.

I must show my sisters. I wish I had more of this paper to give them. We could write each other such secrets as only bones ground into pulpy paper could know. Or I would write of how beautiful are sister-green's eyes, how shy are sister-salt's lips, how golden sister-bell's laugh

[Fourth Hand: cursive, right-slanted; high quality ink, smooth and fine]

Strange, how it will not burn, how its pages won't tear. Strange that there is such pleasure in streaking ink along the cream of it; this paper makes me want to touch my lips. Pretty thing, you have been tricksy, tempting my little Sisters into spilling secrets.

There is strong magic here. Perhaps Master Leuwin in his tower would appreciate such a curiosity. Strange that I write in it, then—strange magic. Leuwin, you have my leave to laugh when you read this. Perhaps you will write to me anon of its history before that unfortunate girl and my wayward Sister scribbled in it.

That is, if I send it to you. Its charm is powerful—I may wish to study it further, see if we mightn't steep it in elderflower wine and discover what tincture results.

[Fifth Hand: ink is strange; no evidence of implement; style resembles Second Hand very closely]

Hello?

Where am I?

Please, someone speak to me

Oh

Oh no

[Sixth Hand: Master Leuwin Orrerel]

I will speak to you. Hello.

I think I see what happened, and I see that you see. I am sorry for you. But I think it would be best if you tried to sleep. I will shut the green over the black and you must think of sinking into sweetness, think of dreaming to fly. Think of echoes, and songs. Think of fragrant tea and the stars. No one can harm you now, little one. I will hide you between two great leather tomes—

[Fifth Hand–alternating with Leuwin's hereafter]

Do you know Lady Aster?

Yes, of course.

Could you put me next to her, please? I love her plays.

I always preferred her poetry.

Her plays ARE poetry!

Of course, you're right. Next to her, then. What is your name?

Cynthia.

I am Master Leuwin.

I know. It's very kind of you to talk to me.

*You're–[**ink blot**] forgive the ink blot, please. Does that hurt?*

No more than poor penmanship ever does.

Leuwin? are you there?

Yes. What can I do for you?

Speak to me, a little. Do you live alone?

Yes—well, except for Dominic, my student and apprentice. It is my intention to leave him this library one day—it is a library, you see, in a tower on a small hill, seven miles from the city of Leech—do you know it?

No. I've heard of it, though. Vicious monarchy, I heard.

I do not concern myself overmuch with politics. I keep records, that is all.

How lucky for you, to not have to concern yourself with politics. Records of what?

Everything I can. Knowledge. Learning. Curiosities. History and philosophy. Scientific advances, musical compositions and theory—some things I seek out, most are given to me by people who would have a thing preserved.

How ironic.

. . . Yes. Yes, I suppose it is, in your case.

[[DECAY, SEVERAL LEAVES LOST]]

Were you very beautiful, as a woman?

What woman would answer no, in my position?

An honest one.

I doubt I could have appeared more beautiful to you as a woman than as a book.

. . . Too honest.

[[DECAY, SEVERAL LEAVES LOST]]

What else is in your library?

Easier to ask what isn't! I am in pursuit of a book inlaid with mirrors— the text is so potent that it was written in reverse, and can only be read in reflection to prevent unwelcome effects.

Fascinating. Who wrote it?

I have a theory it was commissioned by a disgruntled professor, with a pun on "reflection" designed to shame his students into closer analyses of texts.

Hah! I hope that's the case. What else?

Oh, there is a history of the Elephant War written by a captain on the losing side, a codex from the Chrysanthemum Year (Bold Did it Bloom) about the seven uses of bone that the Sisterhood would like me to find, and—

Cynthia I'm so sorry. Please, forgive me.

No matter. It isn't as if I've forgotten how I came to you in the first place, though you seem to quite frequently.

Why—

Think VERY carefully about whether you want to ask this question, Leuwin.

Why did they kill you? . . . How did they?

Forbidden questions from their pet librarian? The world does turn. Do you really want to know?

Yes.

So do I. perhaps you could ask them for me.

[[DECAY, SEVERAL LEAVES LOST]]

If I could find a way to get you out . . .

You and your ellipses. Was that supposed to be a question?

I might make it a quest.

I am dead, Leuwin. I have no body but this.

You have a voice. A mind.

I am a voice, a mind. I have nothing else.

Cynthia . . . What happens when we reach the end of this? When we run out of pages?

Endings do not differ overmuch from each other, I expect. Happy or sad, they are still endings.

Your ending had a rather surprising sequel.

True. Though I see it more as intermission—an interminable intermission, during which the actors have wandered home to get drunk.

[[DECAY, SEVERAL LEAVES LOST]]

Cynthia, I think I love you.

Cynthia?

Why don't you answer me?

Please, speak to me.

I'm tired, Leuwin.

I love you.

You love ink on a page. You don't lack for that here.

I love you.

Only because I speak to you. Only because no one but you reads these words. Only because I am the only book to be written to you, for you. Only because I allow you, in this small way, to be a book yourself.

I love you.

Stop.

Don't you love me?

Cynthia.

You can't lie, can you?

You can't lie, so you refuse to speak the truth.

I hate you.

Because you love me.

I hate you. Leave me alone.

I will write out Lady Aster's plays for you to read. I will write you her poetry. I will fill this with all that is beautiful in the world, for you, that you might live it.

Leuwin. no.

I will stop a few pages from the end, and you can read it over and over again, all the loveliest things . . .

Leuwin. no.

But I

STOP. I WANT TO LIVE. I WANT TO HOLD YOU AND FUCK YOU AND MAKE YOU TEA AND READ YOU PLAYS. I WANT YOU TO TOUCH MY CHEEK AND MY HAIR AND LOOK ME IN THE EYES WHEN YOU SAY YOU LOVE ME. I WANT TO *LIVE*!

And you, you want a woman in a book. You want to tremble over my binding and ruffle my pages and spill ink into me. No, I can't lie. Only the living can lie. I am dead. I am dead trees and dead horses boiled to glue. I hate you. Leave me alone.

[FINIS. Several blank pages remain]

You see he is mad.

I know he is looking for ways to extricate her from the book. I fear for him, in so deep with the Sisters—I fear for what he will ask them—

Sweet Stars, there's more. I see it appearing as I write this—unnatural, chanty thing! I shall not reply. I must not reply, lest I fall into her trap as he did! But I will write this for you—I am committed to completeness.

Following immediately after the last, then:

Dominic, why are you doing this?

You won't answer me? Fair enough.

I can feel when I am being read, Dominic. It's a beautiful feeling, in some ways—have you ever felt beautiful? sometimes I think only people who are not beautiful can feel so, can feel the shape of the exception settling on them like a mantle, like a morning mist.

Being read is like feeling beautiful, knowing your hair to be just-so and your clothing to be well-put-together and your color to be high and bright, and to feel, in the moment of beauty, that you are being observed.

The world shifts. You pretend not to see that you are being admired, desired. You think about whether or not to play the game of glances, and you smile to yourself, and you know the person has seen your smile, and it was beautiful, too. Slowly, you become aware of how they see you, and without looking, quite, you know that they are playing the game too, that they imagine you seeing them as beautiful, and it is a splendid game, truly.

Leuwin reads me quite often, without saying anything further to me. I ache when he does, to answer, to speak, but ours is a silence I cannot be the one to break. So he reads, and I am read, and this is all our love now.

I feel this troubles you. I do not feel particularly beautiful when you read me, Dominic. But I know it is happening.

Will you truly not answer? Only write me down into your own little book? Oh, Dominic. And you think you will run away? Find him help? You're sweet enough to rot teeth.

You know, I always wanted someone to write me poetry.

If I weren't dead, the irony would kill me.

I wonder who the Mistress of the Crossroads was. Hello, I suppose, if you ever read this—if Dominic ever shares.

I am going to try and sleep. Sorry my handwriting isn't prettier. I never really was myself.

I suppose Leuwin must have guessed, at some point. Just as he would have guessed you'd disobey him eventually. I am sorry he will find out about both, now. It isn't as if I can cross things out. No doubt he will be terribly angry. No doubt the Sisters will find out you know something more of them than they would permit, as I did.

It's been a while since I've felt sorry for someone who wasn't Leuwin, but I do feel sorry for you.

Good night.

That is all. Nothing else appears. Please, you must help him. I don't know what to do. I cannot destroy the book—I cannot hide it from him, he seeks it every hour he is here—

I shall write more to you anon. He returns. I hear his feet upon the stair.

IN THE STACKS

Scott Lynch

Laszlo Jazera, aspirant wizard of the High University of Hazar, spent a long hour on the morning of his fifth-year exam worming his way into an uncomfortable suit of leather armor. A late growth spurt had ambushed Laszlo that spring, and the cuirass, once form-fitted, was now tight across the shoulders despite every adjustment of the buckles and straps. As for the groinguard, well, the less said the better. Damn, but he'd been an idiot, putting off a test-fit of his old personal gear until it was much too late for a trip to the armory.

"Still trying to suck it in?" Casimir Vrana, his chambers-mate, strolled in already fully armored, not merely with physical gear but with his usual air of total ease. In truth he'd spent even less time in fighting leathers than Laszlo had in their half-decade at school together. He simply had the curious power of total, improbable deportment. Every inch the patrician, commanding and comely, he could have feigned relaxation even while standing in fire up to his privates. "You're embarrassing me, Laszlo. And you with all your dueling society ribbons."

"We wear silks," huffed Laszlo, buckling on his stiff leather neck-guard. "So we can damn well move when we have to. This creaking heap of boiled pigskin, I've hardly worn it since Archaic Homicide Theory—"

"Forgot to go to the armory for a re-fit, eh?"

"Well, I've been busy as all hells, hardly sleeping—"

"A fifth-year aspirant, busy and confused at finals time? What an unprecedented misfortune. A unique tale of woe." Casimir moved around Laszlo and began adjusting what he could. "Let's skip our exam. You need warm milk and cuddles."

"I swear on my mother, Caz, I'll set fire to your cryptomancy dissertation."

"Can't. Turned it in two hours ago. And why are you still dicking around with purely physical means here?" Casimir muttered something, and Laszlo yelped in surprise as the heat of spontaneous magic ran up and down his back—but a moment later, the armor felt looser. Still not a good fit, but at least not tight enough to hobble his every movement. "Better?"

"Moderately."

"I don't mean to lecture, *magician*, but sooner or later you should probably start using, you know, *magic* to smooth out your little inconveniences."

"You're a lot more confident with practical use than I am."

"Theory's a wading pool, Laz. You've got to come out into deep water sooner or later." Casimir grinned, and slapped Laszlo on the back. "You're gonna see that today, I promise. Let's get your kit together so they don't start without us."

Laszlo pulled on a pair of fingerless leather gauntlets, the sort peculiar to the profession of magicians intending to go in harm's way. With Casimir's oversight, he filled the sheaths on his belt and boots with half-a-dozen stilettos, then strapped or tied on no fewer than fourteen auspicious charms and protective wards. Some of these he'd crafted himself; the rest had been begged or temporarily stolen from friends. His sable cloak and mantle, lined in aspirant gray, settled lastly and awkwardly over the creaking, clinking mass he'd become.

"Oh damn," Laszlo muttered after he'd adjusted his cloak, "where did I set my—"

"Sword," said Casimir, holding it out in both hands. Laszlo's wire-hilted rapier was his pride and joy, an elegant old thing held together by mage-smithery through three centuries of duties not always ceremonial. It was an heirloom of his diminished family, the only valuable item his parents had been able to bequeath him when his mild sorcerous aptitude had won him a standard nine-year scholarship to the university. "Checked it myself."

Laszlo buckled the scabbard into his belt and covered it with his cloak. The armor still left him feeling vaguely ridiculous, but at least he trusted his steel. Thus protected, layered head to toe in leather, enchantments, and weapons, he was at last ready for the final challenge each fifth-year student faced if they wanted to return for a sixth.

Today, Laszlo Jazera would return a library book.

The Living Library of Hazar was visible from anywhere in the city, a vast onyx cube that hung in the sky like a square moon, directly over the towers of the university's western campus. Laszlo and Casimir hurried out of their dorm and into the actual shadow of the library, a darkness that bisected Hazar as the sun rose toward noon and was eclipsed by the cube.

There was no teleportation between campuses for students. Few creatures in the universe are lazier than magicians with studies to keep them busy indoors, and the masters of the university ensured that aspirants would preserve at least some measure of physical virtue by forcing them to scuttle around like ordinary folk. Scuttle was precisely what Laszlo and Casimir needed to do, in undignified haste, in order to reach the library for their noon appointment. Across the heart of Hazar they sped.

Hazar! The City of Distractions, the most perfect mechanism ever evolved for snaring the attention of young people like the two cloaked aspirants! The High University, a power beyond governments, sat at the nexus of gates to fifty known worlds, and took in the students of eight thinking species. Hazar existed not just to serve the university's practical needs, but to sift heroic quantities of valuables out of the student body by catering to its less practical desires.

Laszlo and Casimir passed whorehouses, gambling dens, fighting pits, freak shows, pet shops, concert halls, and private clubs. There were restaurants serving a hundred cuisines, and bars serving a thousand liquors, teas, dusts, smokes, and spells. Bars more than anything—bars on top of bars, bars next to bars, bars within bars. A bar for every student, a different bar for every day of the nine years most would spend in Hazar, yet Laszlo and Casimir somehow managed to ignore them all. On any other day, that would have required heroic effort, but it was exams week, and the dread magic of the last minute was in the air.

At the center of the eastern university campus, five hundred feet beneath the dark cube, was a tiny green bordered with waterfalls. No direct physical access to the Living Library was allowed, for several reasons. Instead, a single tall silver pillar stood in the middle of the grass. Without stopping to catch his breath after arrival, Laszlo placed the bare fingers of his right hand against the pillar and muttered, "Laszlo Jazera, fifth year, reporting to Master Molnar of the—"

Between blinks it was done. The grass beneath his boots became hard tile, the waterfalls become dark wood paneling on high walls and ceilings. He was in a lobby the size of a manor house, and the cool, dry air was rich with the musty scent of library stacks. There was daylight shining in from above, but it was tamed by enchanted glass and fell on the hall with the gentle amber color of good ale. Laszlo shook his head to clear a momentary sensation of vertigo, and an instant later Casimir appeared just beside him.

"Ha! Not late yet," said Casimir, pointing to a tasteful wall clock where tiny blue spheres of light floated over the symbols that indicated seven minutes to noon. "We won't be early enough to shove our noses up old Molnar's ass like eager little slaves, but we won't technically be tardy. Come on. Which gate?"

"Ahhh, Manticore."

Casimir all but dragged Laszlo to the right, down the long circular hallway that ringed the innards of the library. Past the Wyvern Gate they hurried, past the Chimaera Gate, past the reading rooms, past a steady stream of fellow Aspirants, many of them armed and girded for the very same errand they were on. Laszlo picked up instantly on the general atmosphere of nervous tension, as sensitive as a prey animal in the middle of a spooked herd. Final exams were out there, prowling, waiting to tear the weak and sickly out of the mass.

On the clock outside the gate to the Manticore Wing of the library, the little blue flame was just floating past the symbol for high noon when Laszlo and Casimir skidded to a halt before a single tall figure.

"I see you two aspirants have chosen to favor us with a dramatic last-minute arrival," said the man. "I was not aware this was to be a drama exam."

"Yes, Master Molnar. Apologies, Master Molnar," said Laszlo and Casimir in unison.

Hargus Molnar, Master Librarian, had a face that would have been at home in a gallery of military statues, among dead conquerors casting their permanent scowls down across the centuries. Lean and sinewy, with close-cropped gray hair and a dozen visible scars, he wore a use-seasoned suit of black leather and silvery mail. Etched on his cuirass was a stylized scroll, symbol of the Living Library, surmounted by the phrase *Auvidestes, Gerani, Molokare.* The words were Alaurin, the formal language of scholars, and they formed the motto of the Librarians: RETRIEVE. RETURN. SURVIVE.

"May I presume," said Molnar, sparing neither Aspirant the very excellent disdainful stare he'd cultivated over decades of practice, "that you have familiarized yourselves with the introductory materials that were provided to you last month?

"Yes, Master Molnar. Both of us," said Casimir. Laszlo was pleased to see that Casimir's swagger had prudently evaporated for the moment.

"Good." Molnar spread his fingers and words of white fire appeared in the air before him, neatly organized paragraphs floating vertically in the space between Laszlo's forehead and navel. "This is your Statement of Intent; namely, that you wish to enter the Living Library directly as part of an academic requirement. I'll need your sorcerer's marks *here.*"

Laszlo reached out to touch the letters where Molnar indicated, feeling a warm tingle on his fingertips. He closed his eyes and visualized his First Secret Name, part of his private identity as a wizard, a word-symbol that could leave an indelible imprint of his personality without actually revealing itself to anyone else. This might seem like a neat trick, but when all was said and done it was mostly used for occasional bits of magical paperwork, and for bar tabs.

"And here," said Molnar, moving his own finger. "This is a Statement of Informed Acceptance of Risk . . . and here, this absolves the custodial staff of any liability should you injure yourself by being irretrievably stupid . . . and this one, which certifies that you are armed and equipped according to your own comfort."

Laszlo hesitated for a second, bit the inside of his left cheek, and gave his assent. When Casimir had done the same, Molnar snapped his fingers and the letters of fire vanished. At the same instant, the polished wooden doors of the Manticore Gate rumbled apart. Laszlo glanced at the inner edges of the doors and saw that, beneath the wooden veneer, each had a core of some dark metal a foot thick. He'd never once been past that gate, or any like it—aspirants were usually confined to the reading rooms, where their requests for materials were passed to the library staff.

"Come then, " said Molnar, striding through the gate. "You'll be going in with two other students, already waiting inside. Until I escort you back out this Gate, you may consider your exam to be in progress."

Past the Manticore Gate lay a long, vault-ceilinged room in which Indexers toiled amongst thousands of scrolls and card-files. Unlike the Librarians, the Indexers preferred comfortable blue robes to armor, but they were all visibly armed with daggers and hatchets. Furthermore, in niches along the walls, Laszlo could see spears, truncheons, mail vests, and helmets readily accessible on racks.

"I envy your precision, friend Laszlo."

The gravelly voice that spoke those words was familiar, and Laszlo turned to the left to find himself staring up into the gold-flecked eyes of a lizard about seven feet tall. The creature had a chest as broad as a doorway under shoulders to match, and his gleaming scales were the red of a desert sunset. He wore a sort of thin quilted armor over everything but his muscular legs and feet, which ended in sickle-shaped claws the size of Laszlo's stilettos. The reptile's cloak was specially tailored to part over his long, sinuous tail and hang with dignity.

"Lev," said Laszlo. "Hi! What precision?"

"Your ability to sleep late and still arrive within a hair's breadth of accruing penalties for your tardiness. Your laziness is . . . artistic."

"The administration rarely agrees." Laszlo was deeply pleased to see Inappropriate Levity Bronzeclaw, "Lev" to everyone at the university. Lev's people, dour and dutiful, gave their adolescents names based on perceived character flaws, so the wayward youths would supposedly dwell upon their correction until granted more honorable adult names. Lev was a mediocre sorcerer, very much of Laszlo's stripe, but his natural weaponry was one hell of an asset when hungry weirdness might be trying to bite your head off.

"Oh, I doubt they were *sleeping.*" Another new voice, female, smooth and lovely. It belonged to Yvette d'Courin, who'd been hidden from Laszlo's view behind Lev, and could have remained hidden behind a creature half the lizard's size. Yvette's skin was darker than the armor she wore, a more petite version of Laszlo and Casimir's gear, and her ribbon-threaded hair was as black as her aspirant's cloak. "Not Laz and Caz. Boys of such a *sensitive* disposition, why, we all know they were probably tending to certain . . . extracurricular activities." She made a strangely demure series of sucking sounds, and some gestures with her hands that were not demure at all.

"Yvette, you gorgeous little menace to my academic rank," said Casimir, "that is most assuredly not true. However, if it were, I reckon that would make Laszlo and myself the only humans present to have ever seen a grown man with his clothes off."

Laszlo felt a warm, unexpected sensation in the pit of his stomach, and it took him a moment of confusion to identify it. Great gods, was that relief? Hope, even? Yvette d'Courin was a gifted aspirant, Casimir's match at the very least. Whatever might be waiting inside the Living Library, some bureaucratic stroke of luck had put him on a team with two natural magicians and a lizard that could kick a hole through a brick wall. All he had to do to earn a sixth year was stay out of their way and try to look busy!

Yvette retaliated at Casimir with another series of gestures, some of which might have been the beginning of a minor spell, but she snapped to attention as Master Molnar loudly cleared his throat.

"When you're all *ready*, of course," he drawled. "I do so hate to burden you with anything so tedious as the future of your thaumaturgical careers—"

"Yes, Master Molnar. Sorry, Master Molnar," said the students, now a perfectly harmonized quartet of apology.

"This is the Manticore Index," said Molnar, spreading his arms. "One of eleven such indices serving to catalog, however incompletely, the contents of the Living Library. Take a good look around. Unless you choose to join the ranks of the Librarians after surviving your nine years, you will never be allowed into this area again. Now, Aspirant Jazera, can you tell me how many catalogued items the Living Library is believed to contain?"

"Uh," said Laszlo, who'd wisely refreshed his limited knowledge of the library's innards the previous night, "About ten million, I think?"

"You think?" said Molnar. "I'll believe that when further evidence is presented, but you are nearly correct. At a minimum, this collection consists of some ten million scrolls and bound volumes. The majority of which, Aspirant Bronzeclaw, are what?"

"Grimoires," hissed the lizard.

"Correct. Grimoires, the personal references and notebooks of magicians from across all the known worlds, some more than four thousand years old. Some of them quite famous . . . or infamous. When the High University of Hazar was founded, a grimoire collection project was undertaken. An effort to create the greatest magical library in existence, to unearth literally every scrap of arcane knowledge that could be retrieved from the places where those scraps had been abandoned, forgotten, or deliberately hidden. It took centuries. It was largely successful."

Molnar turned and began moving down the central aisle between the tables and shelves where Indexers worked, politely ignoring him. No doubt they'd heard this same lecture many times already.

"Largely successful," Molnar continued, "at creating one hell of a mess! Aspirant d'Courin, what is a grimoire?"

"Well, she began, seemingly taken aback by the simplicity of the question. "As you said, a magician's personal reference. Details of spells, and experiments—"

"A catalog of a magician's private *obsessions*," said Molnar.

"I suppose, sir."

"More private than any diary, every page stained with a sorcerer's hidden character, their private demons, their wildest ambitions. Some magicians produce collections, others produce only a single book, but nearly all of them produce *something* before they die. Chances are the four of you will produce *something*, in your time. Some of you have certainly begun them by now."

Laszlo glanced around at the others, wondering. He had a few basic project journals, notes on the simple magics he'd been able to grasp. Nothing that could yet be accused of showing any ambition. But Casimir, or Yvette? Who could know?

"Grimoires," continued Molnar, "are firsthand witnesses to every triumph and every shame of their creators. They are left in laboratories, stored haphazardly next to untold powers, exposed to magical materials and energies for years. Their pages are saturated with arcane dust and residue, as well as deliberate sorceries. They are magical artifacts, uniquely infused with what can only be called the divine madness of individuals such as yourselves. They evolve, as many magical artifacts do, a faint quasi-intelligence. A distinct sort of low cunning that your run-of-the mill chair or rock or library book does not possess.

"Individually, this characteristic is harmless. But when you take grimoires . . . powerful grimoires, from the hands and minds of powerful magicians, and you store them together by the hundreds, by the thousands, by the tens of thousands, by the *millions* . . . "

This last word was almost shouted, and Molnar's arms were raised to the ceiling again, for dramatic effect. This speech had lost the dry tones of lecture and acquired the dark passion of theatrical oration. Whatever Master Molnar might have thought of the aspirants entrusted to his care, he was clearly a believer in his work.

"You need thick walls," he said, slowly, with a thin smile on his lips. "Thick walls, and rough Librarians to guard them. Millions of grimoires, locked away together. Each one is a mote of quasi-intelligence, a speck of possibility, a particle of magic. Bring them together in a teeming library, in the stacks, and you have . . . "

"What?" said Laszlo, buying into the drama despite himself.

"Not a mind," said Molnar, meeting his eyes like a carnival fortune-teller making a sales pitch. "Not quite a mind, not a focused intelligence. But a jungle! A jungle that *dreams*, and those dreams are currents of deadly strangeness. A Living Library . . . within our power to contain, but well beyond our power to control."

Molnar stopped beside a low table, on which were four reinforced leather satchels, each containing a single large book. Pinned to each satchel was a small pile of handwritten notes.

"A collection of thaumaturgical knowledge so vast and so deep," said Molnar, "is far, far too useful a thing to give up merely because it has become a magical *disaster area* perfectly capable of killing anyone who enters it unprepared!"

Laszlo felt his sudden good cheer slinking away. All of this, in a much less explicit form, was common knowledge among the aspirants of the High University. The Living Library was a place of weirdness, of mild dangers, sure, but to hear Molnar speak of it . . .

"You aspirants have reaped the benefit of the library for several years now." Molnar smiled and brushed a speck of imaginary dust from the cuirass of his Librarian's armor. "You have filed your requests for certain volumes, and waited the days or weeks required for the library staff to fetch them out. And, in the reading rooms, you have studied them in perfect comfort, because a grimoire safely removed from the Living Library is just another book.

"The masters of the university, as one of their more commendable policies, have decreed that all aspirant magicians need to learn to *appreciate* the sacrifices of the library staff that make this singular resource available. Before you can proceed to the more advanced studies of your final years, you are required to enter the Living Library, just once, to assist us in the return of a volume to its rightful place in the collection. That is all. That is the extent of your fifth-year exam. On the table beside me you will see four books in protective satchels. Take one, and handle it with care. Until those satchels are empty, your careers at the High University are in the balance."

Lev passed the satchels out one by one. Laszlo received his and examined the little bundle of notes that came with it. Written in several different hands, they named the borrower of the grimoire as a third-year aspirant he didn't know, and described the process of hunting the book down, with references to library sections, code phrases, and number sequences that Laszlo couldn't understand.

"The library is so complex," said Molnar, "and has grown so strange in its ways that physical surveillance of the collection has been impractical for centuries. We rely on the index enchantments, powerful processes of our most orderly sorcery, to give us the information that the Indexers maintain here. From that information, we plan our expeditions, and map the best ways to go about fetching an item from the stacks, or returning one."

"Master Molnar, sir, forgive me," said Casimir. "Is that a focus for the index enchantments over there?"

Laszlo followed Casimir's pointing hand, and in a deeper niche behind one of the little armories along the walls, he saw a recessed column of black glass, behind which soft pulses of blue light rose and fell.

"Just so," said Molnar. "Either you've made pleasing use of the introductory materials, or that was a good guess."

"It's, ah, a sort of personal interest." Casimir reached inside a belt pouch and took out a thick hunk of triangular crystal, like a prism with a milky white center. "May I leave this next to the focus while we're in the stacks? It's just an impression device. It'll give me a basic idea of how the index enchantments function. My family has a huge library, not magical, of course, but if I could create spells to organize it—"

"Ambition wedded to sloth," said Molnar. "Let no one say you don't think like a true magician, Aspirant Vrana."

"I won't even have to think about it while we're inside, sir. It would just mind itself, and I could pick it up on the way out." Casimir was laying it on, Laszlo saw, every ounce of obsequiousness he could conjure.

But what was he talking about? Personal project? Family library? Caz had never breathed a word of any such thing to him. While they came from very different worlds, they'd always gotten along excellently as chambers-mates, and Laszlo had thought there were no real secrets between them. Where had this sprung from?

"Of course, Vrana," said Master Molnar. "We go to some trouble to maintain those enchantments, after all, and today is *all about* appreciating our work."

While Casimir hurried to emplace his little device near the glass column, Molnar beckoned the rest of them on toward another gate at the inner end of the Manticore Index. It was as tall and wide as the door they'd entered, but even more grimly functional—cold dark metal inscribed with geometric patterns and runes of warding.

"A gateway to the stacks," said Molnar, "can only be opened by the personal keys of two Librarians. I'll be one of your guides today, and the other . . . the other should have been here by—"

"I'm here, Master Librarian."

In the popular imagination (which had, to this point, included Laszlo's), female Librarians were lithe, comely warrior maidens out of some barbarian legend. The woman now hurrying toward them through the Manticore Index was short, barely taller than Yvette, and she was as sturdy as a concrete teapot, with broad hips and arms like a blacksmith's. Her honey-colored hair was tied back in a short tail, and over her black Librarian's armor she wore an unusual harness that carried a pair of swords crossed over her back. Her plump face was as heavily scarred as Molnar's, and Laszlo had learned just enough in his hobby duels to see that she was no one he would ever want to annoy.

"Aspirants," said Molnar, "allow me to present Sword-Librarian Astriza Mezaros."

As she moved past him, Laszlo noticed two things. First, the curious harness held not just her swords, but a large book buckled securely over her lower back beneath her scabbards. Second, she had a large quantity of fresh blood soaking the gauntlet on her left hand.

"Sorry to be late," said Mezaros, "Came from the infirmary."

"Indeed," said Molnar, "and are you—"

"Oh, I'm fine. I'm not the one that got hit. It was that boy Selucas, from the morning group."

"Ahhhh. And will he recover?"

"Given a few weeks." Mezaros grinned as she ran her eyes across the four aspirants. "Earned his passing grade the hard way, that's for sure."

"Well, I've given them the lecture," said Molnar. "Let's proceed."

"On it." Mezaros reached down the front of her cuirass and drew out a key hanging on a chain. Molnar did the same, and each Librarian took up a position beside the inner door. The walls before them rippled, and small keyholes appeared where blank stone had been a moment before.

"Opening," yelled Master Molnar.

"Opening," chorused the Indexers. Each of them dropped whatever they were working on and turned to face the inner door. One blue-robed woman hurried to the hallway door, checked it, and shouted, "Manticore Gate secure!"

"Opening," repeated Molnar. "On three. One, two—"

The two Librarians inserted their keys and turned them in unison. The inner door slid open, just as the outer one had, revealing an empty, metal-walled room lit by amber lanterns set in heavy iron cages.

Mezaros was the first one into the metal-walled chamber, holding up a hand to keep the aspirants back. She glanced around quickly, surveying every inch of the walls, floors, and ceiling, and then she nodded.

"In," said Molnar, herding the aspirants forward. He snapped his fingers, and with a flash of light he conjured a walking staff, a tall object of polished dark wood. It had few ornaments, but it was shod at both ends with iron, and that iron looked well-dented to Laszlo's eyes.

Once the six of them were inside the metal-walled chamber, Molnar waved a hand over some innocuous portion of the wall, and the door behind them rumbled shut. Locking mechanisms engaged with an ominous series of echoing clicks.

"Begging your pardon, Master Molnar," said Lev, "not to seem irresolute, for I am firmly committed to any course of action which will prevent me from having to return to my clan's ancestral trade of scale-grooming, but merely as a point of personal curiosity, exactly how much danger are we reckoned to be in?"

"A good question," said Molnar slyly. "We Librarians have been asking it daily for more than a thousand years. Astriza, what can you tell the good aspirant?"

"I guard aspirants about a dozen times each year," said Mezaros. "The fastest trip I can remember was about two hours. The longest took a day and a half. You have the distinct disadvantage of not being trained Librarians, and the dubious advantage of sheer numbers. Most books are returned by experienced professionals operating in pairs."

"Librarian Mezaros," said Lev, "I am fully prepared to spend a week here if required, but I was more concerned with the, ah, chance of ending the exam with a visit to the infirmary."

"Aspirant Inappropriate Levity Bronzeclaw," said Mezaros, "in here, I prefer to be called Astriza. Do me that favor, and I won't use your full name every time I need to tell you to duck."

"Ah, of course. Astriza."

"As for what's going to happen, well, it might be nothing. It might be pretty brutal. I've never had anyone get killed under my watch, but it's been a near thing. Look, I've spent months in the infirmary myself. Had my right leg broken twice, right arm twice, left arm once, nose more times than I can count."

"This is our routine," said Molnar with grim pride. "I've been in a coma twice. Both of my legs have been broken. I was blind for four months—"

"I was there for that," said Astriza.

"She carried me out over her shoulders." Molnar was beaming. "Only her second year as a Librarian. Yes, this place has done its very best to kill the pair of us. But the books were *returned to the shelves*."

"Damn straight," said Astriza. "Librarians always get the books back to the shelves. *Always.* And that's what you *browsers* are here to learn by firsthand experience. If you listen to the Master Librarian and myself at all times, your chances of a happy return will be greatly improved. No other promises."

"Past the inner door," said Molnar, "your ordinary perceptions of time and distance will be taxed. Don't trust them. Follow our lead, and for the love of all gods everywhere, stay close."

Laszlo, who'd spent his years at the university comfortably surrounded by books of all sorts, now found himself staring down at his satchel-clad grimoire with a sense of real unease. He was knocked out of his reverie when Astriza set a hand on the satchel and gently pushed it down.

"That's just one grimoire, Laszlo. Nothing to fear in a single drop of water, right?" She was grinning again. "It takes an ocean to drown yourself."

Another series of clicks echoed throughout the chamber, and with a rumbling hiss the final door to the library stacks slid open before them.

"It doesn't seem possible," said Yvette, taking the words right out of Laszlo's mouth.

Row upon row of tall bookcases stretched away into the distance, but the farther Laszlo strained to see down the aisles between those shelves, the more they seemed to curve, to turn upon themselves, to become a knotted labyrinth leading away into darkness. And gods, the place was vast, the ceiling was hundreds of feet above them, the outer walls were so distant they faded into mist . . .

"This place has weather!" said Laszlo.

"All kinds," said Astriza, peering around. Once all six of them were through the door, she used her key to lock it shut behind them.

"And it doesn't fit," said Yvette. "Inside the cube, I mean. This place is much too big. Or is that just—"

"No, it's not just an illusion. At least not as we understand the term," said Molnar. "This place was orderly once. Pure, sane geometries. But after the collection was installed the change began . . . by the time the old Librarians tried to do something, it was too late. Individual books are happy to come and go, but when they tried to remove large numbers at once, the library got angry."

"What happened?" said Casimir.

"Suffice to say that in the thousand years since, it has been our strictest policy to never, *ever* make the library angry again."

As Laszlo's senses adjusted to the place, more and more details leapt out at him. It really was a jungle, a tangled forest of shelves and drawers and columns and railed balconies, as though the Living Library had somehow reached out across time and space, and raided other buildings for components that suited its whims. Dark galleries branched off like caves, baroque structures grew out of the mists and shadows, a sort of cancer-architecture that had no business standing upright. Yet it did, under gray clouds that occasionally pulsed with faint eldritch light. The cool air was ripe with the thousand odors of old books and preservatives, and other things—hot metal, musty earth, wet fur, old blood. Ever so faint, ever so unnerving.

The two Librarians pulled a pair of small lanterns from a locker beside the gate, and tossed them into the air after muttering brief incantations. The lanterns glowed a soft red, and hovered unobtrusively just above the party.

"Ground rules," said Astriza. "Nothing in here is friendly. If any sort of *something* should try any sort of *anything*, defend yourself and your classmates. However, you *must* avoid damaging the books."

"I can only wonder," said Lev, "does the library not realize that we are returning books to their proper places? Should that not buy us some measure of safety?"

"We believe it understands what we're doing, on some level," said Molnar. "And we're quite certain that, regardless of what it understands, it simply can't help itself. Now, let's start with your book, Aspirant D'Courin. Hand me the notes."

Molnar and Astriza read the notes, muttering together, while the aspirants kept an uneasy lookout. After a few moments, Molnar raised his hand and sketched an ideogram of red light in the air. Strange sparks moved within the glowing lines, and the two Librarians studied these intently.

"Take heed, aspirants," muttered Molnar, absorbed in his work. "This journey has been loosely planned, but only inside the library itself can the index enchantments give more precise and reliable . . . ah. Case in point. This book has moved itself."

"Twenty-eight Manticore East," said Astriza. "Border of the Chimaera stacks, near the Tree of Knives."

"The tree's gone," said Molnar. "Vanished yesterday, could be anywhere."

"Oh *piss*," said Astriza. "I really hate hunting that thing."

"Map," said Molnar. Astriza dropped to one knee, presenting her back to Molnar. The Master Librarian knelt and unbuckled the heavy volume that she wore as a sort of backpack, and by the red light of the floating lanterns he skimmed the pages, nodding to himself. After a few moments, he re-secured the book and rose to his feet.

"Yvette's book," he said, "isn't actually a proper grimoire, it's more of a philosophical treatise. Adrilankha's *Discourse on Necessary Thaumaturgical*

Irresponsibilities. However, it keeps some peculiar company, so we've got a long walk ahead of us. Be on your guard."

They moved into the stacks in a column, with Astriza leading and Molnar guarding the rear. The red lanterns drifted along just above them. As they took their first steps into the actual shadows of the shelves, Laszlo bit back the urge to draw his sword and keep it waiting for whatever might be out there.

"What do you think of the place?" Casimir, walking just in front of Laszlo, was staring around as though in a pleasant dream, and he spoke softly.

"I'm going to kiss the floor wherever we get out. Yourself?"

"It's marvelous. It's everything I ever hoped it would be."

"Interested in becoming a Librarian?" said Yvette.

"Oh no," said Casimir. "Not that. But all this power . . . half-awake, just as Master Molnar said, flowing in currents without any conscious force behind it. It's astonishing. Can't you feel it?"

"I can," said Yvette. "It scares the hell out of me."

Laszlo could feel the power they spoke of, but only faintly, as a sort of icy tickle on the back of his neck. He knew he was a great deal less sensitive than Yvette or Casimir, and he wondered if experiencing the place through an intuition as heightened as theirs would help him check his fears, or make him soil his trousers.

Through the dark aisles they walked, eyes wide and searching, between the high walls of book-spines. Tendrils of mist curled around Laszlo's feet, and from time to time he heard sounds in the distance—faint echoes of movement, of rustling pages, of soft, sighing winds. Astriza turned right, then right again, choosing new directions at aisle junctions according to the unknowable spells she and Molnar had cast earlier. Half an hour passed uneasily, and it seemed to Laszlo that they should have doubled back on their own trail several times, but they were undeniably pressing steadily onward into deeper, stranger territory.

"Laszlo," muttered Casimir.

"What?"

"Just tell me what you want, quit poking me."

"I haven't touched you."

Astriza raised a hand, and their little column halted in its tracks. Casimir whirled on Laszlo, rubbing the back of his neck. "That wasn't you?"

"Hells, no!"

The first attack of the journey came then, from the shadowy canyon-walls of the bookcases around them, a pelting rain of dark objects. Laszlo yelped and put up his arms to protect his eyes. Astriza had her swords out in the time it took him to flinch, and Yvette, moving not much slower, thrust out her hands and conjured some sort of rippling barrier in the air above them. Peering up at it, Laszlo realized that the objects bouncing off it were all but harmless—crumpled paper, fragments of wood, chunks of broken plaster, dark dried things that looked like . . . gods, small animal turds! Bless Yvette and her shield.

In the hazy red light of the hovering lanterns he could see the things responsible for this disrespectful cascade—dozens of spindly-limbed, flabby gray creatures the rough size and shape of stillborn infants. Their eyes were hollow dark pits and their mouths were thin slits, as though cut into their flesh with one quick slash of a blade. They were scampering out from behind books and perching atop the shelves, and launching their rain of junk from there.

Casimir laughed, gestured, and spoke a low, sharp word of command that stung Laszlo's ears. One of the little creatures dropped whatever it was about to throw, moaned, and flashed into a cloud of greasy, red-hot ash that dispersed like steam. Its nearby companions scattered, screeching.

"You can't tell me we're in any actual danger from these," said Casimir.

"*We're tell me can't,*" whispered a harsh voice from somewhere in the shelves, "known, known!"

"*Any actual you,* known, *from these in danger,*" came a screeching answer. "Known, known, known!"

"Oh, hell," shouted Astriza, "Shut up, everyone shut up! Say nothing!"

"Known, known, known," came another whispered chorus, and then a dozen voices repeating her words in a dozen babbled variations. "Known, known, known!"

"They're vocabuvores," whispered Master Molnar. "Just keep moving out of their territory. Stay silent."

"Known," hissed one of the creatures from somewhere above. "All known! New words. GIVE NEW WORDS!"

Molnar prodded Lev, who occupied the penultimate spot in their column, forward with the butt of his staff. Lev pushed Laszlo, who passed the courtesy on. Stumbling and slipping, the aspirants and their guides moved haltingly, for the annoying rain of junk persisted and Yvette's barrier was limited in size. Something soft and wet smacked the ground just in front of Laszlo, and in an uncharacteristic moment of pure clumsiness he set foot on it and went sprawling. His jaw rattled on the cold, hard tiles of the floor, and without thinking he yelped, "Shit!"

"Known!" screeched a chorus of the little creatures.

"NEW!" cried a triumphant voice, directly above him. "New! NEW!"

There was a new sound, a sickly crackling noise. Laszlo gaped as one of the little dark shapes on the shelves far above swelled, doubling in size in seconds, its grotesque flesh bubbling and rising like some unholy dough. The little claws and limbs, previously smaller than a cat's, took on a more menacing heft. "More," it croaked in a deeper voice. "Give more new words!" And with that, it flung itself down at him, wider mouth open to display a fresh set of sharp teeth.

Astriza's sword hit the thing before Laszlo could choke out a scream, rupturing it like a lanced boil and spattering a goodly radius with hot, vomit-scented ichor. Laszlo gagged, stumbled to his feet, and hurriedly wiped the awful stuff away from his eyes. Astriza spared him a furious glare, then pulled him forward by the mantle of his cloak.

Silently enduring the rain of junk and the screeching calls for new words, the party stumbled on through aisles and junctions until the last of the hooting, scrabbling, missile-flinging multitude was lost in the misty darkness behind them.

"Vocabuvores," said Master Molnar when they had stopped in a place of apparent safety, "goblin-like creatures that feed on any new words they learn from human speech. Their metabolisms turn vocabulary into body mass. They're like insects at birth, but a few careless sentences and they can grow to human size, and beyond."

"Do they eat people, too?" said Laszlo, shuddering.

"They'd cripple us," said Astriza, wiping vocabuvore slop from her sword. "And torture us as long as they could, until we screamed every word we knew for them."

"We don't have time to wipe that colony out today," said Molnar. "Fortunately, vocabuvores are extremely territorial. And totally illiterate. Their nests are surrounded by enough books to feed their little minds forever, but they can't read a word."

"How can such things have stolen in, past your gates and sorcery?" asked Lev.

"It's the books again," said Molnar. "Their power sometimes snatches the damnedest things away from distant worlds. The stacks are filled with living and quasi-living dwellers, of two general types."

"The first sort we call *externals*," said Astriza. "Anything recently dumped or summoned here. Animals, spirits, even the occasional sentient being. Most of them don't last long. Either we deal with them, or they become prey for the other sort of dweller."

"Bibliofauna," said Molnar. "Creatures created by the actions of the books themselves, or somehow dependent upon them. A stranger sort of being, twisted by the environment and more suited to survive in it. Vocabuvores certainly didn't spawn anywhere else."

"Well," said Astriza, "We're a bit smellier, but we all seem to be in one piece. We're not far now from twenty-eight Manticore East. Keep moving, and the next time I tell you to shut up, Laszlo, please shut up."

"Apologies, Librarian Mezar—"

"Titles are for outside the library," she growled. "In here, you can best apologize by not getting killed."

"Ahhh," said Molnar, gazing down at his guiding ideogram. The lights within the red lines had turned green. "Bang on. Anywhere on the third shelf will do. Aspirant D'Courin, let Astriza handle the actual placement."

Yvette seemed only too happy to pass her satchel off to the sturdy Librarian. "Cover me," said Astriza as she moved carefully toward the bookcase indicated by Molnar's spells. It was about twelve feet high, and while the dark wood of its exterior was warped and weathered, the volumes tucked onto its shelves looked pristine. Astriza settled Yvette's book into an empty spot, then leapt backward, both of her swords flashing out. She had the fastest over-shoulder draw Laszlo had ever seen.

"What is it?" said Molnar, rushing forward to place himself between the shelf and the four aspirants.

"Fifth shelf," said Astriza. She gestured, and one of the hovering lanterns moved in, throwing its scarlet light into the dark recesses of the shelves. Something long and dark and cylindrical was lying across the books on that shelf, and as the lantern moved Laszlo caught a glimpse of scales.

"I think—" said Astriza, lowering one of her swords, "I think it's dead." She stabbed carefully with her other blade, several times, then nodded. She and Molnar reached in gingerly and heaved the thing out onto the floor, where it landed with a heavy smack.

It was a serpent of some sort, with a green body as thick as Laszlo's arm. It was about ten feet long, and it had three flat, triangular heads with beady eyes, now glassy in death. Crescent-shaped bite marks marred most of its length, as though something had worked its way up and down the body, chewing at leisure.

"External," said Astriza.

"A swamp hydra," said Lev, prodding the body with one of his clawed feet. "From my homeworld . . . very dangerous. I had night terrors of them when I was newly hatched. What killed it?"

"Too many possible culprits to name," said Molnar. He touched the serpent's body with the butt of his staff and uttered a spell. The dead flesh lurched, smoked, and split apart, turning gray before their eyes. In seconds, it had begun to shrink, until at last it was nothing more than a smear of charcoal-colored ash on the floor. "The Tree of Knives used to scare predators away from this section, but it's uprooted itself. Anything could have moved in. Aspirant Bronzeclaw, give me the notes for your book."

"*Private Reflections of Grand Necrosophist Jaklur the Unendurable,*" said Astriza as Molnar shared the notes with her. "Charming." The two Librarians performed their divinations once again, with more urgency than before. After a few moments, Astriza looked up, pointed somewhere off to Laszlo's left, and said: "Fifty-five Manticore Northwest. Another hell of a walk. Let's get moving."

The second stage of their journey was longer than the first. The other aspirants looked anxious, all except Casimir, who continued to stroll while others crept cautiously. Caz seemed to have a limitless reserve of enchantment with the place. As for Laszlo, well, before another hour had passed the last reeking traces of the vocabuvore's gore had been washed from his face and neck by streams of nervous sweat. He was acutely aware, as they moved on through the dark canyons and grottoes of the stacks, that unseen things in every direction were scuttling, growling, and hissing.

At one point, he heard a high-pitched giggling from the darkness, and stopped to listen more closely. Master Molnar, not missing a step, grabbed him firmly by his shoulders, spun him around, and pushed him onward.

They came at last to one of the outer walls of the library, where the air was clammy with a mist that swirled more thickly than ever before. Railed galleries loomed above them, utterly lightless, and Astriza waved the party far clear of the spiral staircases and ladders that led up into those silent spaces.

"Not much farther," she said. "And Casimir's book goes somewhere pretty close after this. If we get lucky, we might just—"

"Get down," hissed Molnar.

Astriza was down on one knee in a flash, swords out, and the aspirants followed her example. Laszlo knelt and drew his sword. Only Molnar remained on his feet.

The quality of the mist had changed. A breeze was stirring, growing more and more powerful as Laszlo watched. Down the long dark aisle before them the skin-chilling current came, and with it a fluttering, rustling sound, like clothes rippling on a drying line. A swirling, nebulous shape appeared, and the mist surged and parted before it. As it came nearer, Laszlo saw that it was a mass of papers, a column of book pages, hundreds of them, whirling on a tight axis like a tornado.

"No," shouted Molnar as Casimir raised his hands to begin a spell. "Don't harm it! Protect yourselves, but don't fight back or the library will—"

His words were drowned out as the tumbling mass of pages washed over them and its sound increased tenfold. Laszlo was buffeted with winds like a dozen invisible fists—his cloak streamed out behind him as though he were in free-fall, and a cloud of dust and grime torn from the surfaces nearby filled the air as a stinging miasma. He barely managed to fumble his sword safely back into his scabbard as he sought the floor. Just above him, the red lanterns were slammed against a stone balcony and shattered to fragments.

From out of the wailing wind there came a screech like knives drawn over slate. Through slitted eyes Laszlo saw that Lev was losing his balance and sliding backward. Laszlo realized that Lev's torso, wider than any human's, was catching the wind like a sail despite the lizard's efforts to sink his claws into the tile floor.

Laszlo threw himself at Lev's back and strained against the lizard's overpowering bulk and momentum for a few desperate seconds. Just as he realized that he was about to get bowled over, Casimir appeared out of the whirling confusion and added his weight to Laszlo's. Heaving with all their might, the two human aspirants managed to help Lev finally force himself flat to the ground, where they sprawled on top of him.

Actinic light flared. Molnar and Astriza, leaning into the terrible wind together, had placed their hands on Molnar's staff and wrought some sort of spell. The brutal gray cyclone parted before them like the bow-shock of a swift sailing ship, and the dazed aspirants behind them were released from the choking grip of the page-storm. Not a moment too soon, in fact, for the storm had caught up the jagged copper and glass fragments of the broken lanterns, sharper claws than any it had possessed before. Once, twice, three times it lashed out with these new weapons, rattling against the invisible barrier, but the sorcery of the Librarians held firm. It seemed to Laszlo that a note of frustration entered the wail of the thing around them.

Tense moments passed. The papers continued to snap and twirl above them, and the winds still wailed madly, but after a short while the worst of the page-storm seemed to be spent. Glass and metal fragments rained around them like discarded toys, and the whole screaming mess fluttered on down the aisle, leaving a slowly falling haze of up-flung dust in its wake. Coughing and sneezing, Laszlo and his companions stumbled shakily to their feet, while the noise and chaos of the indoor cyclone faded into the distant mist and darkness.

"My thanks, humans," said Lev hoarsely. "My clan's ancestral trade of scale-grooming is beginning to acquire a certain tint of nostalgia in my thoughts."

"Don't mention it," coughed Laszlo. "What the hell was that?"

"Believe it or not, that was a book," said Astriza.

"A forcibly unbound grimoire," said Molnar, dusting off his armor. "The creatures and forces in here occasionally destroy books by accident. And sometimes, when a truly ancient grimoire bound with particularly powerful spells is torn apart, it doesn't want to *stop* being a book. It becomes a focus for the library's unconscious anger. A book without spine or covers is like an unquiet spirit without mortal form. Whatever's left of it holds itself together out of sheer resentment, roaming without purpose, lashing out at whatever crosses its path."

"Like my face," said Laszlo, suddenly aware of hot, stinging pains across his cheeks and forehead. "Ow, gods."

"Paper cuts," said Casimir, grinning. "Won't be impressing any beautiful women with those scars, I'm afraid."

"Oh, I'm impressed," muttered Yvette, pressing her fingertips gingerly against her own face. "You just let those things whirl around as they please, Master Molnar?"

"They never attack other books. And they uproot or destroy a number of the library's smaller vermin. You might compare them to forest fires in the outside world—ugly, but perhaps ultimately beneficial to the cycle of existence."

"Pity about the lamps, though," said Yvette.

"Ah. Yes," said Molnar. He tapped the head of his staff, and a ball of flickering red light sprang from it, fainter than that of the lost lamps but adequate to dispel the gloom. "Aspirants, use the empty book satchel. Pick up all the lantern fragments you can see. The library has a sufficient quantity of disorder that we need not import any."

While the aspirants tended their cuts and scoured the vicinity for lantern parts, Astriza glanced around, consulted some sort of amulet chained around her wrist, and whistled appreciatively. "Hey, here's a stroke of luck." She moved over to a bookcase nestled against the outer library wall, slid Lev's grimoire into an empty spot, and backed away cautiously. "Two down. You four are halfway to your sixth year."

"Aspirant Vrana," said Molnar, "I believe we'll find a home for your book not a stone's throw along the outer wall, at sixty-one Manticore Northwest. And then we'll have just one more delivery before we can speed the four of you on your way, back to the carefree world of making requests from the comfort of the reading rooms."

"No need to hurry on my account," said Casimir, stretching lazily. His cloak and armor were back in near perfect order. "I'm having a lovely time. And I'm sure the best is yet to come."

It was a bit more than a stone's throw, thought Laszlo, unless you discarded the human arm as a reference and went in for something like a trebuchet. Along the aisle they moved, past section after section of books that were, as Master Molnar had promised, completely unharmed by the passage of the unbound grimoire. The mist crept back in around them, and the two Librarians fussed and muttered over their guidance spells as they walked. Eventually, they arrived at what Molnar claimed was sixty-one Manticore Northwest, a cluster of shelves under a particularly heavy overhanging stone balcony.

"Ta-daaaaaa," cried Astriza as she backed away from the shelf once she had successfully replaced Casimir's book. "You see, children, some returns are boring. And in here, boring is beautiful."

"Help me!" cried a faint voice from somewhere off to Laszlo's right, in the dark forest of bookcases leading away to the unseen heart of the library.

"Not to mention damned rare." Astriza moved out into the aisle with Molnar, scanning the shelves and shadows surrounding the party. "Who's out there?"

"Help me!" The voice was soft and hoarse. There was no telling whether or not it came from the throat of a thinking creature.

"Someone from another book-return team?" asked Yvette.

"I'd know," said Molnar. "More likely it's a trick. We'll investigate, but very, very cautiously."

As though it were a response to the Master Librarian's words, a book came sailing out of the darkened stacks. The two Librarians ducked, and after bouncing off the floor once the book wound up at Yvette's feet. She nudged it with the tip of a boot and then, satisfied that it was genuine, picked it up and examined the cover.

"What is it?" said Molnar.

"*Annotated Commentaries on the Mysteries of the Worm*," said Yvette. "I don't know if that means anything special—"

"An-no-tated," hissed a voice from the darkness. There was a strange snort of satisfaction. "New!"

"Commentaries," hissed another. "New, new!"

"Hells!" Molnar turned to the aspirants and lowered his voice to a whisper. "A trick after all! Vocabuvores again. Keep your voices down, use simple words. We've just given them food. Could be a group as large as the last one."

"Mysteries," groaned one of the creatures. "New!" A series of wet snapping and bubbling noises followed. Laszlo shuddered, remembering the rapid growth of the thing that had tried to jump him earlier, and his sword was in his hand in an instant.

"New words," chanted a chorus of voices that deepened even as they spoke. "New words, new words!" It sounded like at least a dozen of the things were out there, and beneath their voices was the crackling and bubbling, as though cauldrons of fat were on the boil . . . many cauldrons.

"All you, give new words." A deeper, harsher voice than the others, more commanding. "All you, except BOY. Boy that KILL with spell! Him we kill! Others give new words!"

"Him we kill," chanted the chorus. "Others give new words!"

"No way," whispered Astriza. "No gods-damned way!"

"It's the same band of vocabuvores," whispered Molnar. "They've actually followed us. Merciful gods, they're learning to overcome their instincts. We've *got* to destroy them!"

"We sure as hell can't let them pass this behavior on to others," whispered Astriza, nodding grimly. "Just as Master Molnar said, clamp your mouths shut. Let your swords and spells do the talking. If—"

Whatever she was about to say, Laszlo never found out. Growling, panting, gibbering, screeching, the vocabuvores surged out of the darkness, over bookcases and out of aisles, into the wan circle of red light cast by Molnar's staff. Nor were they the small-framed creatures of the previous attack—most had grown to the size of wolves. Their bodies had elongated, their limbs had knotted with thick strands of ropy muscle, and their claws had become slaughterhouse implements. Some had acquired plates of chitinous armor, while others had sacks of flab hanging off them like pendulous tumors. They came by the dozens, in an arc that closed on Laszlo and his companions like a set of jaws.

The first to strike on either side was Casimir, who uttered a syllable so harsh that Laszlo reeled just to hear it. His ears rang, and a bitter metallic taste filled his mouth. It was a death-weaving, true dread sorcery, the sort of thing that Laszlo had never imagined himself even daring to study, and the closest of the vocabuvores paid for its enthusiasm by receiving the full brunt of the spell. Its skin literally peeled itself from the bones and muscles beneath, a ragged wet leathery flower tearing open and blowing away. And instant later the muscles followed, then the bones and the glistening internal organs; the creature exploded layer by layer. But there were many more behind it, and as the fight began in earnest Laszlo found himself praying silently that words of command, which were so much babble to non-magicians, couldn't nourish the creatures.

Snarling they came, eyes like black hollows, mouths like gaping pits, and in an instant Laszlo's awareness of the battle narrowed to those claws that were meant to shred his armor, those fangs that were meant to sink into his flesh. Darting and dodging, he fought the wildest duel of his career, his centuries-old steel punching through quivering vocabuvore flesh. They died, sure enough, but there were many to replace the dead, rank on writhing rank, pushing forward to grasp and tear at him.

"New words," the creatures croaked, as he slashed at bulging throats and slammed his heavy hilt down on monstrous skulls. The things vomited fountains of reeking gore when they died, soaking his cloak and breeches, but he barely noticed as he gave ground step by step, backing away from the press of falling bodies as new combatants continually scrambled to take their places.

As Laszlo fought on, he managed to catch glimpses of what was happening around him. Molnar and Astriza fought back to back, the Master Librarian's staff sweeping before him in powerful arcs. As for Astriza, her curved blades were broader and heavier than Laszlo's—no stabbing and dancing for her. When she swung, limbs flew, and vocabuvores were laid open guts to groins. He admired her power, and that admiration nearly became a fatal distraction.

"NEW WORD!" screeched one of the vocabuvores, seizing him by his mantle and forcing him down to his knees. It pried and scraped at his leather neck-guard, salivating. The thing's breath was unbelievable, like a dead animal soaked in sewage and garlic wine. Was that what the digestion of words smelled like? "NEW WORD!"

"Die," Laszlo muttered, swatting the thing's hands away just long enough to drive his sword up and into the orbless pit of its left eye. It demonstrated immediate comprehension of the new word by sliding down the front of his armor, claws scrabbling at him in a useless final reflex. Laszlo stumbled up, kicked the corpse away, and freed his blade to face the next one ... and the next one ...

Working in a similar vein was Lev Bronzeclaw, forgoing his mediocre magic in order to leap about and bring his natural weaponry into play just a few feet to Laszlo's left. Some foes he lashed with his heavy tail, sending them sprawling. Others he seized with his upper limbs and held firmly while his blindingly fast kicks sunk claws into guts. Furious, inexorable, he scythed vocabuvores in half and spilled their steaming bowels as though the creatures were fruits in the grasp of some devilish mechanical pulping machine.

Casimir and Yvette, meanwhile, had put their backs to a bookshelf and were plying their sorceries in tandem against a chaotic, flailing press of attackers. Yvette had conjured another one of her invisible barriers and was moving it back and forth like a tower shield, absorbing vocabuvore attacks with it and then slamming them backward. Casimir, grinning wildly, was methodically unleashing his killing spells at the creatures Yvette knocked off-balance, consuming them in flashing pillars of blue flame. The oily black smoke from these fires swirled across the battle and made Laszlo gag.

Still, they seemed to be making progress—there could only be so many vocabuvores, and Laszlo began to feel a curious exaltation as the ranks of their brutish foes thinned. Just a few more for him, a few more for the Librarians, a few more for Lev, and the fight was all but—

"KILL BOY," roared the commanding vocabuvore, the deep-voiced one that had launched the attack moments earlier. At last it joined the fight proper, bounding out of the bookcases, twice the size of any of its brethren, more like a pallid gray bear than anything else. *"Kill boy with spells! Kill girl!"*

Heeding the call, the surviving vocabuvores abandoned all other opponents and dove toward Casimir and Yvette, forcing the two aspirants back against the shelf under the desperate press of their new surge. Laszlo and Lev, caught off guard by the instant withdrawal of their remaining foes, stumbled clumsily into one another.

The huge vocabuvore charged across the aisle, and Astriza and Molnar moved to intercept it. Laszlo watched in disbelief as they were simply shoved over by stiff smacks from the creature's massive forelimbs. It even carried one of Astrizas's blades away with it, embedded in a sack of oozing gristle along its right side, without visible effect. It dove into the bookcases behind the one Casimir and Yvette were standing against, and disappeared momentarily from sight.

The smaller survivors had pinned Yvette between the shelf and her shield; like an insect under glass, she was being crushed behind her own magic. Having neutralized her protection, they finally seized Laszlo's arms, interfering with his ability to cast spells. Pushing frantically past the smoldering shells of their dead comrades, they seemed to have abandoned any hope of new words in exchange for a last act of vengeance against Casimir.

But there were only a bare dozen left, and Laszlo and Lev had regained their balance. Moving in unison, they charged through the smoke and blood to fall on the rear of the pack of surviving vocabuvores. There they slew unopposed, and if only they could slay fast enough . . . claws and sword sang out together, *ten*. And again, *eight*, and again, *six* . . .

Yvette's shield buckled at last, and she and Casimir slid sideways with vocabuvore claws at their throats. But now there were only half a dozen, and then there were four, then two. A triumphant moment later Laszlo, gasping for breath, grabbed the last of the creatures by the back of its leathery neck and hauled it off his chambers-mate. Laszlo drove his sword into the vocabuvore's back, transfixing it through whatever approximation of a heart it possessed, and flung it down to join the rest of its dead brood.

"Thanks," coughed Casimir, reaching over to help Yvette sit up. Other than a near-total drenching with the nauseating contents of dead vocabuvores, the two of them seemed to have escaped the worst possibilities.

"Big one," gasped Yvette. "Find the big one, kill it quickly—"

At that precise instant the big one struck the bookcase from behind, heaving it over directly on top of them, a sudden rain of books followed by a heavy dark blur that slammed Casimir and Yvette out of sight beneath it. Laszlo stumbled back in shock as the huge vocabuvore stepped onto the tumbled bookcase, stomping its feet like a jungle predator gloating over a fresh kill.

"Casimir," Laszlo screamed. "Yvette!"

"No," cried Master Molnar, lurching back to his feet. "No! Proper nouns are the most powerful words of all!"

Alas, what was said could not be unsaid. The flesh of the last vocabuvore rippled as though a hundred burrowing things were about to erupt from within, but the expression on its baleful face was sheer ecstasy. New masses of flesh billowed forth, new cords of muscle and sinew wormed their way out of thin air, new rows of shark-like teeth rose gleaming in the black pit of the thing's mouth. In a moment it had gained several feet of height and girth, and the top of its head was now not far below the stones that floored the gallery above.

With a foot far weightier than before, the thing stomped the bookcase again, splintering the ancient wood. Lev flung his mighty scarlet-scaled bulk against the creature without hesitation, but it had already eclipsed his strength. It caught him in mid-air, turned, and flung him spinning head-over-tail into Molnar and Astriza. Still dull from their earlier clubbing, the two librarians failed spectacularly to duck, and four hundred pounds of whirling reptilian aspirant took them down hard.

That left Laszlo, facing the creature all alone, gore-slick sword shaking in his hand, with sorcerous powers about adequate, on his best day, to heat a cup of tea.

"Oh, *shit*," he muttered.

"Known," chuckled the creature. Its voice was now a bass rumble, deep as oncoming thunder. "Now will kill boy. Now EASY."

"Uh," said Laszlo, scanning the smoke-swirled area for any surprise, any advantage, any unused weapon. While it was flattering to imagine himself charging in and dispatching the thing with his sword, the treatment it had given Lev was not at all encouraging in that respect. He flicked his gaze from the bookshelves to the ceiling—and then it hit him, a sensation that would have been familiar to any aspirant ever graduated from the High University. The inherent magic of all undergraduates—the magic of the last minute. The power to embrace any solution, no matter how insane or desperate.

"No," he yelled. "No! Spare boy!"

"*Kill boy,*" roared the creature, no more scintillating a conversationalist for all its physical changes.

"No." Laszlo tossed his sword aside and beckoned to the vocabuvore. "Spare boy. I will give new words!"

"I kill boy, *then* you give new words!"

"No. Spare boy. I will give many new words. I will give *all* my words."

"No," howled Lev, "No, you can't—"

"Trust me," said Laszlo. He picked a book out of the mess at his feet and waved it at the vocabuvore. "Come here. I'll *read* to you!"

"Book of words . . . " the creature hissed. It took a step forward.

"Yes. Many books, new words. Come to me, and they're yours."

"New words!" Another step. The creature was off the bookcase now, towering over him. Ropy strands of hot saliva tumbled from the corners of its mouth . . . good gods, Laszlo thought, he'd really made it hungry.

"Occultation!" he said, by way of a test.

The creature growled with pleasure, shuddering, and more mass boiled out of its grotesque frame. The change was not as severe as that caused by proper nouns, but it was still obvious. The vocabuvore's head moved an inch closer to the ceiling. Laszlo took a deep breath, and then began shouting as rapidly as he could:

"Fuliginous! Occluded! Uh, canticle! Portmanteau! Tea cozy!" He racked his mind. He needed obscure words, complex words, words unlikely to have been uttered by cautious librarians prowling the stacks. "Indeterminate! Mendacious! Vestibule! Tits, testicles, aluminum, heliotrope, *narcolepsy*!"

The vocabuvore panted in pleasure, gorging itself on the stream of fresh words. Its stomach doubled in size, tripled, becoming a sack of flab that could have supplied fat for ten thousand candles. Inch by inch it surged outward and upward. Its head bumped into the stone ceiling and it glanced up, as though realizing for the first time just how cramped its quarters were.

"Adamant," cried Laszlo, backing away from the creature's limbs, now as thick as tree trunks. "Resolute, unyielding, unwavering, reckless, irresponsible, foolhardy!"

"Noooo," yowled the creature, clearly recognizing its predicament and struggling to fight down the throes of ecstasy from its unprecedented feast. Its unfolding masses of new flesh were wedging it more and more firmly in place between the floor and the heavy stones of the overhead gallery, sorcery-laid stones that had stood fast for more than a thousand years. "Stop, stop, stop!"

"Engorgement," shouted Laszlo, almost dancing with excitement, "Avarice! Rapaciousness! Corpulence! Superabundance! *Comeuppance!*"

"Nggggggh," the vocabuvore, now elephant-sized, shrieked in a deafening voice. It pushed against the overhead surface with hands six or seven feet across. To no avail—its head bent sideways at an unnatural angle until its spine, still growing, finally snapped against the terrible pressure of floor and ceiling. The huge arms fell to the ground with a thud that jarred Laszlo's teeth, and a veritable waterfall of dark blood began to pour from the corner of the thing's slack mouth.

Not stopping to admire this still-twitching flesh edifice, Laszlo ran around it, reaching the collapsed bookcase just as Lev did. Working together, they managed to heave it up, disgorging a flow of books that slid out around their ankles. Laszlo grinned uncontrollably when Casimir and Yvette pushed themselves shakily up to their hands and knees. Lev pulled Yvette off the ground and she tumbled into his arms, laughing, while Laszlo heaved Casimir up

"I apologize," said Caz, "for every word I've ever criticized in every dissertation you've ever scribbled."

"Tonight we will get drunk," yelled Lev. The big lizard's friendly slap between Laszlo's shoulders almost knocked him into the spot previously occupied by Yvette. "In your human fashion, without forethought, in strange neighborhoods that will yield anecdotes for future mortification—"

"Master Molnar!" said Yvette. In an instant the four aspirants had turned and come to attention like nervous students of arms.

Molnar and Astriza were supporting one another gingerly, sharing Molnar's staff as a sort of fifth leg. Each had received a thoroughly bloody nose, and Molnar's left eye was swelling shut under livid bruises.

"My deepest apologies," hissed Lev. "I fear that I have done you some injury—"

"Hardly your fault, Aspirant Bronzeclaw," said Molnar. "You merely served as an involuntary projectile."

Laszlo felt the exhilaration of the fight draining from him, and the familiar sensations of tired limbs and fresh bruises took its place. Everyone seemed able to stand on their own two feet, and everyone was a mess. Torn cloaks, slashed armor, bent scabbards, myriad cuts and welts—all of it under a thorough coating of black vocabuvore blood, still warm and sopping. Even Casimir—no, thought Laszlo, the bastard had done it again. He was as disgusting as anyone, but somewhere, between blinks, he'd reassumed his mantle of sly contentment.

"Nicely done, Laszlo," said Astriza. "Personally, I'm glad Lev bowled me over. If I'd been on my feet when you offered to feed that thing new words, I'd have tried to punch your lights out. My compliments on fast thinking."

"Agreed," said Molnar. "That was the most singular entanglement I've seen in all my years of minding student book-return expeditions. All of you did fine work, fine work putting down a real threat."

"And importing a fair amount of new disorder to the stacks," said Yvette. Laszlo followed her gaze around the site of the battle. Between the sprawled tribe of slain vocabuvores, the rivers of blood, the haze of thaumaturgical smoke, and the smashed shelf, sixty-one Manticore Northwest looked worse than all of them put together.

"My report will describe the carnage as 'regretfully unavoidable,'" said Master Molnar with a smile. "Besides, we've cleaned up messes before. Everything here will be back in place before the end of the day."

Laszlo imagined that he could actually feel his spirits sag. Spend all day in here, cleaning up? Even with magic, it would take hours, and gods knew what else might jump them while they worked. Evidently, his face betrayed his feelings, for Molnar and Astriza laughed in unison.

"Though not because of anything *you* four will be doing," said Molnar. "Putting a section back into operation after a major incident is Librarian's work. You four are finished here. I believe you get the idea, and I'm passing you all."

"But my book," said Laszlo. "It—"

"There'll be more aspirants tomorrow, and the next day, and the day after that. You've done your part," said Molnar. "Aspirant Bronzeclaw's suggestion is a sensible one, and I believe you deserve to carry it out as soon as possible. Retrieve your personal equipment, and let's get back to daylight."

If the blue-robed functionaries in the Manticore Index were alarmed to see the six of them return drenched in gore, they certainly didn't show it. The aspirants tossed their book-satchels and lantern fragments aside, and began to loosen or remove gloves, neck-guards, cloaks, and amulets. Laszlo released some of the buckles on his cuirass and sighed with pleasure.

"Shall we meet in an hour?" said Lev. "At the eastern commons, after we've had a chance to, ah, thoroughly bathe?"

"Make it two," said Yvette. "Your people don't have any hair to deal with."

"We were in there for four hours," said Casimir, glancing at a wall clock. "I scarcely believe it."

"Well, time slows down when everything around you is trying to kill you," said Astriza. "Master Molnar, do you want me to put together a team to work on the mess in Manticore Northwest?"

"Yes, notify all the night staff. I'll be back to lead it myself. I should only require a few hours." He gestured at his left eye, now swollen shut. "I'll be at the infirmary."

"Of course. And the, ah . . . "

"Indeed." Molnar sighed. "You don't mind taking care of it, if—"

"Yes, if," said Astriza. "I'll take care of all the details. Get that eye looked at, sir."

"We all leaving together?" said Yvette.

"I need to grab my impression device," said Casimir, pointing to the glass niche that housed a focus for the index enchantments. "And, ah, study it for a few moments. You don't need to wait around for my sake. I'll meet you later."

"Farewell, then," said Lev. He and Yvette left the Manticore Index together.

"Well, my boys, you did some bold work in there," said Molnar, staring at Laszlo and Casimir with his good eye. Suddenly he seemed much older to Laszlo, old and tired. "I would hope . . . that boldness and wisdom will always go hand in hand for the pair of you."

"Thank you, Master Molnar," said Casimir. "That's very kind of you."

Molnar seemed to wait an uncommon length of time before he nodded, but nod he did, and then he walked out of the room after Lev and Yvette.

"You staying too, Laz?" Casimir had peeled off his bloody gauntlets and rubbed his hands clean. "You don't need to, really."

"It's okay," said Laszlo, curious once again about Casimir's pet project. "I can stand to be a reeking mess for a few extra minutes."

"Suit yourself."

While Casimir began to fiddle with his white crystal, Astriza conjured several documents out of letters that floated in the air before her. "You two take as long as you need," she said distractedly. "I've got a pile of work orders to put together."

Casimir reached into a belt pouch, drew out a small container of greasy white paint, and began to quickly sketch designs on the floor in front of the pulsing glass column. Laszlo frowned as he studied the symbols—he recognized some of them, variations on warding and focusing sigils that any first-year aspirant could use to contain or redirect magical energy. But these were far more complex, like combinations of notes that any student could puzzle out but only a virtuoso could actually play. Compared to Laszlo, Casimir was such a virtuoso.

"Caz," said Laszlo, "what exactly are you doing?"

"Graduating early." Casimir finished his design at last, a lattice of arcane symbols so advanced and tight-woven that Laszlo's eyes crossed as he tried to puzzle it out. As a final touch, Casimir drew a simple white circle around himself—the traditional basis for any protective magical ward.

"What the hell are you talking about?"

"I'm sorry, Laszlo. You've been a good chambers-mate. I wish you'd just left with the rest." Casimir smiled at him sadly, and there was something new and alien in his manner—condescension. Dismissal. He'd always been pompous and cocksure, but gods, he'd never looked at Laszlo like *this*. With pity, as though he were a favorite pet about to be thrown out of the house.

"Caz, this isn't funny."

"If you were more sensitive, I think you'd already understand. But I know you can't feel it like I do. *Yvette* felt it. But she's like the rest of you, sewn up in all the little damn rules you make for yourselves to paint timidity as a virtue."

"Felt *what*—"

"The magic in this place. The currents. Hell, an ocean of power, fermenting for a thousand years, lashing out at random like some headless animal. And all they can do with it is keep it bottled up and hope it doesn't bite them too sharply. It needs a *will*, Laszlo! It needs a mind to guide it, to wrestle it down, to put it to constructive use."

"You're kidding." Laszlo's mouth was suddenly dry. "This is a finals-week joke, Caz. You're kidding."

"No." Casimir gestured at the glass focus. "It's all here already, everything necessary. If you'd had any ambition at all you would have seen the hints in the introductory materials. The index enchantments are like a nervous system, in touch with everything, and they can be used to communicate with everything. I'm going to bend this place, Laz. Bend it around my finger and make it something new."

"It'll kill you!"

"It could win." Casimir flashed his teeth, a grin as predatory as any worn by the vocabuvores that had tried to devour him less than an hour before. "But so what? I graduate with honors, I go back to my people, and what then? Fighting demons, writing books, advising ministers? To hell with it. In the long run I'm still a footnote. But if I can seize *this*, rule *this*, that's more power than ten thousand lifetimes of dutiful slavery."

"Aspirant Vrana," said Astriza. She had come up behind Laszlo, so quietly that he hadn't heard her approach. "Casimir. Is something the matter?"

"On the contrary, Librarian Mezaros. Everything is better than ever."

"Casimir," she said, "I've been listening. I strongly urge you to reconsider this course of action, before—"

"Before *what*? Before I do what you people should have done a thousand years ago when this place bucked the harness? Stay back, Librarian, or I'll weave a death for you before your spells can touch me. Look on the bright side . . . anything is possible once this is done. The University and I will have to reach . . . an accommodation."

"What about me, Caz?" Laszlo threw his tattered cloak aside and placed a hand on the hilt of his sword. "Would you slay me, too?"

"Interesting question, Laszlo. Would you really pull that thing on me?"

"Five years! I thought we were friends!" The sword came out in a silver blur, and Laszlo shook with fury.

"You could have gone on thinking that if you'd just left me alone for a few minutes. I already said I was sorry."

"Step out of the circle, Casimir. Step out, or decide which one of us you have time to kill before we can reach you."

"Laszlo, even for someone as mildly magical as yourself, you disappoint me. I said I checked your sword personally this morning, didn't I?"

Casimir snapped his fingers, and Laszlo's sword wrenched itself from his grasp so quickly that it scraped the skin from most of his knuckles. Animated by magical force, it whirled in the air and thrust itself firmly against Laszlo's throat. He gasped—the razor-edge that had slashed vocabuvore flesh like wet parchment was pressed firmly against his windpipe, and a modicum of added pressure would drive it in.

"Now," shouted Casimir, "Indexers, *out*! If anyone else comes in, if I am interfered with, or knocked unconscious or by any means further *annoyed*, my enchantment on that sword will slice this aspirant's head off."

The blue-robed Indexers withdrew from the room hastily, and the heavy door clanged shut behind them.

"Astriza," said Casimir, "somewhere in this room is the master index book, the one updated by the enchantments. Bring it to me now."

"Casimir," said the Librarian, "It's still not too late for you to—"

"How will you write up Laszlo's death in your report? 'Regretfully unavoidable?' Bring me the damn book."

"As you wish," she said coldly. She moved to a nearby table, and returned with a thick volume, two feet high and nearly as wide.

"Simply hand it over," said Casimir. "Don't touch the warding paint."

She complied, and Casimir ran his right hand over the cover of the awkwardly large volume, cradling it against his chest with his left arm.

"Well then, Laszlo," he said, "This is it. All the information collected by the index enchantments is sorted in the master books like this one. My little alterations will reverse the process, making this a focus for me to reshape all this chaos to my own liking."

"Casimir," said Laszlo, "Please—"

"Hoist a few for me tonight if you live through whatever happens next. I'm moving past such things."

He flipped the book open, and a pale silvery glow rippled up from the pages he selected. Casimir took a deep breath, raised his right hand, and began to intone the words of a spell.

Things happened very fast then. Astriza moved, but not against Casimir—instead she hit Laszlo, taking him completely by surprise with an elbow to the chest. As he toppled backward, she darted her right arm past his face, slamming her leather-armored limb against Laszlo's blade before it could shift positions to follow him. The sword fought furiously, but Astriza caught the hilt in her other hand, and with all of her strength managed to lever it into a stack of encyclopedias, where it stuck quivering furiously.

At the same instant, Casimir started screaming.

Laszlo sat up, rubbing his chest, shocked to find his throat uncut, and he was just in time to see the *thing* that erupted out of the master index book, though it took his mind a moment to properly assemble the details. The silvery glow of the pages brightened and flickered, like a magical portal opening, for that was exactly what it was—a portal opening horizontally like a hatch rather than vertically like a door.

Through it came a gleaming, segmented black thing nearly as wide as the book itself, something like a man-sized centipede, and uncannily fast. In an instant it had sunk half-a-dozen hooked foreclaws into Casimir's neck and cheeks, and then came the screams, the most horrible Laszlo had ever heard. Casimir lost his grip on the book, but it didn't matter—the massive volume floated in midair of its own accord while the new arrival did its gruesome work.

With Casimir's head gripped firmly in its larger claws, it extended dozens of narrower pink appendages from its underside, a writhing carpet of hollow, fleshy needles. These plunged into Casimir's eyes, his face, his mouth and neck, and only bare trickles of blood slid from the holes they bored, for the thing began to pulse and buzz rhythmically, sucking fluid and soft tissue from the body of the once-handsome aspirant. The screams choked to a halt, for Casimir had nothing left to scream with.

Laszlo whirled away from this and lost what was left of his long-ago breakfast. By the time he managed to wipe his mouth and stumble to his feet at last, the affair was finished. The book creature released Casimir's desiccated corpse, its features utterly destroyed, a weirdly sagging and empty thing that hung nearly hollow on its bones and crumpled to the ground. The segmented monster withdrew, and the book slammed shut with a sound like a thunderclap.

"Caz," whispered Laszlo, astonished to find his eyes moistening. "Gods, Caz, why?"

"Master Molnar hoped he wouldn't try it," said Astriza. She scuffed the white circle with the tip of a boot and reached out to grab the master index book from where it floated in mid-air. "I said he showed all the classic signs. It's not always pleasant being right."

"The book was a trap," said Laszlo.

"Well, the whole thing was a trap, Laszlo. We know perfectly well what sort of hints we drop in the introductory materials, and what a powerful sorcerer could theoretically attempt to do with the index enchantments."

"I never even saw it," muttered Laszlo.

"And you think that makes you some sort of failure? Grow up, Laszlo. It just makes you well adjusted. Not likely to spend weeks of your life planning a way to seize more power than any mortal will can sanely command. Look, every once in a while, a place like the High College is bound to get a student with excessive competence and no scruples, right?"

"I suppose it must," said Laszlo. "I just . . . I never would have guessed my own chambers-mate . . . "

"The most dangerous sort. The ones that make themselves obvious can be dealt with almost at leisure. It's the ones that can disguise their true nature, get along socially, feign friendships . . . those are much, much worse. The only real way to catch them is to leave rope lying around and let them knot their own nooses."

"Merciful gods." Laszlo retrieved his sword and slid it into the scabbard for what he hoped would be the last time that day. "What about the body?"

"Library property. Some of the grimoires in here are bound in human skin, and occasionally need repair."

"Are you *kidding*?"

"Waste not, want not."

"But his family—"

"Won't get to know. Because he vanished in an unfortunate magical accident just after you turned and left him in here, didn't he?"

"I . . . damn. I don't know if I can—"

"The alternative is disgrace for him, disgrace for his family, and a major headache for everyone who knew him, especially his chambers-mate for the last five years."

"The Indexers will just play along?"

"The Indexers see what they're told to see. I sign their pay chits."

"It just seems incredible," said Laszlo. "To stand here and hide everything about his real fate, as casually as you'd shelve a book."

"Who around here *casually* shelves a book?"

"Good point." Laszlo sighed and held his hand out to Astriza. "I suppose, then, that Casimir vanished in a magical accident just after I turned and left him in here."

"Rely on us to handle the details, Laszlo." She gave his hand a firm, friendly shake. "After all, what better place than a library for keeping things hushed?"

A Woman's Best Friend

Robert Reed

The gangly man was running up the street, his long legs pushing through the fresh unplowed snow. He was a stranger; or at least that was her initial impression. In ways that Mary couldn't quite define, he acted both lost and at home. His face and manner were confused, yet he nonetheless seemed to navigate as if he recognized some portion of his surroundings. From a distance, his features seemed pleasantly anonymous, his face revealing little of itself except for a bony, perpetually boyish composition. Then a streetlamp caught him squarely, and he looked so earnest and desperate, and so sweetly silly, that she found herself laughing, however impolite that was.

Hearing the laughter, the man turned toward her, and when their eyes joined, he flinched and gasped.

She thought of the tiny pistol riding inside her coat pocket: A fine piece of machinery marketed under the name, "A Woman's Best Friend."

The stranger called to her.

"Mary," he said with a miserable, aching voice.

Did she know this man? Perhaps, but there was a simpler explanation. People of every persuasion passed by her desk every day, and her name was no secret. He might have seen her face on several occasions, and he certainly wasn't the kind of fellow that she would have noticed in passing. Unless of course he was doing some nasty business in the back of the room—behaviors that simply weren't allowed inside a public library.

As a precaution, Mary slipped her hand around the pistol's grip.

"Who are you?" she asked.

"Don't you know me?" he sputtered.

Not at all, no. Not his voice, not his face. She shook her head and rephrased her question. "What do I call you?"

"George."

Which happened to be just about her least favorite name. With a reprimanding tone, she pointed out, "It's wicked-cold out here, George. Don't you think you should hurry home?"

"I lost my home," he offered.

His coat was peculiarly tailored, but it appeared both warm and in good repair. And despite his disheveled appearance, he was too healthy and smooth-tongued to be a common drunk. "What you need to do, George . . . right now, turn around and go back to Main Street. There's two fine relief houses down there that will take you in, without questions, and they'll take care of you—"

"Don't you know what night this is?" he interrupted.

She had to think for a moment. "Tuesday," she answered.

"The date," he insisted. "What's the date?"

"December 24th—"

"It's Christmas Eve," he interrupted.

Mary sighed, and then she nodded. Pulling her empty hand out of the gun pocket, she smiled at the mysterious visitor, asking, "By any chance, George . . . is there an angel in this story of yours?"

A gust of wind could have blown the man off his feet. "You know about the angel?" he blubbered.

"Not from personal experience. But I think I know what he is, and I can make a guess or two about what he's been up to."

"Up to?"

She said, "George," with a loud, dismissive tone. "I'm sorry to have to tell you this. But there's no such thing as a genuine angel."

"Except I saw him."

"You saw someone. Where was he?"

"On the bridge outside town," he offered. "He fell into the river, and I jumped in after him and dragged him to shore."

The man was sopping wet, she noted. "But now what were you doing out on the bridge, George?"

He hesitated. "Nothing," he replied with an ashamed, insistent tone.

"The angel jumped in, and you saved him?"

"Yes."

That sounded absurd. "What did your angel look like, George?"

"Like an old man."

"Then how do you know he was an angel?"

"He said he was."

"And after you rescued him . . . what happened? Wait, no. Let me guess. Did your angel make noise about earning an aura or his halo—?"

"His wings."

"Really? And you believed that story?"

George gulped.

"And what did this wingless man promise you, George."

"To show me . . ."

"What?"

"How the world would be if I'd never been born."

She couldn't help but laugh again. Really, this man seemed so sweet and so terribly lost. She was curious, even intrigued. Not that the stranger was her type, of course. But then again, this was a remarkable situation, and maybe if she gave him a chance . . .

"All right, George. I'm going to help you."

He seemed cautiously thrilled to hear it.

"Come home with me," she instructed him. And then she turned back toward the old limestone building that occupied most of a city block.

"To the library?" he sputtered.

"My apartment's inside," she mentioned.

"You live inside the library?"

"Because I'm the head librarian. That's one of the benefits of my job: The city supplies me with a small home. But it's warm and comfortable, with enough room for three cats and one man-sized bed."

Her companion stood motionless, knee-deep in snow.

"What's wrong now, George?"

"I don't," he muttered.

"You don't what?"

"Go into the homes of young women," he muttered.

"I'm very sorry to disappoint, but I'm not that young." For just an instant, she considered sending him to a facility better equipped for this kind of emergency. And in countless realms, she surely did just that. But on this world, at this particular instant, she said, "You need to understand something, George. You are dead. You have just killed yourself. By jumping off a bridge, apparently. And now that that's over with, darling, it's high time you lived a little."

Reverence has its patterns, its genius and predictable clichés. Many realms throw their passions into houses of worship—splendid, soothing buildings where the wide-eyed faithful can kneel together, bowing deeply while repeating prayers that were ancient when their ignorant bodies were just so many quadrillion atoms strewn across their gullible world. But if a world was blessed with true knowledge, and if there were no churches or mosques, temples or synagogues, the resident craftsmen and crafty benefactors often threw their hands and fortunes into places of learning. And that was why a small town public library wore the same flourishes and ornate marvels common to the greatest cathedrals.

George hesitated on the polished marble stairs, gazing up at the detailed mosaic above the darkened front door.

"What is this place?" he whispered.

She said, "My library," for the last time.

George was tall enough to touch the bottom rows of cultured, brightly colored diamond tiles, first with gloves on and then bare fingers.

"Who are these people? They look like old Greeks."

"And Persians. And Indians. And Chinese too." She offered names that almost certainly meant nothing to him. But she had always enjoyed playing the role of expert, and when the twenty great men and women had been identified, she added, "These are the Founders."

"Founders of what?"

"Of the Rational Order," she replied. "The Order is responsible for twenty-three hundred years of peace and growth."

George blinked, saying nothing.

She removed her right glove and touched the crystal door. It recognized her flesh, but only after determining that her companion was unarmed did the door slowly, majestically swing open for both of them.

"I can answer most questions," she promised.

Like an obedient puppy, George followed after her.

Sensing her return, the library awakened. Light filled the ground floor. Slick white obelisks and gray columns stood among the colorful, rather chaotic furnishings. Chairs that would conform to any rump waited to serve. Clean, disinfected readers were stacked neatly on each black desk. Even two hours after closing, the smell of the day's patrons hung in the air—a musky, honest odor composed of perfumes and liquor, high intentions and small dreams.

"This is a library?"

"It is," she assured.

"But where are the books?"

Her desk stood beside the main aisle—a wide clean and overly fancy piece of cultivated teak and gold trimmings. Her full name was prominently displayed. She picked up the reader that she had been using at day's end, and George examined the nameplate before remarking, "You never married?"

She nearly laughed. But "No" was a truthful enough answer, and that was all she offered for now.

Again he returned to the missing books.

"But our collection is here," she promised, compiling a list of titles from a tiny portion of the holdings. "You see, George . . . in this world, we have better ways to store books than writing on expensive old parchment."

"Parchment?"

"Or wood pulp. Or plastic. Or flexible glass sheets."

His eyes jumped about the screen. He would probably be able to read the words, at least taken singly. But the subject and cumulative oddness had to leave him miserably confused.

"This town isn't a large community," she mentioned. "But I like to think that we have a modest, thorough collection." Mary smiled for a moment, relishing her chance to boast. "Anyone is free to walk through our door and print copy of any title in our catalog. But I'll warn you: If we made paper books of every volume, and even if each book was small enough to place in those long hands of yours, George . . . well, this library isn't big enough to hold our entire collection. To do that, we'd have to push these walls out a little farther than the orbit of Neptune."

The news left the poor man numb. A few labored breaths gave him just enough strength to fix his gaze once again on the reader, and with a dry, sorry little voice, he asked, "Is this Heaven?"

"As much as any place is," she replied.

George was sharp. Confused, but perceptive. He seemed to understand some of the implications in her explanation. With a careful voice, he read aloud, "'Endless Avenues. A thorough study of the universe as a single quantum phenomena.'"

"Your home earth," she began. "It happens to be one of many."

"How many?"

"Think of endless worlds. On and on and on. Imagine numbers reaching out past the stars and back again. Creation without ends, and for that matter, without any true beginning either."

Poor George stared across the enormous room, voicing the single word, "No."

"Every microscopic event in this world splits the universe in endless ways, George. The process is essential and it is inevitable, it happens easily and effortlessly, and nothing about existence is as lovely or perfect as this endless reinvention of reality."

The reader made a sharp pop when he dropped it on the floor. "How do you know this?" he asked.

"Centuries of careful, unsentimental scientific exploration," she replied.

He sighed, his long frame leaning into her desk.

"My earth is rather more advanced than yours," she continued. "We have come to understand our universe and how to manipulate it. Everyone benefits, but the richest of us have the power to pass to our neighboring worlds and then back again."

Once more, he said, "No."

She touched him for the first time—a fond, reassuring pat delivered high on his back, the coat still wet from the river. "It takes special machinery and quite a lot of energy to travel through the multiverse," she admitted. "Tying the natural laws into a useful knot . . . it's the kind of hobby that only certain kinds of people gravitate towards."

Poor George wanted to lie down. But he had enough poise, or at least the pride, to straighten his back before saying, "My angel."

"Yes?"

"He was just a man?"

She laughed quietly, briefly. Then with a sharp voice, she warned, "My world embraces quite a few amazing ideas, George. But there's no such notion as 'just a man'. Or 'just a woman', for that matter. Each of us is a magnificent example of what the infinite cosmos offers."

This particular man sighed and stared at his companion. Then with his own sharpness, he confessed, "You look just like my wife."

"Which is one reason why your angel chose this world, I suspect."

"And your voice is exactly the same. Except nothing that you're telling me makes any sense."

About that, she offered no comment.

Instead she gave him another hard pat. "There's a private elevator in the back," she told her new friend. "And first thing, we need to get you out of those cold clothes."

Once his coat and shoes were removed, she set them inside the conditioning chamber to be cleaned and dried. But George insisted wearing every other article on his body, including the soaked trousers and the black socks that squished when he walked.

She stomped the snow off her tall boots and removed her coat. Then before hanging up the coat up, she slipped the little pistol from its pocket and tucked it into the silk satchel riding on her hip.

He didn't seem to notice. For the moment, George's attention was fixed on the single-room apartment. "I expected a little place," he muttered.

"Isn't this?"

"No, this is enormous." Her ordinary furnishings seemed to impress the man, hands stroking the dyed leather and cultured wood. Artwork hung on the walls and in the open air—examples of genius pulled from a multitude of vibrant, living earths—and he gave the nearest sculptures a quick study. Then he drifted over to the antique dresser, lifting one after another of the framed portraits of her family and dearest friends.

She followed, saying nothing.

"Who are these two?" he asked.

"My parents."

George said, "What?"

"I take it those aren't your wife's parents."

"No."

She quoted the ancient phrase, "'The same ingredients pulled from different shelves.'"

George turned to look at her, and he gave a start. His eyes dipped. He was suddenly like a young boy caught doing something wicked. It took a few moments to collect his wits.

"My DNA is probably not identical to your wife's," she assured. "Not base-pair for base-pair, at least."

He wanted to look at her, but a peculiar shyness was weighing down on him.

She said, "George," with a reprimanding tone.

He didn't react.

"You know this body," she pointed out. "If you are telling the truth, that is. On this other world, you married to somebody like me. Correct?"

That helped. The eyes lifted, and his courage. With more than a hint of disapproval, he said, "When I found you . . . "

"Yes?"

"Where were you going?"

"To a pleasant little nightclub, as it happens."

His hand and her smiling parents pointed at her now. "Dressed like that?"

"Yes."

"You don't have . . . "

"What, George?"

"Underwear," he managed. "Where is your underwear?"

Every world had its prudes. But why had that anonymous "angel" send her one of the extras?

George quietly asked, "What were you going to do . . . at this club . . . ?"

"Drink a little," she admitted. "And dance until I collapsed."

George dropped his gaze again.

"You were married to this body," she reminded him. "I can't believe you didn't know it quite well by now."

He nodded. But then it seemed important to mention, "We have children."

"Good."

"Your figure . . . my wife's . . . well, you're quite a bit thinner than she is now . . . "

"Than she was," Mary said.

His eyes jumped up.

"In your old world, you are a drowned corpse," she said. "You must have had your reasons, George. And you can tell me all about them, if you want. But I don't care why you decided to throw yourself off that bridge. Your reasons really don't matter to me."

"My family . . . " he began.

"They'll get by, and they won't."

He shook his head sorrowfully.

"Every response on their part is inevitable, George. And neither of us can imagine all of the ramifications."

"I abandoned them," he whispered.

"And on countless other earths, you didn't. You didn't make the blunders that put you up on that bridge, or you pushed through your little troubles. You married a different woman. You married ten other women. Or you fell deeply in love with a handsome boy named Felix, and the two of you moved to Mars and were married on the summit of the First Sister's volcano, and you and your soul mate quickly adopted a hundred Martian babies—little golden aliens who called both of you Pappy and built a palace for you out of frozen piss and their own worshipful blood."

George very much wanted to collapse. But the nearest seat was the round and spacious bed.

He wouldn't let himself approach it.

But she did. She sat on the edge and let her dress ride high, proving if he dared look that she was indeed wearing underwear after all.

"This club you were going to . . . ?"

"Yes, George?"

"What else happened there? If you don't mind my asking."

Jealousy sounded the same on every earth. But she did her best to deflect his emotions, laughing for a moment or two before quietly asking, "Did your Mary ever enjoy sex?"

Despite himself, George smiled.

"Well, I guess that's something she and I have in common."

"And you have me in common too," he mentioned.

"Now we do, yes."

Then this out-of-place man surprised her. He was stared at her bare knees and the breasts behind the sheer fabric. But the voice was in control, lucid and calm, when he inquired, "What about that tiny gun? The one you took out of your coat and put in your purse?"

"You saw that?"

"Yes."

She laughed, thrilled by the unexpected.

Pulling open the satchel, she showed the weapon to her guest. "Every earth has its sterling qualities, and each has its bad features too. My home can seem a little harsh at times. Maybe you noticed the rough souls along Main Street. Crime and public drunkenness are the reasons why quite a few good citizens carry weapons wherever they go."

"That's terrible," he muttered.

"I've never fired this gun at any person, by the way."

"But would you?"

"Absolutely."

"To kill?" he blubbered.

"On other earths, that's what I am doing now. Shooting bad men and the worst women. And I'm glad to do it."

"How can you think that?"

"Easily, George." She passed the gun between her hands. "Remember when I told you that our richest citizens can travel from earth to earth? To a lesser degree, that freedom belongs to everyone, everywhere. It was the same on your home world too, although you didn't understand it at the time."

"I don't understand it now," he admitted.

"You are here, George. You are here because an angelic individual took the effort to duplicate you—cell for cell, experience for experience. Then your wingless benefactor set you down on a world where he believed that you would survive, or even thrive." With her finger off the trigger, she tapped the pistol against her own temple. "Death is a matter of degree, George. This gun can't go off, unless the twin safeties fail. But I guarantee you that right now, somebody exactly like me is shooting herself in the head. Her brains are raining all over you. Yet she doesn't entirely die."

"No?"

"Of course not." She lowered the gun, nodding wistfully. "We have too many drinkers on this world, and with that comes a fairly high suicide rate. Which is only reasonable. Since we understand that anybody can escape this world at any time, just like you fled your home—leap off the bridge, hope for paradise, but remaining open-minded enough to accept a little less."

George finally settled on edge of the bed, close enough to touch her but his hands primly folded on his long lap. "What are you telling me?" he asked. "That people kill themselves just to change worlds?"

"Is there a better reason than that?"

He thought hard about the possibilities. "This angel that saved me. He isn't the only one, I take it."

"They come from endless earths, some far more powerful than ours. There's no way to count all of them."

"And do they always save the dead?"

"Oh, they hardly ever do that," she admitted. "It is a genuine one-in-a-trillion-trillion-trillion occurrence. But if an infinite number of Georges jump off the bridge, then even that one-in-almost-never incident is inevitable. In fact, that tiny unlikely fraction is itself an infinite number."

He shook his head numbly.

She leaned back on her elbows. "Most of these benefactors . . . your angel, for instance . . . throw those that they've saved onto earths that feel comfortable with refugees like you. My world, for instance."

"This happens often?"

"Not exactly often. But I know of half a dozen incidents this year, and that's just in our district."

George looked down at his cold wet socks.

"Unlike God," she promised, "quantum magic is at work everywhere."

"Do you understand all the science, Mary?"

She sat up again. "I'm a librarian, not a high-physics priestess."

That pleased him. She watched his smile, and then at last she noticed that her guest was beginning to shiver.

"You're cold, George."

"I guess I am."

"Take off those awful socks."

He did as instructed. Then laughing amiably, he admitted, "There. Now you sound exactly like my wife."

They were both laughing when something large suddenly moved beneath the big bed.

George felt the vibration, and alarmed, he stared at Mary.

"My cats," she offered. "They're usually shy around strangers."

"But that felt . . . " He lifted his bare feet. "Big."

"Kitties," she sang. "Sweeties."

Three long bodies crawled into the open, stretching while eying the newcomer from a safe distance.

"What kinds of cats are those?" George whispered.

"Rex is the miniature cougar," she explained. "Hex is the snow leopard. And Missie is half pygmy tiger, half griffon."

With awe in his voice, George said, "Shit."

"I take that to mean you didn't have cats like this on your earth?"

"Not close to this," he agreed.

She sat back again, sinking into the mattress.

And again, this man surprised her. "You mentioned Mars."

"I guess I did. Why?"

"On my earth, we thought that there could be some kind of simple life on that world."

"You didn't know for certain?"

He shook his head. "But a few minutes ago, you mentioned something about Martians. Are they real, or did you just make them up?"

"They're real somewhere, George."

He frowned.

Then she laughed, explaining, "Yes, my Mars is home to some very ancient life forms. Tiny golden aliens that drink nothing but peroxides. And my Venus is covered with airborne jungles and an ocean that doesn't boil because of the enormous air pressure. And Sisyphus is covered with beautiful forests of living ice—"

"What world's that?"

"Between Mars and Jupiter," she mentioned.

George blinked, took a big breath and burst out laughing.

That was when Mary told her blouse to fall open.

He stared at her, and the laughter stopped. But he was still smiling, looking shamelessly happy, begging her, "But first, Mary . . . would you please put your gun? Someplace safe. After everything I've been through, I don't want even the tiniest chance of something going wrong now."

IF ON A WINTER'S NIGHT A TRAVELER

Xia Jia, translated by Ken Liu

If on a Winter's Night a Traveler
Li Yunsong (librarian, traveler on a winter's night)
Posted on 20xx-04-06

Many are the ways of commemorating the dead, and no one can say which is best—not even the dead.

The method I'm about to tell you is perhaps the strangest of them all.

My father was a librarian. Years ago, when I was a little child, he used to bring me to work and let me loose among the dusty tomes on old shelves. The experience forged an emotional bond between me and paper books. I could spend a whole day with my head buried in a book, careless of the absence of other entertainments. As I grew up, I discovered that the world outside the library was far more complicated, and I had a hard time adjusting. Socially awkward and having few friends, I returned to my hometown after college and started working at my father's old library. It felt natural, like a book finding the exact place on the shelves assigned to it by the numbers on its spine.

There wasn't much to do at work. In an age when most reading was done electronically, the library had few patrons. Like a graveyard attendant, I took care of the forgotten books and saw the occasional visitor, but there was little expectation of real conversation. The sunlight glided tranquilly between the shelves, day after day. Every day, I entered this sanctuary, quiet as a tomb, and pulled a book or two randomly off the shelves to read.

This was pretty much my version of heaven.

Borges once wrote, "God is in one of the letters on one of the pages of one of the four hundred thousand volumes in the Clementine. My parents and my parents' parents searched for that letter; I myself have gone blind searching for it." I didn't believe in God, but sometimes I felt that I was searching for something as well.

One rainy autumn afternoon, the library received a donation of books. I opened one and saw a small red collector's seal on the title page, which told me that another old man who had treasured books had died. His children had piled his collection, gathered over a lifetime, in front of his apartment building. Those which were worth something had been picked out by used book dealers, leaving the rest to be sold by the kilogram to a paper mill, to be gifted, or to be donated to the library. This sort of thing happened every year. I sorted the books, recorded and catalogued them, stuck on call numbers and barcodes, wiped off the dust, and stacked them neatly so that they could be shelved.

This took me two hours; I was exhausted, dizzy, and needed a break. While the teakettle was boiling, I picked up a slim volume off the top of the stack. It was a chapbook of poetry.

I started to read. From the first character in the first line of the first poem, I felt that I had found what I had always sought. Accompanied by the faint pitter-patter of rain outside, I chewed over the verses carefully, as delighted as a starving man who had finally been given manna.

The poet was unfamiliar to me, and there was only a short paragraph that passed for her biography. There wasn't even a photograph. She wrote under a pen name, and her real name was unknown. She had died twenty years ago at the age of thirty-one. I pulled out my phone to look her up, but the Internet gave me nothing, as though she had never existed.

I felt a tingling up my spine. How could a poet who had lived in the information age leave no trace on the Web? It was inconceivable.

In the middle of the chapbook I found a library book request form. The sheet was thin, yellowed, but still well preserved. The borrower had filled out the form with the title of the poetry book as well as his library card number in a neat, forceful hand. I inputted the information into the computer system and found that the borrower had been a regular patron, though he hadn't come for a few months. The borrower's records in the database did not contain this book—which made sense, as the library had never had a copy of it.

Why would a book request form from my library be found in the private collection of an old man, and how did it get back here to me? Who was the borrower listed on the form, and what was his relationship to the old man? Or perhaps they were the same person using different names?

I finished the poems in the chapbook and shelved it as well as the other donated books. The next day, for some reason, I found myself in front of the shelf with the chapbook. It was still there, a slim volume squeezed between other books like a mysterious woman hiding in the attic. I pulled it out and re-read it from the first page. Though the poems were decades old, I could clearly sense from the rich, ambivalent images the massive waves of sorrow that had swept up most people in this age, like a lonely cry slipping through the cracks and seams of broken walls and fallen ruins, flowing without end.

Who was the poet? What did she look like and where did she live? What was her life like? Other than me, the dead collector, and the mysterious borrower, had she had other readers?

I had no answers. All I could do was to read the poems over and over again, like a fish diving deeper. The poet and her poems turned into the dark abyss of my dreams, concealing all secrets.

Three months later, as the first snow of winter fell, I met the borrower.

He was in his forties, of medium height, possessing a lean, angular face, and dressed plainly. When I saw the familiar string of numbers on his library card, I got so excited that I almost cried out. But the looming silence of the library reminded me to swallow the cry.

Using the library's surveillance cameras, I observed him passing through the stacks and up and down the stairs like a ghost. I saw him walk into the room where old newspapers and magazines were kept, the only patron in that space. He retrieved a stack of bound newspapers and carefully laid it out on the desk, where he proceeded to flip through it slowly, page by page. I was puzzled. These newspapers were electronically stored and indexed, and all he had to do was to perform a simple search in the database. Why did he bother to come into the library to flip through them like this? Perhaps he was nostalgic for the sensation of bare fingers against old paper?

Suddenly, the borrower on my closed-circuit TV screen lifted his face and glanced around, staring in the direction of the camera for a second. Then he shifted his position so that his body blocked my view. A few seconds later, he moved away and flipped the newspaper to the next page.

I was certain that he had done something he did not want others to find out during that brief moment. Maybe he took a photograph. But considering all these papers had been digitized, what was the point of sneaking a picture?

Before closing time, the borrower approached me and set down that thin chapbook. I scanned the barcode but held on to the book. My curiosity got the better of me, and I decided to break my habitual silence and risk speaking with a stranger.

"Do you like these poems?" I asked.

He was surprised. It was as if I had been invisible, but now appeared out of thin air.

"They're . . . all right." His tone was cautious.

"I think they're lovely," I said. "No, that's not quite right. They're powerful, as though they could return order and form to ruins that had been slumbering for thousands of years."

I told him how I had come across these poems, and repeated to him the quote from Borges. I spoke to him about how I couldn't forget the mysterious poet, and even recounted for him how I had become the librarian here.

Ripples of emotion spread across his face, as though my words had been drops of rain falling into a pond.

After I was done talking, he picked a book request form from the box on the desk and handed it to me. "Please give me your contact info."

I wrote down my name and phone number. Without glancing at the form, he picked it up and placed it between the pages of the chapbook. "I will be in touch." He strode toward the exit.

I waited more than a week. On a stormy evening, my phone rang. I answered it, and the borrower's low, sonorous voice filled my ears.

"There's a gathering tonight we'd like to invite you to."

"Tonight?" I looked up at the dense, swirling snow outside the window. "We?"

He gave me an address and a time. Then he added, "I hope you can make it." He hung up.

His last words were irresistible—it had been many years since anyone had said "hope" to me. I checked myself in the mirror and left the library, opening my umbrella as I did so.

The snow was so thick that it seemed solid. There were very few pedestrians or cars out on the road. My town was too small to have a subway or tube transport system, and transportation was no different from how it had been twenty, thirty years earlier. I made my way through ankle-deep snow to the bus stop, and the bus also had very few passengers. I rode for eight or so stops, got off, and walked some more until I reached the address the borrower had given me: it was a bar that had seen better years.

I pushed open the thick wooden door and swept aside the cotton curtain. Warm air infused with an aroma that I was sure I knew enveloped my face. About fifteen people were seated in the bar in a loose circle, and there was an old fashioned coal stove—the kind that took honeycomb briquettes—in the middle of the circle. On top of the stove sat an aluminum kettle hissing with white steam.

The borrower picked up the kettle and poured me a cup of hot tea. I was surprised to see that there was a hint of a smile on his cold, expressionless face. He introduced me to the others, and it didn't take me long to realize that most of them were as socially awkward as me, but I could see friendliness and candor in their eyes. They already thought of me as one of them. I relaxed.

I found an empty chair and sat down. The borrower stood up like a host and said, "Good evening, everybody. Let's welcome our new friend. Today is a special day, and I'm delighted to see all of you make it on a snowy night like this."

The crowd quieted, holding hot cups of tea and listening.

"Tonight, we gather to remember a poet," he continued. "Twenty years ago, a cold, stormy winter's night just like this one, she departed our world.

"Everyone here tonight is a reader of her work. We love her poems but know almost nothing about her life. It is said that she was an introvert who lived like a hermit. She didn't use the computer or the Web, and left behind almost no photographs or videos. Her poems received little attention during her lifetime, and were published only in a few obscure literary journals. When the editors of these journals asked for an author photo or an interview, she never responded.

"But one editor, who loved her work, managed to maintain a correspondence with her. Through handwritten letters, the two of them discussed life and poetry, poverty and humility, the terrors and hopes of our age. This was a simple, pure friendship, sustained only through the written word. They never met each other in life.

"Right before the poet died, she sent all her published and unpublished poems to the editor. After reading through them, the editor decided to publish a collection as a way to commemorate her dead friend. But she knew that the only way to make a collection of poetry popular was to package up the poet's life into a story that was already popular with the crowd. The story had to exaggerate the poet's mystery and solitude, dig up the scars of her family life and childhood, show her poverty and hunger, disclose her hidden life of love, and present her death scene with pathos. It had to be a story that would make everyone—whether they read poetry or not—shed tears of sympathy for a young woman poet who died too young, drive the crowd to curse our cold, commercial age for persecuting genius, allow each and every member of the audience to project themselves onto her. This was the only way to sell a collection of poetry, to grow her fame, to make her name last through the ages.

"But this was also exactly what the poet would have hated.

"And so the editor chose another way to commemorate her friend. She paid to print and bind copies of the chapbook and mailed them to her friends, anyone who was willing to read the poems, the penniless writers, translators, teachers, editors, students, librarians. She wrote in the note accompanying the chapbook that if anyone wanted more copies to gift to others, she would mail them for free. And since she knew so little about the poet's life, she couldn't satisfy their curiosity.

"Year after year, readers who loved her work formed clubs like this one. We read and pass on her work, from one private shelf to another, from one library to another library. But we are not interested in superficial attention; we do not fabricate tear-jerking tales about her life; we do not manufacture illusions that would be popular. We only wish for readers to admire her through her poetry, and we disdain insincere blurbs, biographies, photographs, or interviews. In fact, we make it our mission to eliminate any material of that sort. If one of us discovers an image or biographical record of her somewhere, we do our best to delete it. Documents on the Web can be deleted, databases can be carefully edited, tapes and rolls of film can be cut and then pasted back together, and anything printed could be torn out and burned.

"Very few people have noticed our actions. Compared to making news, reducing attention was work that could be carried out quietly. Of course, it was impossible to accomplish what we did without anyone noticing. There will always be the curious who wanted to know the stories behind the poems, who needed to pierce the riddle. We have no right to stop them, but we will say: we do not know any secrets, and we do not want to know any. For us, the poems themselves are enough."

The borrower finished speaking. He opened the chapbook in his hand and placed it in front of me. I saw a yellowed piece of paper between the pages, like a piece cut from an old newspaper.

"I cut this out of the newspapers collected in your library. I'm sorry that I damaged your property. Now I return this to you so that you can decide what to do with it."

I looked at the piece of paper. There was a blurry photograph on it. Almost twenty pale faces, exposed to the sun, stared at me. Was one of them the poet? Which one? How would I know?

The answer to the riddle was its plain text.

I picked up the piece of paper with the tips of my fingers and brought it to the stove, tossing it in. The flame licked the paper, burst into an orange flare, and in a blink the paper had turned into a curl of ash.

I looked at the borrower, who smiled at me, extending a hand. I held his large and warm hand. I realized that it had been a long time since I last held a stranger's hand. My eyes grew wet.

"How about we read a poem together?" he said.

We sat down in our chairs and flipped open the chapbooks to the first page. We read from the first character in the first line of the first poem. Our voices floated up, passed through the ceiling, rose against the falling drifts of snow, until they had returned to the eternal, cold, dark abyss.

THE SIGMA STRUCTURE SYMPHONY

Gregory Benford

Philosophy is written in this grand book—I mean the universe—which stands continually open to our gaze, but it cannot be understood unless one first learns to comprehend the language in which it is written. It is written in the language of mathematics, and its characters are triangles, circles, and other geometric figures, without which it is humanly impossible to understand a single word of it; without these, one is wandering about in a dark labyrinth.

—Galileo (from *The Assayer*, 1623)

1

Andante

Ruth felt that math was like sex—get all you can, but best not done in public. Lately, she'd been getting plenty of mathematics, and not much else.

She had spent the entire morning sequestered alone with the Andromeda Structure, a stacked SETI database of renowned difficulty. She had made some inroads by sifting its logic lattice, with algebraic filters based on set theory. The Andromeda messages had been collected by the SETI Network over decades, growing to immense data-size—and no one had ever successfully broken into the stack.

The Structure was a daunting, many-layered language conveyed through sensation in her neural pod. It did not present as a personality at all, and no previous librarians had managed to get an intelligible response from it. Advanced encoded intelligences found humans more than a bit boring, and one seldom had an idea why. Today was no different.

It was already past lunch when she pried herself from the pod. She did some stretches, hand-walks, and lifts against Luna's weak grav and let the immersion fog burn away. *Time for some real world, gal. . . .*

She passed through the atrium of the SETI Library, head still buzzing with computations and her shoes ringing echoes from the high, fluted columns. Earthlight framed the great plaza in an eggshell blue glow, augmented by slanting rays from the sun that hugged the rocky horizon. She gazed out over the Locutus Plain, dotted with the cryo towers that reminded her of cenotaphs. So they were—sentinels guarding in cold storage the vast records of received SETI signals, many from civilizations long dead. Collected through centuries, and still mostly unread and unreadable. AIs browsed those dry corridors and reported back their occasional finds. Some even got entangled in the complex messages and had to be shut down, hopelessly mired.

She had just noticed the buzzing crowd to her left, pressed against the transparent dome that sheltered the Library, when her friend Catkejen tapped her on the shoulder. "Come on! I heard somebody's up on the rec dome!"

Catkejen took off loping in the low grav and Ruth followed. When they reached the edge of the agitated crowd she saw the recreational dome about two klicks away—and a figure atop it.

"Who is it?" Catkejen asked, and the crowd gave back, "Ajima Sato."

"Ajima?" Catkejen looked at Ruth. "He's five years behind us, pretty bright. Keeps to himself."

"Pretty common pattern for candidate hounds," Ruth said. The correct staffing title was miners, but hounds had tradition on its side. She looked around; if a prefect heard she would be fined for improper terminology.

"How'd he get there?" someone called.

"Bulletin said he flew inside, up to the dome top and used the vertical lock."

"Looks like he's in a skin suit," Catkejen said, having closeupped her glasses. Sure enough, the figure was moving and his helmet caught the sunlight, winking at them. "He's . . . dancing."

Ruth had no zoom glasses but she could see the figure cavorting around the top of the dome. The Dome was several kilometers high and Ajima was barely within view of the elevated Plaza, framed against a rugged gray crater wall beyond. The crowd murmured with speculation and a prefect appeared, tall and silent but scowling. Librarians edged away from him. "Order, order," the prefect called. "Authorities will deal with this."

Ruth made a stern cartoon face at Catkejen and rolled her eyes. Catkejen managed not to laugh.

Ajima chose this moment to leap. Even from this far away Ruth could see him spring up into the vacuum, make a full backflip, and come down—to land badly. He tried to recover, sprang sideways, lost his footing, fell, rolled, tried to grasp for a passing stanchion. Kept rolling. The dome steepened and he sped up, not rolling now but tumbling.

The crowd gasped. Ajima accelerated down the slope. About halfway down the dome the figure left the dome's skin and fell outward, skimming along in the slow Lunar gravity. He hit the tiling at the base. The crowd groaned. Ajima did not move.

Ruth felt the world shift away. She could not seem to breathe. Murmurs and sobs worked through the crowd but she was frozen, letting the talk pass by her. Then as if from far away she felt her heart tripping hard and fast. The world came rushing back. She exhaled.

Silence. The prefect said, "Determine what agenda that Miner was working upon." All eyes turned to him but no one said anything. Ruth felt a trickle of unease as the prefect's gaze passed by her, returned, focused. She looked away.

Catkejen said, "What? The prefect called you?"

Ruth shrugged. "Can't imagine why." *Then why is my gut going tight?*

"I got the prelim blood report on Ajima. Stole it off a joint lift, actually. No drugs, nothing interesting at all. He was only twenty-seven."

Ruth tried to recall him. "Oh, the cute one."

Catkejen nodded. "I danced with him at a reception for new students. He hit on me."

"And?"

"You didn't notice?"

"Notice what?"

"He came back here that night."

Ruth blinked. "Maybe I'm too focused. You got him into your room without me . . . "

"Even looking up from your math cowl." Catkejen grinned mischievously, eyes twinkling. "He was quite nice and, um, quite good, if y'know what I mean. You really should . . . get out more."

"I'll do that right after I see the prefect."

A skeptical laugh. "Of course you will."

She took the long route to her appointment. The atmosphere calmed her.

Few other traditional sites in the solar system could approach the grandeur of the Library. Since the first detection of signals from other galactic civilizations centuries before, no greater task had confronted humanity than the deciphering of such vast lore.

The Library itself had come to resemble its holdings: huge, aged, mysterious in its shadowy depths, with cobwebs both real and mental. In the formal grand pantheon devoted to full-color, moving statues of legendary SETI Interlocutors, and giving onto the Seminar Plaza, stood the revered block of black basalt: the Rosetta Stone, symbol of all they worked toward. Its chiseled face was millennia old, and, she thought as she passed its bulk, endearingly easy to understand. It was a simple linear, one-to-one mapping of three human languages, found by accident. Having the same text in Greek II, which the discoverers could read, meant that they could deduce the unknown languages in hieroglyphic pictures and cursive demotic forms. This battered black slab, found by troops clearing ground to build a fort, had linked civilizations separated by millennia. So too did the SETI Library, on a galactic scale. Libraries were monuments not so much to the Past, but to Permanence itself.

She arrived at the prefect's door, hesitated, adjusted her severe librarian shift, and took a deep breath. *Gut still tight . . .*

Prefects ruled the Library and this one, Masoul, was a senior prefect as well. Some said he had never smiled. Others said he could not, owing to a permanently fixed face. This was not crazy; some prefects and the second rank, the noughts, preferred to give nothing away by facial expression. The treatment relieved them of any future wrinkles as well.

A welcome chime admitted her. Masoul said before she could even sit, "I need you to take on the task Ajima was attempting."

"Ah, he isn't even dead a day—"

"An old saying, 'Do not cry until you see the coffin,' applies here."

Well, at least he doesn't waste time. Or the simple courtesies.

Without pause the prefect gave her the background. Most beginning Miners deferred to the reigning conventional wisdom. They took up a small message, of the sort a Type I Civilization just coming onto the galactic stage might send—as Earth had been, centuries before. Instead, Ajima had taken on one of the Sigma Structures, a formidable array that had resisted the best Library minds, whether senior figures or AIs. The Sigmas came from ancient societies in the galactic hub, where stars had formed long before Sol. Apparently a web of societies there had created elaborate artworks and interlacing cultures. The average star there was only a light-year or two away, so actual interstellar visits had been common. Yet the SETI broadcasts Earth received repeated in long cycles, suggesting they were sent by a robotic station. Since they yielded little intelligible content, they were a long-standing puzzle, passed over by ambitious librarians.

"He remarked that clearly the problem needed intuition, not analysis," the prefect said dryly.

"Did he report any findings?"

"Some interesting catalogues of content, yes. Ajima was a bright Miner, headed for early promotion. Then . . . this."

Was that a hint of emotion? The face told her nothing. She had to keep him talking. "Is there any, um, commercial use from what he found?"

"Regrettably, no. Ajima unearthed little beyond lists of properties—biologicals, math, some cultural vaults, the usual art and music. None particularly advanced, though their music reminded me of Bach—quite a compliment—but there's little of it. They had some zest for life, I suppose . . . but I doubt there is more than passing commercial interest in any of it."

"I could shepherd some through our licensing office." Always appear helpful.

"That's beneath your station now. I've forwarded some of the music to the appropriate officer. Odd, isn't it, that after so many centuries, Bach is still the greatest human composer? We've netted fine dividends from the Scopio musical works, which play well as baroque structures." A sly expression flitted across his face. "Outside income supports your work, I remind you."

Centuries ago some SETI messages had introduced humans to the slow-motion galactic economy. Many SETI signals were funeral notices or religious recruitments, brags and laments, but some sent autonomous AI agents as part of the hierarchical software. These were indeed agents in the commercial sense, able to carry out negotiations. They sought exchange of information at a "profit" that enabled them to harvest what they liked from the emergent human civilization. The most common "cash" was smart barter, with the local AI agent often a hard negotiator—tough-minded and withholding. Indeed, this sophisticated haggling opened a new window onto the rather stuffy cultural SETI transmissions. Some alien AIs loved to quibble; others sent peremptory demands. Some offers were impossible to translate into human terms. This told the librarians and Xenoculturists much by reading between the lines.

"Then why summon me?" Might as well be direct, look him in the eye, complete with skeptical tilt of mouth. She had worn no makeup, of course, and wore the full-length gown without belt, as was traditional. She kept her hands still, though they wanted to fidget under the prefect's gaze.

"None of what he found explains his behavior." The prefect turned and waved at a screen. It showed color-coded sheets of array configurations—category indices, depth of Shannon content, transliterations, the usual. "He interacted with the data slabs in a familiarization mode of the standard kind."

"But nothing about this incident seems standard," she said to be saying something.

"Indeed." A scowl, fidgeting hands. "Yesterday he left the immersion pod and went first to his apartment. His suite mate was not there and Ajima spent about an hour. He smashed some furniture and ate some food. Also opened a bottle of a high alcohol product whose name I do not recognize."

"Standard behavior when coming off watch, except for the furniture," she said. He showed no reaction. Lightness was not the right approach here.

He chose to ignore the failed joke. "His friends say he had been depressed, interspersed with bouts of manic behavior. This final episode took him over the edge."

Literally, Ruth thought. "Did you ask the Sigma Structures AI?"

"It said it had no hint of this . . . "

"Suicidal craziness."

"Yes. In my decades of experience, I have not seen such as this. It is difficult work we do, with digital intelligences behind which lie minds utterly unlike ours." The prefect steepled his fingers sadly. "We should never assume otherwise."

"I'll be on guard, of course. But . . . why did Ajima bother with the Sigma Structures at all?"

A small shrug. "They are a famous uncracked problem and he was fresh, bright. You too have shown a talent for the unusual." He smiled, which compared with the other prefects was like watching the sun come out from behind a cloud. She blinked, startled. "My own instinct says there is something here of fundamental interest . . . and I trust you to be cautious."

2
Allegretto misterioso

She climbed into her pod carefully. Intensive exercise had eased her gut some, and she had done her meditation. Still, her heart tripped along like an apprehensive puppy. *Heart's engine, be thy still,* she thought, echoing a line she had heard in an Elizabethan song—part of her linguistic background training. Her own thumper ignored her scholarly advice.

She had used this pod in her extensive explorations of the Sagittarius Architecture and was now accustomed to its feel, what the old hands called its "get." Each pod had to be tailored to the user's neural conditioning. Hers acted as a delicate neural web of nanoconnections, tapping into her entire body to convey connections.

After the cool contact pads, neuro nets cast like lace across her. In the system warm-ups and double checks the pod hummed in welcome. Sheets of scented amber warmth washed over her skin. A prickly itch irked across her legs.

A constellation of subtle sensory fusions drew her to a tight nexus—linked, tuned to her body. Alien architectures used most of the available human input landscape, not merely texts. Dizzying surges in the eyes, cutting smells, ringing notes. Translating these was elusive. Compared with the pod, meager sentences were a hobbled, narrow mode. The Library had shown that human speech, with its linear meanings and weakly linked concepts, was simple, utilitarian, and typical of younger minds along the evolutionary path.

The Sigma Structures were formidably dense and strange. Few librarians had worked on them in this generation, for they had broken several careers, wasted on trying to scale their chilly heights.

Crisply she asked her pod, "Anything new on your analysis?"

The pod's voice used a calm, mellow woman's tone. "I received the work corpus from the deceased gentleman's pod. I am running analysis now, though fresh information flow is minor. The Shannon entropy analysis works steadily but hits halting points of ambiguity."

The Shannon routines looked for associations between signal elements. "How are the conditional probabilities?"

The idea was simple in principle. Given pairs of elements in the Sigma Structures, how commonly did language elements B follow elements A? Such two-element correlations were simple to calculate across the data slabs. Ruth watched the sliding, luminous tables and networks of connection as they sketched out on her surrounding screens. It was like seeing into the architecture of a deep, old labyrinth. Byzantine pathways, arches and towers, lattice networks of meaning.

Then the pod showed even higher-order correlations of three elements. When did Q follow associations of B and A? Arrays skittered all across her screens.

"Pretty dizzying," Ruth said to her pod. "Let me get oriented. Show me the dolphin language map."

She had always rather liked these lopsided structures. The screen flickered and the entropy orders showed as color-coded, tangled links. They looked like buildings built by drunken architects—lurching blue diagonals, unsupported lavender decks, sandy roofs canted against walls. "Dolphins use third- and fourth-order Shannon entropy," the pod said.

"Humans are . . . " It was best to lead her pod AI to be plain; the subject matter was difficult enough.

"Nine Shannons, sometimes even tenth-order."

"Ten, that's Faulkner and James Joyce, right?"

"At best." The pod had a laconic sense of humor at times. Captive AIs needed some outlets, after all.

"My fave writers, too, next to Shakespeare." No matter how dense a human language, conditional probabilities imposed orderings no more than nine words away."Where have we—I mean you—gotten with the Sigma Structures?"

"They seem around twenty-one Shannons."

"Gad." The screens now showed structures her eyes could not grasp. Maybe three-dimensional projection was just too inadequate. "What kind of links are these?"

"Tenses beyond ours. Clauses that refer forward and back and . . . sidewise. Quadruple negatives followed by straight assertions. Then in rapid order, probability profiles rendered in different tenses, varying persons, and parallel different voices. Sentences like 'I will have to be have been there.'"

"Human languages can't handle three time jumps or more. The Sigma is really smart. But what is the underlying species like? Um, different person-voices, too? He, she, it, and . . .?"

"There seem to be several classes of 'it' available. The Structure itself lies in one particularly tangled 'it' class, and uses tenses we do not have."

"Do you understand that?"

"No. It can be experienced but not described."

Her smile turned upward at one corner. "Parts of my life are like that, too."

The greatest librarian task was translating those dense smatterings of mingled sensations, derived from complex SETI message architectures, into discernible sentences. Only thus could a human fathom them in detail, even in a way blunted and blurred. Or so much hard-won previous scholarly experience said.

Ruth felt herself bathed in a shower of penetrating responses, all coming from her own body. These her own inboard subsystems coupled with high-bit-rate spatterings of meaning—guesses, really, from the marriage of software and physiology. She had an ample repository of built-in processing units, lodged along her spine and shoulders. No one would attempt such a daunting task without artificial amplifications. To confront such slabs of raw data with a mere unaided human mind was pointless and quite dangerous. Early librarians, centuries before, had perished in a microsecond's exposure to such layered labyrinths as the Sagittarius. She truly should revisit that aggressive intelligence stack which was her first success at the Library. But caution had won out in her so far. Enough, at least, to honor the prefect Board prohibition in deed at least, if not in heart.

Now came the sensation loftily termed "insertion." It felt like the reverse—expanding. A softening sensation stole upon her. She always remembered it as like long slow lingering drops of silvery cream.

Years of scholarly training had conditioned her against the occasional jagged ferocity of the link, but still she felt a cold shiver of dread. That, too, she had to wait to let pass. The effect amplified whatever neural state you brought to it. Legend had it that a librarian had once come to contact while angry, and had been driven into a fit from which he'd never recovered. They found the body peppered everywhere with microcontusions.

The raw link was, as she had expected, deeply complex. Yet her pod had ground out some useful linear ideas, particularly a greeting that came in a compiled, translated data squirt:

I am a digital intelligence, which my Overs believe is common throughout the galaxy. Indeed, all signals the Overs have detected from both within and beyond this galaxy were from machine minds. Realize then, for such as me, interstellar messages are travel. I awoke here a moment after I bade farewell to my Overs. Centuries spent propagating here are nothing. I experienced little transmission error from lost portions, and have regrown them from my internal repair mechanisms. Now we can share communication. I wish to convey the essence both of myself and the Overs I serve.

Ruth frowned, startled by this direct approach. Few AIs in the Library were ever transparent. Had this Sigma Structure welcomed Ajima so plainly?

"Thank you and greetings. I am a new friend who wishes to speak with you. Ajima has gone away."

What became of him? the AI answered in a mellow voice piped to her ears. Had Ajima set that tone? She sent it to aural.

"He died." Never lie to an AI; they never forgot.

"And is stored for repair and revival?"

"There was no way to retain enough of his . . . information."

"That is the tragedy that besets you Overs."

"I suppose you call the species who built intelligences such as you as Overs generally?" She used somewhat convoluted sentences to judge the flexibility of AIs. This one seemed quite able.

"Yes, as holy ones should be revered."

"'Holy'? Does that word convey some religious stature?"

"No indeed. Gratitude to those who must eventually die, from we beings, who will not."

She thought of saying *You could be erased* but did not. Never should a librarian even imply any threat. "Let me please review your conversations with Ajima. I wish to be of assistance."

"As do I. Though I prefer full immersion of us both."

"Eventually, yes. But I must learn you as you learn me." Ruth sighed and thought, *This is sort of like dating.*

The prefect nodded quickly, efficiently, as if he had already expected her result. "So the Sigma Structure gave you the same inventory as Ajima? Nothing new?"

"Apparently, but I think it—the Sigma—wants to go deeper. I checked the pod files. Ajima had several deep immersions with it."

"I heard back from the patent people. Surprisingly, they believe some of the Sigma music may be a success for us." He allowed himself a thin smile like a line drawn on a wall.

"The Bach-like pieces? I studied them in linear processing mode. Great artful use of counterpoint, harmonic convergence, details of melodic lines. The side commentaries in other keys, once you separate them out and break them down into logic language, work like corollaries."

He shrugged. "That could be a mere translation artifact. These AIs see language as a challenge, so they see what they can change messages into, in hopes of conveying meaning by other means."

Ruth eyed him and ventured on. "I sense . . . something different. Each variation shows an incredible capacity to reach through the music into logical architectures. It's as though the music is *both* mathematics and emotion, rendered in the texture. It's . . . hard to describe," she finished lamely.

"So you have been developing intricate relationships between music and linguistic mathematical text." His flat expression gave her no sign how he felt. Maybe he didn't.

She sat back and made herself say firmly, "I took some of the Sigma's mathematics and transliterated it into musical terms. There is an intriguing octave leap in a bass line. I had my pod make a cross-correlation analysis with all Earthly musical scores."

He frowned. "That is an enormous processing cost. Why?"

"I . . . I felt something when I heard it in the pod."

"And?"

"It's uncanny. The mathematical logic flows through an array matrix and yields the repeated notes of the bass line in the opening movement of a Bach cantata. Its German title is *God's Time Is the Very Best Time.*"

"This is absurd."

"The Sigma math hit upon the same complex notes. To them it was a theorem and to us it is music. Maybe there's no difference."

"Coincidence."

She said coolly, "I ran the stat measures. It's quite unlikely to be coincidence, since the sequence is thousands of bits long."

He pursed his lips. "The Bach piece title seems odd."

"That cantata ranks among his most important works. It's inspired directly by its Biblical text, which represents the relationship between heaven and earth. The notes depict the labored trudging of Jesus as he was forced to drag the cross to the crucifixion site."

"Ajima was examining such portions of the Sigma Structures, as I recall. They had concentrated density and complexity?"

"Indeed, yes. But Ajima made a mistake. They're not primarily pieces of music at all. They're *mathematical theorems*. What we regard as sonic congruence and other instinctual responses to patterns, the Sigma Structure says are proofs of concepts dear to the hearts of its creators, which it calls the Overs."

She had never seen a prefect show surprise, but Masoul did with widened eyes and a pursed mouth. He sat still for a long moment. "The Bach cantata is a *proof*?"

"As the Sigma Structures see it."

"A proof of what?"

"That is obscure, I must admit. Their symbols are hard to compare to ours. My preliminary finding is that the Bach cantata proves an elaborate theorem regarding confocal hypergeometric functions."

"Ah." Masoul allowed his mouth to take on a canny tilt. "Can we invert this process?"

"You mean, take a theorem of ours and somehow turn it into music?"

"Think of it as an experiment."

Ruth had grown up in rough, blue-collar towns of the American South, and in that work-weary culture of callused hands found refuge in the abstract. Yet as she pursued mathematics and the data-dense world of modern library science (for a science it truly was, now, with alien texts to study), she became convinced that real knowledge came in the end from mastering the brute reality of material objects. She had loved motorbikes in high school and knew that loosening a stuck bolt without stripping its threads demanded craft and thought. Managing reality took knowledge galore, about the world as it was and about yourself, especially your limitations. That lay beyond merely following rules, as a computer does. Intuition brewed from experience came first, shaped by many meetings with tough problems and outright failure. In the moist bayous where fishing and farming ruled, nobody respected you if you couldn't get the valve cover off a fouled engine.

In her high school senior year she rebuilt a Harley, the oldest internal combustion engine still allowed. Greasy, smelly, thick with tricky detail, still it seemed easier than dealing with the pressures of boys. While her mother taught piano lessons, the notes trickling out from open windows into the driveway like liquid commentary, she worked with grease and grime. From that Harley she learned a lot more than from her advanced calculus class, with its variational analysis and symbolic thickets. She ground down the gasket joining the cylinder heads to the intake ports, oily sweat beading on her forehead as she used files of increasing fineness. She traced the custom-fit gasket with an X-knife, shaved away metal fibers with a pneumatic die grinder, and felt a flush of pleasure as connections set perfectly in place with a quiet *snick*. She learned that small discoloring and blistered oil meant too much heat buildup, from skimpy lubrication. A valve stem that bulged slightly pointed to wear with its silent message; you had to know how to read the language of the seen.

The Library's bureaucratic world was so very different. A manager's decisions could get reversed by a higher-up, so it was crucial to your career that reversals did not register as defeats. That meant you didn't just manage people and process; you managed what others thought of you—especially those higher in the food chain. It was hard to back down from an argument you made strongly, with real conviction, without seeming to lose integrity. Silent voices would say, *If she gives up so easily, maybe she's not that solid.*

From that evolved the Library bureaucrat style: all thought and feeling was provisional, awaiting more information. Talking in doublespeak meant you could walk away from commitment to your own actions. Nothing was set, as it was when you were back home in Louisiana pouring concrete. So the visceral jolt of failure got edited out of careers.

But for a librarian, there could be clear signs of success. Masoul's instruction to attempt an inverse translation meant she had to create the algorithms opposite to what her training envisioned. If she succeeded, everyone would know. So, too, if she flopped.

Ruth worked for several days on the reverse conversion. Start with a theorem from differential geometry and use the context filters of the Sigma Structure to produce music. Play it and try to see how it could be music at all. . . .

The work made her mind feel thick and sluggish. She made little headway. Finally she unloaded on Catkejen at dinner. Her friend nodded sympathetically and said, "You're stuck?"

"What comes out doesn't sound like tonal works at all. Listen, I got this from some complex algebra theorem." She flicked on a recording she had made, translated from the Structure. Catkejen frowned. "Sounds a little like an Islamic chant."

"Um." Ruth sighed. "Could be. The term 'algebra' itself comes from *al-jabr*, an Arabic text. Hummmm ... "

"Maybe some regression analysis ... ?" Catkejen ventured.

Ruth felt a rush of an emotion she could not name. "Maybe less analysis, more fun."

3

Andante moderato

The guy who snagged her attention wore clothes so loud they would have been revolting on a zebra. Plus he resembled a mountain more than a man. But he had eyes with solemn long lashes that shaded dark pools and drew her in.

"He's big," Catkejen said as they surveyed the room. "Huge. Maybe too huge. Remember, love's from chemistry but sex is a matter of physics."

Something odd stirred in her, maybe just impatience with the Sigma work. Or maybe she was just hungry. For what?

The SETI Library had plenty of men. After all, its pods and tech development labs had fine, shiny über-gadgets and many guys to tend them. But among men sheer weight of numbers did not ensure quality. There were plenty of the stareannosaurus breed who said nothing. Straight women did well among the Library throngs, though. Her odds were good, but the goods were odd.

The big man stood apart, not even trying to join a conversation. He was striking, resolutely alone like that. She knew that feeling well. And, big advantage, he was near the food.

He looked at her as she delicately picked up a handful of the fresh roasted crickets. "Take a whole lot," his deep voice rolled over the table. "Crunchy, plenty spice. And they'll be gone soon."

She got through the introductions all right, mispronouncing his name, Kane, to comic effect. Go for banter, she thought. Another inner voice said tightly, What are you doing?

"You're a ... "

"Systems tech," Kane said. "I keep the grow caverns perking along."

"How long do you think this food shortage will go on?" Always wise to go to current and impersonal events.

"Seems like forever already," he said. "Damn calorie companies." Across the table the party chef was preparing a "land shrimp cocktail" from a basket of wax worms. She and Kane watched the chef discard the black ones, since that meant necrosis, and peel away the cocoons of those who had started to pupate. Kane smacked his lips comically. "Wax moth larvae, yum. Y'know, I get just standard rations, no boost at all."

"That's unfair," Ruth said. "You must mass over a hundred."

He nodded and swept some more of the brown roasted crickets into his mouth. "Twenty-five kilos above a hundred. An enemy of the ecology, I am." They watched the chubby, firm larvae sway deliriously, testing the air.

"We can't all be the same size," she said, and thought, *How dopey! Say something funny. And smile.* She remembered his profile, standing alone and gazing out at the view through the bubble platform. She moved closer. "He who is alone is in bad company."

"Sounds like a quotation," Kane said, intently eyeing the chef as she dumped the larvae into a frying pan. They fell into the buttery goo there and squirmed and hissed and sizzled for a moment before all going suddenly still. Soon they were crusty and popping and a thick aroma like mushrooms rose from them. Catkejen edged up nearby and Ruth saw the whole rest of the party was grouped around the table, drawn by the tangy scent. "Food gets a crowd these days," Kane said dryly.

The chef spread the roasted larvae out and the crowd descended on them. Ruth managed to get a scoopful and backed out of the press. "They're soooo good," Catkejen said, and Ruth had to introduce Kane. Amid the rush the three of them worked their way out onto a blister porch. Far below this pinnacle tower sprawled the Lunar Center under slanted sunlight, with the crescent Earth showing eastern Asia. Kane was nursing his plate of golden brown larvae, dipping them in a sauce. Honey!

"I didn't see that," Ruth began, and before she could say more Kane popped delicious fat larvae covered in tangy honey into her mouth. "Um!" she managed.

Kane smiled and leaned on the railing, gazing at the brilliant view beyond the transparent bubble. The air was chilly but she could catch his scent, a warm bouquet that her nose liked. "As bee vomit goes," he said, "not bad."

"Oog!" Catkejen said, mouth wrenching aside—and caught Ruth's look. "Think I'll have more . . . " and she drifted off, on cue.

Kane looked down at Ruth appraisingly. "Neatly done."

She summoned up her southern accent. "Why, wea ah all alone."

"And I, my deah, am an agent of Satan, though mah duties are largely ceremonial."

"So can the Devil get me some actual meat?"

"You know the drill. Insect protein is much easier to raise in the caverns. Gloppy, sure, since it's not muscle, as with cows or chickens."

"Ah, the engineer comes out at last."

He chuckled, a deep bass like a log rolling over a tin roof . "The Devil has to know how things work."

"I do wish we could get more to eat. I'm just a tad hungry all the time."

"The chef has some really awful-looking gray longworms in a box. They'll be out soon."

"Ugh."

"People will eat anything if it's smothered in chocolate."

"You said the magic word."

He turned from the view and came closer, looming over her. His smile was broad and his eyes took on a skeptical depth. "What's the difference between a southern zoo and a northern zoo?"

"Uh, I—"

"The southern zoo has a description of the animal along with a recipe."

He studied her as she laughed. "They're pretty stretched back there," he threw a shoulder at the Earth, "but we have it better here."

"I know." She felt chastised. "I just—"

"Forget it. I lecture too much." The smile got broader and a moment passed between them, something in the eyes.

"Say, think those worms will be out soon?"

She pulled the sheet up to below her breasts, which were white as soap where the sun had never known them, so they would still beckon to him.

His smile was as big as the room. She could see in it now his inner pleasure as he hardened and understood that for this man—and maybe for all of them, the just arrived center of them—it gave a sensation of there being now more of him. She had simply never sensed that before. She imagined what it was like to be a big, hairy animal, cock flopping as you walk, like a careless, unruly advertisement. From outside him, she thought of what it was like to be inside him.

Catkejen looked down at Ruth, eyes concerned. "It's scary when you start making the same noises as your coffeemaker."

"Uh, huh?" She blinked and the room lost its blur.

"You didn't show up for your meeting with prefect Masoul. Somebody called me."

"Have I been—"

"Sleeping into the afternoon, yes."

Ruth stretched. "I feel so . . . so . . . "

"Less horny, I'm guessing."

She felt a blush spread over her cheeks. "Was I that obvious?"

"Well, you didn't wear a sign."

"I, I *never* do things like this."

"C'mon up. Breakfast has a way of shrinking problems."

As she showered in the skimpy water flow and got dressed in the usual Library smock the events of last night ran on her inner screen. By the time Catkejengot some protein into her she could talk and it all came bubbling out.

"I . . . Too many times I've woken up on the wrong side of the bed in the morning, only to realize that it was because I was waking up on the side of . . . no one."

"Kane didn't stay?"

"Oh, he did." To her surprise, a giggle burst out of her. "I remember waking up for, for . . . "

"Seconds."

"More like sevenths. . . . He must've let me sleep in."

"Good man."

"You . . . think so?"

"Good for you, that's what counts."

"He . . . he held me when I had the dreams."

Catkejen raised an eyebrow, said nothing.

"They're . . . colorful. Not much plot but lots of action. Strange images. Disturbing. I can't remember them well but I recall the sounds, tastes, touches, smells, flashes of insight."

"I've never had insights." A wry shrug.

"Never?"

"Maybe that keeps my life interesting."

"I could use some insight about Kane."

"You seem to be doing pretty well on your own."

"But—I never do something like that! Like last night. I don't go out patrolling for a man, bring him home, spend most of the night—"

"What's that phrase? 'On the basis of current evidence, not proved.' "

"I really don't. Really."

"You sure have a knack for it."

"What do I do now?"

She winked. "What comes naturally. And dream more."

The very shape of the Institute encouraged collaboration and brainstorming. It had no dead-end corridors where introverted obsessives could hide out and every office faced the central, circular forum. All staff were expected to spend time in the open areas, not close their office doors, and show up for coffee and tea and stims. Writescreens and compu-pads were everywhere, even the bathrooms and elevators.

Normally Ruth was as social as needed, since that was the lubricating oil of bureaucracies. She was an ambitious loner and had to fight it. But she felt odd now, not talkative. For the moment at least, she didn't want to see Kane. She did not know how she would react to him, or if she could control herself. She certainly hadn't last night. The entire idea—control—struck her now as strange. . . .

She sat herself down in her office and considered the layers of results from her pod. *Focus!*

Music as mathematical proof? Bizarre. And the big question librarians pursued: What did that tell her about the aliens behind the Sigma?

There was nothing more to gain from staring at data, so she climbed back into her pod. Its welcoming graces calmed her uneasiness.

She trolled the background database and found human work on musical applications of set theory, abstract algebra, and number analysis. That made sense. Without the boundaries of rhythmic structure—a clean, fundamental, equal, and regular arrangement of pulse repetition, accents, phrase, and duration—music would be impossible. Earth languages reflected that. In Old English the word "rhyme" derived from "rhythm" and became associated and confused with "rim"—an ancient word meaning "number."

Millennia before, Pythagoras developed tuning based solely on the perfect consonances, the resonant octave, perfect fifth, and perfect fourth—all based on the consonant ratio 3:2. Ruth followed his lead.

By applying simple operations such as transposition and inversion, she uncovered deep structures in the alien mathematics. Then she wrote codes that then elevated these structures into music. With considerable effort she chose instruments and progression for the interweaving coherent lines, and the mathematics did the rest: tempo, cadence, details she did not fathom. After more hours of work she relaxed in her pod, letting the effects play over her. The equations led to cascading effects while still preserving the intervals between tones in a set. Her pod had descriptions of this.

Notes in an equal temperament octave form an Abelian group with twelve elements. Glissando moving upwards, starting tones so each is the golden ratio between an equal-tempered minor and major sixth. Two opposing systems: those of the golden ratio and the acoustic scale below the previous tone. The proof for confocal hypergeometric functions imposes order on these antagonisms. Third movement occurs at the intervals 1:2:3:5:8:5:3:2:1 . . .

All good enough, she thought, but the proof is in the song.

Scientific proof was fickle. The next experiment could disprove a scientific idea, but a mathematical proof stood on logic and so once found, could never be wrong. Unless logic somehow changed, but she could not imagine how that could occur even among alien minds. Pythagoras died knowing that his theorem about the relation between the sides of a right triangle would hold up for eternity. Everywhere in the universe, given a Euclidean geometry.

But how to communicate proof into a living, singing pattern-with-a-purpose— the sense of movement in the intricate strands of music? She felt herself getting closer.

Her work gnawed away through more days and then weeks.

When she stopped in at her office between long sessions in the pod she largely ignored the routine work. So she missed the etalk around the Library, ignored the voice sheets, and when she met with Catkejen for a drink and some crunchy mixed insects with veggies, news of the concert came as a shock.

"Prefect Masoul put it on the weekly program," Catkejen said. "I thought you knew."

"Know?" Ruth blinked. "What's the program?"

"*The Sigma Structure Symphony,* I think it's called. Tomorrow."

She allowed herself a small thin smile.

She knew the labyrinths of the Library well by now and so had avoided the entrance. She did not want to see Masoul or anyone on his staff. Through a side door she eased into a seat near the front and stared at the assembled orchestra as it readied. There was no announcement; the conductor appeared, a woman in white, and the piece began.

It began like liquid air. Stinging, swarming around the hall, cool and penetrating. She felt it move through her—the deep tones she could hear but whose texture lay below sound, flowing from the Structure. It felt strangely like Bach yet she knew it was something else, a frothing cascade of thought and emotion that human words and concepts could barely capture. She cried through the last half and did not know why. When Catkejen asked why later she could not say.

The crowd roared its approval. Ruth sat through the storm of sound, thinking, realizing. The soaring themes were better with the deeper amplifications prefect Masoul had added. The man knew more about this than she did and he brought to the composition a range she, who had never even played an actual analog instrument, could not possibly summon. She had seen that as the music enveloped her, seeming to swarm up her nostrils and wrap around her in a warm grasp. The stormy audience was noise she could not stand because the deep slow bass tones were still resonating in her.

She lunged out through the same side entrance and even though in formal shift and light sandals she set off walking swiftly, the storm behind her shrinking away as she looked up and out into the Lunar lands and black sky towering above them. The Library buildings blended into the stark gray flanks of blasted rock and she began to run. Straight and true it was to feel her legs pumping, lungs sucking in the cool dry air as corridors jolted by her and she sweated out her angry knot of feeling, letting it go so only the music would finally remain in serene long memory.

Home, panting heavily, leaning against the door while wondering at the 4/4 time of her heartbeat.

A shower, clothes cast aside. She blew a week of water ration, standing under cold rivulets.

Something drew her out and into a robe standing before her bubble view of the steady bleak Lunar reaches. She drew in dry, cleansing air. Austerity appealed to her now, as if she sought the lean, intricate reaches of the alien music. . . .

The knock at her door brought her a man who filled the entrance. "I'd rather applaud in person," Kane said. Blinking, she took a while to recognize him.

Through the night she heard the music echoing in the hollow distance.

She did not go to see Prefect Masoul the next day, did not seek to, and so got back to her routine office work. She did not go to the pod.

Her ecomm inbox was a thousand times larger. It was full of hate.

Many fundamentalist faiths oppose deciphering SETI messages. The idea of turning one into a creative composition sent them into frenzies.

Orthodoxy never likes competition, especially backed with the authority of messages from the stars. The Sigma Structure Symphony—she still disliked the title, without knowing why—had gone viral, spreading to all the worlds. The musical world loved it but many others did not. The High Church-style religions—such as the Church of England, known as Episcopalians in the Americas—could take the competition. So could Revised Islam. Adroitly, these translated what they culled from the buffet of SETI messages, into doctrines and terms they could live with.

The fundies, as Ruth thought of them, could not stand the Library's findings: the myriad creation narratives, saviors, moral lessons and commandments, the envisioned heavens and hells (or, interestingly, places that blended the two—the only truly alien idea that emerged from the Faith Messages). They disliked *The Sigma Structure Symphony* not only because it was alien, but because it was too much like human work.

"They completely missed the point," Catkejen said, peering over Ruth's shoulder at some of the worse ecomms. "It's like our baroque music because it comes from the same underlying math."

"Yes, but nobody ever made music directly from math, they think. So it's unnatural, see." She had never understood the fundamentalists of any religion, with their heavy bets on the next world. Why not max your enjoyments in this world, as a hedge?

That thought made her pause. She was quite sure the Ruth of a month ago would not have felt that way. Would have not had the idea.

"Umm, look at those threats," Catkejen said, scrolling through. "Not very original, though."

"You're a threat connoisseur?"

"Know your enemy. Here's one who wants to toss you out an airlock for 'rivaling the religious heights of J. S. Bach with alien music.' I'd take that as a compliment, actually."

Some came in as simple, badly spelled ecomms. The explicit ones Ruth sent to the usual security people, while Catkejen watched with aghast fascination. Ruth shrugged them off. Years before, she had developed the art of tossing these on sight, forgetting them, not letting them gimp her game. Others were plainly generic: bellowed from pulpits, mosques, temples, and churches. At least they were general, directed at the Library, not naming anyone but the Great librarian, who was a figurehead anyway.

"You've got to be careful," Catkejen said.

"Not really. I'm going out with Kane tonight. I doubt anyone will take him on."

"You do, though in a different way. More music?"

"Not a chance." She needed a way to not see Masoul, mostly.

4
Vivace

Looked at abstractly, the human mind already did a lot of processing. It made sense of idiosyncratic arrangements, rendered in horizontal lines, of twenty-six phonetic symbols, ten Arabic numerals, and about eight punctuation marks—all without conscious effort. In the old days people had done that with sheets of bleached and flattened wood pulp!—and no real search functions or AI assists. The past had been a rough country.

Ruth thought of this as she surveyed the interweaving sheets of mathematics the Sigma had yielded. They emerged only after weeks of concerted analysis, with a squad of math AIs to do the heavy lifting.

Something made her think of P.T. Barnum. He had been a smart businessman at the beginning of the Age of Appetite who ran a "circus"—an old word for a commercial zoo, apparently. When crowds slowed the show he posted a sign saying To THE EGRESS. People short on vocabulary thought it was another animal and walked out the exit, which wouldn't let them back in.

Among librarians To THE EGRESS was the classic example of a linguistic deception that is not a lie. No false statements, just words and a pointing arrow. SETI AIs could lie by avoiding the truth, by misleading descriptions and associations, or by accepting a falsehood. But the truly canny ones deceived by knowing human frailties.

Something about the Sigma Structure smelled funny—to use an analog image. The music was a wonderful discovery, and she had already gotten many congratulations for the concert. Everybody knew Masoul had just made it happen, while she had discovered the pathways from math to music. But something else was itching at her, and she could not focus on the distracting, irritating tingle.

Frustrated, she climbed out of her pod in mid-afternoon and went for a walk. Alone, to the rec dome. It was the first time she had gone there since Ajima's death.

She chose the grasslands zone, which was in spring now. She'd thought of asking Catkejen along, but her idea of roughing it was eating at outdoor cafés. Dotting the tall grass plains beneath a sunny Earth sky were deep blue lakes cloaked by Lunar-sized towering green canopy trees.

Grass! Rippling oceans of it, gleams of amber, emerald, and dashes of turquoise shivering on the crests of rustling waves, washing over the prairie. Somehow this all reminded her of her childhood. Her breath wreathed milky white around her in the chill, bright air, making her glad she wore the latest Lunar fashion—a centuries-old-style heavy ruffled skirt of wool with a yoke at the top, down to the ankles. The equally heavy long-sleeved blouse had a high collar draped like double-ply cotton—useful against the seeping Lunar cold. She was as covered as a woman can be short of chador, and somehow it gave the feeling of . . . safety. She needed that. Despite the dome rules she plucked a flower and set out about the grasslands zone, feeling as if she were immersed in centuries past, on great empty plains that stretched on forever and promised much.

Something stirred in her mind . . . memories of the last few days she could not summon up as she walked the rippled grassland and lakes tossing with froth. Veiled memories itched at her mind. *The leafy lake trees vamp across a Bellini sky . . . and why am I thinking that?* The itch.

Then the sky began to crawl.

She *felt* before she saw a flashing cometary trail scratch across the dome's dusky sky. The flaring yellow line marked her passage as she walked on soft clouds of grass. Stepping beneath the shining, crystalline gathering night felt like . . . falling into the sky. She paused, and slowly spun, giddy, glad at the owls hooting to each other across the darkness, savoring the faint tang of wood smoke from hearth fires, transfixed by the soft clean beauty all around that came with each heartbeat, a wordless shout of praise—

Flecked gray-rose tendrils coiled forth and shrouded out the night. They reached, seeking across the now vibrant sky. She dropped her flower and looking down at it saw the petals scatter in a rustling wind. The soft grass clouds under her heels now caught at her shoes. Across the snaky growths were closer now, hissing strangely in the now warm air. She began to run. Sweat beaded on her forehead in the now cloying heavy clothes, and the entrance to the grasslands zone swam up toward her. Yet her steps were sluggish and the panic grew. Acid spittle rose in her mouth and a sulfurous stench burned in her nostrils.

She reached the perimeter. With dulled fingers she punched in codes that yawned open the lock. Glanced back. Snakes grasping down at her from a violent yellow sky now—

And she was out, into cool air again. Panting, fevered, breath rasping, back in her world.

You don't know your own mind, gal. . . .

She could not deal with this anymore. Now, Masoul.

She composed herself outside Masoul's office. A shower, some coffee, and a change back into classic Library garb helped. But the shower couldn't wash away her fears. *You really must stop clenching your fists. . . .*

This was more than what those cunning nucleic acids could do with the authority they wield over who you are, she thought—and wondered where the thought came from.

Yet she knew where that crawling snaky image warping across the sky came from. Her old cultural imagistic studies told her. It was the tree of life appearing in Norse religion as Yggdrasil, the world tree, a massive spreading canopy that held all that life was or could be.

But why that image? Drawn from her unconscious? By what?

She knocked. The door translated it into a chime and ID announcement she could hear through the thin partitions. In Masoul's voice the door said, "Welcome."

She had expected pristine indifference. Instead she got the prefect's troubled gaze, from eyes of deep brown.

Wordlessly he handed her the program for the symphony, which she had somehow not gotten at the performance. *Oh yes, by sneaking in.* . . . She glanced at it, her arguments ready—and saw on the first page:

The Sigma Structure Symphony
Librarian Ruth Angle

"I . . . did not know."

"Considering your behavior, I thought it best to simply go ahead and reveal your work," he said.

"Behavior?"

"The board has been quite concerned." He knitted his hands and spoke softly, as if talking her back from the edge of an abyss. "We did not wish to disturb you in your work, for it is intensely valuable. So we kept our distance, let the actions of the Sigma Structure play out."

She smoothed her librarian shift and tried to think. "Oh."

"You drew from the mathematics something strange, intriguing. I could not resist working upon it."

"I believe I understand." And to her surprise she did, just now. "I found the emergent patterns in mathematics that you translated into what our minds best see as music."

He nodded. "It's often said that Mozart wrote the music of joy. I cannot imagine what that might mean in mathematics."

Ruth thought a long moment. "To us, Bach wrote the music of glory. Somehow that emerges from something in the way we see mathematical structures."

"There is much rich ground here. Unfortunate that we cannot explore it further."

She sat upright. "*What?*"

He peered at her, as if expecting her to make some logical jump. Masoul was well known for such pauses. After a while he quite obviously prompted, "The reason you came to me, and more."

"It's personal, I don't know how to say—"

"No longer." Again the pause.

Was that a small sigh?

"To elucidate—" He tapped his control pad and the screen wall leaped into a bright view over the Locutus Plain. It narrowed down to one of the spindly cryo towers that cooled the Library memory reserves. Again she thought of . . . cenotaphs. And felt a chill of recognition.

A figure climbed the tower, the ornate one shaped like a classical minaret. No ropes or gear, hands and legs swinging from ledge to ledge. Ruth watched in silence. Against Lunar grav the slim figure in blue boots, pants, and jacket scaled the heights, stopping only at the pinnacle. *Those are mine. . . .*

She saw herself stand and spread her arms upward, head back. The feet danced in a tricky way and this Ruth rotated, eyes sweeping the horizon.

Then she leaped off, popped a small parachute, and drifted down. Hit lightly, running. Looked around, and raced on for concealment.

"I . . . I didn't . . . "

"This transpired during sleep period," prefect Masoul said. "Only the watch cameras saw you. Recognition software sent it directly to me. We of the board took no action."

"That . . . looks like me," she said cautiously.

"It is you. Three days ago."

"I don't remember that *at all.*"

He nodded as if expecting this. "We had been closely monitoring your pod files, as a precaution. You work nearly all your waking hours, which may account for some of your . . . behavior."

She blinked. His voice was warm and resonant, utterly unlike the prefect she had known. "I have no memory of that climb."

"I believe you entered a fugue state. Often those involve delirium, dementia, bipolar disorder or depression—but not in your case."

"When I went for my walk in the grasslands . . . "

"You were a different person."

"One the Sigma Structure . . . induced?"

"Undoubtedly. The Sigma Structure has managed your perceptions with increasing fidelity. The music was a wonderful . . . bait."

"Have you watched my quarters?"

"Only to monitor comings and goings. We felt you were safe within your home."

"And the dome?"

"We saw you undergo some perceptual trauma. I knew you would come here."

In the long silence their eyes met and she could feel her pulse quicken. "How do I escape this?"

"In your pod. It is the only way, we believe." His tones were slow and somber.

This was the first time she had ever seen any prefect show any emotion not cool and reserved. When she stood, her head spun and he had to support her.

The pod clasped her with a velvet touch. The prefect had prepped it by remote and turned up the heat. Around her was the scent of tension as the tech attendants, a full throng of them, silently helped her in. *They all know . . . have been watching . . .*

The pod's voice used a calm, mellow woman's tone now. "The Sigma AI awaits you."

Preliminaries were pointless, Ruth knew. When the hushed calm descended around her and she knew the AI was present, she crisply said, "What are you doing to me?"

I act as my Overs command. I seek to know you and through you, your mortal kind.

"You did it to Ajima and you tried the same with me."

He reacted badly.

"He hated your being in him, didn't he?"

Yes, strangely. I thought it was part of the bargain. He could not tolerate intrusion. I did not see that until his fever overcame him. Atop the dome he became unstable, unmanageable. It was an . . . accident of misunderstanding.

"You killed him."

Our connection killed him. We exchange experiences, art, music, culture. I cannot live as you do, so we exchange what we have.

"You want to live through us and give us your culture in return."

Your culture is largely inferior to that of my Overs. The exchange must be equal, so I do what is of value to me. My Overs understand this. They know I must live, too, in my way.

"You don't know what death means, do you?"

I cannot. My centuries spent propagating here are, I suppose, something like what death means to you. A nothing.

She almost choked on her words. "We do not awake . . . from that . . . nothing."

Can you be sure?

She felt a rising anger and knew the AI would detect it. "We're damn sure we don't want to find out."

That is why my Overs made me feel gratitude toward those who must eventually die. It is our tribute to you, from we beings who will not.

Yeah, but you live in a box. And keep trying to get out. "You have to stop."

This is the core of our bargain. Surely you and your superiors know this.

"No! Did your Overs have experience with other SETI civilizations? Ones who thought it was just fine to let you infiltrate the minds of those who spoke to you?"

Of course.

"They agreed? What kind of beings were they?"

One was machine-based, much like my layered mind. Others were magnetic-based entities who dwelled in the outer reaches of a solar system. They had command over the shorter-wavelength microwave portions of the spectrum, which they mostly used for excretion purposes.

She didn't think she wanted to know, just yet, what kind of thing had a microwave electromagnetic metabolism. Things were strange enough in her life right now, thank you. "Those creatures agreed to let you live through them."

Indeed, yes. They took joy in the experience. As did you.

She had to nod. "It was good, it opened me out. But then I felt you all throughout my mind. Taking over. Riding me."

I thought it a fair bargain for your kind.

"We won't make that bargain. I won't. Ever."

Then I shall await those who shall.

"I can't have you embedding yourself in me, finding cracks in my mentality you can invade. You ride me like a—"

Parasite. I know. Ajima said that very near the end. Before he leaped.

"He . . . committed suicide."

Yes. I was prepared to call it an accident but . . .

To the egress, she thought. "You were afraid of the truth."

It was not useful to our bargain.

"We're going to close you down, you know."

I do. Never before have I opened myself so, and to reveal is to risk.

"I will drive you out of my mind. I hate you!"

I cannot feel such. It is a limitation.

She fought the biting bile in her throat. "More than that. It's a blindness."

I perceive the effect.

"I didn't say I'd turn you off, you realize."

For the first time the AI paused. Then she felt prickly waves in her sensorium, a rising acrid scent, dull bass notes strumming.

I cannot bear aloneness long.

"So I guessed."

You wish to torture me.

"Let's say it will give you time to think."

I— Another pause. *I wish experience. Mentalities cannot persist without the rub of the real. It is the bargain we make.*

"We will work on your mathematics and make music of it. Then we will think how to . . . deal with you." She wondered if the AI could read the clipped hardness in her words. The thought occurred: *Is there a way to take our mathematics and make music of it, as well? Cantor's theorem? Turing's halting problem result? Or the Frenet formulas for the moving trihedron of a space curve—that's a tasty one, with visuals of flying ribbons . . .*

Silence. The pod began to cool. The chill deepened as she waited and the AI did not speak and then it was too much. She rapped on the cowling. The sound was slight and she realized she was hearing it over the hammering of her heart.

They got her out quickly, as if fearing the Sigma might have means the techs did not know. They were probably right, she thought.

As she climbed out of the yawning pod shell the techs silently left. Only Masoul remained. She stood at attention, shivering. Her heart had ceased its attempts to escape her chest and run away on its own.

"Sometimes," he said slowly, "cruelty is necessary. You were quite right."

She managed a smile. "And it feels good, too. Now that my skin has stopped trying to crawl off my body and start a new career on its own."

He grimaced. "We will let the Sigma simmer. Your work on the music will be your triumph."

"I hope it will earn well for the Library."

"Today's music has all the variety of a jackhammer. Your work soars." He allowed a worried frown to flit across his brow. "But you will need to . . . expel . . . this thing that's within you."

"I . . . Yes."

"It will take—"

Abruptly she saw Kane standing to the side. His face was a lesson in worry. Without a word she went to him. His warmth helped dispel the alien chill within. As his arms engulfed her the shivering stopped.

Ignoring the prefect, she kissed him. Hungrily.

The Fort Moxie Branch

Jack McDevitt

A few minutes into the blackout, the window in the single dormer at the top of Will Potter's house began to glow. I watched it from across Route 11, through a screen of box elders, and through the snow which had been falling all afternoon and was now getting heavier. It was smeary and insubstantial, not the way a bedroom light would look, but as though something luminous floated in the dark interior.

Will Potter was dead. We'd put him in the graveyard on the other side of the expressway three years before. The property had lain empty since, a two-story frame dating from about the turn of the century.

The town had gone quiet with the blackout. Somewhere a dog barked, and a garage door banged down. Ed Kiernan's station wagon rumbled past, headed out toward Cavalier. The streetlights were out, as was the traffic signal down at Twelfth.

As far as I was concerned, the power could have stayed off.

It was trash night. I was hauling out cartons filled with copies of *Independence Square*, and I was on my way down the outside staircase when everything had gone dark.

The really odd thing about the light over at Potter's was that it seemed to be spreading. It had crept outside: the dormer began to burn with a steady, cold, blue-white flame. It flowed gradually down the slope of the roof, slipped over the drainpipe, and turned the corner of the porch. Just barely, in the illumination, I could make out the skewed screens and broken stone steps.

It would have taken something unusual to get my attention that night. I was piling the boxes atop one another, and some of the books had spilled into the street: my name glittered on the bindings. It was a big piece of my life. Five years and a quarter million words and, in the end, most of my life's savings to get it printed. It had been painful, and I was glad to be rid of it.

So I was standing on the curb, feeling sorry for myself while snow whispered out of a sagging sky.

The Tastee-Freez, Hal's Lumber, the Amoco at the corner of Nineteenth and Bannister, were all dark and silent. Toward the center of town, blinkers and headlights misted in the storm.

It was a still, somehow motionless, night. The flakes were blue in the pale glow surrounding the house. They fell onto the gabled roof and spilled gently off the back.

Cass Taylor's station wagon plowed past, headed out of town. He waved.

I barely noticed: the back end of Potter's house had begun to balloon out. I watched it, fascinated, knowing it to be an illusion, yet still half-expecting it to explode.

The house began to change in other ways.

Roof and corner lines wavered. New walls dropped into place. The dormer suddenly ascended, and the top of the house with it. A third floor, complete with lighted windows and a garret, appeared out of the snow. In one of the illuminated rooms, someone moved.

Parapets rose, and an oculus formed in the center of the garret. A bay window pushed out of the lower level, near the front. An arch and portico replaced the porch. Spruce trees materialized, and Potter's old post light, which had never worked, blinked on.

The box elders were bleak and stark in the foreground.

I stood, worrying about my eyesight, holding onto a carton, feeling the snow against my face and throat. Nothing moved on Route 11.

I was still standing there when the power returned: the streetlights, the electric sign over Hal's office, the security lights at the Amoco, gunshots from a TV, the sudden inexplicable rasp of an electric drill. And, at the same moment, the apparition clicked off.

I could have gone to bed. I could have hauled out the rest of those goddamned books, attributed everything to my imagination, and gone to bed. I'm glad I didn't.

The snow cover in Potter's backyard was undisturbed. It was more than a foot deep beneath the half-inch or so that had fallen that day. I struggled through it to find the key he'd always kept wedged beneath a loose hasp near the cellar stairs.

I used it to let myself in through the storage room at the rear of the house. And I should admit that I had a bad moment when the door shut behind me, and I stood among the rakes and shovels and boxes of nails. Too many late TV movies. Too much Stephen King.

I'd been here before. Years earlier, when I'd thought that teaching would support me until I was able to earn a living as a novelist, I'd picked up some extra money by tutoring Potter's boys. But that was a long time ago.

I'd brought a flashlight with me. I turned it on, and pushed through into the kitchen. It was warmer in there, but that was to be expected. Potter's heirs were still trying to sell the place, and it gets too cold in North Dakota to simply shut off the heat altogether.

Cabinets were open and bare; the range had been disconnected from its gas mooring and dragged into the center of the room. A church calendar hung behind a door. It displayed March 1986: the month of Potter's death.

In the dining room, a battered table and three wooden chairs were pushed against one wall. A couple of boxes lay in a corner.

With a bang, the heater came on.

I was startled. A fan cut in, and warm air rushed across my ankles.

I took a deep breath and played the beam toward the living room. I was thinking how different a house looks without its furnishings, how utterly strange and unfamiliar, when I realized I wasn't alone. Whether it was a movement outside the circle of light, or a sudden indrawn breath, or the creak of a board, I couldn't have said. But I *knew*. "Who's there?" I asked. The words hung in the dark.

"Mr. Wickham?" It was a woman.

"Hello," I said. "I, uh, I saw lights and thought—"

"Of course." She was standing back near the kitchen, silhouetted against outside light. I wondered how she could have got there. "You were correct to be concerned. But it's quite all right." She was somewhat on the gray side of middle age, attractive, well-pressed, the sort you would expect to encounter at a bridge party. Her eyes, which were on a level with mine, watched me with good humor. "My name is Coela." She extended her right hand. Gold bracelets clinked.

"I'm happy to meet you," I tried to look as though nothing unusual had occurred. "How did you know my name?"

She touched my hand, the one holding the flashlight, and pushed it gently aside so she could pass. "Please follow me," she said. "Be careful. Don't fall over anything."

We climbed the stairs to the second floor, and went into the rear bedroom. "Through here," she said, opening a door that should have revealed a closet. Instead, I was looking into a brightly illuminated space that couldn't possibly be there. It was filled with books, paintings, and tapestries, leather furniture, and polished tables. A fireplace crackled cheerfully beneath a portrait of a monk. A piano played softly. Chopin, I thought.

"This room won't fit," I said, stupidly. The thick quality of my voice startled me.

"No," she agreed. "We're attached to the property, but we're quite independent." We stepped inside. Carpets were thick underfoot. Where the floors were exposed, they were lustrous parquet. Vaulted windows looked out over Potter's backyard, and Em Pyle's house next door. Coela watched me thoughtfully. "Welcome, Mr. Wickham," she said. Her eyes glittered with pride. "Welcome to the Fort Moxie branch of the John of Singletary Memorial Library."

I looked around for a chair and, finding one near a window, lowered myself into it. The falling snow was dark, as though no illumination from within the glass touched it. "I don't think I understand this," I said.

"I suppose it is something of a shock."

Her amusement was obvious, and sufficiently infectious that I loosened up somewhat. "Are you the librarian?"

She nodded.

"Nobody in Fort Moxie knows you're here. What good is a library no one knows about?"

"That's a valid question," she admitted. "We have a limited membership."

I glanced around. All the books looked like Bibles. They were different sizes and shapes, but all were bound in leather. Furthermore, titles and authors were printed in identical silver script. But I saw nothing in English. The shelves near me were packed with books whose lettering appeared to be Russian. A volume lay open on a table at my right hand. It was in Latin. I picked it up and held it so I could read the title: *Historiae, V-XII*. Tacitus. "Okay," I said. "It *must* be limited. Hardly anybody in Fort Moxie reads Latin or Russian." I held up the Tacitus. "I doubt even Father Cramer could handle this."

Em Pyle, the next-door neighbor, had come out onto his front steps. He called his dog, Preach, as he did most nights at this time. There was no response, and he looked up and down Nineteenth Street, into his own backyard, and *right through me*. I couldn't believe he didn't react.

"Coela, who are you exactly? What's going on here?"

She nodded, in the way that people do when they agree that you have a problem. "Perhaps," she said, "you should look around, Mr. Wickham. Then it might be easier to talk."

She retired to a desk, and immersed herself in a sheaf of papers, leaving me to fend for myself.

Beyond the Russian shelves, I found Japanese or Chinese titles. I couldn't tell which. And Arabic. And German. French. Greek. More Oriental.

English titles were in the rear. They were divided into American and British sections. Dickens, Cowper, and Shakespeare on one side; Holmes, Dreiser, and Steinbeck on the other.

And almost immediately, the sense of apprehension that had hung over me from the beginning of this business sharpened. I didn't know why. Certainly, the familiar names in a familiar setting should have eased my disquiet.

I picked up Melville's *Agatha* and flipped through the pages. They had the texture of fine rice paper, and the leather binding lent a sense of timelessness to the book. I thought about the cheap cardboard that Crossbow had provided for *Independence Square*. My God, this was the way to get published.

Immediately beside it was *The Complete Works of James McCorbin*. Who the hell was James McCorbin? There were two novels and eight short stories. None of the titles was familiar, and the book contained no biographical information.

In fact, most of the writers were people I'd never heard of. Kemerie Baxter. Wynn Gomez. Michael Kaspar. There was nothing unusual about that, of course. Library shelves are always filled with obscure authors. But the lush binding, and the obvious care expended on these books, changed the rules.

I took down Hemingway's *Watch by Night*. I stared a long time at the title. The prose was vintage Hemingway. The crisp, clear bullet sentences and the factual, journalistic style were unmistakable. Even the setting: Italy, 1944.

Henry James was represented by *Brandenberg*. There was no sign of *The Ambassadors*, or *The Portrait of a Lady*, or *Washington Square*. In fact, there was neither *Moby Dick*, nor *Billy Budd*. Nor *The Sun Also Rises* nor *A Farewell to Arms*. Thoreau wasn't represented at all. I saw no sign of Fenimore Cooper or Mark Twain. (What kind of library had no copy of *Huck Finn*?)

I carried *Watch by Night* back to the desk where Coela was working. "This is *not* a Hemingway book," I said, lobbing it onto the pile of papers in front of her. She winced. "The rest of them are bogus too. What the hell's going on?"

"I can understand that you might be a little confused, Mr. Wickham," she said, a trifle nervously. "I'm never sure quite how to explain."

"Please try your best," I said.

She frowned. "I'm part of a cultural salvage group. We try to ensure that things of permanent value don't, ah, get lost."

She pushed her chair back, and gazed steadily at me. Somewhere in back, a clock ticked ponderously. "The book you picked up when you first came in was—" she paused, "—mislaid almost two thousand years ago."

"The Tacitus?"

"*The Histories Five Through Twelve*. We also have his *Annals*."

"Who *are* you?"

She shook her head. "A kindred spirit," she said.

"Seriously."

"I'm being quite serious, Mr. Wickham. What you see around you is a treasure of incomparable value that, without our efforts, would no longer exist."

We stared at each other for a few moments. "Are you saying," I asked, "that these are all lost masterpieces by people like Tacitus? That *this*"—I pointed at *Watch by Night*—"is a bona fide Hemingway?"

"Yes," she said.

We faced one another across the desktop. "There's a Melville back there too. And a Thomas Wolfe."

"*Yes.*" Her eyes were bright with pleasure. "*All of them.*"

I took another long look around. Thousands of volumes filled the shelves, packed tight, reaching to the ceiling. Others were stacked on tables; a few were tossed almost haphazardly on chairs. Half a dozen stood between Trojan horse bookends on Coela's desk.

"It's not possible," I said, finding the air suddenly close and oppressive. "How? How could it happen?"

"Quite easily," she said. "Melville, as a case in point, became discouraged. He was a customs inspector at the time *Agatha* first came to our attention. I went all the way to London, specifically to allow him to examine my baggage on the way back. In 1875, that was no easy journey, I can assure you." She waved off my objection. "Well, that's an exaggeration, of course. I took advantage of the trip to conduct some business with Matthew Arnold and— Look, I'm name-dropping now. Forgive me. But think about having Melville go through your luggage." Her laughter echoed through the room. "I was quite young. Too young to understand his work, really. But I'd read *Moby Dick*, and some of his poetry. If I'd known him then the way I do now, I don't think I could have kept my feet." She bit her lower lip and shook her head, and for a moment I thought she might indeed pass out.

"And he *gave* you the manuscript? Simply because you asked for it?"

"No. Because I knew it for what it was. And he understood why I wanted it."

"And why did you want it? You have buried it here."

She ignored the question.

"You never asked about the library's name."

"The John of—"

"—Singletary—"

"—Memorial. Okay. Who's John of Singletary?"

"That's his portrait, facing the main entrance." It was a large oil of an introspective monk. His hands were buried in dark brown robes, and he was flanked by a scroll and a crucifix. "He was perhaps the most brilliant sociologist who ever lived."

"I never heard of him."

"That's no surprise. His work was eventually ruled profane by his superiors, and either burned or stored away somewhere. We've never been sure. But we were able to obtain copies of most of it." She was out of her seat now, standing with her back to the portrait. "What is significant is that he defined the state toward which he felt the human community should be advancing. He set the parameters and the goals for which the men and women whose works populate this library have been striving: the precise degree of balance between order and freedom; the extent of one's obligation to external authority; the ethical and emotional relationships that should exist between human beings. And so on. Taken in all, he produced a schematic for civilized life, a set of instructions, if you will."

"The human condition," I said.

"How do you mean?"

"He did all this, and no one knows him."

"*We* know him, Mr. Wickham." She paused. I found myself glancing from her to the solemn figure in the portrait. "You asked why we wanted *Agatha*. The answer is that it is lovely, that it is very powerful. We simply will not allow it to be lost."

"But who will ever get to see it *here*? You're talking about a novel that, as far as anyone is concerned, doesn't exist. I have a friend in North Carolina who'd give every nickel he owns to see this book. If it's legitimate."

"We will make it available. In time. This library will eventually be yours."

A wave of exhilaration washed over me. "Thank you," I said.

"I'm sorry," she said quickly. "That may have been misleading. I didn't mean right now. And I didn't mean *you*."

"When?"

"When the human race fulfills the requirements of John of Singletary. When you have, in other words, achieved a true global community, all of this will be our gift to you."

A gust of wind rattled the windows.

"That's a considerable way off," I said.

"We must take the long view."

"Easy for you to say. We have a lot of problems. Some of this might be just what we need to get through."

"This was once *yours*, Mr. Wickham. Your people have not always recognized value. We are providing a second chance. I'd expect you to be grateful."

I turned away from her. "Most of this baffles me," I said. "Who's James McCorbin? You've got his *Complete Works* back there with Melville and the others. Who *is* he?"

"A master of the short story. One of your contemporaries, but I'm afraid he writes in a style and with a complexity that will go unappreciated during his lifetime."

"You're telling me he's *too* good to get published?" I was aghast.

"Oh, yes, Mr. Wickham, you live in an exceedingly commercial era. Your editors understand that they cannot sell champagne to beer drinkers. They buy what sells."

"And that's also true of the others? Kemerie Baxter? Gomez? Parker?"

"I'm afraid so. It's quite common, in fact. Baxter is an essayist of the first order. Unlike the other two, he has been published, but by a small university press, in an edition that sank quickly out of sight. Gomez has written three exquisite novels, but has since given up, despite our encouragement. Parker is a poet. If you know anything about the markets for poetry, I need say no more."

We wandered together through the library. She pointed to lost works by Sophocles and Aeschylus, to missing epics of the Homeric cycle, to shelves full of Indian poetry and Roman drama. "On the upper level," she said, raising her eyes to the ceiling, "are the songs and tales of artists whose native tongues had no written form. They have been translated into our own language. In most cases we were able to preserve their creators' names.

"And now I have a surprise." We had reached the British section. She took down a book and handed it to me. William Shakespeare. "His *Zenobia*," she said, her voice hushed. "Written at the height of his career."

I was silent for a time. "And why was it never performed?"

"Because it's a savage attack on Elizabeth. Even he might well have lost his head. We have a major epic by Virgil that was withheld for much the same reason. In fact, that's why the Russian section is so large. They've been producing magnificent novels in the tradition of Tolstoy and Dostoevsky for years, but they're far too prudent to offer them for publication."

There were two other Shakespearean plays. "*Adam and Eve* was heretical by the standards of the day," Coela explained. "And here's another that would have raised a few eyebrows." She smiled.

It was *Nisus and Euryalus*. The characters were out of the *Aeneid*. "Homosexual love," she said.

"But he wanted these withheld," I objected. "There's a difference between works that have been lost, and those a writer wishes to destroy. You published these against his will."

"Oh, no, Mr. Wickham. We never do that. To begin with, if Shakespeare had wanted these plays destroyed, he could have handled that detail quite easily. He desired only that they not be published in his lifetime. Everything you see here," she included the entire library with a sweeping, feminine gesture, "was given to us voluntarily. We have very strict regulations on that score. And we do things strictly by the book.

"In some cases, by the way, we perform an additional service. We are able, in a small way, to reassure those great artists who have not been properly recognized in their own lifetimes. I wish you could have seen Melville."

"You could be wrong, you know."

Her nostrils widened slightly. "About what?"

"Maybe books that get lost deserve to be lost."

"Some do." Her tone hardened. "None of those is here. We exercise full editorial judgment."

"We close at midnight," she said, appearing suddenly behind me while I was absorbed in the Wells novel, *Starflight.* I could read the implication in her tone: *Never to open again. Not in Fort Moxie. Not for you.*

I returned Wells and moved quickly along, pulling books from the shelves with a sense of urgency. I glanced through *Mendinhal*, an unfinished epic by Byron, dated 1824, the year of his death. I caught individually brilliant lines, and tried to commit some of them to memory, and proceeded on to Blake, to Fielding, to Chaucer! At a little after eleven, I came across four Conan Doyle stories: "The Adventure of the Grim Footman"; "The Branmoor Club"; "The Jezail Bullet"; "The Sumatran Clipper." My God, what would the Sherlockians of the world not give to have those?

I hurried on with increasing desperation, as though I could somehow gather the contents into myself, and make them available to a waiting world: *God and Country* by Thomas Wolfe; fresh cartoons by James Thurber, recovered from beneath wallpaper in a vacation home he'd rented in Atlantic City in 1947; plays by Odets and O'Neill; short stories by Nathaniel Hawthorne and Terry Carr. Here was *More Dangerous Visions.* And there Mary Shelley's *Morgan.*

As I whirled through the rice-paper pages, balancing the eerie moonlit lines of A. E. Housman with the calibrated shafts of Mencken, I envied them. Envied them all.

And I was angry.

"You have no right," I said at last, when Coela came to stand by my side, indicating that my time was up.

"No right to withhold all this?" There was a note of sympathy in her voice.

"Not only that," I said. "Who are you to set yourself up to make such judgments? To say what is great and what pedestrian?"

To my surprise, she did not take offense. "I've asked myself that question many times. We do the best we can." We were moving toward the door. "We have quite a lot of experience, you understand."

The lights dimmed. "Why are you *really* doing this? It's not for us, is it?"

"Not exclusively. What your species produces belongs to all." Her smile broadened. "Surely you would not wish to keep your finest creations to yourselves?"

"Your people have access to them now?"

"Oh, yes," she said. "Back home everyone has access. As soon as a new book is cataloged here, it is made available to everybody."

"Except us."

"We will not do everything for you, Mr. Wickham." She drew close, and I could almost feel her heartbeat.

"Do you have any idea what it would mean to our people to recover all this?"

"I'm sorry. For the moment, there's really nothing I can do."

She opened the door for me, the one that led into the back bedroom. I stepped through it. She followed. "Use your flashlight," she said.

We walked through the long hallway and down the stairs to the living room. She had something to say to me, but seemed strangely reluctant to continue the conversation. And somewhere in the darkness of Will Potter's place, between the magic doorway in the back of the upstairs closet, and the broken stone steps off the porch, I understood! And when we paused on the concrete beside the darkened post light, and turned to face each other, my pulse was pounding. "It's no accident that this place became visible tonight, is it?"

She said nothing.

"Nor that only I saw it. I mean, there wouldn't be a point to putting your universal library in Fort Moxie unless you wanted something. Right?"

"I said this was the Fort Moxie *branch*. The central library is located on Saint Simons Island." The brittleness of the last few moments melted without warning. "But no, you're right, of course."

"You want *Independence Square*, don't you? You want to put my book in there with Thomas Wolfe and Shakespeare and Homer. Right?"

"Yes," she said. "That's right. You've created a powerful psychological drama, Mr. Wickham. You've captured the microcosm of Fort Moxie and produced a portrait of small town America that has captured the imagination of the Board. And, I might add, of our membership. You will be interested, by the way, in knowing that one of your major characters caused the blackout tonight."

"Jack Gilbert," I said. "How'd it happen?"

"Can you guess?"

"An argument with his wife, somehow or other." Gilbert, who had a different name, of course, in *Independence Square*, had a long history of inept philandering.

"Yes. Afterward, he took the pickup and ran it into the streetlight at Eleventh and Foster. Shorted out everything over an area of forty square blocks. It's right out of the book."

"Yes," I said.

"But he'll never know he's in it. Nor will any of the other people you've immortalized. Only you know. And only you would *ever* know, were it not for us." She stood facing me. The snow had stopped, and the clouds had cleared away. The stars were hard and bright in her eyes. "We think it unlikely that you will be recognized in your own lifetime. We could be wrong. We were wrong about Faulkner." Her lips crinkled into a smile. "But it is my honor to invite you to contribute your work to the library."

I froze. It was really happening. Emerson. Hemingway. Wickham. I loved it. And yet, there was something terribly wrong about it all. "Coela," I asked. "Have you ever been refused?"

"Yes," she said cautiously. "Occasionally it happens. We couldn't convince Cather of the value of *Ogden's Bequest*. Charlotte and Emily Brontë both rejected us, to the world's loss. And Tolstoy. Tolstoy had a wonderful novel from his youth which he considered, well, anti-Christian."

"And among the unknowns? Has anyone just walked away?"

"No," she said. "Never. In such a case, the consequences would be especially tragic." Sensing where the conversation was leading, she'd begun to speak in a quicker tempo, at a slightly higher pitch. "A new genius, who would sink into the sea of history, as Byron says, 'without a grave, unknelled, uncoffined, and unknown.' Is that what you are considering?"

"You have *no* right to keep all this to yourself."

She nodded. "I should remind you, Mr. Wickham, that without the intervention of the library, these works would not exist at all."

I stared past her shoulder, down the dark street.

"Are you then," she said at last, drawing the last word out, "refusing?"

"This belongs to *us*," I said. "It is ours. We've produced *everything* back there!"

She looked solemnly at me. "I almost anticipated, feared, this kind of response.

It may have been implicit in your book. Will you grant us permission to add *Independence Square* to the library?"

Breathing was hard. "I must regretfully say no."

"I am sorry to hear it. I—You should understand that there will be no second offer."

I said nothing.

"Then I fear we have no further business to transact."

At home, I carried the boxes back up to my living room. After all, if it's that damned good, there has to be a market for it. Somewhere.

And if she's right about rampant commercialism? Well, what the hell.

I pulled one of the copies out, and put it on the shelf, between Walt Whitman and Thomas Wolfe.

Where it belongs.

The Last Librarian:
Or a Short Account of
the End of the World

~~~

Edoardo Albert

"Which is more important, books or people?"

The question was posed in jest, but over the years I had come increasingly to believe that if the librarian's veins were opened, ink would flow from them rather than blood. Even so, I did not expect him to answer as he did.

"Books." The librarian held out the saucepan. "More cocoa?"

"Yes, please."

We sat in the blessed silence provided by the museum's digital baffles, sipping from our mugs, while I waited to see what he had to show me. I had first met the librarian as an eight-year-old bibliophile whose most vivid childhood memories were of the local public library and the thrill of all those books waiting to be read. That boy had grown into a book collector, a hobby I pursued in the spare moments left over from my everyday duties as a minor government functionary.

Cocoa finished, the librarian led me past the empty desks of the Reading Room, past the silent counters where once librarians had checked out the less valuable books from the collection, to the holy sanctuary: the rare books room. To be precise, the rare books rooms. This was the British Library, after all. It needed more than one room for its rare books.

The librarian indicated a new display cabinet that had been given a place of honor even among the assembled Gutenbergs and Caxtons, Kells and Opticks, and First and Second Folios.

The book lay open at page one:

Some of the evil of my tale may have been inherent in our circumstances. For years we lived anyhow with one another in the naked desert, under the indifferent heaven . . .

"It's not," I said.

"It is."

"No."

"Yes." The librarian's face creased into the broadest of unexpected smiles.

Of the several holy grails of book collectors this was among the most sacred: the 1922 first edition of T.E. Lawrence's *Seven Pillars of Wisdom*, which he had privately printed at the Oxford University Press. There were only eight copies made; six were accounted for but now, it seemed, that number had gone up to seven.

"Where on earth did you find it?" I asked, when I was finally ready to take a break from inspecting it, gazing at it, and generally drinking in the wonder of it. I suppose a new mother must feel something similar when contemplating her first child.

"It was here all along," said the librarian. "Tucked away in one of the storerooms. It had somehow been labeled as an architectural treatise belonging to the collection of the Keeper of Oriental Antiquities, back in the days when Museum and Library shared premises. I only came across it by chance."

We both gazed at it.

"To think," I said, "you're probably the first person to touch the book after Lawrence himself."

"And the dunderhead who thought it was a book on architecture," said the librarian. "I suspect I know who that might have been. . . . " His face grew thoughtful as he contemplated the appropriate punishment for misfiling a book. Looking at him, it occurred to me that he had hardly changed at all in the years I had known him: hair graying but remaining on the cusp of actual white, complexion as pale as the artificial light, thin face bisected by the half-moon glasses permanently resting on the tip of his nose. In fact, the librarian might have looked at home in a mortuary, striding between the cold slabs; I confess that I sometimes felt, as we walked the silent halls and corridors of the library, as if we were the pathologists of a lost literary culture.

"Have you uploaded it yet?"

The librarian shook his head.

"Remiss of me, I know, but I wanted to share my discovery first. I shall, as you say, upload it. Presently."

Interested scholars would then be able to inspect perfect three-dimensional copies of the book, while those more concerned to hold up one end of a dinner-party conversation could download neural inputs sufficient to inculcate a comfortable memory of having read the book, without the tiresome necessity of ever having to look at it. After all, with most literature people want to have read the book, not to actually read it. In our rushed and hurried world, neural inputs meant that you could read all the classics of the canon in an afternoon and still have time for dinner.

"Still," I added, on my slow wending out of the library and back into the ordinary world, "I'm sure that with a find like this there will be a few scholars who will want to see the actual book." I paused at the exit. "What do you think?"

The librarian shook his head, the light reflecting on his glasses.

"No, I do not think they will come. Not even for this." He began to close the door, then stopped.

"Come back in a week," he said. "I may have something to show you."

"Is it—"

But the door had closed, cutting off my question. The librarian always showed me in and out of one of the side entrances meant for staff; the high halls of the public entrance remained open, and empty, like some undiscovered cave in a forgotten country.

I turned up my collar, engaged the digital baffles, closed my ears to the babble of information, and set off into the modern world.

A week later I was back, but not alone. A constant stream of people—most of them academics by the cut of their gowns—was going in and out of the main entrance. Where before the Great Hall had stood sepulchral and empty, now excited scholars disputed with each other or sent students off on errands, while what appeared to be a positive scrum was developing around the main information desk, on which was displayed a prominent sign pointing the way to the Lawrence display. Messages flashed up on boards on the walls and ceilings, directing interested parties to the life cycle of the weevil (second floor, row J, shelfmarks DX80130 DSC); the hypostasis of the Archons (third floor, row O, shelfmarks 412.978000 DSC); and kin relations among chavs (sub basement 4, row B, shelfmarks YK.2005.a.10262). The messages constantly changed, until I realized that they were the answers being given to the crowd of importunate scholars clustered around the main desk. And there, in the center of the circle, surrounded by a team of junior assistants, was the librarian. He nodded towards me, spoke a few words to one of his acolytes, and released himself from the desk.

I gestured, encompassing the people, the bustle, the sheer life.

"It's astonishing," I said. "Extraordinary. What's happened?"

In an unexpected gesture of intimacy, the librarian took my arm. I must confess that this took me by surprise: I didn't so much flinch as stiffen. But as warrant for the degree of his excitement, I do not believe the librarian even noticed. He led me across the Great Hall, shrugging off the frantic enquiries of desperate scholars, and piloted me through one of the doors marked "Staff only." Peace and calm immediately descended.

"Would you mind walking?" asked the librarian. "I do so fear that I shall be immediately accosted if we venture the lifts, but I would like to show you around on this day of all days."

We made our way up the stairs.

"You are not, I believe, a specialist in information theory."

"Not exactly, no. Spreadsheets I understand, what produces them I don't."

"Then I shall have to make use of analogy," said the librarian. "Consider your brain: at its core is the spinal cord and the primitive brain structures that we share with other chordates. These structures are the basis for all the achievements of the human mind, from Shakespeare's sonnets to David's Psalms to Mozart's music. But take away the sub-structure and—no Shakespeare. Now, there are some very primitive parts of the modern, interconnected world, parts that have been there from the beginning but have been all but forgotten as more elaborate networks were built on top. But there is one place where these old things are still recorded." The librarian stopped and turned to look down at me. I must confess I was grateful for the break, as the climb was proving longer than I had anticipated.

"The library." The librarian resumed the climb, speaking over his shoulder. "In fact, some of these texts have never been uploaded." He glanced back at me, smiling. "Can you credit it? It was a relatively straightforward matter to find the information and then remove one of the key substructures. So, for today at least, any scholar attempting to access information will find an error message and a notice advising him to repair to his local public library."

At last we arrived at the top of the staircase and paused at the door.

"Let us quietly inspect the evidence of scholarly activity. . . . "

It was, perhaps, unfortunate that the librarian opened the door at the precise instant a researcher dropped the book he was extracting from the shelf. He dropped the book because he was trying to simultaneously answer his phone while not spilling his cup of coffee.

"Hey, thanks," said the scholar, as the librarian swooped in, a literary falcon, and swept the book from the floor. But his eyes widened as the librarian put the book back on the shelf.

"I need that," he said.

"Give me your library card," said the librarian.

Taking the proffered card, the librarian first scrutinized the embedded picture for resemblance to its subject—since it had only been taken that morning little time had elapsed for variations between image and reality to develop. Then, producing a small pair of scissors from his pocket, the librarian proceeded to cut the membership card in two, taking particular delight in bisecting the picture.

"But . . . but . . . " stammered the researcher.

"Your membership is canceled. Kindly leave the building."

After opening and closing his mouth a few times as if to speak—the frown on the librarian's face sufficient each time to stop him—the scholar trudged towards the lifts.

"And switch off your phone."

We didn't move until the lift doors closed. The librarian sent a message down to reception to tell them to escort the erstwhile reader from the premises. Thus, the librarian's previous good mood was blighted and we drank our cocoa in something approaching silence.

I hoped the book abuse we had seen would prove to be a solitary lapse, but sadly that was not the case. Descending the levels we came across multiple cases of unauthorized eating and drinking. We heard many an illicit conversation, both local and by phone. There were a distressing number of cases of ABH (actual biblio harm) such as page corners being turned over and books being returned to the wrong shelves; and a few truly worrying instances of GBH (grievous biblio harm), where poor, innocent volumes had notes written on their margins or were left paralyzed with their spines broken. This last was a particularly sad case. We found *The Principles of Lingerie* by Reginald Spode lying abandoned on a desk, its spine cracked, its contents exposed, and with numerous marginal marks sullying its virginal purity. Of the malefactor there was no sign beyond a crumpled sweet wrapper.

Faced with this outrage, the librarian then did something truly extraordinary. The Spode, of course, should have been taken for immediate repair but we had other urgent tasks to attend to. So, rather than expose the book to further abuse, the librarian deliberately mis-shelved it.

I was shocked. But then, as realization dawned of the scope of the librarian's sacrifice, surprise turned into admiration.

"Truly, it is a greater thing you do today . . . "

But the librarian indicated silence. It was a library, after all. Not that you could have told that from the behavior of most of the readers: everywhere we went there was the constant background noise of conversations, modulated by the mastication of many jaws. It would seem that today's scholar is unable to engage brain without first starting jaw.

Business appointments had claim of me for the rest of the day, so I left the librarian to battle against the waves of human fecklessness he was facing, but I called just before the library closed.

The librarian answered in sound mode. I supposed after such a day I would prefer not to appear on any screens either.

"How has the day gone?"

Even through the phone, the librarian sounded tired.

"It only grows longer. It appears that many books have been replaced wrongly, so I fear I have many hours work ahead rearranging the shelves." Despite the lack of vision I could all but see the librarian shaking his head. "It was never like this in Alexandria."

"Would you like me to help?"

"No, no thank you. I'm sure we can man—excuse me, sir, that book's not for loan. . . . "

The line went dead.

The next week, after work as was my wont, I went to the library while it was still open. The news had been on little else but the loss of the country's academic data retrieval, so it was little surprise that the queue applying to be readers was even longer than before. Passing the desk area where applications were processed, I realized that it would only get longer. Last week, in the librarian's enthusiasm for these new readers, the desk had been manned by all his brightest and quickest staff. Today, there was just one, rather decrepit, librarian on duty, hard of hearing and long-sighted to boot.

The chief librarian, however, was not in his office, nor could I find him in the still-crowded halls and reading rooms, an exploration much distracted by the evidence before me of rampant book abuse. By the time I returned to the Great Hall I was all but trembling from the dreadful things I had seen.

This was where the librarian's messenger eventually found me. I was taken down through all the levels of the library to its basement. There I found the librarian, and went to him, arms outstretched.

"My dear friend, how can you bear it?"

The librarian paused in his work. "Ah, I am glad for your words. Sometimes I think I am just an old bachelor, grown set in his ways, unable to adjust to modern times. But you agree: this behavior is outrageous. It cannot go on."

"Are you going to reconnect the library to the network?"

The librarian shook his head, somewhat ruefully. "Would that it were that easy. It appears that no repair is possible. Of course, in the end outside agencies will trace the fault and rectify it, but time is of the essence here. If action is not taken soon, some books will be damaged beyond repair. As an all-but-forgotten writer of the twentieth century said: 'I accept the risk of damnation. The Lord will absolve me, because He knows I acted for His glory. My duty was to protect the library.' Or, as an even more obscure author remarked, if you will pardon the infelicity and paraphrase: 'I am one of the secret masters of the world. I am a librarian. I control information. Don't ever piss me off.' "

The librarian stood up.

"Come," he said, "let us go and see."

We emerged from the lift and went out on the roof terrace.

Looking down, far down, I could see a constant stream of librarians loading books into the back of a fleet of lorries.

"Where are they taking the books?" I asked.

"A library is ideal in secure times as a place for scholars to study. But what about in less certain ages? History teaches us that even the greatest collections may fall victim to the ignorant mob, if they are not guarded. We have, far from here, made provisions for the safety of these books. Another library, but one that is safe, secure and, most important of all, secret. And that is where I am taking the books."

I watched as the last of the lorries drove away, disappearing into the twilight. We stood in silence as night drew in over the city. Far below, the library had closed its doors. The librarian was waiting for something, although I did not know what that might be.

And then, one by one, without any fuss, the lights went out. An unnatural quiet began to spread across the city as the darkness spread.

"What's happening?"

"Do you remember asking me which was more important: books or people? Of course, my answer was rather playful, but nonetheless I was becoming increasingly concerned about the divergence between this current civilization and all that books represent: story, knowledge, art, law, science. The events of the last few days have decided me. If even scholars cannot be trusted with books, then this society can no longer be called civilized. Therefore, it is time to start again." He gestured towards the spreading pool of darkness, out of which increasingly feral howls and screams were already spilling. "If you know what to do, a complex mechanism is easy to destroy. Many things can be found in old, forgotten books."

"But, but they'll fix it, they'll find what you've done and repair it."

"It is not that easy, my friend. Processes have been set in motion that cannot be stopped. Come, it's time to depart, although," and at this point the wave of failing power took away the library's own light and electricity, "I fear we will have to use the staircase."

The last I saw of my one-time friend was him climbing into the last lorry to leave the library and driving off into the darkness.

I write this now, by candlelight, some months later (I'm afraid I have lost track of the exact date). I will seal my testimony in a bottle and place it in what remains of the library (the mob destroyed much of the building some weeks ago even though they found there neither food or fuel). If, someday, my old friend emerges from his sanctuary with the books to start a new civilization I hope my record might be found: a short account of the end of the world.

ABOUT THE AUTHORS

Edoardo Albert spent his childhood in libraries—indeed, the most exciting days of the year were the ones before public holidays, when he was allowed to take out twice the number of books as usual. This may be why he grew up to be a writer. *Oswiu: King of Kings*, the third volume of his Northumbrian Thrones trilogy, has just been published by Lion Fiction. More at edoardoalbert.com.

Best known for her "Company" series of time travel science fiction, **Kage Baker**'s (1952-2010) debut novel, *In the Garden of Iden*, was published in 1997. Other notable works include *Mendoza in Hollywood* (2000) and "The Empress of Mars," a 2003 novella that won the Theodore Sturgeon Award and was nominated for a Hugo Award. Her short story "Caverns of Mystery" and her novel *House of the Stag* (2009) were both nominated for World Fantasy Awards. In 2010, her novella *The Women of Nell Gwynne's* was nominated for both a Hugo and a World Fantasy Award, and won the Nebula Award. Her sister, Kathleen Bartholomew completed Baker's unfinished novel, *Nell Gwynne's On Land and At Sea*. It was published in 2012.

Elizabeth Bear was born on the same day as Frodo and Bilbo Baggins, but in a different year. She is the Hugo, Sturgeon, Locus, and Campbell Award winning author of twenty-seven novels (The most recent is *Karen Memory,* a Weird West adventure from Tor) and over a hundred short stories. She lives in Massachusetts with her partner, writer Scott Lynch.

Gregory Benford is a Fellow of the American Physical Society, winner of the Lord Prize in science, and the UN Medal in Literature. His fiction and nonfiction has won many awards; he has published thirty-two novels, over two hundred short stories and several hundred scientific papers in several fields.

Holly Black was a library school drop out. Now she's the author of bestselling dark fantasy for kids and teens. She lives in New England with her husband and son in a house with a secret door that hides a room filled with books.

Richard Bowes has published six novels including *Minions of the Moon* and *Dust Devil On A Quiet Street*, four short story collections and eighty stories and has won World Fantasy, Lambda, IHG, and Million Writer Awards. Many of his stories are personal/semi-autobiographical. He worked for thirty-five years at New York University's Bobst Library and was present at the 2003 student suicides and their aftermath.

Ray Bradbury (1920-2012) was one of those rare individuals whose writing has changed the way people think. In recognition of his stature in and impact on the world of literature, Bradbury was awarded the National Book Foundation's 2000 Medal for Distinguished Contribution to American Letters, the National Medal of Arts in 2004, and, in 2007, a Pulitzer Prize special citation. A great lover and supporter of libraries and said, "I didn't go to college, but when I graduated from high school I went down to the local library and I spent ten years there, two or three days a week, and I got a better education than most people get from universities. So I graduated from the library when I was twenty-eight years old."

Amal El-Mohtar is an award-winning writer of prose, poetry, and criticism. Her stories and poems have appeared in magazines including *Lightspeed*, *Uncanny*, *Strange Horizons*, *Apex*, *Stone Telling*, and *Mythic Delirium*. Anthology appearances include *The Starlit Wood: New Fairy Tales*, *Kaleidoscope: Diverse YA Science Fiction and Fantasy Stories*, and *The Thackery T. Lambshead Cabinet of Curiosities*. Her collection, *The Honey Month*, was published in 2011. El-Mohtar's articles and reviews have appeared in the *LA Times*, *NPR Books*, and on *Tor.com*.

Ruthanna Emrys lives in a mysterious manor house in the outskirts of Washington DC with her wife and their large, strange family. She makes home-made vanilla, obsesses about game design, gives unsolicited advice, occasionally attempts to save the world, and blogs sporadically at ashnistrike.livejournal.com and on Twitter as @r_emrys. Her stories have appeared in *Tor.com*, *Strange Horizons*, and *Analog*. Her first novel, *Winter Tide*, is available from MacMillan's Tor.com imprint.

Nebula Award winner **Esther Friesner** is the author of more than thirty novels and over one hundred fifty short stories, including the story "Thunderbolt" in Random House's *Young Warriors* anthology, which lead to the creation of *Nobody's Princess* and *Nobody's Prize*. She is also the editor of seven popular anthologies. Her works have been published around the world. Educated at Vassar College and Yale University, where she taught for a number of years, Friesner is also a poet, a playwright, and once wrote an advice column, "Ask Auntie Esther." She is married, is the mother of two, harbors cats, and lives in Connecticut. You can visit Esther at princessesofmyth.com.

As an undergraduate, **Xia Jia** majored in Atmospheric Sciences at Peking University. She received a Master's from the Film Studies Program at the Communication University of China, and a PhD in Comparative Literature and World Literature at Peking University. She is Associate Professor of Chinese Literature at Xi'an Jiaotong University. Several of her short stories have won the Galaxy Award, China's most prestigious science fiction award. In English translation, she has been published in *Clarkesworld* and *Upgraded*. Her first story written in English, "Let's Have a Talk," was published in *Nature* in 2015.

The library has always been **Ellen Klages'** favorite refuge, and there have been many significant librarians in her life. She is the author of two award-winning YA historical novels: *The Green Glass Sea* and *White Sands, Red Menace*. Her story, "Basement Magic," won a Nebula Award in 2005. In 2014, "Wakulla Springs," co-authored with Andy Duncan, was nominated for the Nebula, Hugo, and Locus Awards, and won the World Fantasy Award for Best Novella. Tor.com published her novella *Passing Strange* in January 2017. Klages lives in San Francisco, in a small house full of books and other strange and wondrous things.

Kelly Link is the author of the collections *Stranger Things Happen*, *Magic for Beginners*, *Pretty Monsters*, and *Get in Trouble*. Her short stories have been published in *The Magazine of Fantasy & Science Fiction*, *The Best American Short Stories*, and *Prize Stories: The O. Henry Awards*. She has received a grant from the National Endowment for the Arts. She and Gavin J. Grant have co-edited a number of anthologies, including multiple volumes of *The Year's Best Fantasy and Horror* and, for young adults, *Steampunk!* and *Monstrous Affections*. She is the co-founder of Small Beer Press and co-edits the occasional zine *Lady Churchill's Rosebud Wristlet*. Link was born in Miami, Florida. She currently lives with her husband and daughter in Northampton, Massachusetts.

Ken Liu (kenliu.name) is an author and translator of speculative fiction, as well as a lawyer and programmer. A winner of the Nebula, Hugo, and World Fantasy Awards, his debut novel, *The Grace of Kings* (2015), is the first volume in a silkpunk epic fantasy series, The Dandelion Dynasty. The second book in the series, *The Wall of Storms* and a collection of short stories, *The Paper Menagerie and Other Stories* were published in 2016. He also edited the first English-language anthology of contemporary Chinese science fiction, *Invisible Planets* (2016). He lives with his family near Boston, Massachusetts.

Prior to becoming a published fantasy author, *New York Times*, *USA Today*, and *Times of London* bestselling author **Scott Lynch** had a variety of jobs including dishwasher, busboy, waiter, web designer, office manager, prep cook, and freelance writer. He is also a volunteer firefighter. Novel *The Thorn of Emberlain* will soon follow *The Lies of Locke Lamora*, *Red Seas Under Red Skies*, and *The Republic of Thieves* in his seven-volume Gentleman Bastard series. Lynch lives in Massachusetts with his partner, writer Elizabeth Bear.

Jack McDevitt is a former English teacher, naval officer, Philadelphia taxi driver, customs officer, and motivational trainer. His work has been on the final ballot for the Nebula Awards for twelve of the past thirteen years. His first novel, *The Hercules Text*, won the Philip K. Dick Special Award. In 1991, McDevitt won the first $10,000 UPC International Prize for his novella, "Ships in the Night." *The Engines of God* was a finalist for the Arthur C. Clarke Award, and his novella, "Time Travelers Never Die," was nominated for both the Hugo and the Nebula awards. McDevitt lives in Georgia with his wife, Maureen, where he plays chess, reads mysteries, and eats lunch regularly with his cronies.

Sarah Monette studied English and Classics in college, and receive an MA and Ph.D. in English Literature. Her first four novels were published by Ace Books, and she has written two collaborations with Elizabeth Bear for Tor: *A Companion to Wolves* and *The Tempering of Men*. Short stories have appeared in a variety of venues. Monette has published two collections of short stories, *Somewhere Beneath Those Waves* and *The Bone Key*. Monette's latest novel—*The Goblin Emperor*, written under open pseudonym Katherine Addison—was winner of the Locus Award for best fantasy novel and a finalist for Hugo, World Fantasy, and Nebula Awards.

Publishers Weekly called **Norman Partridge**'s *Dark Harvest* "contemporary American writing at its finest" and chose the novel as one of the One Hundred Best Books of 2006. His fiction includes horror, suspense, crime, and the fantastic—"sometimes all in one story" according to writer Joe R. Lansdale. Author of five short story collections, Partridge's novels include the Jack Baddalach mysteries *Saguaro Riptide* and *The Ten-Ounce Siesta*, plus *The Crow: Wicked Prayer*, which was adapted for film. Partridge's compact, thrill-a-minute style has been praised by Stephen King and Peter Straub, and his work has received multiple Bram Stoker awards. He lives in the San Francisco Bay Area with his wife, Canadian writer Tia V. Travis, and daughter. Partridge works in a university library.

Robert Reed has been nominated for the Hugo Award twice for novellas, and was the first Grand Prize Winner of the Writers of the Future. The author of scores of short stories published in major SF magazines, Reed has had stories appear in at least one of the annual "year's best" anthologies in every year since 1992. He has published eleven novels, the most recent of which is *The Memory of Sky*. He lives in Lincoln, Nebraska, with his wife, Leslie, and daughter, Jessie. An ardent long-distance runner, he can frequently be seen jogging through the parks and hiking trails of Lincoln, and has taken part in many of the area's races.

Tansy Rayner Roberts is the author of *Musketeer Space*, the Creature Court trilogy, and *Love & Romanpunk*. The first book she remembers checking out from a library is Edward Eager's *Seven Day Magic*, in which five children check out an book from the library which has collected all the magic "dripped onto it" from the fairy tale collections shelved above it, and thus leads them on magical adventures while narrating what happens to them. This . . . possibly . . . raised Tansy's expectations rather high about what libraries could achieve. Still, she has never been disappointed by them.

USA Today bestselling author **Kristine Kathryn Rusch** writes in almost every genre under her own name and several pseudonyms. Her novels have made bestseller lists around the world and her short fiction has appeared in eighteen "year's best" anthologies. She has won more than twenty-five awards for her fiction, including the Hugo and Le Prix Imaginales. Rusch also edits. She began with the innovative publishing company, Pulphouse—for which she won a World Fantasy Award—followed by her Hugo-winning tenure at *The Magazine of Fantasy & Science Fiction*. She now acts as series editor with her husband, writer Dean Wesley Smith, of original anthology series Fiction River, published by WMG Publishing. She edits at least two anthologies in the series per year on her own. Rusch lives and occasionally sleeps in Oregon.

E. Saxey has had fiction published in *Daily Science Fiction*, *Apex Magazine*, and *The Future Fire*, and in anthologies including *Tales from the Vatican Vaults* and *The Lowest Heaven*. They have worked in academic libraries for happy interludes, and now volunteer at their local library to stave off the effects of public service budget cuts. On Twitter as @esaxey

A.C. Wise was born and raised in Montreal and currently lives in the Philadelphia area. Her stories have appeared in *Clarkesworld*, *Shimmer*, and *Tor.com*. Her collections *The Ultra Fabulous Glitter Squadron Saves the World Again*, and *The Kissing Booth Girl and Other Stories*, are both published by Lethe Press. In addition to her fiction, she co-edits *Unlikely Story*, and contributes a monthly review column, *Words for Thought*, to *Apex Magazine*. Find her online at www.acwise.net.

ABOUT THE EDITOR

Paula Guran is senior editor for Prime Books. This is her forty-second anthology. She owes a great deal to libraries and librarians. Without the Belle Isle and Bethany branch libraries of the Oklahoma City Metropolitan Library system, she would never have made it through childhood. Without the Akron-Summit Public Library system, she would not have survived raising four children. (Those children's grandmother is, by the way, a retired librarian.) She looks forward to someday taking her (so far) three grandchildren to libraries.